Point Horror

COLLECTION 2

A terrifying trio in one!

Point Horror

COLLECTION 2

A terrifying trio in one!

My Secret Admirer
Carol Ellis

The Accident
Funhouse
Diane Hoh

Scholastic Children's Books,
Scholastic Publications Ltd,
7-9 Pratt Street, London NW1 0AE, UK

Scholastic Inc.,
555 Broadway, New York, NY 10012-3999, USA

Scholastic Canada Ltd,
123 Newkirk Road, Richmond Hill,
Ontario, Canada L4C 3G5

Ashton Scholastic Pty Ltd,
PO Box 579, Gosford, New South Wales,
Australia

Ashton Scholastic Ltd,
Private Bag 92801, Penrose, Auckland,
New Zealand

First published in this edition by Scholastic Publications Ltd, 1993

My Secret Admirer
First published in the USA by Scholastic Inc., 1989
First published in the UK by Scholastic Publications Ltd, 1991
Copyright © Carol Ellis, 1989

The Accident
First published in the USA by Scholastic Inc., 1991
First published in the UK by Scholastic Publications Ltd, 1992
Copyright © Diane Hoh, 1991

Funhouse
First published in the USA by Scholastic Inc., 1990
First published in the UK by Scholastic Publications Ltd, 1991
Copyright © Diane Hoh, 1990

ISBN 0 590 55480 8

Printed by Cox & Wyman Ltd, Reading, Berks

All rights reserved

10 9

Contents

MY SECRET ADMIRER

Chapter 1

Jenny never knew what woke her up. One minute she was in the middle of a deep sleep and the next she was wide awake, the lightweight quilt tangled around her legs, and her heart drumming in her ears. The silence around her was as deep as her sleep had been. It couldn't have been traffic that woke her; the house was miles from the main road. Maybe it was the moonlight. With no other houses close by, they hadn't been in a hurry to put up shades, and a shaft of moonlight spread across her pillow like a milky white ribbon. Jenny was grateful for the moon tonight. Instead of spending a few panicked seconds in total darkness, trying to figure out where she was, she could see around her well enough to know that she was home.

Home. Well, not exactly. Not yet, anyway. She and her parents had moved into the house two and a half weeks before, and Jenny knew from experience that it would be much longer than that before it felt like a home. If it got the chance to, that is.

Four moves in the last six years, she thought, lying back on her pillow. No wonder she had trouble remembering where she was in the middle of the night. Living with a father whose job as a freelance consultant to shaky businesses took him all over the country and a mother whose feet started tapping after more than a year in one place was enough to make anybody lose their bearings.

A movement at the end of the bed interrupted Jenny's thoughts. Stretching her legs out, she prodded an odd-looking lump with her big toe and got a noise in return, something between a snort and a cough.

"Peaches? You awake?"

The lump moved again and heaved a deep sigh.

Jenny laughed softly and gave it another nudge. "You're awake, all right. You can't fool me."

Finally, the lump sat up. Peaches, an old dog, whose pale, sandy-pink hair was fast turning gray, heaved another sigh and blinked groggily. She'd been a roly-poly puppy and was still chubby in her old age. The closest she got to rolling these days, though, was onto her side for a snooze.

Jenny reached down and gave the dog a hug. "Come on," she said, before Peaches could collapse into sleep again, "I'm wide awake. Let's take a tour."

Taking a tour had become Jenny's solution to sleeplessness. It always happened when they moved, waking up at some strange hour, not knowing where she was, and then not being able to get back to sleep once she remembered. In two or three more weeks, she knew she'd be sleeping her usual dead-to-the-world eight hours, but until she got used to a new house, a nocturnal tour was a better way to pass the time than lying in bed staring at whatever new ceiling she happened to be under.

She slipped on a pair of worn flip-flops and made her way out of the room and down the hall to the stairs, a reluctant Peaches waddling and yawning noisily at her side. On the main floor, she turned into the kitchen, poured herself a glass of milk, and gave Peaches a dog biscuit for being such a good sport. Leaving her pet gnawing happily on the cool tile floor, Jenny took her milk and wandered into the living room.

This was the room that had sold her parents on the house, and Jenny understood why. Stretching from front to back, it took up almost half the first floor and had a soaring beamed ceiling, a stone fireplace, and at the back, a wall of windows that looked out over hills covered with pine and aspen. Beyond that, bathed in the milky moonlight, was a rocky bluff that ringed the town of Rimrock on three sides and gave it its name.

Jenny had been told that the rimrocks were a great place for hiking and learning to climb, in case you got the urge to pit yourself against the mountains that made this part of the country famous. So far, Jenny hadn't felt that urge. In fact, she hadn't even visited the rimrocks yet and wasn't sure she wanted to. If anyone asked, she'd agree that they were beautiful and awesome; privately, they gave her the creeps. She was sure they were full of snakes and coyotes, maybe even a few bears. But it wasn't just the possibility of unfriendly wildlife that bothered her about the bluff, it was the bluff itself. It was like a menacing shadow in a horror story or an evil giant in a fairy tale. It *loomed*.

It was a dark hulk now, but at the end of the day, Jenny had seen its pale, pinkish sandstone turned bloodred by the setting sun. It probably happens at sunrise, too, she thought, shivering as she peered through the tall windows.

She shivered again and then jumped when something cold touched her bare leg. Peaches, who'd ambled in hoping for another late-night treat, sat back with a guilty look on her face.

Jenny shook her head and laughed. "It's okay, Peach. I'm just jumpy. You can't help it if your nose is cold and wet. Let's go back to bed."

The dog was all for that. Bed was even better than a biscuit. It was better than the view, too, Jenny thought, giving the rimrocks one last look before she rinsed her glass and went back upstairs. Maybe that's what kept waking her up at night in this house; maybe that mass of rock that loomed over her new home had somehow worked its way into her sleep, hovering there until she woke up and faced it.

"What you really ought to do, Jen," Richard Fowler said, "is face it during the day sometime."

He stuck some bread in the toaster and poured himself a cup of coffee. Then he leaned against the counter and grinned at the look on Jenny's face. "You go over there and climb around those rocks a few times, and I guarantee that nothing'll wake you during the night. You'll be too tired to do anything but sleep."

Jenny couldn't help smiling back. She should have known her father would have an answer; he always did. It wasn't always the right answer, of course, but he never let that bother him.

"Dad, all I said was I wasn't crazy about the rimrocks. I didn't mean I had any deep, morbid fear of them that needed conquering."

"I didn't mean you did, either," he said, buttering the toast and handing it to her. "I just meant you might sleep better if you got more exercise." He fed two more pieces of bread into the toaster. "Unpacking boxes and putting things away isn't the same as getting outside and stretching your legs. In fact, we could all do with some real exercise. I think I just hit on a good idea."

Her father's voice was enthusiastic, and Jenny knew what was coming. By lunchtime, he'd have the three of them standing at the bottom of the bluff, outfitted in climbing gear, and ready to conquer the forces of nature. Her mother wouldn't mind, she knew; in fact, Grace Fowler would probably head the expedition. Jenny had inherited her mother's blonde hair and freckles and her father's brown eyes and long legs, but somehow they hadn't managed to pass on their go-get-'em, I-can-do-anything attitude to her. Her mother said she was too cautious and waffled back and forth about everything. Jenny guessed it must be annoying that their only child was so different from them, but she couldn't help it. She just approached things more slowly and thought a lot about something before she did it. Especially something like climbing that mini-Matterhorn out there.

"Richard!" Mrs. Fowler's voice bounced off the still-bare walls, and they heard her footsteps slapping rapidly down the stairs. In a couple of seconds, she bustled into the kitchen, her eyes bright with excitement. "Good news!" she announced. "I just got off the phone with the real estate agent, and we've sold the other house!"

"Great!" Mr. Fowler lifted his coffee cup in a toast. "For once we won't be carrying two mortgages."

Mrs. Fowler reached for the telephone book and started paging through it. "I just hope I can get a reservation," she muttered.

"Where are you going?" Jenny asked.

"Well, we've still got things in that house, you know," her mother reminded her. "And there might be some snags in the closing or something. Somebody should be there to make sure everything goes smoothly."

Jenny nodded. Her mother couldn't stand watching from the sidelines.

"Make two," Mr. Fowler said as his wife punched the phone number.

"Two what?"

"Reservations," he said. "I was going to fly back in a week or so anyway, to firm up that consulting deal. Might as well kill two birds with one stone."

"Good idea," Mrs. Fowler agreed. "I'll make two. *If* they have them."

Jenny cleared her throat. "Aren't you forgetting somebody?"

Her mother stopped jabbing at the phone and slapped her forehead. "Of course!" she cried. "The painters."

"What painters?" Jenny asked. "I was talking about me."

Confusion. "You?"

"Me," Jenny said. "Your daughter, remember?"

More confusion. Plus a little guilt. Had she forgotten something important about her daughter?

Jenny decided to come to the rescue. "I was talking about *my* reservation," she said. "You'd better make one for me, too. Unless you want me to stay here."

"That's it!" Mrs. Fowler jumped on Jenny's last thought. "You can deal with the painters." She raised an eyebrow, slightly exasperated. "Honestly, Jenny, of course we didn't forget you. You don't want to go."

There was no question mark in her voice. It was a flat statement. Her mother tended to do that, much to Jenny's annoyance. Assume things about what people wanted or didn't want. Unfortunately, she was often right.

She was right this time, too. Jenny really did not want to go. They'd just moved their entire household. They were barely unpacked. Just the thought of repacking even a suitcase brought on an attack of exhaustion. And if she stayed, she could arrange her room, hang some pictures, shelve some books, and generally putter around without the parental cheering section urging her to move a little faster. Or worse, organizing a hike.

On the other hand, she wasn't crazy about the idea of staying alone. True, she was a boringly responsible sixteen, and if they'd just been here a couple of months longer, she wouldn't have minded. But she wasn't used to the place yet, especially the night noises. And she didn't know anybody. School didn't start for another three weeks.

Her parents were giving each other "the look," trying to communicate without words. Actually, they were pretty good at it. And Jenny was pretty good at interpreting it. Neither one of them would insist that she stay, but they hoped she would. Her mother wanted someone here for the painters; her father wanted someone to keep an eye on the house, since the nearest neighbors were a mile and a half away. And both of them were getting impatient because she was taking so long to think about it.

Be decisive, she told herself. Be bold. "You're right," she said. "Taking a trip is the last thing I want to do. You go, and I'll stay and handle the painters."

Great relief. Her mother went back to the phone. Her father poured himself more coffee. Jenny reached down to pet Peaches, who had stationed herself under the table hoping for a handout and dozed off before she got one. "Wake up, Peach. You're going to have to be a watchdog for a couple of days."

Mr. Fowler snorted. "That dog can't watch anything, including her weight. You should take her for some long walks. Hey, take her with you when you go climbing, that'll work some of the fat off."

"It might give her a heart attack, too," Jenny pointed out. "Besides, it's dangerous to climb alone. I'll wait."

"Never mind." Her father laughed. "You're right about climbing alone, so you and the mutt just keep the home fires burning. Remember, though," he added, his eyes twinkling, "the rimrocks will still be there when we get back."

As it turned out, they couldn't get plane seats for two days, so they could have gone climbing after all. But her mother wanted to get some more things done in the house, and her father had some papers to look over, so Jenny was spared.

She wasn't spared, though, from the "getting-ready-to-go-someplace" attitude of her parents. Fortunately, she was used to it, and instead of getting sucked into their controlled frenzy of listmaking and double-checking, she offered to drive into town and pick up some supplies. Her mother, happily adrift in a sea of lists, surfaced just long enough to hand her the car keys and tell her to drive carefully, then dove back into her preparations.

Rimrock was a tiny town; people did their big shopping in Mount Harris, twenty-five miles away, where there was a mall big enough to get lost in. Even though Jenny knew plenty of rich people lived in the area, Rimrock itself didn't look it. Its trendiest store was a shop that sold candles and hand-painted greeting cards. The rest of the businesses were strictly the necessary ones — a small grocery, a veterinarian, a post office, a clothing store that dealt mostly in Levis, a drugstore, and a diner.

Jenny liked it, though. She had to admit that the bluff made a beautiful setting for a town, and since she'd never lived anywhere near a place that didn't bustle, she enjoyed the small-town quiet. Of course, it was going to be a different story in the winter, when she wouldn't be able to drive or bike into town (she'd heard alarming rumors of three-foot snows and storms that lasted for days), but right now it was warm, and the air was clear and smelled of pine.

She bought the things her mother had asked for, got some snacks and two frozen pizzas for herself, checked to see if the grocery's paperback rack had anything new, which it didn't, then headed back to her car.

She was fumbling in the pocket of her shorts for the keys when she heard the unmistakable clip-clop of horses' hooves. Then a girl's voice said, "Hi! I bet you're our new neighbor."

Jenny turned. It definitely *was* a horse, a big, shiny brown one, and the girl on it had short, curly hair to match. She was riding bareback and she didn't seem the least bit self-conscious about being on a horse in the middle of a paved street lined with cars.

"I'm Sally Rafino," she said. "I've been visiting my grandparents in Ohio, and I just got back yesterday. The first thing Mom told me was that somebody had moved into the house up the road from ours, and they had a girl who looked my age. You've just got to be the one."

"If the road's narrow and steep and doesn't have a name, then you're right." Jenny laughed and introduced herself, and after a couple of minutes, she found out that she and Sally were the same age and would both be juniors when school started.

"I thought maybe I was the only teenager around," Jenny said, after they'd chatted for a few minutes. "We've been here two weeks, and you're the first one I've even seen. I was starting to feel like an endangered species."

"Don't worry, you're not alone," Sally told her. "It's just that in the summer everyone sort of scatters. Vacations and jobs and stuff. When school starts, it'll be different. We get together all the time then."

Jenny knew about Evergreen High, of course; it was supposedly one of the best high schools in this part of the country, and her parents were constantly telling her she was lucky to be going there. Going to it was one thing, Jenny thought, *staying* at it was another. If her parents managed to stay put long enough for her to get through her junior and senior years in one place, then she didn't really care if it was an award-winning school or not.

"I guess all the kids are pretty close, huh?" she said, hoping they weren't so close that she'd feel shut out. "I mean, the whole school's only got about two hundred and fifty kids, doesn't it? You must kind of stick together."

"Yeah, most of us do." Sally tilted her head and wrinkled her up-turned nose, as if thinking of someone she'd rather not be stuck together with. "But don't worry. Everybody's pretty friendly. You'll get along fine. As long as you pass the test," she added.

Jenny stared at her.

Sally grinned. "I'm kidding. Really. Believe me," she said, "there's not enough of us for there to be an in crowd and an out crowd. There's just the crowd. Except for airheads and deadheads, of course, and I can tell you don't belong in those categories, so you're safe."

Jenny laughed, liking her.

"And," Sally went on, "tomorrow night, you'll get to see for yourself how great most of us are. If you're free, that is."

"My datebook's not exactly filled up," Jenny said, laughing again. "What's going on tomorrow night?"

"The scavenger hunt. We have it every summer, and tomorrow's the only time when almost everyone will be around," Sally said. "I would have come up to your house and invited you if I hadn't run into you here."

"Thanks, Sally, I'll definitely come," Jenny said. "It sounds like fun."

"Oh, it's great," Sally agreed. "We get one of the teachers to make up the list, and it's getting wilder every time. Last year we had to find a Mountain Lion."

Jenny tried not to look panicked. A scavenger hunt was a game, not really a hunt, wasn't it?

"No, no," Sally said, seeing the look. "The Mountain Lions are the team from Mount Harris High. Nobody could talk one into coming over here, though, so nobody got everything on the list."

Jenny was relieved. At least she hadn't joined a bunch of rifle-toters.

"Anyway," Sally went on, patting her horse's neck, "I've got to get Emma home before she does something I'll have to clean up. Do you ride?"

"Not much," Jenny said. "I don't think I'd break my neck, though."

"Good. We have four horses," Sally said. "One of them's really gentle. We can ride over to the rimrocks some time. Take a picnic and climb around. Do you climb?"

Jenny shook her head. "Not yet."

"It's not as bad as it looks from a distance," Sally

told her. "You don't need climbing gear or anything, not for most of it. It's fun up there; you'll love it once you get used to it."

Jenny watched her ride off, smiling wryly to herself. There was no getting around it, she guessed. Sooner or later, she was going to have to climb those rimrocks.

Chapter 2

"A 'cedilla'? Would somebody please tell me *where* we're supposed to find a cedilla?"

"Never mind where it is; first we have to figure out *what* it is."

"And what about this?" somebody groaned. " 'A Countenanced Pumpkin.' That's a jack-o'-lantern, right? Who's got a jack-o'-lantern in August?"

"Who has a pumpkin?" someone asked. "And what devious mind is responsible for this list?"

Loud laughter and lots of good-natured complaining greeted the scavenger hunt list. Jenny glanced at it, but she was too busy watching everyone and trying to keep names and faces straight to pay much attention to it.

"It's gotta be Latham," someone else said. "I see his tricky hand all over it."

"Not guilty," a quiet voice said. "I tried, of course, but since Mr. Mayes refuses to use a computer, there was no way I could have any influence on this list."

15

"Mr. Mayes is one of the history teachers," Sally told Jenny. "And that's Dean Latham," she added, tilting her head toward the boy who'd just denied having anything to do with the list. "He's the class brain. Really into computers. I heard his room looks like an electronics lab."

At that moment, Dean Latham, a sandy-haired boy with pale blue eyes, was being teasingly pummeled by another guy who easily outweighed him by fifty pounds. His name was Brad Billings, Jenny remembered; Evergreen High's one and only football star. "The team stinks," Sally had said cheerfully. "But don't tell Brad I said so. He absolutely refuses to face reality."

Sally had already introduced Jenny around. Sally was a fount of information, telling everyone where Jenny came from, which house she lived in, how she was trying to talk her into going climbing. Even the fact that Jenny's parents were leaving town for a few days wasn't left out: Sally kept reminding people to call Jenny so she wouldn't be lonely.

Jenny didn't say much; Sally didn't give her a chance. But people seemed friendly, and she felt welcomed and glad she'd come.

Now, while the group read and joked about the list, Sally continued giving Jenny a quick character sketch of everyone gathered in the high school parking lot: Alice bordered on being an airhead, but she was genuinely nice; Marc thought he was every girl's dream of the perfect date, but Sally went out with him once and all he talked about was how he planned to make a killing in the stock market like his father; Karen was the one who'd probably make the killing; she was almost as smart as Dean.

It was obvious that Sally had everyone pegged. It was also obvious that she was something of a gossip, but there was nothing really malicious in what she said. Jenny figured that once she got to know these people, she'd form her own opinions. In the meantime, she was enjoying Sally's thumbnail sketches. It was sort of like reading the back cover of one of those fat, gothic paperbacks she'd looked at in drugstores — "Jessica, the heiress whose passionate nature matched her fiery red hair; Alexander, the dark-eyed stranger whose secret vow of revenge had hardened his heart. . . ."

"Who's that?" Jenny said suddenly as a couple drove up and got out of a slightly battered Toyota.

"Where . . . ?" Sally glanced in the direction Jenny was looking. "Oh, that's Diana Benson." Sally lowered her voice. "She just broke up with Brad. And it wasn't a friendly split, either. Brad's got this possessive thing — sometimes I think he should have lived in the fifties. And Diana's . . . well, the less said, the better. You can bet the two of them won't be partners in the hunt."

Jenny gave Diana a quick glance — very pretty, blonde, great figure — but Jenny's eyes lingered on Diana's companion. "And, uh, who's that with her?" she asked, hoping she sounded extremely casual. Talk about dark-eyed strangers. The boy walking with Diana had the darkest eyes she'd ever seen, and a lanky, long-legged build. Lanky, long-legged boys were one of Jenny's many weaknesses.

"Oh, you noticed, huh?" Sally chuckled. "I don't blame you. He's not really handsome, but there's something about him, isn't there? And he's nice, too. Kind of quiet, but nice."

"Are you going to tell me his name or not?" Jenny asked.

"David," Sally said. "David Howell. And if you're interested, which I can see by the gleam in your eyes that you are, then I'll see what I can do to get him out of Diana's clutches." With that, she took off.

"But Sally, I . . ." Jenny stopped. Sally was already with David and Diana, gesturing wildly and talking a mile a minute. Jenny wanted to drop out of sight, but even if she could have figured out a way, it was too late: Sally was already on her way back, David and Diana in tow.

"This is Jenny Fowler," she said, smiling brightly. "Jenny, meet David and Diana."

Up close, Diana wasn't just pretty; she was almost beautiful. Jenny had dressed carefully in her favorite faded jeans and a rich brown cotton sweater that she thought made her hair look blonder, but next to Diana, she felt distinctly pale and dishwatery.

A smile would have made Diana even better looking, but she wasn't smiling. She seemed annoyed at the whole world, Jenny included. "I hope you like it here in Rimrock," she said without a trace of sincerity. "You're a fool if you do, of course." Her violet eyes flicked over Jenny. "You're not a fool, are you?"

Jenny laughed a little. "I hope not."

"Mmm." Diana swung her silky hair over her shoulder. "If you're not, what are you doing here tonight?"

"Come on, Diana," David said.

Jenny didn't know what Diana's problem was, but she felt a spurt of anger. "I could ask you the same question," she said.

Diana's lovely face hardened. "I'd be careful if I were you," she said. "You're not getting off to a very good start."

Jenny tried to think of a comeback, but before she could, Diana had spun around and walked over to Dean somebody; Jenny couldn't remember his last name. The genius.

There was an embarrassed silence, which Sally finally broke. "Well," she said brightly, "it's a good thing Diana's not in charge of the welcoming committee. Listen," she went on, "I promised Brad I'd start out with him, so I'll see you two later. Bye!"

Jenny's face was flushed, she could feel the heat. She glanced at David.

"Sorry about that," he said. "Diana's not the warmest person in the world. She isn't usually that bad, though. She had something on her mind; I'm not sure what."

Jenny shook her head. "It doesn't matter."

"Sure it does," he said. "But try not to let it get

to you. You've got to be clear-headed if you're going to be my partner."

"Well, I don't . . ." Jenny hesitated. He was probably being nice because he felt sorry for her. "I mean, okay, if you don't mind."

"Why should I mind?" David asked. "The only thing I'd mind is having a fool for a partner. And the only fool around here just walked off with Dean Latham."

He laughed, and Jenny found herself laughing with him. She felt better and shoved the ugly moment with Diana to the back of her mind.

"Okay!" somebody shouted. "Let's get going! First ones to finish build the fire!"

"Fire?" Jenny asked as she and David headed for the Toyota. "What do you do, burn the lists after it's over?"

"No, but that's not a bad idea," David said. "Didn't Sally tell you? We always have a cookout at the bottom of the rimrocks when we're done. Whoever finishes first — or gives up first — gets the fire going and then we have hotdogs and stuff."

"That sounds like fun."

"It is," he agreed. Then his eyes gleamed. "But the hunt — that's the real fun."

Jenny had never been on a scavenger hunt, but she got into the swing of it fast enough. The entire town seemed prepared for them; at every house they went to, people were helpful, offering to climb to their attics or hunker into their crawl spaces to find some small item, like an attachment to play a

45 record. The clue for that had been "Platter Player. Hint: Pre-CD." Jenny had finally figured it out.

"For a girl who's been stung by the Queen Bee of Evergreen High, your mind is working amazingly well," David commented as he dropped the little piece of plastic into their bag.

Jenny didn't answer, but she didn't mind his teasing, either. He'd been doing it ever since they started, and not just about the scene with Diana. He had a wry sense of humor, and Jenny responded to it, which he seemed to enjoy. In fact he seemed to enjoy her a lot, and Jenny found herself attracted to more than just his looks.

Every time they unlocked a clue and added another item to their bag, they giggled together like little kids who'd found a prize buried at the bottom of the cereal box. Except they weren't little kids, and the prize wasn't a trinket covered with Cheerio dust. To Jenny, the prize was just being together. In between stops, as they walked from house to house or drove to another neighborhood, they talked as if they'd known each other a long time ago and were catching up on each other's lives. He learned almost everything about her family's many moves, her hopes that this would really be the last one before college, her dream of someday sinking her roots down so deep that it would take an act of Congress to get her to move again. She learned that he'd lived in Rimrock for ten years, that he thought he might like to teach someday, but he wasn't sure, that he loved climbing the bluff (Jenny decided not to hold that against him), and that a lot of his favorite things were blue: the color blue, blueberry pie, and blue jeans. She also learned that she'd never liked someone so much, so fast, as she liked David Howell.

That was how *she* felt, anyway. She wasn't positive about David's feelings, but she had a couple of clues. For one thing, even though everyone had divided into groups at the beginning of the hunt, the groups turned out to be very loose. They kept running into the others on their search, naturally, and each time, Jenny noticed that the alignments had changed. Dean and Karen and Diana were together when they'd raced toward one house to see if the owners were possibly harboring a stuffed owl. The next time she saw them, Karen and Dean were together, and Diana was with Alice and Marc. Then she saw Sally and Brad and Marc dumping a telephone book into Brad's car, and she figured that Diana had gone back to Dean. Alice, she assumed, was on her own for the moment.

"I don't get it," Jenny had commented. "If everyone keeps changing teams, who knows who won?"

"We trade off sometimes," David explained. "Somebody might have two of something, so you make a trade with somebody else to help your team."

"Why haven't we done that?"

He smiled, his eyes on the list. "We don't need to," he said. "We're doing fine on our own."

Jenny stood on tiptoe, peering over his shoulder at the list. She saw that they had ten of the twenty items. She also saw that his hands looked strong, with long, tapering fingers.

Were they doing fine on their own? She had no idea. But she did know that they were the only team that had stayed together from the beginning. If he wasn't attracted to her, she thought, he would have suggested switching by now. Wouldn't he?

David lifted his head, and Jenny felt his dark brown hair brush against her cheek. He took a step away, turned and looked at her, his lips still curving in a smile.

Jenny thought he was going to kiss her, which made her nervous. Not that she didn't want to, but she wasn't a master of the romantic moment yet. She tucked her hair behind her ear and cleared her throat.

"I think we're in luck," he said, poking a finger at the list. "Look at Number 13."

So much for the romantic moment. Well, it was too soon, anyway. She guessed.

" 'A flown coop,' " she read, " 'a.k.a.: a syndrome for parents of college freshmen.' " She looked at David. "An empty nest, right?"

He nodded. *Then* he kissed her.

"I've been wanting to do that for an hour," he said, and she felt his breath on her hair.

Jenny smiled, her face against his shoulder. "We only met an hour ago."

"I fall fast." He laughed, pulled away, and shook

out the list. "Okay, an empty nest. Like I said, we're lucky."

"I give up," Jenny said. "Why are we lucky?"

"The bluff's the best place to find an empty bird's nest," he said. "And the lucky part is — I just happen to be one of the best climbers around."

"And you're modest, too," she commented.

"I said *one* of the best, didn't I?" He put his hand on her shoulder and spun her toward the car. "Come on, let's get going."

"Let's?" Jenny didn't budge. "You might be a good climber, but the only thing I've ever climbed was a street in San Francisco," she said. "It was steep, but it was paved."

"That's okay." He put his arm around her shoulder and nudged her forward. "I won't laugh if you slip."

Jenny reluctantly got into the car. "Who said anything about slipping?" she asked as he slid into the driver's seat. "I'm talking about a major fall. The kind that breaks bones."

"That won't happen," he said, starting the car and pulling away. "I'll be right behind you."

"You mean you're going to make me go first?" Jenny kept up the joking tone, but her hands were getting clammy. Definitely not good for climbing.

"I mean I'll *let* you go first," he explained. "That way, if you do fall, you'll fall on me and I'll be the one with the broken bones."

"But that's not going to happen, right?"

"Right," he agreed with a laugh. "Don't worry, it'll be fine."

Jenny took a deep breath and surreptitiously wiped her sweaty palms on her thighs. Just think, she told herself, if you make it, you can tell Mom and Dad and maybe they won't bug you to go up with them for a while. *If* you make it. Great way to put it, Jenny.

She took another deep breath, closing her eyes for a moment. When she opened them, something had changed. The sky in the west had been filled with fluffy white clouds; they were still fluffy, but now they were crimson. "It's not my imagination, is it?" she asked. "Isn't the sun setting?"

"Yeah, but it takes a while," David said. "We'll have plenty of time. Believe me, I wouldn't climb around up there in the dark."

"Well, that's good to know," Jenny said. She wished the sun would just drop quickly out of sight instead of putting on such a long show.

They were on a straight dirt road that led to the bottom of the bluff now, and Jenny could see that it had turned a fiery red like the clouds.

"It's a beautiful sight, isn't it?" David said, pulling the car to a stop. "I've probably seen it like this thousands of times, but I don't think I'll ever get tired of it."

Jenny couldn't argue with that. The bluff really *was* beautiful. Bathed in crimson light, it soared toward the sky like some monument to a primitive god, and she suddenly thought of those flat-topped pyramids of ancient South American cultures. Then she tried to remember if those were the ones used for human sacrifices. Then she realized she'd better stop thinking like that or she'd turn into a mass of quivering nerves and buckling knees and she'd fall for sure.

"Ready?" David said.

Jenny straightened her shoulders and breathed deeply. "Ready."

The first thing she noticed was that the rocks were warm, which shouldn't have surprised her, since the sun was shining directly on them and had been all day. But she'd expected them to be cold, and somehow their heat made them less frightening. Of course, any snakes that happened to live around there might still be out, warming themselves, she remembered. And if they weren't out, then they were in the shadowed nooks and crannies, which she eyed very carefully.

The second thing she noticed was that David wasn't always below her. In fact, most of the time he was above her, stopping now and then to reach out a hand and pull her up to some minute space which he claimed was level. His hands *were* strong, and in spite of being scared, Jenny enjoyed the contact.

"I think I see something," David said suddenly as they perched next to each other on a small jutting platform of sandstone.

"How?" Jenny asked. And that's when she noticed the third thing: The light had changed again. The rocks were still warm, but she couldn't feel the sun's heat on her back anymore; the shadows had lengthened and a wind had come up. "I see something, too," she said. "It's getting dark."

"Don't worry, it won't last long."

"It won't? I always thought it lasted about twelve hours," Jenny said.

"This isn't night yet," David told her. "It's dark because of the clouds."

Sure enough, when Jenny looked behind her, she saw a mass of dark clouds rolling over the western side of the bluff. "Those are not the same cottony clouds that were here half an hour ago," she remarked. "Those clouds are definitely wicked-looking."

David laughed. "They're all bark and no bite," he assured her. "You've been in Rimrock long enough. You must have noticed the late-afternoon storms we get. A big wind, lots of dark clouds, and about three drops of rain?"

"I've noticed," she said. "But not from up here. This is a whole new perspective." She tried to smile, but her mouth wasn't up to it.

"It'll be over in about ten minutes, you'll see." David slipped his arm around her shoulder. The movement required a whole readjustment of their feet, and for once, Jenny didn't welcome his touch.

"Listen," she said. "It's time for a confession. I'm terrified. I've been terrified ever since we set foot on this amazingly beautiful rock formation, and the little storm that's brewing isn't doing anything to calm me down." She tried to stop it, but her voice kept rising until she was almost shouting. "What'll calm me down is feeling flat ground underneath my feet!"

David got the point, and to Jenny's relief, he didn't click his tongue or shake his head in disgust. His fingers tightened briefly on her shoulder. "You're right," he said. "It's stupid staying up here in a storm. We'll forget the nest. Let's get down."

Wishing wouldn't get them down, of course. Only an agonizingly slow process would do that. The hand and footholds they'd used on the way up seemed to have shifted position, or else the darkening sky made them harder to find, and Jenny spent a lot of time clinging precariously to the side of the bluff while David scrambled below her, found a secure spot, then helped her inch her way down to him.

The wind was stronger now, whipping Jenny's hair around her face and blowing grit into her eyes and mouth, but so far, the rain had held off.

"Not much farther," David said as Jenny scrunched down behind him on a narrow, sloping ditch between two massive boulders, her drawn-up knees poking him in the back.

He turned his head to say something more, and Jenny saw his shoulders tense and his mouth snap shut.

"What?" she asked.

"Thought I heard something." He listened again, his head cocked to one side.

Jenny thought she heard what he did. A gutteral rumbling, like a far-off drum-roll. "Thunder," she said. But not so far off, because it was followed in seconds by a flash of lightning.

David nodded, but kept listening for a moment. Then he gave a little shake of his head. "Stay here a sec. I'm going down a few feet. I'll be back."

Jenny managed a smile, but since he was already scooting over the edge of their little slope, he didn't see it. She pulled a piece of hair out of her mouth, wrapped her arms around her knees, and waited. The thunder kept rolling and she did her best to ignore it.

Then there was a sharp crack, followed almost immediately by a real flashbulb of lightning, and the rain hit. It was more than three drops this time. Jenny's hair was plastered to her head in seconds, and the patch of sandy dirt she'd hunkered down on quickly turned to mud.

"David?" Jenny's voice was swallowed up by another crack of thunder. She eased up onto her knees, steadying herself with one hand on the slippery rock beside her. "David!" she shouted. "David!"

The thunder was her only answer.

Chapter 3

Just wait a minute, Jenny ordered herself. David's on his way back, he just has to go slower because the rocks are wet. Don't panic.

She waited. She didn't panic, although it was very tempting. She hunkered back down and stuck her hands up the sleeves of her sweater and waited. For a minute.

When there was a pause in the thunder, she called again. "David! David, you okay?"

There was still no answer, and in the silence between thunder cracks, a gory picture formed in her mind: David, unconscious and bloody, lying on some jagged rock.

One voice told her not to be ridiculous. He knows these rocks like the back of his hand, it said. He's just waiting until the storm passes. She shook the picture away, and then another voice said, then why doesn't he answer you?

"Daa-viid!" she called, stretching his name out on a long breath. "Daa-viid!"

The thunder answered again. Jenny opened her mouth to shout, then stopped. Beneath the fading rumble of the thunder, she thought she heard a voice.

"David!" she called. "Is that you?!" She tried to block out the whistling wind and the deep-throated beginnings of another thunderclap. Every muscle tense, she listened for an answer, praying that she hadn't imagined the whole thing.

There it was! It was muffled by the noise, but it was definitely a voice. Jenny rose to her knees again and cupped her hands around her mouth. "David! I'm still here! This way!"

Just as the thunder reached its crescendo, Jenny heard an answering shout. She scrambled to her feet, ready to call again, when the lightning flashed around her like a sheet of white neon, and she heard a scream. She clapped one hand over her mouth, thinking she was the one who'd screamed, but the sound went on for a moment, then blended into the shrieking wind.

Jenny took her hand away, knowing now that she hadn't actually screamed hysterically, and shouted again. "David! I'm still here! Are you all right?! David!!"

But there was no answer. Only the wind and the rain and the thunder building again.

He was hurt, Jenny knew it. And then she *did*

scream. "David! Can you hear me?!"

If he could, he couldn't answer, and Jenny decided she had to move. She had to get down, get into town, and get help.

She scooted to the edge of her little ditch, turned around and stuck a leg out behind her, poking around with her foot and praying she'd hit something besides air. When her foot touched something solid — slippery, but solid — she could have cried with relief. Slowly, she lowered her other leg, her hands dragging in the muddy gravel, and then inched herself over and down until she could stand.

After three more maneuvers like the first, Jenny finally found herself in a place where there was enough room to turn around. Her back against a slab of dripping stone, she looked out over a wide sloping area of rocks and gullies that led to the bottom of the bluff and the low scrubby bushes that grew at its base. This time, the tears did come. Almost there, she told herself. Almost safe.

But there was still David to take care of, so Jenny wiped her muddy hands, sat down on her rear, and started scooting. Going forward felt absolutely wonderful.

The storm seemed to be fading a little; the breaks between thunderclaps were getting longer, but the rain kept coming steadily, and Jenny knew there wouldn't be any last-minute clearing of the skies like she'd seen on other days. The darkness that had closed in was there to stay, at least for the night. That would make it harder to find David, she thought. But the town of Rimrock had to have some special rescue crew; this couldn't be the first time somebody had gotten lost or hurt up here.

The picture flashed into her mind again, of David lying helpless, and she scooted faster, barely feeling the bruising bumps she was taking in the backside. After a couple of minutes, she finally reached the part of the slope where she could stand and walk.

She took a step on the rocky, gentle slope, and then stopped so suddenly she fell backward again, banging her elbow painfully.

"Jenny!" David said. "Hey, you made it down okay!"

It was definitely David, dark eyes, lanky build, and all. He was wet to the skin, like she was, and he was muddy. But he wasn't bloody. Relief flooded her, followed almost immediately by anger. In his hand, she saw that he was clutching a sopping mass of twigs and weeds. An empty bird's nest.

Jenny scrambled up, wiped her hair out of her eyes, and hollered at him. "Where *were* you?! Didn't you hear me calling? Was that stupid nest so important you left me stuck up there in the middle of a storm?"

"Wait, wait." David held up his hands. "I didn't leave you up there, at least I didn't mean to," he said. "I admit I'd gone a little farther than I'd planned, and I was just about to come back for you when the storm got really wild. It took me a while, but I made it." He gave her a curious look. "You weren't there."

"Of course I was there!" Jenny said. "Where else would I be?"

"That's what I wondered."

Jenny couldn't believe it. Did he really think she'd decided to go exploring on her own? In the middle of a storm? "You probably went to the wrong place," she said, trying to keep her voice even. "Or else you got there after I'd already left."

"Yeah, I guess. Maybe."

Maybe, nothing, Jenny thought. "Anyway, why didn't you answer me?" she went on. She wasn't hollering anymore, but her voice was still plenty loud. "I called and called, and then I thought I heard a scream." The tears were back, and she wiped at them furiously. "I was scared out of my mind. I thought you were dead! Why didn't you answer me?"

"I didn't hear you. I didn't hear anything but thunder," he said, quietly, walking over to her. Even in the dark, Jenny could see that his eyes were bright, watching her alertly. "I didn't scream. Are you sure you heard one? Maybe it was the wind. It had to be the wind."

"I already thought of that," Jenny snapped. "No, I'm not sure I heard a scream. But I'm not sure I *didn't* hear one, either." She shut her eyes and tried to bring the moment back. Yes. A shout, then a scream. Definitely. Why was David so eager to make her think it was the wind? Had he slipped and screamed in panic and was ashamed to say so? If that was it, then she'd gotten him all wrong.

David put a hand on her shoulder, but Jenny shrugged it off. She was glad he was all right, but she was too shaken up to be calm and cool. She'd spent the last half-hour being terrified, and the terror still hadn't completely faded. She took another look at the dripping bird's nest. "Well, at least you completed your mission," she remarked. "I'm sure you're happy about that."

"Jenny." David gave a helpless laugh. "I just found it, right when I was starting back for you. Come on, I know you were scared. I was, too, but it's over now. Let's go, okay?" He wiped the rain off his face and hunched his shoulders against the wind. "There's not going to be any cookout tonight, that's for sure. I'll take you home."

"Now, you're sure you know what to say to the painters?" Mrs. Fowler asked. She stopped poking around in her carry-all and glanced sharply at Jenny. "You've got the number where we're staying, in case there's any problem?"

Jenny nodded. "You left it next to every telephone in the house, remember?"

"Everything will be fine, Grace. Just fine." Mr. Fowler spoke heartily, but his eyes lingered on Jenny's face. "She's got the number, she's got the mutt, and we've got a plane to catch."

"Attention passengers," the announcer intoned. "Interstate Flight 473 is now boarding at Gate 4."

"That's us," Mr. Fowler said. He kissed Jenny on the top of her head, then picked up the two carry-on cases. "See you in a few days, sweetie."

"Bye Dad. Have fun."

Jenny's mother gave her a hug. "We'll call tonight," she said. "And you be sure to call if . . ."

"I will." Jenny managed a laugh. "Don't worry. I'll handle the painters so well they'll move us to the top of their list and give us a rock-bottom price."

Her mother looked insulted. "I meant to call if you need us," she said. "I may sound like I care more about the painters than you, but it's not true."

"Grace, we've still got the security gate to get through," Mr. Fowler interrupted.

"Go on, Mom." Jenny helped her mother hoist the canvas bag onto her shoulder and kissed her cheek. "Have a safe trip."

A couple of minutes later, Jenny watched her parents shuffle through the security gate. She waved a last good-bye, then turned and headed for the parking lot. They were okay, she thought. Sometimes they drove her crazy, but in general, they were pretty good at being parents.

As Jenny walked to the car she thought about the night before. The ride home from the rimrocks had been quiet, to say the least. Jenny was silent, still not over the scare she'd had, and David must have decided that any attempt at conversation would be futile; except for asking directions to her house, he hadn't said a word.

A long, hot bath helped soak most of the aches out of her, but the fear had lasted all night, and was still with her in the morning. Which was why her parents kept looking at her, then at each other. Jenny read their signals, as usual, and knew they were trying to figure out what was wrong.

Jenny slid into the car and started it up. It was a sunny, cloudless day, and all she had to show for her battle with nature were a couple of scratches and a bruised elbow. She turned on the radio and laughed out loud when "Don't Worry, Be Happy" came on. She decided to follow the advice.

Jenny stayed cheerful for the entire twenty-five miles back to Rimrock, but she was a born worrier, and as soon as she pulled into town, she started to fret. She fretted about the painters, who she was sure were going to be hardnosed and high-priced. She fretted about being alone in the big house at night, even though she knew that if anything bad happened, it would probably be something like a toilet backing up. Mostly, though, she fretted about David.

She had to admit, she'd treated him harshly. It wasn't his fault that a storm came up, after all. Or that she was scared of the rimrocks and that being stuck up there was like a nightmare come true. Of course, he could have tried to be a little more understanding. He could have admitted that he'd yelled and not blamed it on the wind. They might even have joked about it, instead of driving home in unfriendly silence.

The worst part was that they'd been so attracted to each other, Jenny thought. Well, *she'd* been attracted, anyway. But so had he, she was sure of it.

She was good at reading signals, and even if he hadn't kissed her, his signals would still have been very positive.

So what now? Should she just forget it, write him off as nice, but not quite right? Let him write her off as a bad sport, nice, but not worth the trouble?

Pulling into the driveway, Jenny turned off the car, but she didn't get out. Instead, she listened to the motor tick and thought for a moment. It would be easy to let him write her off. After all, even though they'd been attracted to each other, it wasn't exactly a long-term passion she was dealing with. In a few days, the memory would fade away.

But even if nothing would ever come of their mutual attraction, Jenny decided she should at least do something about the rotten impression she'd made. She'd been upset, too upset to really think about what she was saying. Now, though, she figured she owed him an apology. After that, she'd just have to see what happened. If he apologized, too, which she thought he should, then maybe they could start over.

Having decided to clear her conscience, Jenny thought she might as well get it over with as soon as possible. Howell was a common name, but Rimrock probably only had a couple. She'd find his number and call him right away.

Peaches greeted her at the door, her stumpy tail wagging. "Hi, Peach," Jenny said. "You get lonely?" She dropped her purse on the hall table and gave the dog a hug. "It's just you and me, now, Peach.

We're in charge, you know, so you have to be on your best behavior. No wild parties, okay?"

Peaches waddled into the kitchen and looked longingly at her feeding dish.

"You're too fat," Jenny said sternly. She opened the refrigerator and took out a cold chicken leg. "I'm allowed," she explained, when Peaches whined. "I'm not a blimp and besides, I didn't have any breakfast." Then she relented and put a couple of bites into the dish.

She opened the telephone book, found one Howell, and copied the number onto a piece of notepaper. She reached for the phone, then stopped. She ought to plan exactly what she was going to say, that was much better than a bunch of umm's and uh's.

Still eating, she wandered into the living room, trying to decide whether to try to be funny about it, maybe try to make him laugh, or just keep it straight and to the point.

There was a desk in the living room, a beautiful, oak rolltop that had been her great-grandfather's. It was the one piece of furniture that always went with the Fowlers on their numerous moves, and Jenny loved all its tiny drawers and cubbyholes.

She sat at the desk and rolled up its top, revealing a sleek, slate-gray telephone with a built-in answering machine, looking very out-of-place on the polished, golden wood. Sort of like a spaceship in a cornfield, Jenny thought. Then she noticed that there were three messages on the machine.

She punched the play button and leaned back in the chair to listen. Maybe David had called. Maybe he'd decided she had a good reason for yelling at him, and wanted to see her again. It would sure make things a lot easier.

The tiny tape clicked to a stop, there was a beep, and then a garbled voice saying something about the eleventh, between nine and four. There was a tremendous clanging in the background, but Jenny thought she heard the name McPherson. If she did, then it meant the painters were coming the day after tomorrow, and she should stick around the house, even though they probably wouldn't get there till three-forty-five.

There was a pause, then another beep. "Hi, it's Sally," Jenny heard. "How'd you like the hunt? Kind of wet, huh? Or did Mr. H. keep you dry?" Laughter. "Anyway, I feel terrible. I hope you didn't drown or anything. We never get rain like that here. Anyway, since there wasn't a cookout, I'm trying to get everybody together tomorrow. You know the diner in town? That's where. But I'll talk to you before then. I'll call you back. Or you call me when you get home. Bye. Wait." More laughter. "You need my number. It's 555-0071. Bye again."

Jenny smiled. Some people got tongue-tied talking to a machine, but Sally obviously wasn't one of them. She had a feeling Sally was never at a loss for words.

Another pause, another beep. Another voice. A boy's this time.

"You're going to think I'm crazy, Jenny," it said. "And I guess I am. Crazy about you, that is. Don't laugh. This isn't a joke. You're really incredible. Maybe someday I'll be able to tell you face to face. Until then, I'll just keep my eye on you. And believe me, that's one spectacular view. Bye, Jenny. For now."

As Jenny had listened, she'd slowly straightened up until she was leaning over the telephone, her finger ready to punch the save button so she wouldn't lose the message.

Who was it? Did any of the boys she'd met yesterday really have such a soft, silky voice? Or was he just putting it on? Was it a joke, in spite of what he'd said?

The tape stopped, and she set it going again, listening impatiently through McPherson and Sally. Then she curled up in the chair and waited, determined to catch any false note, like a muffled laugh or something, anything that would give the voice away and tell her it was a crank call.

But all she heard the second time around was the same soft message, spoken in that smooth, quiet voice with just a hint of shyness in it. That shy quality made it even more appealing.

Jenny listened to it a third time, then saved the whole tape and went back into the kitchen to think about it while she finished the drumstick.

It wasn't a crank call, she decided. He knew her name for one thing. For another, they weren't even listed yet, so he had to have asked information, not just picked a number out of the book. And it couldn't be a prank, a joke on the new girl in town. That was the kind of thing twelve-year-olds did. And that caller was no twelve-year-old.

Jenny smiled to herself. So someone was going to keep an eye on her, was he? It was silly, but it was flattering, too. How often did she get a message like that, after all? Never, that's how often. She'd gone on her share of dates, but for the most part they'd been extremely boring or else they'd turned into wrestling matches in the front seat of the car. And nobody'd ever said he was crazy about her.

Jenny laughed and rummaged in the refrigerator for some more chicken. The call had come at a perfect time, considering the disaster of the night before. Who cared if it was just a game? It could turn out to be fun.

Peaches ambled over, hoping for another handout, and Jenny laughed again. "Guess what, Peach? I've got a secret admirer."

Chapter 4

When the phone woke her the next morning, Jenny leaped out of bed and dashed down the hall to her parents' room. Maybe it was him, her secret admirer. All the day before she'd hung around the house, mainly because she didn't have any reason to leave, but also because she half expected *him* to call again. He hadn't, and she'd gone to bed feeling strangely disappointed.

Breathless and rumpled, she grabbed the phone and flopped down on her parents' bed. "Hello?"

"Hi, sweetie."

It was her father. Jenny stifled a yawn.

Her father chuckled. "I heard that. It's ten-thirty, you know. What'd you do, leave a few lights blazing and keep yourself awake?"

"Something like that," Jenny said, deciding not to tell him exactly how many lights. "How was your trip? I thought you'd call last night."

"Everything's okay," he said. "We tried to call

during the day a couple of times, but the line was busy."

That must have been when she was trying to reach David or Sally, Jenny thought. She hadn't gotten either of them.

"Then the O'Dell's took us out to dinner," her father went on, "and it was past one when we got back. How's everything?"

"Okay," Jenny reported. "Tell Mom the painters called. They're coming tomorrow, so wish me luck."

"Just tell 'em what we want and get an estimate. Don't argue with them, they're the only painters within a fifty-mile radius. Just a second." Jenny heard her mother's voice in the background, then her father came back on. "Your mother says don't let them intimidate you."

"I won't," Jenny said. "She thinks I'm a total pushover. I can handle them."

"Sure you can," he said. "Well, is the mutt earning her keep? Guarding the homestead?"

Peaches hadn't budged when Jenny tumbled out of the bed. "Give her a break, Dad. After all, you two gave her to me, remember? So, how long do you think you'll be there?"

"Couple of days, tops," he said. "We'll let you know when to meet us. Take care, sweetie."

"I will, Dad. Bye."

Jenny hung up the phone and headed for the shower. She'd just finished pulling on shorts and a faded blue T-shirt when the doorbell rang. Dragging a comb through her wet hair, she ran down the stairs to the front door and found Sally standing on the porch, red-cheeked and out of breath.

"I just rode my bike up here," Sally puffed. "I forgot how steep that hill is. Remind me to take Emma next time."

"Come on in," Jenny said, stepping aside. "I was just going to find something to eat. You hungry?"

"Always."

"I tried to call you back yesterday, but you weren't there."

"I know. My mother sent me on about a thousand errands. Hey!" Sally peered into the living room on the way to the kitchen. "That's a great view. Sort of makes you feel like you're all alone with nature."

"Don't remind me," Jenny said. She opened a box of Blueberry Pop Tarts and put two in the toaster. "I'm still trying to get used to how isolated this house is. The worst time is at night. It's hard getting to sleep with all the creepy noises I hear outside. And it's even worse now that my parents are gone."

"Yeah, I can tell by the shadows under your eyes," Sally said. "But I figured it was David who kept you up, not night noises."

Jenny smiled, but didn't answer. She didn't want to talk about David yet. "You want coffee?"

"Are you kidding?" Sally opened cabinets until she found juice glasses and took two out. "I'm hyper enough as it is. If I drink any coffee, I'll never stop talking, and then I'll never hear how it went with you and David."

Sally sure was persistent, Jenny thought. "Oh

. . ." she shrugged, still not wanting to talk about it. First she wanted to clear things up with David. She was saved from answering by the entrance of Peaches, who'd come downstairs to inspect the company. Sally went into raptures over the dog, who wriggled and wagged in ecstasy over all the attention. "She's a love. Kind of fat, though."

"Shh," Jenny whispered. "She's very sensitive about it."

They were just starting in on the Pop Tarts and orange juice when the phone rang. Jenny grabbed for it, but it was definitely not her admirer. "This is McPherson," a deep voice said. "Let me talk to Mrs. Fowler, please."

"She's not here," Jenny told him. "You're the painter, right?"

"Right, and who's this?"

"Jenny Fowler. Her daughter," she said. "Are you still coming tomorrow?"

"Well, yeah, I was just calling to confirm," he said. "Make sure somebody'd be there."

"Fine, well, they will," Jenny said. "I mean, I will."

"Not your folks?" he asked.

"My parents are out of town," Jenny said. "They asked me to show you what needs to be done."

He gave a low chuckle. "So, you're on your own, huh? All by your lonesome."

Jenny frowned at the phone. Was this guy for real? "You're coming tomorrow, then?" she asked coolly.

"Oh, yeah." Another chuckle. "See you then, Miss Fowler."

Still frowning, Jenny hung up and told Sally about the man's comments. "Just what I need," she said. "A painter who thinks he's Don Juan."

"Gee, Jenny," Sally said. "Why'd you tell him your parents were away? Don't you know you're not supposed to let people know you're alone?"

"Come on, I'm sure he's harmless." Jenny laughed, but she felt slightly uneasy. Admitting she was alone hadn't been very bright, she guessed, but she wished Sally hadn't brought it up. And why did Sally care? She'd broadcast Jenny's 'single' status to the entire group at the scavenger hunt.

"Well, never mind," Sally said breezily. "It's too late, now, anyway." She sipped her juice and smiled. "Let's get back to David. Do you like him? Does he like you?"

"Sure. I mean, I guess," Jenny said. "It's too soon to tell." She could see that wasn't going to satisfy Sally, so she held up her hand. "Let's forget David for a minute," she said. "I think he likes me, but there's somebody else who I *know* likes me. Come on." She led Sally into the living room. "Listen to this and tell me what you think," she said, turning on the message tape.

First the painters, then Sally herself, then the mystery voice. Jenny watched Sally's eyes widen in surprise, then narrow in concentration, her mouth curving into a gleeful smile. "Well?" Jenny asked, when the message was over. "I have no idea who it is. Do you?"

"Somebody with an extremely sexy voice," Sally said dreamily.

"I already know that," Jenny told her. "But who?"

"Play it again," Sally directed. When it was over, she shook her head. "It's weird. You'd think I'd be able to tell, but I can't. Somebody's doing a really good job of disguising his voice."

"Take a guess."

"David, I suppose," she said, "even though he's not the type to make a call like that. At least I don't think he is." She gave Jenny a curious smile. "I can tell you think it's impossible for it to be him. What happened with you two on the hunt, anyway? You keep avoiding the subject."

"Oh, we had an argument about something," Jenny said, still reluctant to give a blow-by-blow account. "It was dumb. But he's probably decided I'm a real pain, so I don't think he'd leave me a message like that."

Sally nodded, as if she understood, and it was Jenny's turn to smile curiously. "There's something I want to ask you," she said. "You seem to think David's terrific, and you haven't mentioned a boyfriend, so I wondered . . ."

"Do I want David?" Sally finished for her.

"To be perfectly nosy, yes," Jenny admitted.

Sally's brown eyes clouded over for a second,

48

then she gave a short laugh. "Well, I did, let's put it that way," she said. "But he's . . . I'm . . . oh, I don't know, it's hard to say." She sighed and twisted her hair around a finger. "He's kind of quiet and thinks a lot. Not that I don't think, but you must have noticed that I tend to run off at the mouth."

Jenny couldn't argue with that, but she decided not to say so.

"I think it really bothered David," Sally said. "The couple of times we went out, I think I drove him crazy. I thought opposites were supposed to attract, but I guess it doesn't always work out that way." She sighed again, and then gave herself a little shake. "Anyway, I'm all over that, so let's figure out who's crazy about you."

Was Sally over it? Jenny couldn't tell for sure, but she thought she'd pried enough. "Okay," she said. "Let's say for now that it's not David. Who else could it be? What's his name—the hulk—Brad? Or that guy you said was so smart?"

"Dean," Sally said. "I don't know. He doesn't seem the type, either. It's possible that he thinks you're incredible, but he'd probably send you a computer printout about it if he did." She reached down and scratched Peaches, who'd followed them into the living room. "Maybe Brad. But he usually comes right out and tells people what he thinks—he's not the most subtle guy in the world. Diana can tell you that. Of course, Diana's no gem, either, I'm sure you know. If you're interested in David, you better move fast, or she'll beat you to him."

"She's interested in him?" Jenny asked. She hadn't known that.

"She's interested in guys, period," Sally said. "For a while. And then she moves on." Her eyes darkened and her face lost its sunny look, as if the thought of Diana were like a cloud drifting across her mind. But it passed quickly. "Anyway, back to you and your mysterious caller."

Jenny was still wondering about Diana and David. Was he interested in Diana? "Forget it," she said to Sally. "I mean, probably nobody's crazy about me. This has to be a joke."

"Maybe," Sally said. "But it would have fooled me."

"Well, if he really is serious, then he'll call again," Jenny decided. "I guess I'll just have to wait and see."

"You can, but I won't." Sally drained her juice glass and headed back toward the kitchen. "I'm going to try to figure it out," she said over her shoulder. "And this afternoon's the perfect time to do it. Everybody'll be there."

"Be where?"

"Oh, right, we never did get that straight," Sally said, setting her glass in the sink. "The diner. We're all going to meet there around three for hamburgers, since the cookout was a washout. Well, I couldn't get a hold of Diana, but I'm sure she's heard about it by now. She shows up at everything, no matter how stupid she says it is. I couldn't believe the way she talked to you. You must hate her. Anyway, can you come?"

"Sure." Jenny walked with her to the front door. "But you're not going to start quizzing people about the call, are you? I really don't want the whole world to know about it."

"I'm insulted," Sally said dramatically. "I may talk a lot, but I'm not a complete blabbermouth. Trust me, Jenny."

Later in the day, Jenny got ready to go into town. Leaving on her white cotton shorts, she changed into a royal blue tanktop. David liked blue, she remembered. She studied herself in the mirror, then pulled the top off and rummaged in the drawer for something else. Wearing blue wasn't going to make any difference. She'd apologize for yelling at him and see what happened. What *should* happen would be for him to apologize, too, to say that he shouldn't have dragged her up on the rimrocks. Then they'd go on from there. She hoped it turned out that way, but if they ever did have a relationship, it would have to be based on more than his favorite color.

She put on a yellow top, then went downstairs and filled the dog dish so Peaches would have something to occupy at least three minutes of her time while she was alone. Peaches loved to ride in the car, her ears flapping in the breeze, and always put up a fuss when she got left behind, so Jenny hurried outside before the dog figured out what was happening.

As Jenny drove, she thought about the people who'd be there. Everyone, Sally had said, which would be nice, since she hadn't really gotten to know any of them. Of course, everyone included Diana, and Jenny hoped she'd be in a better mood this time. She wondered if Diana was as calculating as Sally seemed to think, or if Sally was just jealous. Probably a little of both. Maybe Sally's gossiping wasn't quite as harmless as it had seemed at first. Jenny decided she'd better not rely on anyone's opinion but her own.

The inside of the diner was as un-trendy as the rest of the town, but its red-leather booths looked comfortable and the smells coming from the kitchen made Jenny's stomach rumble. She spotted her group at a couple of pushed-together tables near the back. David was already there, she saw. And Sally, and the computer guy, Dean. Plus another girl whose name she couldn't remember. Brad wasn't there yet. Neither was Diana, Jenny noticed with a slight sense of relief. "Jenny!" Sally saw her and waved her over. She pulled out an empty chair between her and David and patted it. "You're just in time."

Jenny smiled at everyone and sat down. "Just in time for what?"

The girl sitting next to Dean — Karen, Jenny suddenly remembered — rolled her eyes. "Sally's got us playing this ridiculous game," she said. " 'Whose Voice Am I?' We shut our eyes and somebody talks in a different voice and the others try to guess who it is."

Jenny shot Sally a look, but Sally ignored it. "It's not ridiculous," Sally said. "It's fun. I'm learning a lot."

"About what?" David asked. He'd glanced at Jenny when she sat down, but he didn't seem overly thrilled to see her, she thought. They hadn't had a chance to talk yet, though. She wondered if they'd get one.

"About what lousy actors we all are," Sally said. She turned to Jenny. "We tried doing bored voices, and everybody was able to guess who was talking."

"Probably because we *weren't* acting," Karen said.

"Okay, then let's try a . . . a nasty voice," Sally suggested. "You know, the kind you'd use to put somebody down with."

Next, Jenny knew, she'd ask for a shy-but-sexy voice. Karen was right — this *was* ridiculous. If one of the boys here had made that call, he'd hardly give himself away so easily.

"I'm not sure I can do that at all, Sally," Dean said, and in spite of herself, Jenny listened carefully as he talked. "Putting someone down just doesn't come naturally to me." He said this with a straight face, but his light blue eyes sparkled just enough to show he was joking. "I yam what I yam," he said, and launched into a terrible rendition of Popeye's song.

Jenny laughed along with the others, although she noticed that they seemed surprised to be laughing at something Dean had said. He obviously wasn't the class comedian. But was he her secret admirer? His voice was soft, but slightly thin and a little on the high side.

"Give it up, Sally," David said. "I'm not sure why you have the urge to play this game, but I'm afraid it's a real dud."

"Okay, okay, I know when to quit," Sally said. "The nastiest voice isn't here yet, anyway."

Jenny was pretty sure she was talking about Diana. She couldn't see David's reaction, but Dean stared at the table as if he were embarrassed.

Sally wasn't embarrassed at all. Smiling brightly, she said, "So, Jenny, what did you think of our scavenger hunt?"

Jenny cleared her throat. "It was fun. I liked it."

Dean raised his eyes and looked at her. "How far did you get on the list before the rain came?" he asked.

"Oh . . ." Jenny glanced sideways at David. He was busy with his Coke.

"Oh, that's right," Karen said. "You and David were together, weren't you?"

"They were at the beginning," Sally said with a grin. "Who knows about the end?"

Jenny blushed, but David just smiled tightly. "The end was a washout. Right, Jenny?"

"Right," she agreed, wondering if he was playing

a word game. "I'm afraid I'm not much of a climber, not even in good weather."

"Wait. Are you saying you were on the rimrocks when the storm hit?" Sally said.

"A lot of us went up there," Dean reminded her.

"Not me," Karen said.

"Well, sure," Sally said to Dean. "I mean, there's always at least one thing on the list that you can find on the rimrocks. Brad actually insisted that we go up there to find a bird nest, but we didn't go in the middle of the thunderstorm."

"I'm sure David and Jenny didn't plan it that way," Dean told her. He looked at Jenny again. "Did you?"

"Why don't you drop it, Dean?" David said suddenly. "We got rained on, and we didn't plan it, okay?"

"Yeah, you're embarrassing them," Sally said. "Especially David. After all, he's the number one climber around here. It must be very uncool for a good climber to get caught in a storm."

"Sure." Dean leaned back in his chair and smiled. "I was just curious, but I'll drop it. Didn't mean to embarrass anyone."

There was a short silence, and then Karen asked, "What about you, Dean? Where were you when the sky opened up?"

Before Dean could answer, a waitress came to take their food orders. Jenny snuck a look at David, wondering why he'd snapped at Dean. She didn't believe he was embarrassed. Was there some kind of rivalry between these two? Dean had left on the hunt with Diana. Was David jealous about that? You don't know him, she reminded herself.

By the time they finished ordering, the tension had passed. Dean and Karen were discussing a college placement course they both were going to take, and Sally was bending David's ear about one of her horses. Jenny was trying to decide whether she should be apologizing to David or not. For some reason, he was awfully touchy about that night; maybe it would be better to just let it slide. Since everyone else was busy talking, Jenny was the first one to see Brad come in the door.

The only time she'd seen him was on the night of the hunt. A big guy, with a round face and a swaggering walk. But not swaggering now, Jenny noticed. And his round face was filled with emotion.

Sally saw him next. She started to wave, but her hand stopped in mid air. "Something's wrong," she said. "Something terrible's happened."

"Sally, don't be so drama — " Karen broke off and stared at Brad.

Moving woodenly, he made his way over to them and grabbed hold of the back of Dean's chair.

"Diana," he said, and his voice broke. He took a deep breath. "Did you hear about Diana?"

"Sit down," Dean told him. He reached across the aisle and dragged over an empty chair. Brad slumped into it and leaned his head in his hands. "They found her. Yesterday," he said.

"Found her?" Karen asked. "You sound like she's dead or something."

Brad shook his head. "In a coma."

"What happened?" Sally breathed.

Brad looked up, and Jenny saw that his green eyes were bloodshot. "A couple of climbers found her on the rimrocks. She was unconscious and her head was all — " his deep voice cracked. "She fell."

No one said anything for a moment, least of all Jenny. Her nightmare *had* come true. For Diana. As she sat there, the cool, comfortable interior of the diner faded, and she was back on the bluff, the thunder rolling and the lightning crackling around her. She saw herself yelling for David, and then she remembered the scream she thought she'd heard. She came back to reality with a jolt.

"I can't believe it!" Karen was saying. "I think I was the last one to see her. We'd been with you, Dean, remember? And then you went off to try to find a zither. And Diana — she was in a really foul mood — said she was going home."

"Yeah, well she must have changed her mind," Brad said. "When was that, Karen?"

"I don't know. About a half hour or so before the storm."

"Gee, she went up on the bluff alone?" Sally said. "What a dumb . . . never mind."

"She wasn't the only one to go up there, remember?" Dean said. He looked at David. "She must have screamed when she fell. It's amazing nobody heard her."

"I might . . ." Jenny cleared her throat. "I might have heard her."

She'd spoken softly, but no one missed it. They stared as if she'd shouted. David didn't look surprised, naturally. But she noticed that his eyes narrowed and didn't move from her face.

Brad leaned forward tensely. "What do you mean?"

"Well, I'm not sure if I'm right," Jenny said. "I mean, I . . . David and I got caught up there in the storm and — "

"Yeah, okay," Brad said impatiently. "Just tell us what you heard."

Jenny closed her eyes in concentration. "I'd just shouted for David, and then . . ."

"I thought you were together," Sally said.

"We got separated for a few minutes," David told her.

"Who cares about that?" Brad asked. "Come on, Jenny, what did you hear?"

"There was a big thunderclap," Jenny said, closing her eyes again, "but just before it came, I heard somebody yell . . ."

"Yell what?" Brad asked.

Jenny opened her eyes. "I don't . . ." she shook her head helplessly. "I can't remember." What had the voice said? She remembered almost everything else, why had the words disappeared? She shook her head again.

"Come on," Brad urged. He was across from Jenny, now he leaned forward even farther, his big hands almost touching hers. "Think, can't you? It's important!"

Jenny sat back a little. The look on his face scared her. "I'm trying," she said.

"Well try harder!" His right hand closed in a fist and his eyes glittered with anger. "How can you just forget something like that? Come on, you've got to remember!"

"Brad . . ." Sally said softly.

"What?" He swung his head toward her. "You think it doesn't matter? She could have been the last person to see . . . to hear Diana ali — " He broke off before he said it, then slapped the table with the palm of his hand.

"Take it easy, Brad," Dean said calmly. His pale eyes were sympathetic. "Remember what Jenny said. She was up there in the middle of the thunderstorm. You must have heard it. It sounded like the inside of a bowling alley." He tapped his mouth with his forefinger and glanced at Jenny before looking back to Brad. "Don't you think it's possible — even probable — that she didn't hear anyone? That it was just the wind and the thunder playing tricks with her ears?"

"That's what David thought," Jenny said, and David nodded, his eyes still watching her. But she knew it wasn't true. She *did* hear somebody yell something. At the moment, though, she wasn't going to argue about it. Brad was really agitated, and she remembered what Sally had told her, about how Diana had just broken off with him. He must be feeling guilty, she thought. He was probably so mad at her, he hoped something awful would happen. And it had.

"Yeah." Brad slumped back into his chair and wiped a hand over his face. "I guess that might be it."

Jenny knew she would remember what she'd heard; it would come back to her one of these days. But she kept that thought to herself. She didn't want to set Brad off again.

She smiled gratefully at Dean. He was the one who'd calmed Brad down and taken the spotlight off her, and she wanted him to know she appreciated it even though he was wrong about her imagining things.

Dean smiled back, which didn't surprise her. What surprised her was that he gave her a wink along with the smile. And it wasn't just a friendly one, either. She'd never been much of a sucker for winks, but if she had, Dean's slow, seductive one might have done the trick. Sally sure has him pegged wrong, she thought. He doesn't need a computer printout *or* an answering machine to get his message across.

Slightly flustered, Jenny glanced away. The others had been talking quietly of Diana; no one seemed to have noticed Dean's little eyeplay, and she was glad. The timing just wasn't right for a come-on, and besides, she wasn't interested, even though he seemed nice enough.

She took another look at David. He was awfully

quiet. Of course, she didn't blame him for that. He was worried about Diana.

But if it was Diana he was thinking about, then why did he sit so still, his eyes never leaving Jenny's face, like a cat at a mousehole?

Chapter 5

Around four, everyone but Jenny started to leave. No one had felt like hanging around any longer; after a few attempts at changing the subject, they always came back to Diana, and finally, there was nothing left to say. Diana was in a coma; they'd just have to wait and see what happened.

Jenny was going to leave, too, but then she changed her mind. She hadn't ordered anything before and there was nothing at home she wanted to eat, so she decided to get a hamburger. But she wanted to wait until everyone else had gone first. She felt slightly guilty that she had an appetite while the rest of them had barely touched their Cokes.

David left first, then the others got up and headed for the door. Jenny had just started to relax when Dean came back. Remembering his wink, she was afraid for a second that he'd decided to join her.

But he barely glanced at her. "I think I left my keys," he said, stooping to look under the table.

When he straightened up, he patted the pockets of his jeans. Jenny heard a jingling sound.

"Sounds like keys to me," she said.

He pulled a handful of coins from his pocket and held them out for her to see. "Sounds like you heard wrong."

"Okay." Jenny shrugged and smiled. "I get the point."

"What point is that?"

"That I heard wrong on the rimrocks, too."

He raised his eyebrows. "What's *your* point? That you didn't hear wrong?"

Jenny just shook her head, shrugging again. "I wasn't making any point at all," she said.

"Neither was I." Dean put the change back in his pocket. "Except that sound can fool your mind. Make it play tricks on you, make you think you heard one thing when it was really something else." He reached into the other pocket and took out his car keys. Looking at them, he smiled slightly. "Guess I didn't leave them after all. Bye, Jenny."

Jenny shook her head again as she watched him go. What an oddball. Well, he was supposed to be a genius. Maybe that explained it.

She ordered a burger and had just doused it with ketchup and taken a huge bite when a shadow fell across the table. Her mouth full, she looked up into David's dark eyes.

She swallowed as quickly as possible and wiped her mouth. "Hi," she said. "I thought you'd gone."

"I came back," he said, slightly out of breath. He

pulled out a chair and sat down, stretching his long legs under the table. "I saw you were still here so I decided to come in. I felt like talking."

Jenny nodded and waited for him to start. But he kept quiet, so she picked up her burger again. "I can't help it," she said. "I'm starving."

"You don't have to explain," he told her. "Some people eat when they're upset."

"I know, but I'm not one of them. I just eat when I'm hungry. Not that I'm not upset," she added.

He leaned his elbows on the table and cupped his chin in his hands, watching her.

"Actually I'm feeling guilty," she went on. "I mean we were up there when Diana fell. I even heard her. Of course, I was busy worrying about my own situation, but afterward — when I met up with you again — that's what's bothering me."

"What do you mean?"

"Well, if I just hadn't ripped into you," Jenny said. "I was going to apologize to you for that, by the way," she added. "Anyway, if I'd just insisted that *somebody* was up there, then maybe Diana would have been found sooner. I know she still would have been hurt, but at least . . ." Jenny heard herself running on and stopped. David still hadn't taken his eyes from her and she was beginning to feel uncomfortable. "Anyway," she said again, "that's what I was feeling."

"Guilty?"

Jenny nodded, not liking the sound of the word.

"Then you don't think Dean was right?" he asked. "You don't think you imagined that shout?"

Jenny started to say no, and then changed her mind. Was he giving her a way out of feeling guilty? Even though it wasn't true, she decided to take it. "I guess I'll never be absolutely sure," she said.

"Maybe not." David leaned back, crossed his arms over his chest, and flashed a quick smile.

Jenny was glad he'd come, but she couldn't think of anything else to say. This was hardly the time for small talk, and besides, he was the one who said he felt like talking. She decided to keep quiet for a while and give him a chance.

Another quick smile lit up David's face, and then he said, "What did you think of Diana?"

"I don't know her," Jenny reminded him with a little laugh. "I only met her that one time, before the scavenger hunt. Of course, she wasn't exactly friendly to me then, so I can't say I liked her. But like you said, she had something on her mind."

"Yeah, she did," he agreed with a frown. Jenny couldn't tell if the frown was because of Diana's bad mood, or because of his opinion of Diana. He'd never said how he felt about her. "And you didn't talk to her at all after that, while we were running around?"

"You know I didn't," she said, wondering what he was getting at. "You and I were together the whole time."

No smile this time, just a straight look that Jenny

couldn't read at all. She suddenly wished he would go. He was tense and preoccupied, and his mood was making her edgy.

As if he could read her mind, David scraped his chair back and stood up. "I'm not good company right now," he said. "I'll see you, Jenny." Then he hurried out of the diner like someone late for a crucial appointment.

Jenny stared at the remains of her burger and sighed. Why had he acted so strangely? Was it just because he was upset about Diana? Or did he secretly think she *had* heard that shout? Did he agree with her — that she'd wasted time yelling at him on the rimrocks that night, time that could have been spent helping Diana? After all, he'd asked what she thought of Diana. Did he honestly believe she might be glad the girl was lying in a coma? If he did, then he didn't know her very well. But she didn't know him, either.

After a few more minutes, Jenny paid for her meal and headed for home. She couldn't avoid seeing the rimrocks on her way — half of them turned a brilliant red again — and that didn't help her mood any. By the time she pulled up to the house, she was wishing desperately that she'd gone with her parents. What was the big deal about packing one small suitcase? And so what if they missed the painters? They could live with a salmon pink living room for a little while longer.

Jenny got out of the car and kicked a couple of small rocks to the edge of the driveway. "Stop wallowing in self-pity," she said out loud. "It's truly disgusting." It was also easier said than done, and her shoulders were still slumping as she climbed the steps to the flagstone porch. Her head was down, too, so when she went up the last step, she didn't see the basket of flowers until it brushed against her hair.

It was hanging from one of the curly pieces of wrought-iron attached to the porch pillars. They were just right for hanging flowerpots, and Jenny's mother had been talking about getting some. Now she wouldn't have to.

Jenny untangled a strand of hair and looked at the basket. It was filled to overflowing with a fantastic assortment of flowers, most of which she'd seen growing by the side of the road or in fields. Driving by them in a car, they hadn't been that impressive, but massed together in the basket, they made one of the most beautiful bouquets she'd ever seen.

She reached up and poked around in the flowers for a card, thinking it might be from the Welcome Wagon, or maybe from the real estate agent who'd sold them the house. The last agent had given them discount coupons to the local stores; Jenny thought the flowers were much nicer.

There was no card, though. And there was no pot inside the basket, which was odd. The flowers had been put in without any dirt at all, and some of them were already starting to wilt.

Strange, Jenny thought, unlocking the front

door. If I'd been much later getting home, I would have found a bunch of dead flowers waiting for me. Somebody goofed at the flower shop.

"Hi, Peach!" Jenny bent down and patted the dog, who'd come to greet her. "Did you see who brought the flowers? Did you bark real loud or did you run and hide?"

Wagging her short tail in circles, Peaches led the way into the kitchen. Jenny poured dry food into the bowl, then walked into the living room, kicking off her sandals as she went.

The answering machine was aglow again: A red number one showed that one person, at least, had tried to call. Jenny pressed the button and stood at the tall windows, frowning out at the bluff.

"Hi, Jenny. It's me again." The same soft, sexy-shy voice. "Did you see the flowers? I hope you like them. They reminded me of you, and I couldn't resist picking them." A short laugh. "I just thought — I guess couldn't resist picking you, either." There was a pause, then, almost as if he was in a hurry, the caller said, "I better go, Jenny. Bye."

She'd almost forgotten. After David's cool attitude and the awful news about Diana, and her own sense of guilt, Jenny had almost forgotten about her secret admirer.

She'd stopped frowning the minute she heard his voice, and now, with what she knew was a silly smile on her face, she hurried out to the porch and brought the basket of flowers inside. Then she rummaged

68

around in the packing cartons that were still lined up along one wall of the kitchen until she found a tall, cut glass vase. She unrolled it from its wrapping of dishtowels, filled it with water, and put in all the flowers that hadn't completely wilted. She knew they wouldn't last long, but maybe with water they'd have a better chance of making it through the night.

Back in the living room, she set the vase in the middle of the stone mantel over the fireplace and stepped back to look at it. It looked great.

What a nice end to a rotten day. That made it twice now that he'd called and raised her spirits just when they were dragging along the ground. Was he psychic or was his timing just lucky? Jenny spun around and flopped down on the couch, still grinning. Almost immediately she hopped up and played the tape again, hoping for some clue that would let her in on the boy's identity.

It couldn't be David, or Dean. Or Brad, either, she thought. David had been so distant, and Dean wasn't the shy computer freak she'd thought he was. Nobody who could make a wink look that suggestive would bother with anonymous phone calls. And if it was Brad, then Brad had a problem. To be so angry that he'd come close to hitting her and then to turn right around and compare her to a bunch of beautiful wildflowers was an awfully twisted thing to do. Besides, she'd gotten the first call before Diana's accident. So if it was Brad, he wouldn't have kept it up. Except as some kind of nasty game. Which was pretty twisted, too, when she thought about it.

No, it had to be someone else. She couldn't remember the names of everyone she'd met at the hunt. She'd have to ask Sally. Or maybe she'd even get the chance to ask her secret admirer himself. She had to stay home all day tomorrow for the painters; if he called, she'd be ready with as many questions as it took to find out who he was.

She stretched and pulled herself up out of the soft cushions of the couch, feeling relaxed and peaceful for the first time since she'd heard about Diana. Having a secret admirer was the perfect cure for jangled nerves.

So was a shower. Checking to make sure the door was locked, Jenny went upstairs, stripped, and stood under the warm needles of water, humming and smiling to herself. By the time she got out, the sky was finally darkening. She left the lights off in her room while she toweled off and dressed, still feeling funny about not having curtains or shades, even though no Peeping Tom in his right mind would pick this house to spy on.

Wrapped in a short white terrycloth robe, Jenny trotted downstairs to check out what was on television. Their reception wasn't very good because the antenna was still lying on its side up on the roof like some broken pieces of an erector set, but maybe she'd get lucky and find a station that didn't look like it was in the middle of a desert sandstorm.

She was still turning the dial when the phone rang. Twice in one day, maybe, she thought hopefully.

"Hi, Jenny." A tired-sounding Sally.

"Hi." Jenny wasn't really disappointed. Sitting in front of a grainy-screened television wasn't an exciting way to spend an evening, and waiting for the secret admirer to call again would be like waiting for water to boil.

A sigh came over the telephone. "I just got back from the hospital," Sally reported. "A few of us went, but they wouldn't let us see her."

Jenny curled up on the couch next to Peaches. "I take it there hasn't been any change."

"No, nothing." Sally sighed again. "I thought Brad was going to punch a hole in the wall." She laughed a little. "Better the wall than your head, I guess. Did he call and apologize to you for the way he acted at the diner?"

"Uh, no. Why, did he say he was going to?"

"Not exactly. We told him he ought to," Sally said. "He came on like a real Neanderthal. You must think he's nuts."

"The thought did cross my mind," Jenny admitted. "But I guess he was just really upset."

"And feeling guilty, I'll bet," Sally added. "Diana breaks up with him and he's thinking terrible things about her, and then boom — something terrible happens to her."

"That's what I figured," Jenny said. "I'm just glad Dean managed to calm him down."

"He calmed him down at the hospital, too," Sally told her.

"Oh, he was there?"

"Yeah, and Karen. I suppose some more will go tomorrow. I might, too."

Jenny thought it was a little odd that Sally would keep watch at the hospital, considering the way she felt about Diana.

"Well," Sally went on, "I wanted to find out if you got any more anonymous, sexy calls." She laughed. "My voice game wasn't too successful."

Jenny rolled her eyes. It hadn't been too subtle, either. She started to mention the latest call, but then she suddenly noticed that Peaches had lifted her head and sniffed the air. Then the dog tumbled off the couch and moved in the direction of the front door. "Listen," Jenny said to Sally, "my parents are still out of town, you know. And I love my dog, but she's not much of a conversationalist. Why don't you come over tonight and we can . . . I don't know . . . make some popcorn and talk. Watch TV if I can get something on it." Sally might be annoying at times, but Jenny wanted company and there wasn't anyone else to ask.

"I can't," Sally said. "One of our horses has a cold and the vet's coming by to give her a shot. I've got to stick around until he comes and I have no idea when that'll be."

"Your vet makes house calls?"

"Yeah. Dr. Jacobsen is really great," Sally said. "The kind of vet who takes care of stray animals and tries to find them a home. You'll meet him probably, whenever you have to take Peaches in for her shots. Uh-oh, I gotta go," she said quickly. "My mom has to use the phone. Bye, and don't worry about being alone tonight — remember, the perverted painter doesn't come till tomorrow."

Thanks for reminding me, Jenny thought as she hung up. Maybe no company was better after all. She headed for the kitchen, thinking she might make some popcorn, and found Peaches standing by the front door, shifting from side to side.

A nature call, Jenny thought. She took the leash down from the coatrack and snapped it on the dog's collar. Once Peaches got to know the territory, Jenny wouldn't have to walk her. But she had visions of her pet wandering off and not being able to find her way back, or of being on the losing side of an argument with a raccoon, so she still didn't let her out alone.

Jenny opened the door and gave a startled gasp. Standing on the porch was Brad Billings. His green eyes were still bloodshot, but this time she could smell beer, and she knew he'd been drinking.

"Jenny," he said thickly. "I came to . . . I don't know. Apologize. Didn't mean to jump on you at the diner."

Jenny swallowed and stepped outside, pulling the dog with her. She didn't want Brad in the house.

He squinted at her. "You sure you can't remember what you heard that night?"

Jenny decided to lie rather than get into it with

him. "I've thought about it and I realized Dean was right — it was just the storm. I didn't hear anyone else at all."

He kept staring at her. She couldn't tell what he was thinking.

"Listen," she told him, "you didn't have to apologize. And you sure didn't have to come all this way to do it."

He waved his hand as if batting her words away. "I was driving around anyway. Thinking."

"Well." Jenny cleared her throat. "Thanks for coming." Now go, she thought.

But Brad stayed, his big body swaying a little. "I was thinking about Diana. She was . . . is . . ." he laughed a little, ". . . sometimes she's a real pain, you know? I mean a *real* pain, cold and mean."

Jenny kept quiet. If she didn't talk, maybe he'd leave faster.

"You know what she did to me?" Brad asked. He didn't wait for an answer. "Made me think she cared, then dropped me like I was a piece of garbage. Said she'd made a mistake." He put a hand on the wall and leaned toward Jenny. "That wasn't right!" he shouted. "You don't treat people like that!"

Jenny flinched and edged away.

"I hated her after that," he went on loudly, "but I never wanted anything like this to happen! I just wanted to . . . oh, I don't know." He took his hand away and stepped back.

Jenny waited, not sure what he was going to do,

afraid she'd set him off if she said anything.

Brad tilted his head back and took several gulps of air. When he looked at her again, he blinked, as if surprised to see her there. He ran a hand over his face and mumbled, "Sorry, Jenny." Turning around, he stepped off the porch and walked to the end of the driveway.

When she heard a car start, Jenny let her breath out. She realized as he pulled away, she shouldn't have let him drive. But he was gone so quickly. Brad's visit had shaken her and she would have gone right back inside, except that Peaches was whining again.

"Come on." Jenny gave a gentle tug on the leash and the two of them went down the front steps. It was almost completely dark, but the moonlight was strong and the cool breeze felt good on her bare legs. Peaches must have liked it, too. She stopped halfway down the walk and sniffed the air again.

A small gust of wind ruffled the dog's fur and Jenny's still-damp hair. Clouds blew across the moon and blotted out its light. Jenny heard a strange rumble; for a second she thought it was a faraway truck. Then she realized it was Peaches. The dog was growling.

Jenny listened carefully. She could hear the wind high up in the tops of the pine trees, and she thought she heard a rustle of weeds down at the edge of the road. A raccoon or a deer. Or Brad? She'd heard his car start, but maybe he hadn't gone far. Maybe he'd walked back.

Giving the leash a not-so-gentle tug this time, Jenny whirled around and ran back inside, locking the door with shaking fingers. Once unleashed, Peaches sat down in front of the closed door and stared at it.

Jenny took a deep breath, determined not to get nervous again. Brad had been drinking, she told herself. He wasn't thinking straight. He didn't mean what he said about hating Diana, and he didn't come here to scare me. He'll be embarrassed when he remembers what he said. *If* he remembers.

She went into the kitchen, got the popcorn, and poured it into the popper. She'd do what she planned — make some popcorn, try to find something on television, read a little. And forget about Brad.

As Jenny was dribbling melted butter over the popcorn, she caught a movement out of the corner of her eye. The kitchen windows were at the front of the house, and like all the others, they were still uncovered. That's where she'd seen something move.

Feeling extremely exposed, Jenny set the butter down, walked over to the doorway and turned off the light. Telling herself it was only an animal, not someone out roaming the foothills, and not Brad, she crept over to one of the windows and peered out. But it was pitch dark outside, and all she could see was the pale reflection of her white bathrobe.

Her reflection! That must have been what she'd seen before. She turned the light back on and started pouring the butter again. Sure enough, when she circled her hand above the bowl, the reflected movement caught her eye.

She finished with the butter, and then realized that something was missing — Peaches. The dog loved popcorn, but instead of coming in and begging for some, she'd stayed at her post by the door. Jenny tried to entice her with a few unbuttered pieces, but the dog didn't budge.

Her arms around the bowl of popcorn, Jenny closed her eyes and listened. Except for the sighing of the wind, everything was quiet. So why was her dog acting so strange?

Forget it, Jenny told herself. If you keep this up, pretty soon you'll be looking in every closet and then building booby traps in front of the doors. She'd done that once a few years before. After watching a grisly horror movie on television, she'd built a pyramid of soup cans topped with silverware against her bedroom door, so she'd at least be awake when the killer came to do her in. And when the pyramid had toppled, it was her mother, coming to wake her up the next morning.

Well, there wasn't going to be any horror movie tonight, she thought. And if Brad did come back, he couldn't get in.

Jenny picked up the bowl of popcorn, turned out the light, and started for the stairs. Peaches glanced at her, but didn't follow.

In the second-floor hall, Jenny rummaged in a box of books and found a copy of *Rebecca*, which she'd never read. She piled the pillows high against her headboard, set the popcorn at just the right reaching distance on her bedside table, got under the quilt, and opened the book. She could hear Peaches downstairs, still snuffling and whining at the door, and she could hear the wind rustling the tops of the trees outside, but by the time she reached the bottom of the first page, she was hooked, and soon the only sound she was aware of was the beating of her own heart.

Chapter 6

Jenny woke with a jerk, her heart no longer thumping steadily but racing with fear. She'd slipped sideways in her sleep and so had the book, and one corner of it was poking her in the cheek. She pushed herself up onto her pillows and rubbed her face. It was sweaty, and her arms ached as if she'd been clenching her fists.

What a dream! The rimrocks and the wind and Manderley and the sea had gotten all jumbled up. And Jenny had turned into Diana, not unconscious, but wide awake and clinging to a rock that kept crumbling in her hands. And all the time, she kept hearing someone shouting at her. She couldn't understand the words, but something about them terrified her.

Jenny rubbed her eyes and pushed back her hair. It was damp and tangled. *Rebecca* had been a mistake, she guessed. If she'd wanted to get Diana and the awful rimrocks out of her mind, she should have picked a joke book and saved weird, obsessed Mrs.

Danvers for another time. Daytime, not night.

She heard a shuffling sound from somewhere, and her heartbeat, which had almost returned to normal, suddenly speeded up again. The wind was still blowing outside, and something skittered across the roof of the house. Probably a twig, she thought, straining her ears for the shuffle again.

There it was. Not a shuffle, though. It was more like somebody panting, but trying to hide it by breathing through his nose. Somebody . . . Brad?

She'd kept telling herself that he hadn't meant to scare her, but what if he had? What if he'd just been acting? After all, before he'd gone on about what a rotten person Diana was, he'd asked Jenny about the shout. Had he known she was lying when she said she agreed with Dean? Had he come back again to try to force her into remembering?

Jenny shut off her reading lamp, slid out of bed, and moved soundlessly toward the door, the mood of the dream still clinging to her like a thick fog. The shuffling, or panting, kept on going, and it wasn't until she was almost at the head of the stairs that she realized what it was: a pudgy, aging dog who thought there was something outside and was doing her best to smell it through the solid wood thickness of the front door.

Jenny tightened the belt on her robe and hurried downstairs. She glanced into the kitchen; the clock over the stove said it was two-fifteen. Peaches was actually pawing at the door now. She turned her head and whined at Jenny, then went back to her hopeless task.

Jenny had often read about people going cold with fear, but what she felt was a sudden rush of heat that made her break into a sweat all over again. Something — or someone — *was* outside the house. Jenny couldn't remember Peaches ever pawing frantically at a door. Something was out there, and the dog wanted to get at it.

Jenny was so scared her heart was thudding in her ears like a bass drum. She wished it would stop. She couldn't hear anything else but it, and if she couldn't hear the enemy, whatever it was, how would she know it was about to jump on her?

Stop it, stop it, stop it! Nobody's going to jump on you, she thought. How could they? They'd have to get in first and how can they get in unless you open the door? Not even Brad's big enough to break down the door.

Immediately, Jenny took a quick mental tour of the house. The front door was locked. Back door? Yes, she remembered checking it before she went into town earlier, and she hadn't used it since. Same with the door leading in from the garage. She'd left the car in the driveway after she drove her parents to the airport; she hadn't used the garage at all. But what about the garage door itself? What if the automatic lock hadn't worked?

The thudding in her ears got louder than ever. When she took Peaches out earlier, when Brad was there, she'd left the door open. Someone could have stolen in then. It couldn't be Brad though. Or could it? After he'd left, she'd stayed out with Peaches. He could have come back. He — or someone else — could be in the house right now. Jenny spun around. All she could see were the stairs and part of the living room. Behind her, Peaches was whimpering, a high-pitched, anxious sound that made Jenny bite her lips, mainly to keep from whimpering herself. There was the basement, too, she thought. Piled with unpacked boxes, it was the perfect place to hide out.

Wait, wait, wait! Jenny turned around again. Peaches wasn't whimpering or pawing anymore, she was just sitting and staring at the door. Her ears were pricked up, but her tongue was hanging out the side of her mouth, as if she were taking a quick breather, just waiting to see what move her opponent on the other side of the door was going to make.

On the other side of the door. If someone were in the house, Peaches wouldn't be glued to the door like that. Whoever or whatever was out there, was *out there*.

They have to be, Jenny thought. And the thought made her heart slow down. She didn't feel safe, but she wasn't on the verge of panic, either. The thudding in her ears started to fade a bit, and she could hear other sounds — *normal* sounds — like the hum of the refrigerator and the dripping of water in the kitchen sink. She leaned over and patted

Peaches on the head, then went into the kitchen and tightened the faucet. She stood in the dark for several seconds, listening, and heard nothing out of the ordinary. That didn't mean much, though. Someone sneaking around outside a house in the middle of the night would try to be as quiet as possible.

Wincing at every noise she made, Jenny opened a cabinet and pulled out several cans of corn, soup, and tuna, and a couple of jars of spaghetti sauce. She opened a drawer and scooped up a handful of silverware, then put everything into a plastic grocery bag.

Peaches was still at the front door, head cocked, eyes trying to bore a hole through the wood. Jenny left her and went down the hall to the basement door, were she built a pyramid of cans and topped it with several strategically placed spoons.

Back to the bottom of the stairs where she erected another booby trap, then into the kitchen and the door that led to the garage.

She saved the front door for last. After carefully placing a fork on top of a can of vegetable soup, she pulled Peaches into her arms and scratched her between the ears. The dog was quivering with tension, and Jenny's heart started to speed up again. She tried to talk down the rising sense of panic. *It doesn't have to be some*one. *It's probably some-thing. An animal. A broken branch. In the morning, you'll find out, and then you'll laugh about it.*

It was almost three o'clock. Only about three more hours, Jenny thought, and then the sun will come up, and then everything will be okay. Three hours. You can make it.

She was wringing wet, but a shower was completely out of the question. Jenny gave Peaches another pat, then went into the living room and sat on the couch. Her heart just wouldn't stop thudding, and she had to strain her ears to hear above it.

She pulled her legs up and leaned sideways, letting her head rest on one of the throw pillows, suddenly so tired her eyes were starting to close. She forced them open and stared across the room at the desk and the telephone. The red number one glowed on the machine. The message from her secret admirer — she'd saved it, of course. She was afraid to play it now, afraid to make any noise at all, but just remembering the sound of his voice calmed her for a moment.

Suddenly a piece of silverware clanged, and Jenny was on her feet, her secret admirer forgotten, her heart racing faster then ever. Her mouth was dry and her knees were actually weak. Which trap had fallen? Where had the sound come from?

Clutching a pillow, she forced herself to move across the living room and into the front hall. She'd left a light on at the top of the stairs, and its faint glow just reached the bottom of the front door. There was the tower of cans, and there, lying on the tiles, was the fork. The door was still closed, still chained. Peaches was still there, too. Sniffing the fork.

Jenny swallowed hard and felt the blood start

moving in her legs again. There was still the rest of the night to get through, but at least she knew who'd sprung this trap.

She replaced the fork, then pointed to the tower and said "no" a couple of times, using her sternest voice. The dog barely glanced at her; she was busy worrying at the door again.

After checking the other doors, and finding nothing disturbed, Jenny went back into the living room. She headed for the couch, then stopped and took the iron poker from the stand of fireplace tools. Gripping it tightly, she sat back down and waited for the night to end.

It was the poker that woke her this time, slipping from her hand and banging to the floor. Jenny's eyes flew open, then blinked at the brightness of the room. Morning, finally.

She sat for a minute, listening to the silence around her. Not a perfect silence, though. She heard a very familiar sound and turned her head to see Peaches curled up on the other end of the couch, snoring softly. Jenny didn't know when the dog had joined her. The last time she'd checked the clock, it was four-thirty, and Peaches had still been at the front door.

Well, none of the booby traps had been sprung, so whoever or whatever must still be outside. Or else they'd gone away. There was no doubt in Jenny's mind that *something* had been out there, though. And the thought of spending another night alone in the house was already starting to make her anxious.

Suddenly Peaches lifted her head and pricked her ears.

Not again, please, Jenny thought. She couldn't go through that again.

But Peaches tumbled off the couch and trotted to the front door. Just as she reached it, somebody rang the bell and then called out. Peaches wagged her rear end, toppling Jenny's soup-can tower.

Jenny's neck was stiff, her eyes felt gritty, and just remembering the night made her scalp prickle with fear. She got up, reached for the poker, and headed slowly for the door.

Then someone called out again, and Jenny recognized Sally's voice. "I heard a crash in there!" Sally said. "I hope nobody's wounded or anything."

"I'm not wounded," Jenny called back. "Just barricaded. Wait a sec." She toed some cans away, sending them rolling noisily across the tile, then unchained and unbolted the door.

Sally walked in, holding a package in her hands. It was about the size of a shoebox, wrapped in crimson paper and topped with a white silk bow. She clutched it to her chest and silently surveyed the rolling cans, scattered silverware, and Jenny's droopy, disheveled appearance.

"Wild night, huh?" she finally said.

Jenny didn't feel like joking, and not just because she was tired. She was still frightened. It *had* been a wild night, but not the way Sally meant it.

Sally poked her head into the kitchen. "Gee, another barricade in there," she said. She eyed the poker in Jenny's hand, and raised an eyebrow. "What *did* happen? Don't tell me somebody tried to break in."

"No. I don't know. I thought they might." Jenny relaxed her grip on the poker and took a shaky breath. Then she told Sally what had happened. She started to mention Brad, then changed her mind. If he hadn't been the one, then she didn't want Sally gossiping about his visit. "I should feel better now that it's morning," she said, "but I don't. Daylight doesn't seem to help. I've never been so scared in my life."

"Yeah, I can see why," Sally said. They'd moved into the living room, and she sat down on the couch. Peaches jumped up beside her and whined. "It sounds like one of those movies," she went on, scratching the dog between the ears. "You know, where the girl's all alone in the house and the next thing you know there's blood all over the place."

"Did you have to say that?" Jenny shivered. "That's all I thought about all night long. I'd like to forget it."

"Sorry." But Sally didn't look sorry at all. "Anyway, you should have called me. The vet didn't come until really late. If you'd called, at least you would have had an ear-witness for when the killer started coming for you." She held an imaginary phone to her ear. "Jenny?! Jenny, why are you screaming like that?! Answer me, Jenny!!"

Jenny stared at her. Why did Sally insist on joking? Didn't she realize how scared Jenny had been? How scared she still was, for that matter? Obviously not. She suddenly wished Sally would leave. But she looked very comfortable on the couch, with Peaches next to her. Jenny tried to shake off her annoyance and pointed to the package Sally was still holding. The dog was whining and sniffing at it. "What's that?"

"This?" Sally glanced down at the box. "Oh. It was on the porch when I got here. I don't know what it is. Why don't you open it and find out?" She lifted it away from Peaches's nose and held it out to Jenny. "Must have something tasty in it . . . ah-ha!" She snapped her fingers triumphantly. "You *did* have a visitor last night! Somebody who's probably very sexy, but also extremely shy? So he makes phone calls and drops off little presents in the middle of the night?"

Her secret admirer. Not once during the long, horrible night had Jenny considered that it might be him out there. But it made sense, now that she thought about it. She traced her finger along the silky bow and felt her lips curve in a smile. Well, he'd scared her half out of her mind, but maybe it was going to be worth it.

"So?" Sally got up and stood next to her. "Don't just look at it. Open it!"

Eager now, Jenny pulled off the ribbon. "I wonder what it is," she said, ripping off the red paper. "If I ever meet him, remind me to thank him. Remind me to tell him, however, not to deliver presents in the middle of the night, not unless he likes his girls terrified."

"Hurry up," Sally urged. "I haven't had any breakfast. Maybe it's chocolate, or a bunch of cookies or something."

"Why food?" Jenny used her thumbnail to slit the tape that held the lid on.

"Because of your dog," Sally explained. "She's sitting there drooling like it's got a steak in it. Maybe it *is* a steak."

"That's not very romantic," Jenny said. She slit the last piece of tape and fumbled with the lid. "But I guess it would be original. There!"

The lid was finally off. Jenny let it drop to the floor and pulled out several wads of white tissue paper. One last piece. She lifted it off. And froze.

At the bottom of the box, nestled on a bed of more white tissue paper, was a rattlesnake. A dead rattlesnake. Jenny knew it was dead, because its severed head had been placed carefully on top of its limp, lifeless body.

Chapter 7

Jenny felt her stomach churn; she screamed, a short, high-pitched scream, and flung the box across the room. It hit one of the tall windows and dropped to the floor with a soft thunk. She didn't wait to see what happened to the snake. Whirling around, she ran into the kitchen and gulped down some water, holding the glass with both shaking hands.

Sally was right behind her. The two of them stared at each other for a second, both of them looking slightly sick. Sally recovered first. She took a big breath and then let it out in a whoosh. "Talk about your unusual gifts," she said. "That has to be the grossest thing I've ever seen. Some admirer you've got."

Jenny shook her head. "It couldn't be from him. Yesterday he left me flowers." She went back into the living room and pointed at the vase on the mantel. Some of the flowers were drooping badly, but most had made it through the night. "See?" she said. "And he called, too, and he sounded just as nice as he did the first time. Nobody sends flowers and then follows it up with a dead snake. It's someone else."

"I guess you're right. Somebody must be playing a joke." Sally agreed. "But whoever it is sure has a weird sense of humor."

"Sick, you mean." Jenny shivered in disgust and risked a glance at the box. Peaches was nosing around it, sniffing loudly. "Peaches, stop it!" She said it roughly, and the dog slunk away.

"Hey, you didn't tell me he called again," Sally said, obviously trying to change the subject. "What'd he say? I take it he hasn't revealed his identity yet."

"Not yet." Jenny was still eyeing the box. Had Brad come back and left it?

Sally was looking at the box, too, and suddenly a grin broke out. "Now that I think about it, that's a great way to let somebody know how you feel about them."

"It's not! It's disgusting!" Jenny cried. "How can you laugh about it?"

"Sorry," Sally said. She stopped smiling, but her eyes were still twinkling. "I can't help it. I always laugh at the wrong time."

Jenny barely heard her. Her skin was still crawling, and she couldn't shake off the feeling that she might be sick. "Who would do that to me?" she asked. "To anyone?"

"Nobody. I mean, nobody that I know," Sally said. "Everyone I've talked to says they think you're nice, pretty, good things like that. Not that we've been gossiping or anything," she added. "But you know, when somebody new moves in, you can't help talking about them a little."

Jenny nodded. "They've said good things? Even Brad?" She took a deep breath and finally told Sally about his visit. She didn't go into detail, just told her that he'd been drinking and was still upset. "I wasn't going to say anything, but now . . . do you think he did it?"

"Brad," Sally said thoughtfully. "He does still have this idea that you heard something on the rim-rocks that night. Dean and Karen and everybody keep telling him to forget it. But he's really bull-headed. And after what he did last night, I guess he could be the one."

"But it doesn't make any sense," Jenny said. "Why would he leave me a dead snake?"

"Somebody who'd do something like that isn't making sense in the first place. And Brad's not famous for his brainpower." Sally looked curiously at Jenny. "Did you really hear something up there?"

"I thought I did." Jenny's mind flashed back to that moment on the bluff. "No, I'm *positive* I did," she said. "I keep going over it and over it. I even dreamed about it last night. But everytime I get to that part, I can hear the voice, but I can't hear what it said."

"What was the voice like?"

"I don't know." Jenny shook her head. "It was loud, shouting."

"Mad? Scared?" Sally asked. "Seems like you'd be able to tell that much."

Why was Sally pushing? Jenny wondered.

"What difference does it make?" Jenny said defensively. "Diana shouted and then she fell and screamed. It happened all at once, almost. There wasn't anything I could have done."

"No, but maybe Brad thinks there was," Sally said. "Like I said, he's obsessed about it, so maybe he decided you *could* have done something, and he sent you a chopped-up snake to let you know how he feels about you."

Jenny shuddered. She remembered Brad's strong hands reaching across the diner table toward her, and the way he'd leaned over her last night. He'd been so angry. Was he still so angry that he'd do something like this? "Do you really think it was him?"

"I think it's possible," Sally said.

"Wait!" Jenny snapped her fingers. "Maybe it's somebody in junior high. This has a real junior-high, prank-type feeling to it, don't you think?" She suddenly felt hopeful. She could deal with a junior-high prank. It was revenge she couldn't handle.

"Well, like I said, anything's possible," Sally said, "but actually, I'd put my money on Brad."

Why was she so eager to blame Brad? Jenny wondered. Weren't they friends? "I guess I'll never know for sure," she said. "But I'd rather believe it was a bad junior-high joke."

"Suit yourself."

"Speaking of bad jokes." Jenny tilted her head toward the box. "I don't suppose you want to help me get rid of it?"

"You're a great hostess, you know that?" Sally joked. "Sure, I'll take care of it. As long as it's dead, it doesn't bother me."

She went into the kitchen and came back with a handful of paper towels. Turning the box over, she gingerly used the towels to scoop the two pieces of snake back into it. "There," she said, fitting the lid back on. "Out of sight, out of mind, right? I have to go, so I'll put it in that big garbage can next to the garage."

"Wait." Sally was already heading for the front door and Jenny followed her. "You never said why you came in the first place."

"I knew I forgot something!" Sally said. "I came because my mother was on one of her marathon calls, so I couldn't use the phone, and I wanted to see if you'd like to go horseback riding."

"Now?"

"Well, you probably ought to change first," Sally suggested, looking pointedly at Jenny's robe. "But yes, soon. I've only got about an hour or so and then I have to do about a thousand other things."

"I'd love to go," Jenny said. Right now, she'd do anything to get out of the house. Then she heard the unmistakable sound of a truck pulling into the driveway. She peered out the front door, then turned back to Sally. "But I can't. The painters are here."

Sally looked out at the truck and grinned. "Well, just offer them coffee and fried rattlesnake. That'll get rid of them fast!" she said as she was leaving.

Jenny didn't mention the snake, but she did offer McPherson and Son coffee, expecting them to refuse. They accepted. They followed her into the kitchen and seated themselves at the table as if this were the usual way of doing business. McPherson the elder blew on his coffee and settled back in the chair. "So, young lady. Who do we talk to?"

"Talk to? Oh," Jenny said, realizing he expected to deal with her parents. "Me. I'll show you what we want done and you can give me a price."

McPherson the younger was about thirty, Jenny thought, and she noticed that he hadn't taken his eyes off her bathrobe since he'd come in the house. "You're still alone here, then?" he asked.

"Yes." Jenny cleared her throat. "For the moment," she added. The guy made her nervous. Why had she bothered with the coffee? "Look, I'm expecting someone in just a few more minutes. Why don't you bring your cups with you and I'll show you the rooms."

Without waiting for an answer, Jenny strode into the entry hall. "This," she said, gesturing at the walls. She turned and went into the living room. "And this." Turning again, she went back to the entrance and pointed up the stairs. "And the hallway up there."

The two of them started up the stairs. Halfway

up, the younger man glanced down at her and smiled. "You're not coming?"

Jenny shook her head and stayed by the front door.

"Oh, right, you're expecting company." He smiled again, as if he were on to her lie, and followed his father up the stairs.

Jenny waited, wishing somebody *would* come. A friendly face would be very welcome right about now.

The McPhersons were back in a couple of minutes. The elder gave her the price and Jenny nodded. "That sounds fine," she said, even though it seemed outrageously high. "I'll tell my parents and let you know tomorrow."

"Don't wait too long," the younger man told her, letting his eyes drift over her bathrobe again. "We can slot you in in ten days, but after that, who knows?"

"I'll just have to take my chances," Jenny said. She pulled the door open wide and stepped back to let them through. "Thanks for coming."

"Oh, it was our pleasure," he said.

Jenny shut the door behind them and leaned against it for a second. Then she raced upstairs and into the shower. It felt so good to finally be taking one that she didn't even think about the snake until she was blowing her hair dry. She shuddered, but her stomach stayed steady.

Back downstairs and dressed at last, Jenny took Peaches outside, then brought her in and gave her some unbuttered popcorn as a peace offering for yelling at her. She deserved it. After all, she'd heard something and kept watch almost the entire night.

"Wait till Dad hears about it, Peach," Jenny said, patting her as she wolfed down the popcorn. "He won't be making any more cracks about what a fat, lazy good-for-nothing you are. And if he does, we'll just remind him of The Night You Smelled the Snake."

Jenny's stomach churned again, but not from the memory of her surprise package. While she filled the dog dish with kibble, she thought about what she'd eaten in the last sixteen hours: no dinner to speak of and no breakfast at all. It was past noon now, so no wonder her stomach was acting up. She was famished.

Well, there was plenty of soup and canned vegetables, she thought wryly. Also a couple of frozen pizzas, guaranteed to taste like oregano-sprinkled cardboard. And there was peanut butter. She didn't want any of it, so she decided to go into town and buy something she did want.

It felt good to be out of the house and driving. She turned up the radio and cranked down the window, enjoying the feel of the wind in her hair. There was never any traffic on this road, and her mind drifted. She refused to think about the snake, or Brad, or anything unpleasant. Instead, she thought about what kind of food she'd buy and whether she should get her hair cut chin-length. And she thought about her secret admirer. She was halfway into

Rimrock before she noticed the car behind her.

A blue Toyota, a little worse for wear, and very familiar. It was David's car; Jenny recognized it the minute she turned onto the main street. Had he been following her or was this just a coincidence?

Finding a parking place was no problem, as usual. She had her pick and pulled into one right in front of the grocery store. The Toyota pulled in next to her. Jenny got out and so did David. Tall, loose-limbed, dark-eyed David.

"I tried to call you a little while ago," he said, joining her on the sidewalk.

No "Hi, how's it going?" she noticed. No small talk. "I guess I was . . . ?" Where? She hadn't left the house since late yesterday afternoon. "Oh. In the shower. But we have a machine." Except there hadn't been any new message on it when she left.

"I know. I didn't use it. I hate those things."

Loose-limbed, dark-eyed, old-fashioned David, she thought. "Well. So. Why did you call?" No beating around the bush for her, either.

He stuck his hand into the pocket of his jeans and pulled something out. A bracelet, woven of narrow, multi-colored strands of cloth. "I found this in my car this morning," he said, holding it out to her. "I guess it fell off some time that night."

No need to ask *what* night. Jenny remembered now that she'd worn it, but she hadn't missed it at all. "Well. Thanks." She slipped it over her hand and smiled at him. She'd been complimented on her smile a few times in her life; supposedly it brought out a dimple at the corner of her mouth, although she'd never been able to see it. According to her mother, it also lit up her face and made people want to smile back. Jenny always thought her mother was just prejudiced, and now she was sure of it, because David wasn't smiling back at all. She cleared her throat. "Have you . . . um . . . been to see Diana?"

"I've been to the hospital," he said. "But nobody can see her except her family."

"Is she still the same?"

He nodded.

"That's too bad." That sounded awfully weak, but Jenny couldn't think of anything else.

However, David didn't seem to be listening to her lame conversation. He was looking at her again the way he had in the diner, as if she were fascinating but frightening.

Jenny stood it as long as she could and then laughed nervously. "Is there something stuck on my teeth?" she finally asked. "If there is, please tell me and I'll get rid of it."

This time he did smile, and little pinpoints of light flashed in his nearly black eyes as they took in her cutoffs and faded blue workshirt. "No, you look great, Jenny."

"Well, that's good. The way you were staring at me, I felt like I was under a microscope."

"Sorry," he said, running a hand through his hair. "I've been thinking."

Jenny waited.

David looked at the sky, as if he were inspecting it for signs of rain. The sky was clear. Finally he said, "About that night."

Back to that, Jenny thought. She guessed she couldn't blame him, but she really didn't want to talk about it.

"You remember, when I found you . . . or you found me, or whatever, you said you'd heard a scream? And then, at the diner," he went on, "you said it again. Brad was all over you about it and you changed your mind and said it was the wind. You said that when I came back, too. When you were eating."

"I didn't exactly say that," Jenny reminded him. "I said I'd probably never know. And before, when Dean said it must have been the storm, I went along with it because I didn't feel like getting punched or strangled."

"Okay, good."

"Good?"

"Yeah, you didn't change your mind, you just backed off." David's eyes were slits now and his voice was quiet and intense. Jenny felt like she was under a hot spotlight.

"What's good about it?" she asked.

"It means you *did* hear something," he said. "And I want to know what it was. It's like trying to put a puzzle together, you know? Only a piece is missing. And you've got it."

"*You're* the puzzle, David," Jenny gave another nervous laugh. He was so edgy he almost scared her. "I mean, okay, so I heard a scream or a shout or something. But I can't remember what it was. I've tried, but I just can't." She fiddled with the cloth bracelet, twisting it around her wrist. "And . . . this is going to sound really heartless, I know, and I don't mean it to — but what difference does it make what I heard?"

"It's . . ." he shook his head impatiently. "Look, I can't get into it. But it could make a lot of difference."

Suddenly he reached out with both hands, as if he were going to take her by the shoulders and shake her. He didn't do it, but Jenny could tell he still wanted to.

"I don't see why," she said. She was uncomfortable, but her nervousness was fading and she was starting to get annoyed. "She probably yelled 'help' or 'oh, no,' or something like that. Whatever it was, she said it right before she fell, and there was nothing anybody could do, unless maybe they'd been standing next to her."

"That's what I'm . . ." Another quick shake of the head. "You don't understand, Jenny."

"Well, explain it to me, then! I'm not dense."

"I can't!" This time David did grab her shoulders. "I just wish you'd try to remember. It's important!"

She shook herself free and stepped back. "First Brad and now you," she said. "I'm sorry I ever mentioned it in the first place, and I'm sick of feeling guilty about something that wasn't my fault!"

"That isn't — "

"Look, let's just forget it," she interrupted. "I don't want to talk about it." She turned to leave and then spun around. "I heard something, but I can't remember what it was, and I'm not going to try anymore! I wish I'd never been up there in the first place!"

Jenny spun back toward her car, just in time to see a group of kids coming down the sidewalk toward them. Karen and Dean and a girl she didn't recognize. She'd been shouting at the end, and she could tell by the looks on their faces that they'd heard what she'd said, but she marched back to her car without a word, her face blazing hot. Let David be the one to explain why she'd been shrieking at him on the street.

If the main street of Rimrock hadn't been paved, she would have roared off in a cloud of dust, but she had to be satisfied with just gunning the motor before she pulled away. She didn't want to give him the satisfaction of looking back, but she did glance discreetly in the rearview mirror. There he was, hands stuffed in his pockets, talking to the others.

Probably telling them a complete lie, she thought. Oh, he was tricky. All that cute, little-boy stuff he'd pulled at first — looking at the sky, running his hand through his hair — he'd done everything but scuff the toe of his sneaker in the dirt. And all the time he was just working up to making her feel guilty about Diana. He'd conveniently forgotten, of course, that when they'd met up on the rimrocks that night, *he* was the one who suggested that the storm had played tricks with her hearing. And now that they knew what had happened to Diana, he wanted Jenny to remember, so he could wallow in a bunch of "If only's."

Well, too bad. She wasn't going to accommodate him. She was through trying to remember what she'd heard, and she was going to do her best to bury that night at the bottom of her memory pile.

Jenny's anger carried her most of the way home. It wasn't until she was on the long, empty stretch of road that led to her turnoff that she calmed down enough to notice how fast she was driving. She eased up on the gas pedal, even though she knew it wouldn't matter. Not once on this road had she ever seen a police car. In fact, the first time she'd encountered any car was earlier, when she'd seen David's Toyota behind her.

Not quite furious anymore, but still plenty mad, Jenny sped up the hill to her house and all but stomped inside. Peaches was waiting, as usual, looking as if she'd just waked up.

She gave the dog an absent-minded pat, walked into the living room, and was all set to fling herself onto the couch when she noticed that the answering machine had a message on it.

If she ever needed an admiring phone call, this would be the time. She punched the button eagerly, crossing her fingers and wondering what he'd say. Would he finally reveal who he was, or was he going to keep the tantalizing game going a little longer?

Chapter 8

But instead of the soft, enticing voice of her secret admirer, Jenny heard her father's voice boom out: "Jen! Looks like we'll be a few days longer than we thought. The house deal hit a couple of snags, nothing that can't be worked out, although your mother is ready to throttle everybody in sight. As soon as we know when we're coming back, we'll give you the word. Call and tell us how you're doing, but not tonight. We'll be out. Hope the mutt's earning her keep."

Oddly enough, the first thing that occurred to Jenny was not that she'd have to spend two, maybe three more nights alone in the house. Her first thought was the painters. She'd promised to call them tomorrow. *Then* she thought about being alone in the house and a shiver ran through her.

"First things first," she said out loud. She checked the number where her parents were staying and dialed it.

"Mom, hi, I just got Dad's message."

"And you've called to offer your condolences, I hope." Mrs. Fowler sounded harried, to say the least. "These people! They actually want us to include that gorgeous lighting fixture in the asking price!"

"What gorgeous lighting fixture?"

"The one in the dining room. The one from Italy?" Jenny's mother made it sound as if she'd made a special trip to Italy just to buy it, when she'd actually found it at a neighborhood garage sale. It wasn't gorgeous, either, not in Jenny's opinion. It was kind of hideous, now that she thought about it — lots of fat globes that needed dusting all the time.

"Well, I'm sure you'll work it out," Jenny said.

"You sound like your father," Mrs. Fowler sighed. "The lamp isn't the only thing they want, you know."

"Okay, well then, call off the deal," Jenny suggested.

Her mother gasped. "Do you realize what that would mean?" she asked. "The real estate market isn't exactly booming here; if we don't sell it now, we'll . . ."

"Mom!" Jenny broke in. "I didn't call about the house. I called about the painters."

That got Mrs. Fowler's attention. "All right," she said, as if expecting the worst. "Let me have it."

"It's highway robbery," she announced when Jenny had finished. "But tell them we agree. Of course, if this house deal falls through, we'll just have to live with salmon walls for the next twenty years."

Jenny swallowed a laugh and decided not to mention that they could do the painting themselves. Which would be a lot better than having that creep McPherson in the house. But her mother obviously wasn't in the mood for solutions. She was enjoying the problems too much.

"Well." Mrs. Fowler sighed again. "Anything else?"

"That's all," Jenny said. No need to mention headless snakes and sleepless nights. Her mother would pooh-pooh the whole thing as the product of somebody's small mind, not worthy of worry. And she'd be right, Jenny told herself firmly. "Just let me know when you'll be coming back so I can meet you."

"Oh, we will. If we ever do get back." On that optimistic note, her mother said she had to go. Back to the battle, Jenny supposed.

As soon as she hung up, the thought of the empty house leaped into her mind, but she pushed it away. Busy, she decided. She'd keep so busy she wouldn't have time to get scared.

First she called McPherson & Son, left word on their answering machine that the Fowlers of Rimrock would be ready to have them start painting as soon as possible, and asked them to call back and tell her the exact date.

Next she called Sally. "Another ten seconds and you'd have missed me," Sally said. "I was just on my way out the door. What's up? Don't tell me you got another charming present."

"No, and please don't mention it again," Jenny told her. "I'm trying to erase it from my memory. I'm also trying to pretend that being alone here is perfectly wonderful."

"And it's not?"

"Well, so far it's okay, but that's because it isn't dark yet," Jenny said. "When the sun goes down, I just might turn into a blubbering idiot, so I thought I'd see if you wanted to come spend the night." Sally wasn't perfect, but Jenny couldn't be picky. "We could listen to music, and I think I can figure out how to hook up the VCR, so we could watch a tape. All you'd have to bring is yourself. And some food," she added, suddenly remembering that she never did make it to the grocery store. "Unless you'd be satisfied with frozen pizza and peanut butter."

"Sorry," Sally said.

"I don't blame you," Jenny said. "Maybe you could buy some stuff and then come over. I'd pay you back."

"No, I mean I'm sorry I can't come," Sally told her. "I wish I could, believe me. Some friends of my parents are having a cookout. They do it every summer and it's extremely boring. But since they live fifty miles away and we hardly ever see them, I have to go. We won't be getting back until really late. Sorry," she said again.

"Oh, that's okay." Jenny tried to sound unconcerned. "It's dumb for me to be scared, anyway. Nothing's going to happen."

"Right," Sally agreed. "Brad or whoever wouldn't play another prank so soon after the first one. They'll wait awhile until they're sure you've forgotten all about it. *Then* they'll spring the second one on you."

"Thanks a lot."

"Whoops — forget I said that. Listen," Sally went on. "I can't help you out tonight, but how about tomorrow morning?"

"Assuming I'm still alive?" Jenny asked. Maybe joking about it would help.

"Come on," Sally said. "Just lock all the doors and leave all the lights on. Anyway, why don't we go riding in the morning? Early, like for breakfast? I'll supply the horses and the food and we'll ride to the bottom of the bluff and build a fire and fry bacon and eggs."

Jenny didn't have to think about it twice. "I'll be ready," she said. "And we can go as early as you want, since I just might stay awake all night."

"Then you'd better ride Alice," Sally said. "She's practically geriatric, so you'll be able to take a nap on the way."

They finished making their plans, and when Jenny hung up, she realized she was ravenous. The thought of tomorrow's bacon and eggs made her stomach rumble wildly, and she wished she had some now. If it hadn't been for meeting David, she probably would.

An image flashed into her mind: David standing close to her on the sidewalk, the lights in his eyes like two piercing spotlights as his strong hands reached for her. And she saw in the image something she hadn't noticed at the time it was happening. He was anxious and upset, yes, but he was also . . . what? Scared? Desperate? She couldn't give a name to the emotion she saw in his eyes, and that bothered her. Maybe if she hadn't lashed out at him, if she'd given him a chance to explain, then their meeting might have ended in a different way.

Her glance strayed to the telephone, but as it did, the image of David changed. The confusing emotion in his eyes faded; all she saw was the anger, and she felt his fingers digging hard into her shoulders again.

Of course he wasn't scared, she thought. She'd only been imagining it. And he hadn't seemed about to offer any explanations.

She blinked, and David's image faded completely. The only vision in her mind now was a table spread with food. Peaches at her heels, she went into the kitchen and unearthed two cans of chili and a box of instant rice. Ten minutes later, she poured the chili over the rice and dug in. Nothing had ever tasted so good, and she'd made so much there'd be enough for later that night, when she was sure to be hungry again.

But if Jenny's stomach rumbled for more food later that night, she didn't hear it. After shelving books for a few hours, something she'd been planning to do ever since her parents left, she hooked up the VCR, put on a movie — an inane comedy, with absolutely no hint of scariness to it — and stretched out on the couch to watch it. She might have seen ten minutes of it, but that was all. Her eyelids drooped, and she forced them open a few times, but then they closed for good. When she woke, it was just past seven in the morning.

By eight-thirty, she and Sally were astride Emma and Alice, plodding their way slowly toward the base of the rimrocks. The sun wasn't up very high yet. It would get hot later on, but right now the air was cool and fresh.

Jenny smiled to herself. It was amazing what eleven hours of sleep could do for a person, she thought. Eleven hours of sleep made it easy to believe that nothing weird, like a dead snake arriving in a giftbox, would ever happen again. Sleep made it hard to believe it really *had* happened. It made Brad seem pathetic, and turned the argument with David into a bad but fading memory. Even the thought of spending a couple of more nights alone in the house wasn't as terrible.

Mostly, eleven hours of sleep and not enough food made her wish Alice wasn't quite as slow as Sally had promised. "Hey, I'm starving!" she called out. "I think I can manage not to fall off if we speed up the pace a little!"

"Okay, then just give her a tap with your heels," Sally instructed. "And don't forget to hang on."

"To what?" Jenny asked. They were riding bareback.

"To her mane," Sally said. "Or wrap your arms around her neck."

One tap of Jenny's heels put Alice into a jaw-rattling trot, and Jenny had to clutch her mane tightly or she would have ended up on the ground. But with a second tap, Alice broke into an easy, rocking-horse lope. It felt wonderful, and Jenny was almost sorry when they had to slow down so the horses could pick their way around the rocks at the bottom of the bluff.

"That was fantastic," she said as she slid to the ground. "Let's do it again. Like tomorrow, maybe."

"I can't tomorrow." Sally took the knapsack off her back and ran her fingers through her curly hair. "I won't be here tomorrow."

"Oh? Where are you going?"

"My aunt's," Sally said shortly. "She's a pain. Come on, let's get going."

For once, Sally didn't seem talkative. "So you're leaving in the morning?" Jenny asked.

"Late this afternoon." Sally hoisted the knapsack to her shoulder again. "Come on, let's find a good spot to eat."

Jenny looked uncertainly at the horses.

"Don't worry," Sally told her, sounding annoyed. "They won't wander, and anyway, we're not climbing far. Pick up some dry twigs on the way; we'll need them for the fire." With that, she was gone, urging Jenny to hurry up.

Sally knew her way around the rimrocks as well as David, Jenny noticed, as she watched her scramble nimbly up the side of what looked like a completely smooth boulder. Jenny found a gully beside it and used that instead. "You'll never learn to climb that way," Sally said. "And it's taking you forever."

"What's the rush?" Jenny asked, slowly pulling herself up beside Sally.

"Nothing, never mind." Sally set the knapsack down. "We're here."

Jenny stood up and looked around. The rock they were on was very wide and almost flat on top, except for some little basin-type indentations that would be perfect for a fire. The sun was higher up now, but there was a huge outcropping of rocks several feet above that gave them shade and still left them room to stand. Jenny walked gingerly to the edge of their rock and looked over. They hadn't climbed high enough for her to see the town, but she could see Emma and Alice, not very far below, still munching the apples Sally had brought for them.

Jenny took a deep breath. She thought she'd hate being up here again, but they were on the opposite side from where she and David had been. Besides, it was beautiful in the morning. It would be a perfect place for a date. A breakfast date, she thought. David's lean, handsome face came to mind immediately, and she thought again about calling him. She'd decided this morning not to. Sure, she'd lost her temper, but he was the one who'd started the whole thing by acting so strangely. Let him do the calling. Now, though, she was starting to lean the other way. She sighed and shook her head, wishing she could for once make up her mind and have it stay made up.

She heard a sound behind her and turned. Sally had gathered the twigs together and was setting a match to them. Her hair was falling in her face, and she had her tongue clamped between her teeth in concentration. Jenny hadn't mentioned the sidewalk encounter with David. Should she tell Sally? Of course, Sally probably knew already. She seemed to know everything that went on. But if she knew, she probably would have brought it up by now. She wasn't the type to hold back out of politeness. But Sally seemed edgy this morning. She seemed to have something on her mind. Jenny wondered what it was and realized that she didn't know her all that well. She usually talked a lot, but not about feelings or things like that. Maybe she was just what she seemed to be — frank and friendly, with no murky, hidden feelings at all.

"Hey."

Jenny turned and saw that Sally had the fire going and was digging into the knapsack for the food. She tossed Jenny the packet of bacon. "Open that, why don't you?"

Jenny tackled the bacon, glad she'd decided not to talk about David. She was beginning to wish she hadn't come, and wondered why Sally had bothered, since she was in such a bad mood.

Sally hadn't brought eggs; there was only one

left in her refrigerator. But she'd brought a loaf of Italian bread and a chunk of cheddar cheese, and when the bacon was done, they made enough sandwiches for six people. Jenny ate hungrily, but Sally just picked at the food.

"I'm so stuffed I can't move," Jenny said when she'd finished. "I may just have to stay up here all day."

"I do sometimes," Sally said. "Or I stay for hours, anyway. I love it up here." She was standing at the edge of the rock, keeping an eye on the horses. She checked her watch, then said, "Come on over here. The view's great."

Jenny scooted over and sat next to her. "I can see why you love it. Now," she added, "the other night, I hated it."

"Well, nobody in their right mind would like it in a storm," Sally said. "A couple of kids say they're afraid of it after what it did to Diana."

"I take it you're not one of them."

"Do I look afraid?" Sally asked.

Jenny started to say that she looked worried, but she changed her mind. If Sally wanted to talk, she would. "How is Diana?" she asked.

"The same." Sally checked the time again, then shoved her hands in the back pockets of her jeans.

"Do you want to go or something?" Jenny asked.

Sally flushed. "Why?"

"Well, you keep looking at your watch," Jenny said. "If you've got to leave, then just say so."

"It's my aunt," Sally said quickly. "I keep checking the time because I keep hoping it's magically slowed down. My aunt's a pain. I don't want to go visit her."

"I guess everybody has at least one relative like that." Jenny lay back on the rock and squinted up at the sky. She was just about to say more when she heard a faint, swishing sound, and suddenly her face was covered with dust and grit. "Where'd that come from?" She reached up to brush it off.

"What?" Sally was still gazing at the horses.

"This . . ." Jenny stopped as she heard something else. A grating, rattling noise, almost like marbles rolling along a floor. She sat up and twisted around, just in time to see a virtual avalanche of small pebbles pouring over the edge of the rock outcropping above them. The last of the pebbles wasn't so small, though. In fact, it wasn't a pebble at all, it was more the size of a bowling bowl.

Jenny scrambled to her knees. "Sally, look out!"

Sally turned, but not fast enough. The large rock sailed through the air and hit her in the shoulder with enough force to spin her around. She grabbed her shoulder, completely off balance, one foot skidding off the edge of their breakfast spot. There was nothing to grab on to; if she fell, she'd fall ten feet before she hit more rocks below.

Jenny shot out her hand, grabbed a fistful of denim and pulled back with all her strength. Sally teetered at the edge for one more terrible second, then fell backward, her elbow jabbing Jenny painfully in the cheek as she landed half on top of her.

Sally rubbed her shoulder. Jenny rubbed her cheek. Both of them were gasping as if they'd been in a race.

"Thanks," Sally said after a moment.

"You're welcome." Jenny got to her feet and started stuffing things into the knapsack. She wanted to leave, fast.

Sally sat up, slowly. She looked shaken, but she tried for a joke. "Somebody ought to put some falling rocks signs around here."

Jenny didn't laugh. The rocks hadn't fallen, she knew that as surely as she knew her own name. When she'd looked back, before, she'd seen something besides a bunch of rocks tumbling down. She'd seen a shadow. A human shadow. The rocks hadn't fallen. They'd been pushed.

Chapter 9

Sally didn't believe her, not at first. "It was a cloud," she said as they rode the horses away from the rimrocks. She gestured over her head; the wind was skittering several puffy clouds across the sky. "They make funny shadows on the ground, you know that."

"It wasn't a cloud," Jenny said. "I know what cloud shadows are like and this wasn't one of them. And don't try to tell me it was a bear."

Sally hooted. "We're not in the complete wilderness out here, no matter what some people think. Of course it wasn't some bear."

"Right. It was some*body*." Jenny was too worried to feel relief that there were no bears around. "It was another prank, I'm sure of it."

"Come on! Pranks are harmless," Sally said. "Ugly, maybe, like that snake, but harmless."

"You're saying those rocks just fell by themselves?" Jenny asked. "Just kind of slipped over the edge without any help?"

"Well, they had to have help," Sally said. "But it didn't have to be human help." She pulled Emma up so Jenny could ride alongside. "It could have been geological. You know, something like an earthquake. A little one that nobody could feel. Or maybe there was a sonic boom that shook the rocks up. It could have been anything."

"I didn't hear any sonic boom," Jenny said. "And a 'little' earthquake wouldn't be enough to move that rock, Sally. And no matter what you say, not all pranks are harmless. What about all those deaths you read about from fraternity hazings?" She took a deep breath. "I saw a shadow — a human shadow!"

"Okay, okay! Calm down," Sally said. "Maybe you're right. Weird things do keep happening to you, so maybe somebody *is* behind it all."

"But who?!" Jenny cried. "Brad? Do you think Brad did it?"

"That's for you to find out, isn't it?"

It was a strange answer, Jenny thought. Either Sally didn't really believe her and was just humoring her, or else. . . . Jenny gave her a sidelong glance. Sally was looking ahead, smiling to herself. Did she know? Did Sally know who was behind it all?

No, it couldn't be true. Sally was a little shallow, maybe, a little uncaring, but she wasn't mean. Was she?

Suddenly, all Jenny wanted to do was get home. She pushed her horse into a faster pace and held on tight, letting the pounding gait drive all the unanswered questions from her mind for the moment.

At the turnoff to Sally's house, Jenny slid off Emma's back. "I'll see you when you get back," she said. "I hope your visit's not too awful."

"Thanks," Sally said. "And thanks for grabbing me up there. I probably would have broken some bones if I'd fallen." She waved as she rode off on the winding dirt road to her house. "I'll call you in a few days!" came floating back on the dusty air.

Jenny watched until Sally and the horses rounded a bend, then hiked up the road to her house. She let herself in, patted the dog, and went straight to the answering machine.

McPherson. The younger. "Miss Fowler," he said. "Still alone, huh? Too bad."

"How do you know I'm still alone?" Jenny said out loud, hating the crude chuckle in his voice. She stopped the machine. She remembered his eyes, riveted to her bathrobe, and shivered. How *did* he know she was alone? He couldn't, unless . . . no. No, he was just guessing. Wasn't he?

Jenny started the tape again and heard him say they could start in ten days, at eight in the morning. He didn't mention her being alone again. Maybe somebody had come in while he was talking, she thought, and he couldn't say what he really wanted to say.

No, stop it. You're acting paranoid. Jenny gave herself a shake and shut off the machine. That was the only message. Nothing from her parents. And nothing from her secret admirer. Jenny wondered if he'd decided to give up. It had been a while since his last contact; maybe he'd had second thoughts. Or maybe he felt like an idiot for making the calls and sending her flowers in the first place. She wanted to tell him to keep it up. Better yet, she wanted him to march up to her door and introduce himself.

"Oh, well. Maybe he will."

Peaches, stationed at Jenny's feet, perked her ears up and whined.

Jenny smiled at her. "Have you been lonely, Peach?"

The dog wagged her stump of a tail.

"Okay. I've got dust in my hair so I'm going to take a shower," Jenny said. "Then we'll drive into town and buy some food."

Ecstasy. *Drive* and *food* were two of Peaches' favorite words.

Jenny showered off the dust and grit, and decided to let her hair dry naturally. It would look like a gone-to-seed dandelion, but she didn't want to stay in the house. She wished she had someplace to go besides the grocery store, some friend's house where she could feel comfortable and safe. Sally was leaving, but she wouldn't do, anyway. After the way she'd acted before, Jenny wasn't sure she'd ever feel comfortable with her again. And there wasn't anybody else. The store was her only escape. Later, she'd have to stay in the house whether she liked it or not. Then she could mess with her hair if she wanted to. And she might want to. There was an entire night ahead to get through; shelving books would get boring after awhile. So, she could hang pictures, put away clothes, maybe even cut her hair if she got up the nerve. That ought to take her until at least midnight. Then a movie. Then sleep. Maybe.

Peaches was delighted to be getting out. She took off toward the car in a cross between a trot and a roll, looking like a furry, stubby-legged barrel. Jenny actually had to hoist her into the back seat.

"You're pathetic," she said affectionately.

Peaches took up her usual position, her nose poking out the partially open window, her ears blown back by the wind, as Jenny, singing along with the radio, drove them into Rimrock. As usual, the road in was deserted, so Jenny was surprised to see so few parking places once they arrived in town.

The spots in front of the grocery store were all taken, so she drove up two blocks, then around, and finally found one in front of the card shop. "Come on, Peach. We're here."

A faint snore emanated from the back seat. Peaches was asleep.

Jenny shook her head, then looked around. The car wasn't in the shade. But she wouldn't be gone long and there *was* a breeze. If she left the windows down, Peaches would be fine. Besides, she remembered that the grocery store had three round stickers on its doors. One had a cigarette, one had a pair of bare feet, the third had the silhouette of a dog.

All of them had diagonal red bars through them. Peaches couldn't go in anyway.

Jenny rolled all the windows down halfway, then slid out of the car and closed the door as quietly as possible so Peaches wouldn't wake up and whine to come with her. The dog didn't budge; maybe she'd sleep the whole time. Jenny hoped so. Peaches loved a drive, but being left in the car, even for five minutes, made her howl as if she'd been abandoned for good.

The last time Jenny had been in the grocery store, she'd been the only customer there. Today it was actually crowded. Not jammed like the supermarkets she was used to, but there were enough people in the aisles to make it tricky getting her cart around. She kept an eye out for familiar faces, then realized there wasn't anyone she really wanted to see. That was when she saw Dean.

He was walking by outside, and as he glanced in the window, Jenny waved to him. He stared at her so long, she started to think he'd forgotten who she was. Finally he raised an arm and pointed to his watch, as if he didn't have time to stop. Then he turned and left.

Jenny shrugged. She didn't want to talk to him anyway. He seemed kind of aloof. But after he'd gone, she felt more alone than ever.

Bumping her way through the aisles, she bought fruit, eggs, frozen waffles, chocolate chip ice cream, cheese and crackers, hamburger meat and rolls, sliced turkey, salad makings, and a chicken to cook for when her parents came back. Then she got in one of the two checkout lines. Then she waited.

Half an hour later, she was still waiting. It wasn't a computerized supermarket. Not only that, but the man three carts ahead of Jenny had bought enough food to last at least a month. She glanced at her cart and started to think about what to put back so she could get in the express line. Then she remembered there was no express line. She sighed, hoping Peaches wasn't howling and creating a disturbance, then she pulled a tabloid from the rack. The place wasn't so old-fashioned that it didn't have tabloids.

Halfway through a story about a woman who'd been to Mars and back, and seen Elvis en route, Jenny felt a hand on her arm, and looking up, she saw Brad.

His eyes were clear this time, she noticed, and his round face was pale. "Jenny," he said quietly, "I don't really remember too much about the other night. But I think I made a fool of myself. I'm sorry."

Jenny stared at him. He seemed to mean it, but she couldn't be sure.

"Well . . ." he turned to go.

"Wait," Jenny said. "You didn't happen to leave anything at my house, did you?"

"No." He looked confused. Either that, or he was a good actor. "At least, I don't think so."

"Okay." There was no point in going on, Jenny decided. Either he'd left the snake or he hadn't. And if he had, he wasn't going to admit it.

"Well . . . okay. Bye, Jenny." Still looking slightly baffled, Brad left the store. Jenny wasn't sorry to see him go.

Finally, her turn at the checkout came. She bagged her own groceries, which seemed to surprise the girl at the cash register, but another thirty minutes had crept by, and Jenny just knew Peaches was awake by now, putting on her abandoned-animal act.

With one bag under each arm, Jenny finally left the grocery store and hurried the two blocks back to her car, straining her ears every step of the way for the howls of a miserable dog. She didn't hear them, and when she reached the car, everything was quiet.

Relieved, Jenny set her bags down and glanced in the back window. She couldn't believe it, but Peaches was still asleep, the sun picking out the pinkish highlights in her hair. Jenny laughed and rapped loudly on the window. The window . . . it was up. All the way up. She'd left it halfway down, hadn't she?

She reached for the driver's door. Locked. And its window was up, too. All the windows were up. What was going on? She fumbled in the pocket of her shorts for the keys, unlocked the door, and pulled it open. A puff of ovenlike air enveloped her bare legs: the inside of the car was baking hot.

"Peaches, what happened, you must be . . ." Jenny stopped. The dog hadn't moved. "Oh, no!"

Jenny reached over and unlocked the back door, then slid outside and yanked it open. Peaches still hadn't moved, but as she leaned in, she saw that Peaches was breathing. Barely. "Oh, Peach!"

Heat stroke. She'd read about it, knew the dog might as well have been shut in an oven, knew she was dying. Jenny heard a horrible, rasping sound and realized it was her own ragged breathing. She reached for the dog, tears filling her eyes, and felt the hot fur in her hands. Dying. Peaches was dying. *Would* die, unless. . . .

A vet. There was a veterinarian around here someplace, but where? Where! She'd have to drive around until she spotted it. She pulled back out of the car, hitting her head so hard on the roof that everything went black for a sickening moment. Gasping in pain and terror, she stumbled toward the front seat. Have to hurry, she thought. Can't stop. Can't waste a second.

Just as she was about to slide in, Jenny spotted a woman coming down the sidewalk. "The vet's!" she shouted, her throat thick with tears. "Where is it? Where's the vet?!"

The woman must have seen the panic on Jenny's face because she didn't waste words. "Middle of the next block, the sign's out front. Dr. Jacobsen."

Faster on foot. Jenny reached into the back seat, slid her arms under Peaches and pulled her out. The dog was limp and heavy, but Jenny cradled her as close as she could, then half trotted, half shuffled her way down the sidewalk. "It's okay, you'll be okay," she crooned over and over. Hurry! She had to hurry. Oh, God, poor Peach!

The waiting room was empty, but Jenny knew someone must be around because she could hear a cat meowing pitifully and a man's voice saying something soothing. She hurried over to the desk and called out, "Please, I need help! It's an emergency!"

The cat kept yowling, but Jenny heard footsteps, and in seconds a man in a white coat, liberally sprinkled with animal hair, came into view. They ought to wear brown coats, Jenny thought wildly, the hair wouldn't show so much.

"It's my dog!" she said. "She was in the car and it was hot. . . ."

The man, Dr. Jacobsen, she figured, lifted a hinged section of the desk and stepped out. Without a word, he took Peaches from Jenny's arms and strode back into the examining room, out of sight.

Jenny's shirt was pasted to her chest and her arms were shaking. She let them hang limply at her sides until they stopped. Then she sat down in a chair and waited.

The doctor was back in half an hour. He didn't waste words either. "She'll make it," he said.

Jenny didn't know she'd been holding her breath until she let it out. She stood up. "Thank you," she said in a shaky voice.

Dr. Jacobsen was about her father's age, she thought, with graying-blond hair and bright blue eyes. He would have been handsome if he'd smiled, but he wasn't smiling. "I know you didn't mean for this to happen," he said, "but I have to tell you that it was a stupid thing to do. There's just no other word for it."

"I — "

"I know, I know, you don't want a lecture," he interrupted. "Believe me, I don't like giving one, either. But it's part of the job. You just don't leave the animal in a car on a hot day like this. That's what causes heat stroke, which is what your dog has, and which could have killed her."

Jenny shook her head. "The windows . . . I left — "

"You left them cracked," he interrupted again. "You should have put them halfway down at least. Better yet, you shouldn't have left her there at all. Don't do it again."

Jenny stopped trying to explain. What could she say? The truth would just sound like a lie, like she was trying to worm her way out of feeling guilty.

The doctor must have seen the misery in her face, because his expression changed. His eyes softened and so did his voice. "End of lecture," he said. "I'll keep her here tonight and watch her tomorrow. But you should have her back on Monday." He smiled for the first time. "She seems to be basically healthy, except for a weight problem. But we can talk about that when you pick her up."

Jenny couldn't smile back. She was afraid she'd burst into tears. The best she could manage was another thank you on her way out.

Her car was exactly as she'd left it, two doors open, grocery bags dumped beside it. The frozen waffles would probably survive; she wasn't sure about the meat. But the ice cream was now a vanilla puddle topped with melting chocolate chips. Jenny found a rag in the trunk and cleaned up the mess as well as she could, then got in the car and headed home.

The tears finally came as she left town and started down the long empty stretch of road that led to her turnoff. At first she tried to blink them back, then she gave up. There were no other cars to run into anyway. She wiped her face with one hand, steered with the other, and tried to figure out what had happened.

This was no prank, she knew that. Putting someone's pet in danger wasn't prank material. Had Brad done it? He'd been in town. But so had Dean — he didn't have anything against her, did he? Plenty of other people had been around. It didn't have to be someone she knew, doing something hateful. It could have been an accident. A good deed gone wrong. Maybe Peaches had woken up, started howling and throwing herself against the doors, and then some passerby had rolled up the windows to keep her from leaping out. It was hard to believe that whoever did it could be totally ignorant about the temperature inside a closed car, but it was possible, she guessed. She didn't want to believe that someone had done it deliberately.

For a few minutes, Jenny kept reliving the whole

thing, felt the heat wash out from the car, saw Peaches's nearly lifeless form on the backseat, remembered the awful helpless feeling as she sat in the waiting room. But finally she was able to push the images away by reminding herself that Peaches was going to be all right. That was the most important thing.

The tears had dried up, and she was feeling much calmer when the car stopped. On its own. No sputtering or coughing to let her know something was wrong, either. It just coasted a few feet in silence before finally refusing to move another inch. Jenny tried to restart it, got out and looked under the hood, checked the tires, got back in, and turned the key one more time. That's when she noticed that the gas gauge was on empty. Below empty, to be more precise.

"Oh, no." She put her head against the steering wheel, not sure whether to laugh or start crying again. It was only two-thirty in the afternoon. If the rest of the day kept up like this, it was going to be the longest twenty-four hours on record.

If she just sat here for a while, somebody would come by, wouldn't they? Of course they would. But judging from the traffic on this road, it would be two or three days at least. If she was lucky.

Feeling very tired, Jenny got out and stood beside the car. Your house isn't that far away, she told herself. Three miles? Maybe less. You can do it.

She stood another minute or two, then pocketed

the keys and started down the road. That does it for the meat, she thought, glancing back at the car. She'd have to dump it the minute she got it home. Whenever that miraculous event occurred.

For the first few minutes, Jenny kept listening hopefully for the sound of another car, but after that, she became resigned to the fact that it wasn't going to happen. She didn't know where all the Saturday shoppers lived, but it obviously wasn't out this way. Nobody seemed to live out this way except her and Sally. She brightened up at that. Sally said they were leaving later this afternoon. Maybe she was still home. She'd go there first and see if they had any gas. If they didn't, at least they could drive her back to her car after she'd called a gas station.

That thought brought a little energy back to her legs, and she picked up her pace and actually smiled. When she saw the telephone booth, the smile widened into a grin.

She must have passed it every time she'd driven into town, and she'd completely forgotten about it. But there it was, set back in a little place where the road widened for cars to pull off so their drivers could make calls. Important calls, like the one she was about to make.

Jenny dug down into the bottom of her purse, which was where all the change ended up, and fished out four quarters and three dimes. Then she forgot how tired she was and started running toward the telephone booth.

Chapter 10

When she was just a few yards from the phone booth, she heard the whine of a distant engine. She stopped in her tracks and looked back down the road, ready to wave her arms and flag the driver down. This might be the only car she'd see out here, and she wasn't about to trust her luck and let it go by. The way her luck was running, the phone would be out of order.

The whine was getting louder; Jenny stepped into the middle of the road. She'd let the driver see her from a distance and have plenty of time to slow down. She was glad she was wearing white shorts and a rainbow-striped T-shirt. She'd be hard to miss.

Finally the car came into view. No, not a car, a motorcycle. As long as it has wheels, Jenny thought. And plenty of gas. She raised her arms above her head and started waving them up and down in big arcs. The motorcycle got closer.

It was black, Jenny could see now, and its rider

had on a black helmet, a sleek, space-age type that hid his face and made him look like Darth Vader. She thought of him as a he, anyway, but she couldn't really tell. She didn't really care, either, just as long as he stopped.

A few more seconds had passed when Jenny suddenly realized that the rider had no intention of stopping. He was moving toward her very fast, the whine of the engine had become a roar, and Jenny knew there was no way he could have missed seeing her bright shirt and frantically waving arms. But the engine's roar only got louder, the driver didn't slow down, and as Jenny moved quickly toward the side of the road, she felt such a rush of anger that she wanted to scream.

She *did* scream, but not in anger. She'd just reached the safety of the roadside when she turned and saw the motorcycle coming straight at her. Her scream was one of fear, and she leaped back, bumping against a corner of the phone booth and scraping her bare arm painfully on its metal edge. The motorcycle swerved, kicked up a shower of dirt and gravel, and roared off.

It had been deliberate. There was no doubt in Jenny's mind about that. She leaned against the booth, her knees actually weak and her heart pounding so loud in her ears that at first the other noise didn't even register as anything but a noise. Then she realized what it was, that it was the high-pitched whine of the motorcycle getting louder and louder. It was coming back.

She glanced around wildly, her breath coming in short little gasps. Then she felt the warm glass of the phone booth on her back, and without even thinking about it, she got herself inside and slammed the door shut.

The whine turned into a roar again, and Jenny could see the motorcycle through the glass, heading straight for the booth. She closed her eyes and sank down to the gritty cement floor, her knees jammed up against her chest. When the roar reached its highest peak, her eyes flew open, just in time to see the motorcycle swerve again, miss the booth by inches, and tear off in the other direction.

Would he come back? How much time did she have before he did? Jenny straightened up, facing the direction he'd come from if he came, and reached into her pocket for the change she'd put there when she'd been waving her arms in the middle of the road and thinking that help was on the way. Her hand shook and all the coins spilled to the floor.

Down on her knees again, she scrabbled for the money. Then she heard the motorcycle again.

She couldn't. She couldn't stay in this glass box and wait for that maniac to bear down on her again like some giant black insect homing in on its prey. She'd get out and run into the woody field behind; he wouldn't be able to follow her in there. That's where she should have gone in the first plàce.

As the sound of the motorcycle grew louder, Jenny grabbed the door handle and pulled. It didn't open. She tugged again, harder, then again, almost sobbing in frustration. The door was jammed. She was trapped.

Four more times Jenny looked on in terror as the motorcycle rushed toward her. She tried not to watch, but not seeing was worse, somehow. She tried to get one of the quarters into the coin slot, but her hands were slick with sweat and shaking so badly she kept dropping the money. She finally remembered that she didn't need money to make an emergency call, but by then the driver wasn't even bothering to ride off. He just turned around a few yards from the booth, the roar of his engine making it impossible to hear anything, especially an operator who'd want to know her name and location. Finally Jenny gave up and sat on the floor, her whole body tense and shaking, as the rider played his insane game. The sun beat through the glass walls of the airless booth, making it almost unbearably hot, reminding her of Peaches trapped and helpless in the baking car.

She was still thinking of Peaches when she realized that the motorcycle hadn't come back. She lifted her head and listened. No sound, except her dry, gasping breaths. She waited a minute, and when nothing happened, when no whine broke the silence, she slowly got to her feet. She carefully slotted a quarter into the phone, and punched the number of the gas station, which was conveniently displayed on a sticker on the inside of the receiver.

Busy. Jenny sobbed again in frustration and slammed the phone down. He could still come back;

he might just be waiting, letting her think she was safe.

The sweat was pouring down her body now, and the air in the booth was so steamy it hurt to breathe. Jenny grabbed the door handle and pulled, willing it to open. Her sweaty hands slipped and she fell backward, crashing into the hot glass behind her.

Hurry. She had to hurry. She had to get out or get help. She got her coins, slotted them again, and dialed.

"Bill's Texaco."

"I . . ." Jenny swallowed. Her throat felt thick.

"Yeah?" The man sounded impatient, hurried.

Jenny's words came out in a quavering whisper. "I need help! I'm stuck!"

"Lady, speak up."

"I . . . can't!" Sobbing again, Jenny held onto the phone like a lifeline.

"I can't help you if I can't hear you, lady."

Jenny tried to stop, but her stomach muscles seemed to have taken over. In and out, again and again, dry, rasping sobs that hurt her chest and wouldn't stop. She didn't know how she could keep breathing, it was so hot. So hot!

She let the phone slide from her hands and reached for the door handle. She had to get out! Her hands slipped off the handle, and she wiped them on her shorts, then grabbed the handle again and pulled. Her head felt like it might burst from the pounding, and she heard a hoarse, rhythmic, guttural sound, like an animal grunting, and realized it was coming from her. She wiped her hands again, gripped the handle, and pulled, her voice rising in pitch with the effort until she was screaming. And then, with a hideous grating of metal, the door opened.

Jenny fell backward, banging her head on the glass, and slid to the gritty floor of the booth. Too tired to move yet, she closed her eyes and felt the cooler outside air wash over her legs.

Move. She had to move. Get up and get out. She opened her eyes and was pushing herself up when she heard a tinny, distant voice. "Lady? Hey, what's going on? You all right? Lady!"

Jenny took a deep, shaky breath, got to her knees, and reached for the dangling receiver.

It was late afternoon when Jenny finally turned the car into the driveway of her house. She shut the engine off and reached for the door handle. Peaches had been in all day, she thought, she'd need a walk. Then she remembered that Peaches wasn't home, and she sank back against the car seat, closing her eyes in exhaustion. Her head was pounding and her clothes were still damp with sweat. She needed a shower, some aspirin, something cold to drink. But for the moment, all she could do was sit.

She'd told the man from the gas station to come to the phone booth. To walk down the road to her car, risking another encounter with the madman on the motorcycle, was impossible for her, like stepping into the unknown. So she'd stayed with the known — the hot, stinking telephone booth — and waited. When the Jeep arrived, Jenny knew she'd be grateful to Bill's Texaco for the rest of her life.

The man had definite opinions about everything, all of which he shared, and none of which Jenny heard. If she told him what had happened, she was sure he'd give her his opinion about that too, but she just sat dully in his Jeep, nodding from time to time as he drove her back to her car. He'd probably tell her to call the police, and she knew she should. But later. After she got home and locked the doors. After she was safe.

Now, sitting outside in the driveway, Jenny closed her eyes. She could barely think of going into that house and being alone again. She hadn't felt safe there since they'd moved to Rimrock. And the police? What would they say when she told them what she'd decided: that what had happened with the motorcycle wasn't an isolated incident, that starting with the headless snake, someone was trying to scare her. And that someone was succeeding.

The police would want to know why, and at the moment, Jenny didn't have an answer. But it was true, she knew it. She should have known it all along.

She put her hands to her temples and rubbed, trying to ease the pounding, telling herself to get out of the car, but her body just wouldn't cooperate. She felt herself sinking into a doze and when she heard the music, she thought she must be dreaming.

She opened her eyes. The music didn't stop. It wasn't quite music, though, just a few notes, hauntingly beautiful, drifting through the air.

Jenny slid out of the car and started for the house, mystified and enchanted with the sound. When she reached the porch, she saw the wind chime. Six long metal tubes suspended from a small circle of smooth wood, moving slowly in the gentle breeze. It was hanging from the same piece of wrought iron where she'd found the basket of wildflowers, and Jenny knew exactly who'd put it there. For the first time in this endless day, she remembered that she had an admirer.

She touched the chimes, setting off another peal of notes, then unlocked the front door and went inside to see if he'd called, too. There was a message, but it was from her father: everything had been worked out; he and her mother would be arriving tomorrow at six in the evening. Maybe the next call would be from her secret admirer, and she'd be home, and the two of them would actually talk. More than anything else right now, Jenny wanted someone to talk to.

Moving like a sleepwalker, she dragged herself upstairs, peeled off her filthy clothes and stepped into the shower. She'd done this just a few hours before, she remembered, but it seemed like days. Her head was still aching when she finished, so she swallowed an aspirin. Then she put on her oldest, softest pair of jeans and a dark-green, oversized

T-shirt, wrapped her wet hair in a towel, and went back downstairs.

If Mom was here, she'd tell you to eat, Jenny thought. She went back outside to the car and got the food, threw out the chicken, the turkey, and the hamburger meat, and forced herself to eat some cheese and an apple. Part of an apple. She couldn't finish it. She was hungry, but her mind had started working again and the thoughts that whirled around inside didn't go well with food.

Nobody was playing pranks: harmless, innocent pranks. Someone wanted to scare her, to frighten her so badly that she'd . . . what? Leave town? That's what she felt like doing. If she could, she'd move away and never come back.

But why? Why would anyone want to do that to her? What had she done to make someone hate her so much? And who was that someone?

The house was too quiet. She was getting jumpy again, so she unwrapped her hair and went out on the porch. The sun was getting low, but as long as there was light, she felt safe. She sat on the steps, only three feet from the door in case she wanted to run back inside, and listened to the soothing sounds of the wind chime.

Be logical. Organize your ideas. That's what teachers were always saying, not to mention her parents. Of course they were talking about research papers, not hate-filled maniacs, but that was beside the point. Jenny combed her fingers through her wet hair and tried to get her thoughts in order.

The snake. It had started with the snake. So what had she been doing before the snake arrived? Recovering from an almost-sleepless night. Her first night alone in the house, when Peaches had heard something outside. The day before, she'd taken her parents to the airport, and then what? Then she'd heard about Diana.

The air was still warm, but Jenny shivered as she remembered. She'd gone into town, to the diner, and at first, everyone was happy, joking over their hamburgers. Jenny shivered again. Then Brad had come, and the happy crowd learned that Diana had fallen on the rimrocks. And Jenny told everyone about the shout she'd heard and the scream. And Brad had been furious because she couldn't remember the words. She still couldn't remember. Was he still so furious that he wanted to hurt her? Just because she couldn't remember? Remembering wouldn't help Diana, he had to know that.

Jenny shivered again and wrapped her arms around her knees. The awful things had started happening the day after she'd told everybody about the shout. The shout. She squeezed her eyes shut and tried to hear it again, not the words, just the sound, the feeling.

It wasn't hard to bring the feeling back to life. The wind and thunder and lightning. Her own fear, and her own shouts for David. She squeezed her eyes tighter. There'd been a big flash of lightning, and she'd screamed, then she'd heard someone shout. And then she'd heard someone scream. Someone else.

Jenny's eyes flew open, but she didn't see anything except the dark, rain-drenched rocks of the bluff. The wind chime was still making its haunting music, but she heard nothing except the shout and the scream. And the voices. Not just one. *Two* voices. She'd heard two different voices. One shouted and one screamed. Two different people. Not just Diana, alone, but two people up there. And then Diana fell. And whoever was with her knew it, and left her there, knowing she was hurt. Knowing she might die.

Jenny's heart sped up, sending a rush of blood to her face, a rush of fear. Then you came along the next day, she told herself, talking about what you'd heard. And whoever was up there with Diana was listening to every word. And got scared that you'd remember. Diana was in a coma; *she* wouldn't say anything. The only person to worry about was bigmouthed Jenny Fowler. And the thing to do was make sure she didn't remember. To play tricks on her and scare her so badly she wouldn't think of anything but what was happening to her.

Well, it had almost worked. Jenny had tried her best to forget that night on the rimrocks, anyway. She'd even tried to convince herself that there was some idiot, junior-high prankster behind all the tricks, laughing up a storm. Whoever was behind them wasn't laughing, though. He or she was deadly serious.

Suddenly Jenny jumped up, unable to sit still any longer. She was so scared she wanted to run. But where could she run to? Who could she run to? She was alone. Just like he wanted.

He? Brad? Jenny thought again of the big, good-looking football player and the desperation on his face when she couldn't remember what she'd heard. And that visit he'd made to her house, when he'd said how he hated Diana. Jenny had been scared then, scared of the fierceness in his eyes and the way they glittered whenever he looked at her. But that fear was nothing compared to what she felt now, now that she knew someone was out to get her. Someone crazy with anger, so crazy he'd pushed Diana off the rimrocks. That someone could be Brad.

Sally thought Brad had sent the snake. But Sally had been the one to deliver it. She said she'd found it on the porch, but she could have brought it. And she'd acted so strange this morning, up on the rimrocks, so nervous. Looking at her watch, like she was waiting for something to happen. Could she have arranged the fall of rocks, not knowing it would go wrong? Could she be in it with someone else? With Brad?

Jenny shook her head. It was hard to believe. But it was hard to believe that any of this was happening at all. It *was* happening, though. If she wanted to be safe, she'd better figure out who was doing it.

Jenny paced the porch, her mind racing, flitting

back and forth over the people she knew, until it finally landed on Dean. Dean Latham. In spite of that wink he'd given her, Jenny thought he was a cold fish. So calm, so rational, so logical when he'd talked about how sound could play tricks. And Jenny had agreed, thinking he was just trying to be nice. Her mind hadn't played any tricks, though, she knew that. But Dean might be. And he'd been in town today, she'd seen him. He could have shut the windows of her car. If he'd pushed Diana, or left her there, then he'd want to be very sure about what Jenny heard.

There was someone else who wanted to be sure, too, and Jenny's mind finally turned to David. She'd been putting him off, not wanting to face it, not wanting to admit that he could be the one. But he could. He'd been as anxious, as desperate as Brad for her to remember what she heard. And he'd been with her on the rimrocks. And that time they'd been separated was when he could have been with Diana, instead of looking for a bird's nest, like he said.

Jenny stood up, shaking her head. Not David, she told herself. Not him. But why not? Just because he'd kissed her? Just because she was half crazy about him twenty minutes after they first met?

What about the second time they met, when he'd come back to the diner, and the third, when he'd followed her into town? She thought he was mad at her those times, or had changed his mind about her. But now she realized there might be another reason for the way he'd acted. Pushing her to remember what she'd heard, asking her if she'd seen Diana, acting so jumpy, so secretive — he could have a secret, all right. A deadly one.

"You don't really know him," she said aloud. "You don't really know any of them."

The breeze picked up, blowing the wind chime and making its bell-like notes ring out more clearly. Jenny listened gratefully to the sound, wishing it were even louder, so loud it would drive everything else from her mind. She didn't want to be thinking these thoughts, suspecting people, feeling terrified. If she told anyone, they'd probably think she was crazy.

Half an hour before, she probably would have agreed. But not now. Not since she'd remembered that other voice, and knew that someone had been with Diana on the bluff. No one could convince her she was crazy now. But there was no one to tell, either.

Again, Jenny felt an overwhelming urge to run — anywhere — but there was nowhere to go. If only she had a friend, a safe place to go to, just for a while, until she could decide what to do. Her eyes burning, her throat dry, she stumbled into the house and gulped down two glasses of water, then bent over the sink as her stomach heaved. She didn't get sick, but she felt so lightheaded that she lurched into the living room like a cartoon-drunk and fell onto the couch.

Finally her head stopped spinning, and she sat

up and looked around. Through the windows, she could see the rimrocks blazing red from the setting sun. She turned away from them, and as she did, she saw that the answering machine's light was on. While she was out on the porch, so caught up in her horrible, logical thinking that she wouldn't have heard the ringing phone, someone had called and left a message.

She pushed herself off the couch, walked to the desk, and punched the button.

"Jenny? Did you like the music? When I saw the chime and heard the sound it made, I thought of you. I hope you like it. That's why I'm calling."

There was a pause. Jenny stared at the phone, feeling her tension start to ease. His voice was so friendly, so warm, she wished it could keep her company all night long. All night? Could she really stay in this house alone for another night, knowing what she knew?

"No." His voice was a little stronger now. "That's not why I'm calling. Not the only reason, anyway. I think . . . I know these phone calls and the presents must seem like a joke to you. I hope they don't, but I wouldn't blame you if they did. They're not a joke, Jenny, but they are getting laughable."

Another pause, and Jenny heard him take a breath. She took one, too.

"So will you meet me? It's almost six now. If you get home any time in the next hour, will you meet me? I know I should come to your house, but I have to be at my job by seven-thirty, and it's in the opposite direction, almost in Mount Harris." He took another breath and laughed softly. "Also I . . . well, you've probably figured out that I'm not Mr. Outgoing. I mean, ringing the doorbell, making conversation with your parents, I'd probably make a rotten first impression. Couldn't we just be together first, someplace quiet? After all, you might not like me. But if you do, I'll come to your house next time and make the best impression I can. Promise." A slight pause, then he went on. "There's a place I like. It's on the way to my job. You could come and we could talk. Face to face, finally."

He went on to describe the place he liked, and as she listened, Jenny realized he was talking about the rimrocks.

When he finished giving directions, he took another deep breath. "I hope you come, Jenny," he said. "I'll be waiting for you. If you can't make it, don't worry, I'll understand. But I sure hope you can."

The message was over. Before it could erase itself, Jenny pressed the save button, thinking that she'd listen to it again.

Instead, she found her purse, took out her billfold and stuffed it in the pocket of her jeans. Then she ran through the house, turned on every light, turned on the radio loud enough so anyone coming by would think there was a party in progress, and ran out the door.

She wanted someplace to run to and her admirer's message had made her think of one: the airport in Mount Harris. She'd go there and wait through tonight and tomorrow for her parents' flight to come in. Plenty of people spent the night in the airport, and if anyone asked, she'd just tell them she missed a connection.

First, though, she'd make a stop at the rimrocks. A quiet place, a quiet talk with a shy, gentle-voiced boy. Someone who cared, who she could feel safe with. A boy so gentle that he had said he would understand if she didn't meet him. That was what she needed now, someone soothing, quiet, and caring.

She wasn't even afraid of the rimrocks if her secret admirer was there.

Chapter 11

By the time Jenny turned her car onto the bumpy drive that led to the bottom of the bluff, the sun was almost down. But she knew it would be a while yet before all the light left the sky. They'd have plenty of time to sit and talk and get to know each other.

She stopped the car and got out, looking around. The rimrocks weren't so bloodred now; they'd faded to a soft, pale pink, with purplish shadows created by overhanging rocks. The breeze was still blowing, and the air smelled of pine, even though there weren't any trees around. It was nice now, she decided. A perfect setting, something she might see in a movie.

It *was* kind of like a movie, now that she thought about it. Shy boy finally gets up the courage to meet the girl he's been worshiping from afar. Picks the most romantic place he knows, a place with soft lighting and gentle breezes and . . . Jenny shook her head and smiled. She was getting carried away. First she had to meet the guy. Then she'd see if this meeting had Hollywood potential.

She was sure he'd be there already, very visible, but as she picked her way through the low bushes and scattered rocks toward the bottom of the bluff, she didn't see anyone waiting for her. He couldn't be hiding, she thought. Nobody was *that* shy. Could he have changed his mind?

She stopped walking and looked behind her. Hers was the only car there. She listened, hoping to hear another one coming, but everything was quiet. She looked toward the rimrocks again, and picked out the place he'd told her to come to. It was easy to spot, an enormous flat-topped rock right in the middle of the center section of the U-shaped bluff. It was about ten or fifteen feet up, but very easy to get to. He said she couldn't miss it, and she didn't. What she missed was someone sitting on it, waiting for her.

He'd decided not to come. No he hadn't; he'd just gotten held up or something; stop jumping to the bleakest conclusions and give him a chance, at least. Jenny argued back and forth with herself a few more times, and then finally started walking toward the rendezvous point. She couldn't believe he wouldn't show up, but even if he didn't, she felt comfortable. Which was strange, considering the way she'd always felt about the rimrocks. Maybe it was just the time of day. Or maybe she was just so tired she didn't have the energy to worry about anything. Whatever it was, she decided to climb to the rock and wait. For a while.

She reached the flat-topped rock in about fifteen minutes, using her usual climbing method of skirting every boulder in the way and walking up the gullies instead. Her stomach was back to normal and rumbling; she wished she'd eaten more than the warm cheese and apple. But maybe he'd bring a picnic. Food was always a good icebreaker.

The rock was still warm from the sun. If it had been soft, Jenny would have stretched out on it and closed her eyes. She was really tired. A single day wasn't long enough for everything that had happened. The things she'd gone through should be stretched out over a couple of weeks, at least.

But she didn't want to think about that. Later, when she wasn't so fuzzy-headed, she'd decide what to do. Right now, she just wanted to keep her mind empty and let her secret admirer fill it with whatever he wanted.

She wasn't wearing her watch. When she left the house, it had been almost six-thirty. He'd called at six. Anytime within the next hour, he'd said. The hour must be almost up. She sat cross-legged on the warm rock and looked down below. Her car was still all by itself, a dusty brown shape among the lengthening shadows.

She put her head in her hands and closed her eyes for a few seconds. It was a chancy thing to do. She'd never slept sitting up before, but the heat from the rock and the soft wind through her hair made up for the hardness of the seat. Her head dropped lower, and she brought it up with a jerk. If she sat here much longer, she'd really fall asleep and probably roll right off her perch.

She stood up and stretched. The rock was big enough for pacing, so she tried that for a while, then sat down again. The rock wasn't as warm as before. And the light was changing, too. Pretty soon she wouldn't be able to see her car. It was still peaceful, but as far as she was concerned, the peace ended when the sky got dark. If he didn't show up in a few more minutes, she was leaving.

"Jenny?"

What was he, a mind reader? She stood up again, brushing off the seat of her jeans. She hadn't seen him coming, and she had a bird's-eye view of the territory. "I'm here," she called. "Where are you?"

She heard a small sound that might have been laughter. "Up here, above you."

Jenny turned and looked, but couldn't see anything. Another rock jutted part way over the one she was on and blocked her view. She ran her fingers through her hair, wishing she'd thought to stick a comb in her pocket when she'd gone tearing out of the house.

"Don't bother with that," he called. "You look fine."

Jenny dropped her hands, feeling like she'd been caught at something. "Where'd you come from?"

"The top."

Of course, she thought, the bluff's flat on top. There's even a road up there. Maybe he lived up that way.

She started to fiddle with her hair again, then stopped. "This isn't fair," she laughed. "I can't see you. Come on down, why don't you?"

"I've got a better idea. You come up here to me," he told her. "Getting up's easier than getting down at this point."

Jenny had her doubts about that. "I'm not much of a climber," she said. "And it's getting hard to see."

"You'll do fine," he assured her. "And I'll start down, so we'll meet halfway, okay?"

It was funny, Jenny thought. She'd been shouting almost, but his voice was still the same soft, gentle one she'd heard on the phone. And it was still unrecognizable. Each time he spoke, she tried to place it, but couldn't. She wanted to see his face, so she might as well climb.

"Okay," she said. "Just tell me which way to go. All I can see from here is another rock. And it doesn't have any steps carved into it."

Another soft sound. Definitely a laugh. "Just get off the rock, the side with the gully on it," he said. "You'll be able to follow the gully for a while before you have to do any serious climbing. And by then, I'll be down to you. It's not hard, Jenny, believe me."

Jenny didn't like the sound of the words "serious climbing," but she decided to go as far as she could.

"Okay," she called. "I'm on my way."

"So am I," he called back.

Jenny scooted off the rock and into the gully, which was about six inches wide and full of pebbles. But he was right, it did go on for quite a distance. Sometimes she had to scramble over a group of big rocks, but she always found the path again. Every once in a while she called out to make sure he was still coming, and he'd call back and say yes, he was on his way.

She kept her eyes on her feet most of the time, so she didn't notice how much darker it was getting until the gully finally ended. She looked up then and found herself facing what looked like a smooth wall of stone. It seemed to go up forever. There was no way she could climb up that.

As if he'd read her mind again, he said, "It's not as bad as it looks, Jenny. Just move a few feet to your right, and you'll see a kind of gap in the rock, a split. There are plenty of footholds in there."

Jenny did as he said and found the gap. But it was shadowy. The whole place was shadowy now.

"Come on Jenny," he said. "I'm almost down to you. I'll be able to give you a hand in a minute."

At least he's right about that, Jenny thought. His voice was much closer now. She braced her hands on either side of the split in the rock, put her foot up, found a hold, and dragged the other one up beside it. The rock wasn't as straight up as it looked. It slanted just enough so that she didn't feel like a fly on a wall. Not quite, anyway. "This must be the serious climbing you were talking about," she commented.

"You're doing great," he said. "Not much farther."

One foot up, wedge it in, bring the other foot up. Good thing she was wearing jeans or she wouldn't have any skin left on her knees. Jenny was feeling almost confident when her wedged foot came unwedged and slipped out. She gasped and clung to the rock with both hands, found her foothold again, and steadied herself.

"You okay?"

"Yes." Jenny swallowed a few times. "But listen, I don't like this," she said. "I think I want to go back down. I'd feel a lot happier with something flat under my feet."

"But you're almost here."

"Almost isn't there, though. I don't like this," she said again. "Why don't I wait while you come the rest of the way down to me? Or I could go all the way down and you could go all the way up and we could meet somewhere. Like at the diner, maybe. It's got a floor."

She'd been talking in a joking way, so she wouldn't sound whiny and chicken, and she expected him to chuckle at least. But he didn't.

"Come on, Jenny. Don't quit now." His voice was still soft. Soft and encouraging.

"I'm not quitting," Jenny said, starting to feel annoyed. "I just don't like the idea of climbing around here in the dark anymore. That's not why

I came, you know. I came to meet you."

"Then do it."

"What for?" Jenny couldn't believe it; they were arguing and they hadn't even met yet. "By the time I get up there, it'll be really dark, and I won't be able to see your face anyway. I'm going down."

"No, don't! You can't stop now, Jenny!" He was yelling, his voice no longer soft and intriguing, but hoarse with desperation. "I was counting on you!"

The words bounced off the rocks, and Jenny stopped, listening as they echoed in her mind. Closing her eyes, she heard them again. But not an echo this time. A memory. A memory of a few nights before when windswept rain had battered the bluff, when lightning tore across the sky and the thunder seemed to shake the rocks. And she'd been cowering in a little ditch, shouting for David, calling over and over until she finally heard what she thought was an answering shout.

"I was counting on you!" That's what she'd heard. Words shouted in fury, in a voice that cracked with anger and fear. But not shouted to her, to Jenny. They were shouted at Diana. The very same words, shouted by the very same voice.

"You." It came out on a rush of breath; she hadn't meant to say it.

But he'd heard. "Me what? Me what, Jenny?"

"Nothing. I . . . nothing." He was the one, Jenny was thinking. He was the one with Diana that night, and he was the one who'd called Jenny all those times, pretending he cared. He'd left Diana to die and now he was after Jenny. Because she'd heard. And now she remembered.

"Oh, Jenny." He almost moaned her name. "You know, don't you? You remember."

Jenny didn't answer. She was poking her foot around, trying not to think about anything but finding the foothold below. Where was it?! "Remember what? I don't know what you mean."

"You can't run, Jenny. It's too late for that. I know this place and you don't."

Jenny heard a movement above her and knew he was coming down. She couldn't see him. She could hardly see anything. She finally got her toe into a hole and eased herself down. A cascade of pebbles bounced from above, landing on her head and shoulders. He was coming.

"If you hadn't remembered, I wouldn't have done anything," he said, and his voice was closer. "I just wanted to talk and sound you out. I heard you up here that night, but I was hoping you hadn't heard me. But you had. So I tried all those other things, the snake and the motorcycle and that fat mutt of yours, to get you so crazy and scared, you'd leave. Just pack up and take off."

The same one, Jenny thought. The shy, warm boy on the phone and the crazy guy who'd terrorized her were the same one. And she'd never guessed. She gritted her teeth; she couldn't find the next toehold. She bit her lips and felt wildly with her foot, stretching her leg as far down as it would go.

"But it didn't work," he said. "You didn't go

away. And it's really too bad, Jenny."

Jenny found the toehold. At the same time, she heard a swift, brushing sound almost on top of her. Before she had a chance to look up, she felt a strong hand on her shoulder. With one big push, her secret admirer sent her tumbling back off the face of the rimrocks.

Something kept tickling her face. Something feathery soft and maddeningly persistent. Dog whiskers, maybe. Peaches?

Jenny reached her hand up and brushed her cheek, felt the soft something drift down her neck and into her shirt, and came fully awake. To darkness.

It took only a second to remember. She wasn't in bed, with Peaches nuzzling insistently at her to wake her up and be taken out. She was somewhere on the bluff, and part of its gritty dust was still sifting down her face.

She brushed off as much as she could, then closed her eyes again, taking stock. She was almost in a sitting position, her back up against a very hard rock. There was a sore, burning feeling along her backbone and throbbing on the side of her head. Her palms stung and one elbow ached, but the ache didn't get any worse when she moved it. She must have twisted somehow on the way down, bracing herself with her feet and hands and scraping her back along the rocks as she fell.

Fell. That was hardly the right word for it. She

opened her eyes and sat up straighter, her heart beating faster as she remembered that awful moment when she felt his hand push against her shoulder. Her secret admirer's hand. The one person she thought she didn't have to fear.

She'd been so stupid! Where was her mind? She let herself be seduced by a soft voice and actually followed it up here! Followed it just minutes after she'd told herself that she couldn't trust anyone, not even Sally.

Well, she was pretty sure Sally was out of the picture. But her "admirer's" identity was still a secret. Sure, she'd heard his voice, but that didn't mean a thing. He'd probably disguised it, given it a different pitch or something. There must be patterns in his speech he couldn't disguise; someone who knew him well probably wouldn't be fooled. But, as she'd told herself not too long ago, she didn't know anyone here that well. Not even David.

Jenny shifted around, but the rocks and sand underneath her started slipping, and she did, too. It was so dark, there wasn't even a moon. What if she slipped some more, right into the air?

If her mouth and throat hadn't been so dry and full of grit, she might have screamed. She felt like it, felt like screaming and screaming until somebody heard and came to help.

She shifted again, carefully, and heard rocks clattering down. They seemed incredibly loud, probably because everything else was so quiet. The only other sound she could hear was her own breathing.

It wasn't steady, but at least she was doing it. At least she was alive.

Did he know she was alive? He must have checked after he pushed her, Jenny thought. He must have come down and checked. But if he'd done that, then he would have known she wasn't dead.

Did he think she was in a coma, like Diana? No, he couldn't have taken a chance on that. If he'd seen she was still alive, he would have killed her.

He couldn't have seen, then. He didn't know for sure. He must not have been able to get to her. He must be waiting. Waiting until there was just enough light to see by. Then he'd make his move.

Jenny put her hands over her mouth and gulped down the sound that was trying to escape. She had to be quiet. But she also had to move, get down, get away. She didn't know what time it was, it could be hours before the first light, or it could be minutes. She had to move now. And she had to do it without him hearing her.

Chapter 12

In spite of the urge to start scrambling down immediately, Jenny forced herself to sit still for a few more minutes. The darkness was almost total; her eyes had adjusted enough so that she could make out shapes close by, but when she tried to see for any distance, it was as if a thick black cloak had been thrown over the world. It must be cloudy, she thought. She couldn't even see any stars above her, just more darkness.

She stretched her arms out wide, trying to get a feel of the place where she'd landed, and whether or not there were any sheer drops in store for her when she made her first move. Her hands met with rocks, and after she'd pulled on one to make sure it wasn't going to come loose and fall with her, she held on tight and started to roll over onto her knees. That's when she felt the pain in her right ankle. The sharpness of it made her hiss through her teeth and sweat broke out on her forehead. When the pain eased into a dull ache, she reached down and felt her ankle, gently.

It felt puffy. Did broken bones swell? She didn't know. Probably it was sprained; she must have twisted it when she landed. She couldn't let it hold her back, though, broken or not. She might have to move even more slowly than she'd planned, but she still had to move.

She grabbed hold of the rock again and rolled over. She poked around with her good foot until she felt it come up against something solid, then took a deep breath and slowly let herself slide down.

She had no idea how high she'd climbed before he'd pushed her, but she kept hoping to find that gap in the rock. After a few minutes, though, during which she covered about two feet, she knew she wasn't going to. She thought she'd fallen straight backwards, but when she twisted, she must have twisted in the opposite direction from the way she'd come. Her foot never slid into any familiar holes, and she had no other landmarks to go by. If she could just see, she'd probably see that the gap was only a few feet to one side or the other. But there was no way of telling in the darkness, and she wasn't about to start scrambling around searching for it. Her ankle wouldn't cooperate, and even if it weren't hurt, she was no fleet-footed mountain goat. She grabbed hold of another well-planted rock and slid backwards and down another few inches.

Every move Jenny made created a small landslide of rocks and gravel. Their skittering noise drove her crazy. If she could hear it, so could he. She'd move, wait for the noise to stop, try to hold her breath, and listen for some other sound. She never heard one, but that didn't mean anything. He was there, she knew it. He was waiting, probably hearing every move she made. He had to hear her, she was clattering around like a one-woman band.

So what was he waiting for? Why didn't he come and get it over with? Was he just hoping she'd fall? Or was he standing there at the bottom, listening to her trying to be quiet, waiting until she got down to him?

If that was it, Jenny knew she didn't have much of a chance. She couldn't run, not on her bad ankle. She stopped and rested, breathing in rock dust, trying to figure out what to do. She couldn't go up. But she couldn't stay put, either. Even if he was down there, she had to keep going. She couldn't outwait him; she'd go crazy if she stayed still.

It seemed endless. Between the sliding and the resting, the groping around for something solid to hang on to, and the waiting for the pain in her ankle to ease, Jenny figured a snail could have outraced her. It was impossible to go straight down; three or four times her foot had hit nothing but air, and she had to heave herself sideways until she found a safer route. But with all the slipping and scrabbling, she never came across that gap in the rock. She had no idea where she was. Down was the only direction she was certain about.

It was during one of her rest-stops that she felt

something had changed. Not the rocks, they were just as hard as ever. Not her ankle, it was still on a regular cycle of sharp pain and dull ache. But something was different. She tilted her head back, tired of inhaling dust, and that's when she figured it out: the sky had changed. It was still dark, but not the pitch-black darkness of before. Here and there her eyes were able to pick out a difference in shading, and she knew she was seeing the clouds. Morning was coming, and the sky was going to get lignter. It would be gradual, but it wouldn't be long before the light would be bright enough for Jenny to see by. And to be seen by.

She had to try to move faster now. She'd started out hating the dark, but after a while she realized it was about the only thing going for her. It was like a cover, and once morning came, that cover would be ripped off. She wouldn't be able to sneak back to her car then, or find some crevice to crawl into and hide. There hadn't been much chance of that to begin with, but once the light came, the chance would be completely gone. He'd see her, no matter where she was.

Moving faster was something she could only do in her mind, though. Her heart raced, but the rest of her just plodded along at the same agonizing slow pace. She was afraid to look up again, afraid to see even more light; she focused her eyes on the rocks about two inches from her nose and tried to forget everything else.

After a few more minutes, Jenny's foot hit air

again. She reached out with her left arm and felt a smooth, flat surface. She couldn't tell how far it went on, but to the right there was just more air, so she stuck out her left foot and managed to slide a few feet until she felt solid rock underneath. She felt to the left again. More flat rock. And more. Maybe it was the rock where she'd first come to meet him. If it was, then the gully was over to her left. And once she got to that, she could stand up and walk the rest of the way down. No, she couldn't do that, not on her ankle. She'd have to crawl. But that wasn't so bad; she should keep low, anyway.

It was still quite dark, and as she turned over on her seat and started scooting to the other side of the rock, Jenny felt a surge of hope. She was certain he was waiting for her, but if she'd actually made it down off the face of the cliff before the first light, then she might have a chance after all.

She scooted a few feet, then stopped. Her ankle was killing her and her good leg was cramping from holding all her weight. She stretched it out and rubbed it frantically. She couldn't stop now.

There. It was okay. She got ready to move, braced herself on her hands, and pushed up on her good leg. And stopped in that position, not moving, not even breathing.

She'd heard something. A sound, but not one she'd made. Silently, she eased herself down and listened.

There it was again. A rock clattering on another

one, followed by a soft swish of smaller pebbles. She knew that sound, all right, she'd been making it all night. But she hadn't made this one. Someone else had.

Automatically, Jenny reached around until her fingers closed over a loose rock. It was perfect, rough and uneven, just the right size for her hand. Then she waited again.

She heard another clattering, and then a voice, calling her name. "Jenny? Jenny!"

She bent her head, and for a second, her eyes filled with tears. He hadn't bothered to disguise his voice this time. Why should he? It didn't matter anymore, not to him. But it mattered to her. The voice she'd heard belonged to David.

"Jenny?"

She remained perfectly still, listening. She was now dry-eyed and thinking hard. He was over to her left somewhere, not to the right where the gully was. More than anything, she wanted to keep moving to the right. But she knew she had to go left, and wait for him to get her near her. Near enough so she could use the rock.

"Jenny!" He wasn't shouting, but there was fear in his voice.

Good, she thought. Maybe he thinks he's lost you. So let *him* be scared. Let him be the one who's afraid.

Quietly, she began moving toward the sound of his voice. When she reached the edge of the flat rock, she scooted back as far as she could go, got on her knees, braced herself with her good foot, and waited.

It didn't take long. She heard the shifting of gravel again, and then she could hear his breathing. It was lighter now, and she saw him move. He was climbing toward her.

"Jenny? Are you up here? If you can, answer me!"

When his head was almost level with hers, Jenny gave her answer. Her arm was already back, and with every bit of strength she had, she brought the rock crashing down on his head. She cried out at the sickening thud, but David didn't make a sound. He fell where he was, a trickle of blood already seeping down his forehead.

She didn't know when she'd started crying, but her face was wet with tears and her hand shook as she wiped them away. She rolled to her side, away from the sight of David, and lay there, wishing she could be magically transported a million miles from there to a soft bed with clean sheets. She'd made it, she was safe, but she was suddenly so exhausted she wasn't sure she could move another inch.

She had to, though. Had to get all the way down and hobble to her car, drive to the police. She forced her eyes open, and for the first time was able to pick out actual shapes. She *was* on the rock she'd first climbed to. The light was coming fast now; if she sat up, she might even be able to see her car.

Keeping her face turned away from David, Jenny

pushed herself up and looked out below. There was her car, barely visible. The sight of its shadowy bulk cheered her up, and she smiled. She could make it.

"There you are."

Nothing could have startled her more; Jenny yelled at the sound of the voice and looked around wildly. David?

"Over here, Jenny."

It was Dean Latham. Standing in the gully on the other side of the rock, his calm, pale eyes gazing at her steadily.

"What . . ." Jenny's voice cracked. She tried to clear her throat. "What are you doing here?"

"Looking for you."

"But . . ." she had to swallow again. "Why? I mean, what . . ." Jenny shook her head. Had she left her mind somewhere up on the bluff? She couldn't hold onto a single thought long enough to get it out.

"Don't bother talking," Dean told her. "It's probably better if you don't say anything."

"I have to talk," Jenny managed to blurt out. "You don't know . . . or do you? You must. Why else would you be up here looking for me?"

"I don't know what?"

"What's been happening!" Jenny flung her hand out, gesturing at David. She was still clutching the rock she'd hit him with, and she held onto it, turning it over and over in her hands as she tried to put a coherent sentence together. "He was after me. He tried to kill me. And he would have if I . . ."

"If you hadn't bashed him in the head?" Dean smiled at her and his voice was cool. "Poor David."

"Poor . . . ?" Jenny couldn't help feeling outraged. His sympathy was definitely in the wrong place. She was the one who'd just gone through hell. And what about Diana?

Dean had moved up onto the rock and was standing there, still watching her. Jenny frowned at him. He was awfully calm for somebody who'd just found out that one of his friends was an almost-murderer. Of course, he might be in shock. But he didn't look shocked. In fact, he looked satisfied, even pleased. Pleased with himself, as if he'd just solved a tricky problem.

She frowned at him again. She hadn't noticed it before, but now Jenny saw that Dean was dressed in black. Black jeans, black sneakers, a black, long-sleeved pullover. The only light spots were his hair and face. And his hands, clenched into fists.

Jenny's head was clearer now, and as she stared at Dean, her mind filled with questions. "I don't understand," she said.

"Understand what?"

"Why you were looking for me. And how you knew where to look." She gestured toward David. "Why you're not more upset about him, why you don't seem the least bit worried, or relieved, or whatever you should be feeling now that it's — "

"Now that it's over?" He smiled again. He said, "But it's not over, Jenny. Not yet. Haven't you figured that out?" His voice had changed while he talked, back to the one Jenny had heard when she'd come running to meet him, and earlier, on the answering machine. Back to the soft voice of her secret admirer.

Now it made sense. The black clothes, the sudden, unexplained appearance, the cool comment about David. It was Dean who'd called her up here, Dean who'd pushed her, who'd waited until daybreak to find her again. Jenny's eyes widened as she realized the danger she was in.

"I see you've figured it out now," Dean said. "I probably shouldn't have waited until you did. It would have been easier on you. But I guess I just wanted to see it through."

While he spoke, Jenny slowly got to her feet. She staggered, trying not to put any weight on her ankle, then got her balance. Dean watched her, the thin, polite smile never changing.

"In case you're wondering," he said, "I didn't push Diana. She fell by accident. It worked out very conveniently for me, though. Until you started talking about what you heard that night."

Jenny tried not to listen. Soft as it was, his voice was distracting. It kept her from thinking, and she had to think.

"Poor David," he said again. "I really do feel sorry for him. He didn't know what he was getting into."

Jenny didn't take her eyes off him. She had to be ready.

"But actually, he makes it easier for me," Dean

went on. "Everybody knew you two had hit it off. At first. And then plenty of us heard you screaming at him in town." He took a step toward Jenny. "They'll probably decide it was some kind of lover's quarrel. The two of you met and argued. The argument got physical." He moved toward her again, unclenching his hands. "They'll decide it was an accident, too. A tragic accident." He laughed, almost soundlessly. "Three accidents in a week. It's going to give this place a bad name. Everybody'll shake their heads and say they always knew how dangerous the rimrocks were. And for a while, nobody will climb up here. But then everything will get back to normal. People will forget. They always do."

Come on, come on! Jenny thought. Just a little closer.

Dean looked at her and sighed, as if she were a bothersome child who wouldn't leave him alone. He took another step. Then, finally, he glanced away from her, up to the sky, checking the light.

"Well, Jenny."

He started to say something more, but Jenny didn't give him a chance. She drew her arm back, pushed off with her good foot, and lunged at him, swinging the rock down toward his head.

Dean reached up to block her arm, his ice-blue eyes not calm any longer, but wide with surprise. Jenny tried to spin away from his grasping hand, but her ankle wouldn't support her and she fell, landing hard on her knee. She pushed with her hands, trying to get up fast, ready to fight.

But the fight was already over. Dean's balance had been off to begin with, and he never got it back. As Jenny was scrambling to her feet, she heard a small, sharp gasp. That tiny intake of breath was the only sound Dean made as he fell backward toward the rocks below.

Chapter 13

Jenny kept expecting to get hysterical. Or cry, at least. After all, it was over. She'd spent an endless night doing things the wishy-washy Jenny Fowler of a few days ago could never have done. Wasn't reaction supposed to set in now? She might even have killed someone. Shouldn't she feel something besides this strange calm that left her mind blank?

Almost blank. As she stood there, breathing deeply, the first image that came to mind was a tall glass of ice-cold water. Maybe that was hysteria, she thought.

Her eyes felt rusty from sand and lack of sleep. She blinked them, then started to rub them, and realized she was still gripping the rock. She looked at it for a moment and was still looking at it, still not really thinking about anything, when she heard a low groan off to the side.

David was struggling to his feet, and Jenny dropped the rock and limped toward him. She felt so much relief that her eyes finally filled, and she knew her emotions were waking up.

"You're all right," she said. "I'm so glad you're all right."

"Uh-huh." He touched his head gingerly, wincing as he felt the bump on it.

Jenny winced, too, in sympathy. "I'm sorry," she said. "I thought you . . . I didn't know."

But he was already up on the rock with her, his arms around her. She felt him take a deep, shaky breath and let it out, and she knew his emotions were working, too.

They stood together for a minute, not saying anything, and then Jenny pulled away and pointed. "Dean's down there," she said. "He fell. I don't know if he's dead or not." She swallowed hard and felt her knees start to shake. Now reaction was setting in.

A look of amazement in his eyes, David went to the edge of the rock and peered over. After a minute, he said, "He's alive. I can see him moving a little. I don't think he's fully awake, though."

"We have to call an ambulance," Jenny said.

David nodded. "I used my dad's car." He smiled faintly. "I'd have found you faster if I'd had a flashlight. There *is* a C.B. in the car, though. I'll use it to get an ambulance here." He helped her sit down. "I'll be back for you in a few minutes."

Jenny scooted herself to the edge of the rock and watched him run, leaping over rocks and bushes, all the way to his car. She hadn't seen it earlier; it was parked on the other side of hers. He wasn't in it long. Soon, he was hurrying back, carrying something floppy, probably a blanket. She saw him go to Dean and kneel beside him, and then she turned her eyes away.

The clouds were starting to break up, and a big section of the rimrocks was turning rosy. It was going to be a sunny day, she thought. Her parents would have good flying weather. She thought about going to bed and setting her alarm in time to meet them, then decided she'd better not. Once her head hit a pillow, she was going to sleep for a long, long time. A brass band outside her window might wake her, but an alarm clock didn't stand a chance.

She could hear David's voice. Dean must be awake, she thought. But she still didn't look at them. She didn't want to see Dean. She knew he needed help, psychiatric help, and she hoped he'd get it, even though she hadn't recovered enough to feel sorry for him yet. She was angry, but not so angry that she was afraid she might hit him or yell at him. She simply didn't want to see him, ever again.

In a few minutes, she heard David coming back. She looked up and saw that his face was working, as if he were trying not to cry. He and Dean were friends, she remembered. Maybe not close ones, but they'd known each other a long time. She didn't blame David for being upset. It was the kind of reaction she'd expected from Dean, earlier. To find out that someone you'd known and gone to school with for years was a completely different person than you thought — it was going to hit everybody hard.

David's face was calm by the time he reached her.

"Is he . . . how is he?" Jenny asked.

"I'm not sure. I think just his leg's broken, but I was afraid to move him," David said. "I told him what happened and that there'd be an ambulance soon."

Jenny was still shaking. David came and sat beside her, putting a washed-out denim jacket around her shoulders. They looked at each other and then they both spoke at the same time.

"What happened?"

"You first," David said.

She spoke carefully, trying not to leave anything out. She told him about the scary things that had happened — the snake and Peaches and the motorcycle — and how she'd finally figured out that they were because of what she'd heard up here that night. She told him about the admiring phone calls and the presents, and how happy they'd made her. How glad she was when she got the one last night.

"I felt so alone," she said. "I didn't trust anybody, obviously." She looked at the wound on his forehead, and he smiled. "I guess I was so scared and confused that I wasn't thinking straight. If I had been, I never would have come up here. It just never entered my mind that one person was doing both things."

"It probably wouldn't have entered anybody's

mind," David said. "Not anybody normal, anyway."

"Maybe. And then his voice!" Jenny went on. "I've heard Dean talk before, not much, but enough. He changed it some way, though. I just didn't recognize it. And I didn't think he was my secret admirer because of the way he winked at me that time."

"What time?"

"In the diner, just after everybody had heard about Diana," Jenny said. "My secret admirer was bashful, and anybody who winks like that isn't bashful."

"Dean's not bashful," David said. "He's always been kind of standoffish, though. Cold, I guess I'd say now. But he's not a winker, either. It must have been part of his plan. To fool you."

"Well, it worked," Jenny said. She shuddered and David put his arm around her shoulders.

They sat quietly for a minute, and then they heard the siren in the distance. "I know you're wiped out," David said, "but we've got to go. Can you make it?"

Jenny nodded and shrugged her arms into the jacket. He helped her up and across the rock. Then he lifted her down into the gully. He grabbed her around the waist, she draped an arm around his neck, and then he walked and she hopped away from the rimrocks.

It was slow going. They were only halfway to the cars when the ambulance pulled up. David helped her sit and went to join the men who came running toward them.

Jenny closed her eyes, her mind blank, while the medical crew took care of Dean. She didn't want to see him being carried away, and she only opened them again when she heard the siren start up. By then, David was beside her, helping her up.

"I said you just twisted your ankle and didn't need to ride in an ambulance," he told her. "I hope I was right. I just didn't think you'd . . ." his voice trailed off and he gestured at the white van that was speeding away.

Jenny hadn't even considered the possibility that she might ride to the hospital with Dean. The idea was so horrifying, it was almost funny, like black comedy, and she found herself laughing a little. "Thanks," she said. "I hadn't thought of that."

They went a little farther toward the cars, and when they stopped a second to catch their breath, Jenny remembered something.

"You said you told Dean what happened," she said. "Now tell me."

"That's right, I never got my turn, did I?"

"No. So tell me," Jenny said. "How did you know where to come looking for me? And *why* were you looking for me? And why didn't you seem surprised when I was telling you about Dean?" She'd just thought of that. Her mind really was not working well at all.

"You left out the fight we had the other day,"

David reminded her. "Don't you want to know why I've been acting so weird?"

"I want to know everything," Jenny said. "I've been in the dark long enough, excuse the pun."

"Okay." David took a deep breath. "First things first. Diana woke up."

"She did?" Jenny felt genuinely glad for the girl. "That's great, David. And she's going to be all right?"

"She's all right already," he said. "Anyway, she told about what happened to her. How she and Dean were arguing and she fell."

"He told me that, that it was an accident," Jenny said. "I didn't believe him."

"I guess he's not a total liar," David said, and his face looked sad for a moment. "He didn't push her, but he left her there. Just walked off and left her. Diana doesn't know that yet."

He was quiet for a moment as they started hobbling along. Then he said, "Dean's a computer freak."

"Yes, Sally told me."

"Well, he's a really bright guy and his family's the kind that pushes, you know? Gotta be the best, gotta get the best grades, get into the best college."

"Wasn't he?" Jenny asked. "The best, I mean?"

"According to Diana, his grades were dropping. I don't know why, maybe he just got tired of it. Anyway, it looked like he might not get into Harvard or Stanford or wherever. But he's not just your average computer nut, he's a brilliant one and he figured out how to tap into the school's system."

"I get it," Jenny said. "Instant A's."

David nodded. "Diana found out, and he begged her not to tell, she said. She felt sorry for him at first, and said she wouldn't. But then the school got wind of something funny going on and they started asking questions. Diana works in the office and she knew it wouldn't be long before they found out about him. Maybe about her, too."

"So she decided to tell?"

"Yes, but first she just wanted to lay it out to him, maybe convince him to confess," David said. "And he freaked. Just went crazy, yelling that he'd be ruined, that he'd been counting on her."

I was counting on you. Jenny didn't think she'd ever forget the words.

They reached the cars, and David helped her into his, saying he'd come back for hers as soon as he could.

"I have to pick my parents up at the airport later," Jenny said. "At six. They'll be expecting me."

"You'll be there," he told her. "I'll drive you."

Jenny leaned back in the seat and smiled. "At last," she said, "something besides rocks to sit on. This is dangerous, though. I may never get up."

"If you really want to walk, hop, I mean. . . ."

"Forget it," she said. "Just tell me now, about why you, all of a sudden, got so . . . I don't know, so distant. You acted like you hated me after what happened to Diana. And then you started bugging me to remember what I heard. What was going on?"

David put the key in, but didn't turn it. His dark eyes looked confused, as if he wasn't sure himself what had been going on. "That night at the scavenger hunt, remember? I gave Diana a lift. She was really upset, told me she was worried about something. She wouldn't tell me what, just said she had to work it out and it wasn't going to be easy. Then she went off with Dean. And after that, I didn't know what happened."

He shook his head, and a look of shame came into his eyes. "This is hard to say, Jenny, but I might as well be honest. There were a couple of times there when I thought it might be you." He swallowed, and then went on in a rush. "She isn't exactly the nicest person in the world, and she'd been pretty nasty to you when you met. I thought maybe after I left you on the bluff that you started climbing up, and ran into her and argued, or something. I knew you wouldn't have pushed her, but I thought . . ."

" . . . it might have been an accident?" Jenny finished.

He nodded. "Everything kept pointing to Dean, though," he went on quickly. "And I didn't want to believe it." He pounded softly on the steering wheel. "I mean, he's a friend, was a friend, I don't know. Anyway, it's not every day you suspect a friend of leaving someone to die. It made me a little crazy. I guess it was easier to think it might be you. I don't expect you to understand, but I kept telling myself I didn't really know you."

"I did, too," Jenny told him. "When I finally realized somebody was trying to scare me, I suspected everyone, even Sally. Even you," she added, glancing at his forehead. "How could I not understand why you thought those things about me, David?" she said. "I didn't trust you, either. And it's true, we *don't* know each other."

"No. I guess not," he said. They were both quiet for a minute. Then David went on, "So, anyway, there I was, thinking rotten thoughts and feeling rotten for thinking them. Then when Diana woke up and told us about Dean, I felt even worse. I came over to your house to tell you about her, but mostly I just wanted to apologize and to talk."

"But I wasn't there," Jenny said. "Why did you come looking for me here? Why were you even worried?"

David leaned his head back and grinned. "I broke into your house."

"You what? You didn't."

"Right, I didn't. You forgot to lock the door," he said.

"And you just walked right in? Not that I'm complaining," Jenny said quickly, "but what made you do that?"

"Because the place was lit up like the Fourth of July, and it sounded like a party was going on," he explained. "But I knew your parents were out of town, and nobody answered the door. So I decided to investigate."

"It's a good thing my dog wasn't there."

"Why, would it have bitten me?"

"No." Jenny giggled. "She probably would have fainted from fear. At least I know she's safe and well at the vet's." She suddenly thought of something. "You didn't go into my room, I hope. It's a mess. Don't tell me you went into my room."

"No, I didn't go into your room. What are you worrying about your room for?" He was laughing. "I went into your *living* room, so relax. It was very neat. I noticed there was a message on your machine and I thought maybe it would give me a hint about where you were."

"And it did, and you rushed over here," Jenny said. Then she thought of something else. "Wait a minute. You went to my house last night. You didn't get here until sunrise practically. I don't mean to sound picky, but . . ."

"What took me so long?" he finished. "I didn't know who'd called you. I thought you had a boyfriend."

"I just moved here, how could I have a boyfriend already?"

He looked at her, his eyes gleaming. "It's been known to happen."

"Yes. I guess it has." Jenny was suddenly very conscious of the way she must look. Her jeans were ripped, her ankle was the size of a small cantaloupe, every piece of exposed skin was scratched, and she didn't even want to think about her hair. She must be getting back to normal, she thought, if she was worrying about her hair.

David grinned at her again, as if he knew exactly what she was worrying about. "Anyway, I went home," he said. "Everybody was on the phone that night, talking about Diana and Dean. Brad called, Karen called; if Sally'd been here, she would have talked nonstop. I don't know why, but I decided to call Dean. I didn't know if he knew. That Diana had come out of the coma, I mean. I thought somebody ought to tell him and give him a chance to go to her. Apologize, maybe." He laughed softly, almost sadly.

"And he wasn't there."

David nodded. "Nobody knew where he was. That's when I figured out that he was the one you'd gone to meet. I got here as fast as I could."

That was it. There wasn't anything more to tell. David started the car, but before he drove away, he reached over and took her hand. "I should have talked to you before," he said. "If I'd told you what was on my mind, I might have saved you a lot of . . ." he sighed " . . . *trouble* is not the right word, but you know what I mean."

"Yes." Jenny held tight to his hand. "But I understand why you didn't. Don't start thinking 'What if.' I'm not going to. It's over. Let's just go on from here."

"Deal," he said. "On one condition" — he leaned across and brushed some dust from her face, then kissed her softly on the forehead — "We both said we didn't really know each other. Let's get to know each other better, okay?"

"Deal," Jenny said.

David put the car into gear and pulled away. As they drove, Jenny looked back toward the rimrocks. The sun had climbed higher; the rocks were losing their vivid rose color and fading back to sandy pink.

They still loomed, Jenny thought. But they hadn't been the cause of her nightmare. The nightmare was over, and she knew without a doubt that the rimrocks would never disturb her sleep again.

THE ACCIDENT

Chapter 1

The heat was oppressive, settling down on the village of Lakeside, smothering it like a wet woolen blanket. A pale charcoal sky hung low over the lake and the tall pine trees surrounding the navy-blue water like giant sentries. For days the dark sky had promised, but refused to deliver, the relief of a cooling rain.

The students at Philippa Moore Senior High School in Lakeside complained constantly about the heat, unusual for the last weeks of May. "It's never this hot this early," they said, their clothing sticking to their skin like damp tissue paper.

Philippa Moore, an old but still-beautiful structure of antique brick and white pillars, was not air-conditioned. On days when heat rays radiated up from the sidewalks outside, and chalk grew moist and sticky inside, sitting in one of its classrooms was like being roasted over hot coals.

Class cutting became rampant. Even those students who seldom skipped gave in to the temptation to escape the stifling classrooms.

Jenny Winn, sixteen; her fifteen-year-old sister, Barbie; and their best friend, Cappie Cabot, cut their final class of the day on a Wednesday afternoon. "The woods on the other side of the lake will be cooler," Jenny said. "We'll go there."

They put the top down on the big old yellow convertible, a legacy from their older brother Gene when he went off to college. The car had fins that looked like wings. While tiny Jenny would have preferred a cute little sports car to tool around town in, when given the elephantine vehicle she had said, "Wheels are wheels," and had quickly learned to handle the car like an expert.

"We should have asked Megan and Hilary to come along," Cappie said as Jenny confidently guided the car down the highway. "But Megan probably wouldn't have cut, and Hilary said she had to go to the drama department after school."

"I think Megan had stuff to do for her birthday party," Barb said, her long, blonde hair blowing around her freckled face. "She's so excited about it. Wish *I* was turning sixteen."

"You will."

The big yellow car moved along the road beside the lake, creating a breeze that was thick and hot, aimed straight at them.

But they all agreed it was better than being in one of Philippa's classrooms.

"It had better be cool in the woods," Jenny muttered, easing into the curve at Sutter's Bend. "If Miss Beech finds out I deliberately cut class, she'll hang me out to dry. So this little excursion had better be worth it."

As she always did when she reached the sharp elbow in the road, Jenny eased up on her speed and kept a firm grip on the wheel. She had driven this curve hundreds of times since she got her license in January. It was part of her trip to and from school every day.

On her right lay the lake, still too cold for swimming, guarded by stately pine trees. Big old houses and smaller, rustic cabins were scattered along its shores. The woods were off to her left, and a dry open road lay ahead of her like a flat gray ribbon. There was no oncoming traffic and no one tailgating her. Taking the curve should have been as simple as brushing her teeth.

But it wasn't. When she turned the steering wheel, it moved too easily, too rapidly, too loosely. And the car refused to obey. It continued moving in a straight line. Jenny tried again, using more force this time. The steering wheel spun uselessly, as if it had nothing whatsoever to do with the car.

She hunched over the wheel, saying in a low, tense voice, "Barb, something's wrong."

Barbie glanced up, unconcerned. "What? What's the matter?" When she realized that the big yellow car wasn't following the curve, she jerked upright. "Jenny — "

Everything happened very quickly, no longer than the blink of an eye.

The car left the road, heading directly toward a

utility pole on their right. And Jenny made a bad mistake. In her panic to regain control of the car, the foot she intended for the brake pedal slammed down instead on the gas pedal.

The car shot forward.

The three girls screamed, their hands flying up instinctively to protect their faces.

The car hit the utility pole, and the sound of metal crashing into wood echoed out over the quiet, peaceful lake.

The impact sliced the pole in two. Its upper section tipped in slow motion and descended onto the crumpled pile of yellow metal. Sparks danced about as the wires came into contact with the steel and the road.

Barbie, upon impact tossed like a rag doll from the convertible, lay stunned, not quite conscious, on the grassy area above the lake, safe from the spitting wires. She was murmuring her sister's name.

The only sign of the girl whose name Barbie kept repeating was a bare and bloodied arm draped lifelessly over what was left of the driver's door. Cappie was hidden within the bent and broken car.

Then Barbie lost consciousness, and the only sound breaking the ominous silence was the faint hissing of the electrical wires.

190

Chapter 2

Megan Logan stood before the free-standing, oval, wooden-framed cheval mirror in her bedroom, listening to the whippoorwills outside her open window and wondering if the blue-green dress she was trying on should be shortened for her party. The bird song was nearly drowned out by the constant humming and chugging of boat engines on the lake behind her house and by the sound of the television downstairs. But Megan was very good at filtering out sounds that didn't interest her and hearing only those she chose, like the call of the whippoorwills.

The blue and cream slant-ceilinged bedroom at the rear of the house was stuffy and hot, not conducive to trying on clothes. Old houses like this one, her mother's inheritance from Megan's grandmother Martha, had no air conditioning. Normally the breeze off the water cooled the house, but during this heat wave, even the breeze was oven-warm. The silky fabric of the dress clung uncomfortably to her moist skin.

But she had to check out the dress. The Sweet

191

Sixteen party her parents were throwing for her was coming up soon, and there was still a lot to do.

Her parents had said, "We'll give you a big party for your sixteenth birthday, Megan, but only if you buckle down and pull up your grades."

Megan had pulled up her grades, but it hadn't been easy. It wasn't that she didn't care about school. She did. She just had trouble concentrating, that was all.

"Megan is a dreamer," her English teacher, Miss Bolt, had told her parents during their most recent conference. "She's bright enough, but she spends too much time gazing out the window. When I call on her, she always looks so surprised, as if she isn't sure exactly where she is. The thing is, she almost always knows the right answer. And *that* surprises her, too."

A stern lecture from her father had followed, and then Megan's renewed effort to pay attention in class, and now the party was in the works.

A week from Sunday she would reach that magical age: sixteen. All of her friends were excited about the party. But no one more than Megan.

In spite of the excitement, an uneasy feeling had plagued Megan all day. She had no explanation for it. Maybe it was just the heat. But at the back of her mind, she felt that *something* was wrong.

Megan surveyed the dress with a critical eye. It had to be exactly right for her Sweet Sixteen party. The party would be held here, at the big white house on the lake. Her family had moved in just three months before, after her grandmother's death.

Megan swept her thick dark hair up, away from her shoulders and held it high with one hand. The frothy mass of gentle curls, dark as crows' wings, framed her oval face and sea-green eyes. It always seemed to Megan to be a wonderful mistake. Shouldn't someone as shy and quiet as she have plain, straight, brown hair? Didn't this hair belong on someone more outgoing, more dramatic? She'd been told it was just like her grandmother Martha's had been when she was young.

Wasn't the full, short skirt of the turquoise dress half an inch too long? It might make her look shorter than she actually was. She hadn't been lucky enough to get the hair *and* height. Maybe she should buy higher heels. Justin was tall enough. Not that she'd asked him yet to be her date. But she would. Any day now. Her best friends, Hilary Bench, Jenny Winn, and Cappie Cabot, had said it was up to her to ask, because she was the guest of honor. "You get to choose," Hil had said firmly.

I choose Justin Carr, Megan thought to herself.

As if on cue, the blue telephone on the nightstand in front of her window rang, and Justin's deep voice answered her quiet hello.

"So, are you hitting the books in preparation for the bio quiz tomorrow?" he asked. "Old Ollie had that gleam in his eye today when he warned us about it. You know, that look he gets behind his glasses when he's been plotting The Attack of the Killer Quiz. Boy, how that guy loves to see us sweat!" He laughed. "Sorry. Poor choice of words. Who needs help in that department now that Lakeside has become the Overpowering Inferno?"

Megan laughed. During the past year, Justin had become one of her best friends. He made her laugh. And he listened. Most boys didn't. He never teased her about preferring jazz to rock music, or for taking long walks by herself, or for being late repeatedly to the first-period science class they shared. The last time she'd come in late, walking into class sweaty and breathless, it had been because she'd stopped to pick wildflowers. When she had unthinkingly blurted out that truth to Old Ollie, the entire class had roared with laughter. Except Justin. He had smiled at her and gone to the sink at the back of the room to fill a beaker with water, which he then presented to her with a flourish. Flushing with embarrassment, Megan had thrust the black-eyed Susans into the beaker. Justin carefully installed the bouquet on his lab table, where it remained until the petals turned gray-brown and began to fall.

No one in the room had laughed when he did that. People didn't laugh at Justin. People took him seriously. Having him on her side was wonderful.

She had fallen in love with him that day.

But she still hadn't asked him to be her date for the party.

Because Justin Carr, who was tall and thin like one of the reeds in the shallower coves of the lake, Justin with his sandy, wavy hair and his gray eyes behind his wire-rimmed glasses, Justin with a smile that said, "The world's a crazy, interesting place, isn't it?" could invite any girl to any party, and that girl would be dashing out to buy a new dress before he'd even finished asking. So why would he want to go to a party with someone who was just a friend? And maybe not the most exciting friend in the world, either. Another thing she'd inherited from her grandmother Martha was shyness. She hated being shy, but there didn't seem to be anything she could do about it.

Hilary always insisted, "Justin is crazy about you, you dope. You're the only one who doesn't see it. He's just afraid of scaring you off by making a move on you. Asking him to your party will let him know how you feel. Then you can both relax."

To which Megan always replied, "Silly Hilly. We're just friends." And wished like crazy that it weren't true.

"I just opened my book a minute ago," Megan told Justin, flopping across her bed unmindful of the blue-green party dress and opening her biology book. "Are you ready for the quiz?"

Justin laughed again. "I was born ready."

"Lots of people are blowing it off." Megan rolled over onto her back. The dress rustled a protest. "There are tons of people out on the lake. I guess it's cooler out there. I'm sure I heard Karen Tucker's laugh, and she's in Ollie's class."

"Well, if she's planning on batting her eyelashes and telling him her book fell in the water and got ruined so she couldn't study, she'd better get real. Ollie isn't impressed by those sexy types."

Megan's eyes closed in pain. He thought Karen

Tucker was sexy? What was it that Karen had that she, Megan, didn't? As if I didn't know, she thought. Karen has the art of flirting down to a science and a great figure. She *is* sexy.

A siren sounded in the distance. Then another. But they were too far away to be the Lake Patrol. So it wasn't a boating accident. A fire in town? A car wreck?

That uneasy feeling she'd had all day kicked her in the stomach. Sirens meant something, somewhere, was very wrong.

"Megan? You still there?"

"Listen, Justin, I can't sit here and talk to you all night." She was still stinging from the "sexy type" remark. She didn't care if he heard it in her voice. "You may have this quiz aced, but I don't. I've got to go."

"Oh. Okay." Was that disappointment in his voice? Then why didn't he say, "I'll miss you when you hang up"?

Because Justin never said stuff like that to Megan Logan. He talked to her about books and music and metaphysics and the power of the universe, but he never said, "Megan Logan, you make the sun shine for me," which happened to be exactly what she wanted to hear.

"See you at lunch tomorrow?"

"Sure," she murmured, her voice lake-water cool. "I mean, I guess so. I always do. See you at lunch, I mean." She groaned silently. Brilliant. Positively brilliant. She really should see an agent about some heavy-duty public speaking. She'd make a fortune.

There was a brief silence. Then Justin asked quietly, "You okay?"

She was being stupid and childish. Justin hadn't done anything wrong. Karen Tucker *was* sexy. Everyone said so. But she still didn't feel like asking him to her party, not right now. Maybe later. "Sure. I'm fine. Just hyper about the quiz, that's all. I'd better go. See you tomorrow."

The minute she hung up, she was angry with herself for not asking him about the party. It was only eleven days away, and the birthday girl still didn't have a date.

Maybe I'll go stag, she thought, switching on her radio. But Mom would have a fit. "Honestly, Megan," she'd say in exasperation, "why didn't you ask Justin? I suppose you put it off and put it off until it was too late. What am I going to do with you?"

Gram had always defended her. Whenever Megan's parents threw up their hands in despair because their only daughter had "her head in the clouds," Gram would say mildly, "Megan marches to a different drummer, that's all. All creative people have their heads in the clouds. Maybe she'll write a great novel one day. She's fine. Leave her alone."

But Gram was gone, five months now.

Megan still missed her.

She got up, smoothing out the turquoise skirt, just as the music on her radio was replaced by an announcer's deep voice saying, *"This word just in. There has been a serious automobile accident at Sutter's Bend just west of town. Three people have been taken by Emergency Medical Services to Lakeside Medical Center after their vehicle hit a utility pole. Residents are urged to avoid the area as live wires pose a safety threat. The names of the injured, whose families have been notified, are sisters Jennifer and Barbara Winn, ages sixteen and fifteen, and Catherine Cabot, sixteen."*

Megan's hand flew to her mouth. She stood stock-still in the center of the room, frozen in shock. Jenny? And Barb? And Cappie? Hurt?

She couldn't move. The sirens had not wailed for some poor stranger, after all. They had been shrieking for three of her closest friends. And the announcer had clearly said, *"A serious accident." How* serious?

The telephone shrilled again, startling her. Numbly, she reached down and picked up the receiver.

"Meg? Megan, is that you? It's me, Hilary. Megan, *say* something!"

All the people out on the lake had gone home, leaving it peaceful and quiet. Downstairs, the television her parents and her ten-year-old brother, Thomas, were watching droned on. The whippoorwills were quiet. Everything, except the suffocating heat, was as it always was.

Except that something horrible had just happened.

"Hil," she said slowly. "Jenny and Barb . . ."

"I know. I heard. That's why I'm calling."

"What happened? Jenny's a really good driver."

"My dad thinks a tire blew. He said that when the pavement's hot as a barbecue grill for more than a few days, it's hard on tires. He said a blowout on such a big car would make it really hard for someone as tiny as Jenny to control."

"Oh, God, Hil, this is awful! Have you heard how bad they're hurt?"

"No, not yet. But it *sounds* really bad. Dad said that when wires are down at an accident, it takes longer to get the . . . the victims out. Too dangerous for emergency personnel."

"I just can't believe it, Hil!"

"And Jenny was so excited this afternoon." Hilary swallowed hard. "She'd asked Rob Lyle to your party. And he'd said yes. . . ."

Both girls fell silent, wondering if Jenny Winn would even be attending the party eleven short days away. How serious was "serious"?

"I can't talk about this anymore," Hilary said, breaking the silence. "Call me if you hear anything, okay?"

"I will. You, too."

When the blue phone was back in its cradle, Megan sat on the bed, lost in shock and disbelief. Was it really true? Had her friends smashed into a utility pole? How scared they must have been! She couldn't stand to think about them in pain, hurting, maybe scarred, maybe . . . dead? No, that couldn't be. The announcer hadn't mentioned a fatality. But "injured" was bad enough.

Shaking, she got up to remove the party dress. That made her wonder if Jenny had found "the perfect party dress" she'd been hunting for, and Megan burst into tears.

Suddenly Megan felt the temperature in her room plunge. The lights dimmed, sending the room into near-darkness, and the radio fell ominously silent.

Mouth and eyes wide open, Megan clutched at a bedpost. What was happening? An earthquake? A storm?

She was about to bolt for the door when a soft voice whispered, "Why are you crying, Megan Logan?"

Megan stopped in her tracks, unable to breathe.

The voice was faint and hollow, like the distant echo Megan's own voice returned to her when she called out across the lake late at night.

"I said, why are you crying?"

Chapter 3

Megan looked slowly around the room. There was no one in it but her.

But when her eyes moved to the big oval mirror, she gasped, her hands flying to her mouth. She backed rapidly away from the mirror until she bumped into the dresser, its fat white knobs poking her rudely in the back. And there she stood, transfixed. And completely, utterly terrified.

Instead of her own image, the glass was filled with a wispy, shadowy plume, faintly purple in color, weaving gently back and forth in the glass. Gradually, as Megan continued to stare with horror-stricken eyes, the plume began to take on a vaguely human shape. There were no facial features, only a bright golden glow where a person's eyes, nose, and mouth would normally be. No arms or legs were apparent on the gauzy purple stream. It was like looking at a person from a great distance through a sheer, delicate veil.

I've fallen asleep, I'm having a nightmare, Megan told herself to silence her galloping heart.

"I asked why you were crying. You look very sad."

Megan was freezing. The air coming in the window behind her was toaster-warm, yet within her room, it was as cold as an underground cavern. Every inch of her body was paralyzed with fear.

Megan struggled to find her voice. "What's going on?" she whispered. "What's happening?"

An eerie silvery glow began to surround the lavender plume, lighting it from behind. "I need to talk to you, Megan Logan. Don't be scared. I won't hurt you."

"Who . . . what are you?" Megan croaked hoarsely. Her legs weren't going to hold her up much longer. She felt that at any second she was going to collapse to the floor, completely helpless. Willing herself to remain upright, she repeated shakily, "What *are* you?"

The answer came softly, sweetly. "I am Juliet."

Megan had spent countless hours sitting on the terrace roof shaded by the branches of the huge old oak tree. There she watched the clouds drifting in over the lake. She always found something interesting in each wad of cottony white, each slab of pale or dark gray, each sunset-pinked gossamer trail.

But now, staring in terror at the shapeless, wavy stream of lavender in her mirror, she saw nothing familiar, nothing ordinary, nothing to still her hammering heart. The only thing she could be sure of was that the voice coming from the wispy column was, like her own, feminine.

202

"Juliet? But . . . but . . ." Megan sank down on the bed, shivering. The room was so cold. Yet a stream of stultifying, breath-defying hot air continued to crawl in sluggishly through her open window.

This wasn't happening. This *can't* be happening, Megan thought.

The voice was soft as cobwebs. "You think I shouldn't have a name?"

Without taking her eyes off the mirror, Megan slowly reached out and pulled the comforter from her bed, wrapping herself in it. The lighting in the room remained dim, while the silvery glow in the mirror seemed to deepen. "Go away," Megan whispered. "Whoever — whatever you are, I don't want you here. You don't belong here."

"I can't. I've got to talk to you, Megan. And you've got to listen to me. It's important."

"No," Megan said in a mere whisper. She wanted to cry out for her parents, or her brother, but she knew the shout would never escape her frozen throat. "I don't want to."

Sadness sounded in the voice, and bitter disappointment. "You won't listen to me? No, oh, no, that can't be! I was sure you would. I've waited so long. So very long . . ." The voice trailed off, the silvery glow began to dim.

"You've waited? For me?" Confusion added to Megan's fear. "Where? Where did you wait? Where did you come from?"

"I come from another time, another place. I'm here now, that's all that matters."

"How did you get into that mirror?"

The voice gathered strength as Megan began to respond. The silvery light throbbed, brightening again. "The mirror isn't important. It doesn't mean anything. I'm only using it so you can see me."

"But I don't *want* to see you!" Megan cried. "I don't want you here! Just go away!"

"Please, Megan, please, all I ask is that you listen. It would mean so much to me."

Only the possibility that she had fallen asleep and was caught in a horrible nightmare kept Megan from fleeing the room. That, and the mesmerizing quality of the plume's plaintive voice as it begged her to listen.

"You're getting ready for your party?" the voice said. "Pretty dress."

Megan said nothing.

"You're wondering how I know about your birthday. I know because it's my birthday, too. We share that. That's one of the reasons I can talk with you. But we weren't born in the same year."

Megan was seized by a fresh chill. The thing in the mirror had had a birthday? It had once been born, had lived, had maybe been a young girl like Megan?

But . . . if that was what it had *been*, what was it *now*?

Struggling, she managed to ask, "When? When *were* you born?"

"Nineteen thirty."

"Nineteen thirty?" Sixty-one years ago. But the voice was not that of a sixty-one-year-old woman. It was as young as Megan's.

204

"That dress really is pretty."

Megan looked down in surprise, as if someone had slipped the dress on her when she wasn't looking. The blue-green skirt peeked out from beneath the blue print comforter.

They had both been speaking in near-whispers, but now, the voice in the mirror gained strength. "I had a new dress for my sixteenth birthday party, too," it added wistfully. "My dress was blue like yours, but a darker shade, like the night sky. It was taffeta. It crackled when I walked. I loved that sound. I was having an orchestra at my party, and colored lanterns strung above the lawn, and napkins with my initials on them."

Megan was clenching her fists so tightly around the comforter, her knuckles looked bleached. The . . . thing in the mirror had had a birthday party?

Suddenly the plume became very agitated, jerking erratically from side to side. "But I never had my party," the voice said mournfully. "It was canceled."

A wave of skin-scorching heat blew in Megan's window, but she scarcely noticed. The agitation in the mirror terrified her. It . . . the plume . . . Juliet . . . was becoming very upset. I should leave, she thought numbly. I should run, right now, get out of this room. But fear had turned her body to stone.

An anguished sob filled the room. "There was an accident. A bad one."

The light around the plume dimmed, and the room became lost in shadow. An owl in the oak tree beside the terrace hooted. Megan jumped, startled by the sound. She spoke automatically, as if in a trance. "An accident?"

"A boating accident. Out there on the lake, in that cove just around the bend. Do you know the place?"

Megan knew it well. Most lake people avoided it because of the rocks, some jutting up above the water, most hidden beneath it. At the bottom of the lake there was a treacherous tangle of undergrowth and weeds lying in wait to imprison whatever might come its way. The cove had a history of boat wrecks and drownings.

Was this . . . Juliet . . . saying she was a part of that tragic history?

Megan waited with growing dread. Something terrible had happened to the thing in the mirror. She knew it. She didn't want to know what that something terrible was.

"Our boat hit a rock. I hadn't had time to learn to swim, but it wouldn't have helped. I was thrown overboard and knocked unconscious. My body became tangled in the undergrowth. By the time I was pulled from the water . . . it was too late. . . .

"I never made it to my party," the voice whispered sadly. "But . . . it was all a long time ago. Forty-six years ago. Such a long time . . ."

When Megan still said nothing, the thing called Juliet added, "I would have been sixteen the day of my party. Like you, Megan. Sweet sixteen . . ."

The wispy plume began spinning like a top. Soft, anguished sobs filled the room with pure pain. "I'd been planning that party for ages. I was sure it meant all the fun would begin. The best time of my life. I was pretty and very popular." The spinning stopped, but the voice was heavy with distress. "Everyone said I had so much promise. But that horrid accident took my life from me before I ever had a chance to live it."

Megan was struck by the horror of Juliet's words. Fresh tears streamed down her face, and her eyes were full of pain. "No, oh, no," Megan whispered. Then, lifting her head, she said, "But this isn't happening. This is *not* happening."

"Oh, dear, I've made you cry again. I shouldn't have upset you. I'll leave now, but I'll come back another time. Thank you for listening to me. . . . Most people wouldn't have."

And before Megan could cry out, the light dimmed, went out, and the mirror was clear again. There was nothing in it but the reflection of a girl, shaking violently beneath a blue print quilt, her face streaked with tears.

The lights came up to full power, and the radio came back on, as if Juliet had flicked a switch as she left. Once again, the room became suffocatingly hot.

Megan trembled for a long time. After a while, she removed the comforter, took off the party dress, and hung it carefully on a hanger in her closet. She got ready for bed, moving the entire time in stunned slow-motion. When she crawled up underneath the canopy, she pulled the pale blue sheet up over her in spite of the suffocating heat, unable to shake the chill left by the wraith in her mirror and the words the wraith had spoken.

I dreamed the whole thing, she told herself, staring up at the yellowed ceiling. I'm dreaming right now. I'm dreaming that I'm just going to bed, when the truth is, I've been asleep for hours.

The thought was comforting. It allowed her to relax and go to sleep.

The next morning when she awoke and remembered, her eyes flew to the mirror.

Except for Megan's own sleepy-eyed, tousle-haired reflection, the mirror was empty.

Chapter 4

On Thursday morning, Lakeside residents awoke to disappointment. The sky was still a sullen gray, the sun hidden, the heat still suffocating the town.

Megan felt like she'd slept in a sauna. Her head ached, her skin felt sticky, and her hair was matted to her head.

After checking the mirror and finding it empty, she thought immediately of her friends. Were they okay? She hoped her parents had heard something. Maybe her mother had talked to someone at the hospital.

As she got ready for school, her eyes returned repeatedly to the big mirror. Although there was nothing there, the feeling of a foreign presence lingered in the room. Something that didn't belong had entered her room, uninvited. It was gone now, but the sense of it remained.

But I *did* dream that whole thing, she told herself after her shower. She pulled on white shorts and a pale yellow top. I dreamed it because I was so upset about the accident that nearly killed three of my friends. So I dreamed about someone my age who *had* died in an accident.

It had been so real, though. She remembered clearly every second of it. Slipping her feet into a pair of sandals, she pulled her thick mass of curls into a ponytail and fastened it with a yellow clip. Her morning shower had done nothing to ease the headache. The pounding behind her eyes was relentless.

Megan deliberately kept her back to the freestanding mirror as she halfheartedly applied a touch of blush and mascara. But as she left the room, her biology book in her arms, her blue denim shoulder bag hanging from one wrist, she couldn't resist glancing one more time into the wooden-framed glass.

There was nothing in it but the reflection of a pale-faced girl in yellow and white. I look like a wilted daisy, Megan thought in disgust. When she closed the bedroom door behind her, she hoped she was closing out all memory of the strange wraith and its tragic story. And she hoped that when she came home later that day, her room would feel like her own again.

The early-morning mist on the water had already cleared as Megan pedaled her bicycle to school, using the bike path above the lake. Glancing up at the granite-colored sky, she told herself it was going to be another skin-sticky day. Everyone at school would be moaning and groaning about the weather.

Unless they were preoccupied with last night's accident.

Megan crossed the highway to Philippa Moore High School, where groups of teenagers in shorts and tank tops milled about on the lawn. Her mother hadn't had any news about the physical condition of her friends. She had found out only that they were all still alive. Locking her bicycle in the rack beneath the huge flagpole, Megan quickly searched for someone who could give her more information about Jenny, Barb, and Cappie.

But no one knew anything until lunch period, when Megan met Justin and Hilary and learned that Hilary had called the hospital and talked to Mrs. Winn.

"Barb's okay," she told Megan and Justin. "She was thrown clear and landed on grass. She's going home today. Cappie has a broken wrist and a lot of bruises. But Jenny wasn't so lucky. She has a really awful head injury, and her collarbone was shattered. There weren't any seat belts in the car because it was so old. Mr. Winn had ordered some, but they hadn't come in yet." Hilary paused, then added quietly, "Mrs. Winn was crying the whole time we were talking."

Megan shuddered. Her nasty headache persisted. My friends could all have been killed, she told herself, believing it for the first time. They could have died.

Like poor Juliet.

Except Juliet wasn't real. She was just a dream. An awful dream.

What was almost worse than the dream was the feeling now that she was being watched. She felt eyes on her, following her every move. Her skin itched. It had started when she walked up the school steps, and it stayed with her. She had to keep fighting the urge to glance over her shoulder. When she did look around nervously, no one was paying any attention to her.

The student body at Philippa Moore was sprawled across the back lawn on the embankment sloping down to the lake. The air was thick and sluggish, making any sort of movement an effort. Too wiped out by the suffocating heat to play volleyball or toss a Frisbee, everyone studied or talked softly while they ate.

But the disturbed quiet across campus had nothing to do with the heat. It was the direct result of three of their own narrowly escaping death. The students were trying to deal with the grim fact of the accident.

"I don't get it," Justin said. "Jenny's a good driver, and it wasn't raining yesterday. No slippery roads. Anybody hear how it happened?"

Hilary, sitting on the ground with her legs crossed, leaned forward. Her thick, straight blonde hair was cut short and square around her ears in a shining cap, her round face pink-cheeked and healthy looking. "Mrs. Winn told me that when they hit that curve, Jenny aimed the car around it just like she always did. At least she tried to. But nothing happened. Barbie told her mother that the car just wouldn't turn. It went straight into that utility pole like it had a mind of its own."

"Sounds like the steering went," Justin commented.

Hilary shrugged. "Maybe. Mrs. Winn said the sheriff is checking out the car."

Justin frowned. His sandy hair curled softly across his forehead. He was wearing khaki shorts and a white short-sleeved T-shirt. His warm gray eyes were pensive behind his wire-rimmed glasses. "Jenny could be out of commission for a long time. She's going to go stir-crazy in that hospital."

"Well," Megan said, "as soon as she can have visitors, we'll just have to see that she doesn't get lonely."

Justin smiled at her. "If anybody can cheer her up, you can. You're good at that."

"Well, I think it all stinks!" Hilary complained. "School's almost over, and Jenny won't get to finish out the year."

After a moment or two of somber silence, Hilary sat up straighter and said, "Let's not talk about this anymore. Too depressing." She made a face of disgust as she said, "Guess who asked me out this morning?" Hilary could switch moods as easily as she changed a T-shirt.

"Who?" Justin asked. "Who do we know without a single shred of taste?"

Hilary crossed her eyes at him. "Donny Richardson. He asked me to a movie. Isn't that a hoot?"

"What did you tell him?" Megan asked, knowing

perfectly well that short, squat, mustached Donny was definitely not Hilary's type. He wasn't tall enough or cute enough. He wasn't athletic, and he wasn't popular. Definitely not Hilary Bench's type.

"I said, 'Not in this lifetime.' The guy has the personality of a hangnail."

"Hilary, did you have to be so cruel?" Megan asked. It wasn't hard to imagine the pain of that kind of rejection. If Justin ever treated her like that, she'd die. "You could have been a little bit nicer."

"If you're polite with guys like Donny, they never give up."

"Well," Justin said, "I think you could have been more tactful." He grinned. "Although we know that tact isn't among your limited virtues, Bench. Donny's not a bad guy, and the girls in this school treat him like dirt. He probably has his limits, like everyone else. I was with Jenny a couple of weeks ago when Donny asked her to a movie. She turned him down. She was more polite than you, Hil, but he stomped off down the hall like he was squashing bugs. He was *not* happy."

Megan frowned. "He asked Jenny out? Jenny Winn?"

"Yeah."

"I think he asked Cappie out, too," Hilary said. "I saw them arguing in the hall last week. Donny yelled something about girls who say they have to wash their hair when anyone with eyes can see their hair isn't the least bit dirty." Hilary grinned. "I thought it was pretty funny." The grin disappeared.

214

"Now I'm not so sure." Her blue eyes narrowed.

"I feel sorry for Donny," Megan said. "Nobody likes him, and I think his home life stinks. His parents are divorced, and he moves back and forth between two different homes. That can't be much fun."

"My parents are divorced, too," Hilary said airily, "but I'm not a dweeb like Donny."

"Sure you are," Justin said lazily, grinning. "You're just prettier than Donny."

"It must be awful to be so unpopular," Megan said slowly. She was remembering the dream, hearing Juliet say again that she'd been popular. Donny wasn't. But he was still luckier than Juliet had been. He just didn't know it.

"Oh, Megan," Hilary said in exasperation, "You're always feeling *sorry* for people! You just don't get it that there are some really crummy people out there who don't have good excuses for the rotten way they act. Get with the program, will you?"

"But that's what makes her so lovable," Justin said lightly, giving Megan's arm a reassuring squeeze. "That's part of her charm."

Megan smiled up at him. Hilary made a gagging gesture, but she grinned as she did it.

Before they went back into school, Megan turned and looked back at the lawn. No one seemed to be paying any particular attention to her. So why did she have this feeling that she was a specimen under a microscope? It gave her goose bumps.

215

Later, passing Donny Richardson in the hall on her way to art class, she found herself smiling at him with more warmth than usual.

He looked surprised, and his skinny black mustache remained in place, refusing to curve into a return smile. Megan had a feeling that even if he had smiled, it wouldn't have reached his eyes. They seemed so cold and empty.

When she reached the art room, she went straight to her assigned cubbyhole at the rear of the room. There was a square of red construction paper sticking halfway out, sandwiched between her latest drawing and her box of pastels.

She hadn't used red construction paper lately.

Curious, she slid the paper out of the cubbyhole and looked at it. What she saw was a crude, childish drawing of a large yellow car with no top, filled with a strange cargo.

Megan walked over to the big window to look at the picture in better light.

It was horrible. Seated in the driver's seat of the crudely drawn car was a . . . horse? Wearing a string of pink beads around its throat. On the passenger's side of the front seat sat what looked like a large candy bar beside a fat yellow-and-black-striped blob with wings. A bumblebee.

What on earth . . . ?

Her eyes moved to the backseat. A hat of some kind was drawn there. It had a visor with an emblem on it. A baseball cap? There was a small, green ball beside it. A green baseball? No. It looked more like an oversized green pea.

216

As people began to file into the big art room, Megan studied the picture carefully. It was a simple puzzle. The car was clearly Jenny's. The candy bar and the bumblebee were easy: Bar. Bee. Barbie. And the cap and the pea meant Cappie. But why was there a horse in the driver's seat?

What kind of twisted mind would draw such a sick picture about a tragic accident?

And why was it in Megan's cubbyhole?

Was it a joke? If it was, someone at Philippa had a very bizarre sense of humor.

Shivering, Megan crumpled the picture angrily and tossed it into the wastebasket.

On her way out of class fifty minutes later, Megan plucked the wrinkled drawing from the trash and stuffed it into her notebook. She didn't know why she did it. She only knew that it seemed like a good idea.

When she got home, Megan approached her bedroom door with hesitation, wondering nervously if the room would still feel strange. It had been almost a whole day since the dream. Her bedroom should feel like her own room again by now.

Megan slowly pulled the door open. Instead of closing it behind her, she stood in the doorway, listening, and searching all four corners with her eyes. The room, its flowered wallpaper faded and peeling slightly in spots, would ordinarily be filled with sunshine at this time of day, but because of the slate-colored sky, it looked dreary and gray.

Megan's searching eyes found nothing out of the ordinary. The unmade bed seemed to hold no secrets, the lace curtains hanging from her canopy and on her windows waited patiently for her to enter the room, and the clothes lying on the floor in small, scattered heaps were as familiar as the stuffed animals cluttering the white shelves at the far end of the room.

Megan stepped inside and closed the door.

At last, she let herself glance into the full-length mirror.

It was empty.

Of course it is, she told herself, and went to her desk to remove a sheaf of papers from a drawer.

She had just turned around, papers in hand, when the curtains began blowing wildly and she was hit by a blast of frigid air. Her room darkened and became shrouded in shadow.

"What are you doing, Megan Logan? Is it something fun?"

Chapter 5

Shivering with renewed fear, Megan forced her eyes to the mirror.

Juliet had returned.

I wasn't dreaming after all, Megan thought, her breath frozen in her throat. She sank down on the bed, drawing the comforter around her against the chill. "What . . . what are you *doing* here?" she whispered.

"I came to talk. Will you listen, Megan Logan? Please?"

The gauzy purple image became sharper. The head was wide at the top, narrow at the bottom, the eye sockets sunken and lit by a golden glow, the body no more than a transparent stream of lavender waving about in the glass.

While the light in the mirror grew brighter, the room itself became murky with shadows, a dark, icy place unknown to Megan. She wanted desperately to leave it, but she was afraid. And beneath the fear, curiosity stirred.

219

"Why are you here?" she asked softly. "You don't belong here."

"Why can't you accept me?" the voice asked. "I'm not going to hurt you."

"Leave me alone. You're scaring me."

Someone outside on the lake laughed. Megan wished fiercely that she could suddenly, magically, be transported out there to join them.

"Well, I'm not trying to scare you. I thought you'd talk to me because you have an open mind. I know that about you. I know everything about you. When I found out that we shared a birthday, I knew that I'd have to know everything. So I studied you carefully."

Megan remembered the feeling of being under a microscope. "You . . . you've been watching me?"

"I had to. When I found out that you were a dreamer, I knew that would make it easier for you to hear me."

If only she were daydreaming now. Because Megan didn't want this . . . thing . . . this Juliet . . . to be real.

"I've been waiting forever for someone who could hear me," Juliet said, her voice excited. "I can't talk to just anyone. Has to be someone exactly my age. Someone near the lake, where I died. Someone with an open mind and a kind heart. Someone with imagination and a belief that anything's possible. Someone just like you, Megan Logan." The plume waved gently back and forth in the mirror, illuminated in the darkened room only by the strange silvery glow surrounding it. "But I made myself wait to talk to you, so you'd have time to settle into this house. I was scared that if I showed up too soon, I'd frighten you off." Juliet hesitated, then added, "This was your grandmother's house. Martha's house. She left it to your mother when she died a while ago."

How could . . . Juliet . . . know so much about her? All Megan knew about the thing in her mirror was that it had lived, and died, and it was lonely.

A sigh echoed from the mirror. "It's been hard not to give up hope! All this time . . ."

Nervously fingering the edges of the comforter, Megan asked, "Hope of what?"

"Of having someone to talk with. Of reaching someone. Of . . . trading."

Mesmerized by Juliet's velvety voice, Megan failed to notice that her own body had stopped trembling, her hands were no longer shaking, and the lump in her throat had dissolved. "Trading? Trading what?"

"Nothing. Never mind. Let's talk about your party."

"But . . . you can't be here. This can't be happening." Megan's voice was remarkably steady. "How did you *get* here?"

"It was easy. I *had* to be here. You're my only chance."

"But it's . . . it's not possible."

"Anything is possible, Megan. You believe that, don't you? Isn't that what your grandmother Martha always said?"

It was. Gram had said, "Believe in everything, Megan, until you learn otherwise. Anything is possible in this world. You remember that."

But had she been talking about wispy columns of smoke in a mirror? What would she say about this visit from Juliet? Megan knew the answer to that question. Gram would say, "Do whatever you think is right, Megan. Trust yourself. Make up your own mind."

Like snow on a sun-warmed slope, the icy, mind-numbing fear began slowly, slowly, to melt away from Megan. As it ebbed, it was replaced by complete bewilderment.

Megan shifted on the bed, remembering suddenly how long ago Juliet had . . . died. "Did you . . . did you know my grandmother? Before . . . before your accident, I mean."

"Everyone knew the Logan family."

Realizing that Juliet had known her grandmother stirred an inner warmth in Megan. She had more in common with the image in her mirror than just a shared birthday. "What was she like when she was a teenager?"

"I didn't know her very well. I wasn't here, on the lake, that long. I think she was like you. Quiet, dreamy." The voice lowered, heavy again with sadness. "How I envy you, Megan! You'll have the wonderful party I never had. You'll get to live those years full of fun. Parties, dances, boyfriends . . . I missed all of that."

Tears pooled in Megan's eyes. Jenny Winn, Barb, and Cappie; all had nearly lost their lives, like this . . . like Juliet. What would that be like, to have your life end so young? The thought made her pull the comforter more closely around her, as if it could somehow protect her from harsh reality.

"Are you cold, Megan?"

"No. Just feeling sad. It . . . it isn't fair that your life ended . . . so early."

"You're nice. I knew you'd understand. I think it was unfair, too. That's why I can't be at peace. . . ." the voice moaned. "If only . . . no, never mind. You're not ready. It's too soon."

Megan frowned. "If only what?"

The light around the plume deepened, easing the shadows surrounding Megan. "Well, I really think you need more time. But since I don't have much, I'll go ahead and explain. I know you won't understand right away, but maybe after you've thought about it, we can talk again."

Megan stirred. "Understand what?"

"My life ended too soon, Megan. That's not ever supposed to happen. But I have a chance to make up for that now. If I can find someone who shares a birthday with me, and if that person can hear me, I can ask her to switch places with me for just one short week. I can ask for her willing consent to let me live her life for seven days and seven nights. That's what I want to ask of you."

Megan could not take in what she was hearing. Juliet's words whirled round and round in her head. Trade places? With . . . with *that*?

Megan felt the darkened room begin to spin around her. The dark shadows began to move, to reach out for her with cold, clammy fingers. Instinctively she pushed backward on her bed until her back was pressed up against the headboard and she could go no further. "What," she whispered hoarsely, "are you talking about?"

"It's really easy, Megan." Juliet's voice became stronger. "And it would only be for a week. A week when I'd have the chance to live the most fun time in a girl's life. Compared to a lifetime, a week really isn't much. But it would be enough for me. At the end of the week, I'd go away. I'd be at peace then, forever."

Megan was unable to speak. Not a muscle moved, not an eyelash blinked as she sat frozen under the canopy of her bed. The room grew deathly quiet.

"Megan?" Juliet said finally. "Megan?"

But Megan could not find her voice.

"I've scared you. I'm sorry. I knew I shouldn't have told you so soon. But I don't have very much time. Just think about it, please? Remember, Megan, *anything is possible.* I'll come back again, after you've had time to think. Thank you for listening to me."

The light in the mirror faded and vanished. Megan was alone.

She sat on the bed and stared at the wooden-framed glass. The voice had been real. Juliet had been real. Nothing had been imagined or dreamed. Even for someone like Megan, who created stories out of images she saw in clouds, it was difficult to accept. But she *had* accepted Juliet's presence.

Yet what Juliet had proposed was so strange and frightening that Megan could barely believe it. Could something like that actually be possible?

224

Megan had never had any trouble following her grandmother's advice: "Believe in everything until you learn otherwise." But this was too strange, too crazy to think about.

After wrestling with it for hours, the only thing Megan was sure of was that something *had* been in her mirror.

All evening, she waited for something more to happen. She couldn't read or study or concentrate on television. And she couldn't seem to move from her room.

But nothing happened.

The glass remained glass, nothing more.

Chapter 6

When Hilary called later, it was easy for Megan to keep silent about Juliet. One word about her and practical-minded Hilary would think Megan was losing her marbles.

Fortunately Hilary had other things on her mind. "Jenny's regained consciousness," she told Megan. "They think she's going to be okay. My mom talked to Mrs. Winn today. But . . . the worst thing, Megan, is that it wasn't an accident. Somebody screwed up the steering on Jenny's car."

Megan inhaled sharply. Someone had deliberately tried to hurt her friends? "Hilary, are you sure?"

"Sheriff Toomey's sure. My parents are really freaked-out. Three of my best friends are in the hospital, so my mom thinks I might be next. I could be grounded forever. She says, 'Better safe than sorry.' "

"This is unreal," Megan breathed. "Who would do something so horrible?"

"Maybe a rejected boyfriend? Like the famous

Donny Richardson, for instance? Practically every girl in school has turned him down lately. Maybe he hates all of us. And doesn't he work in his brother's garage? It has to be someone who knows auto mechanics."

"Hilary, practically everyone at Philippa took auto mechanics, including most of the girls."

Hilary's voice became testy. "Well, I don't know about you, Megan, but when *I* took it, I certainly didn't learn how to kill someone by sabotaging a car!"

When Megan had hung up, she focused on Hilary's final remarks about how lucky Jenny was. "At least she's alive," she'd said.

Unlike poor Juliet, Megan thought, flinching in pain as she pictured a fifteen-year-old girl being thrown from a boat and sinking rapidly into the deep, dark waters of the lake.

What was really tough to swallow was the horrifying news Hilary had given her. Someone had deliberately caused the car wreck? Whoever it was couldn't possibly have known the three girls would survive. The tampering had been intended to kill.

Suddenly Megan remembered the crude crayon drawing of the yellow car and its weird cargo. It was still in her notebook. She had thought of it as a cruel, sick joke. Now she realized it had been more than that.

I cut art on Tuesday, she remembered. Hilary talked me into a spur-of-the-moment trip to the mall. I never checked my cubbyhole that day. It could have been in there then, before the accident ever happened. Which would make it *not* a cruel joke but . . . a warning.

If she took the drawing to Sheriff Toomey, would he laugh? He was a nice man, but if she brought him evidence that looked like a child's drawing, he might think she was wasting his time. She would have to think about it.

Exhausted, Megan began getting ready for bed.

Lost in worry, she had just slipped into a pair of white shortie pajamas when the temperature in her room plummeted again. She wrapped a blanket around her shoulders and turned to face the mirror. It began to glow, and Juliet took shape.

"Megan. I hope what I told you before didn't upset you. You've been so nice, listening to me."

Still wary, Megan sat on the floor in front of the mirror. "What do you want from me?" she asked cautiously. "I hope you don't think I'm going to do that . . . trading thing that you talked about."

"You won't even consider it?" Juliet asked sadly. "But I thought you had an open mind, Megan. I thought you believed anything was possible, as Martha did."

Megan shook her head vigorously. "Not that. Not . . . what you said — about trading. I don't believe *that's* possible." I don't *want* it to be, she added silently.

"Oh, but it is! And it's so simple."

"Simple how?" Megan asked suspiciously.

"You would step into the mirror, and I would step out. As you. What could be simpler?"

228

"It can't be that easy!"

Juliet sighed deeply. "All of the hard parts come first, Megan. Finding someone near the lake who shares my birthday. Getting her to listen. Almost no one will listen. And getting her consent to switch is the hardest thing of all. People are too afraid of the unknown."

"That's for sure," Megan agreed. The thought of becoming, even temporarily, what Juliet was — a smoky, incandescent purple plume — made her flesh feel as if a thousand tiny spiders were making their home on her skin.

"It would only be for a week, Megan," the voice pleaded. "And it's not so bad in my world. . . . You wouldn't need to worry about stubbing a toe or catching cold. Nothing from your world could touch you."

Right then, that sounded kind of appealing to Megan. "But . . . if you would look like me, does that mean I would look . . . like you?"

"You wouldn't have any physical form at all. I'm only like this so you can see me. I would be able to hear you, and you could talk to me at any time. But no one else would see or hear you."

Megan shook her head again. She would become invisible? "It's just too strange, Juliet. You need someone braver than me."

"You *are* brave, Megan, or you wouldn't have heard me in the first place. Oh, Megan, I thought you understood, I can't use anyone else. Only you. Because you live here. Because of our shared birthday. And because you listened to me."

The sadness and yearning in Juliet's voice touched Megan to the core. She thought again how horrible it would be to have your life cut short at such a young age. Wasn't that, after all, what everyone at school had been thinking about? That it could have been *their* car, their accident, and that they might not have been so lucky. They might not have survived.

As Juliet hadn't.

"Don't you believe that anything is possible?" Juliet asked. "I thought you did."

Megan remembered Hilary's phone call then. "Even if I were willing, which I'm not," she said, "this would be the wrong time to trade places with me. Someone deliberately hurt some of my friends. My best friend Hilary's mother thinks Hil might be next, but it could be me. *I* could be next. If we did this . . . trading thing, you'd be putting yourself in my place. That's not a good place to be right now."

"I don't have any choice!" Juliet's voice took on a note of desperation. "You have to be my *exact* age — fifteen. So even one minute past your sixteenth birthday is too late for me. We only have until the clock strikes midnight on Saturday. Unless I get your consent before then, my one perfect chance will disappear. I don't get another chance. If you won't help, I'll disappear forever, and I'll never know peace. So the danger you talk about doesn't matter to me. I'm willing to take that risk."

"But what about me?" Megan asked. "If I decided to trade with you and something bad happened to my body while you were in it, what would become of me?"

"Actually, Megan, you'll be safer. I can sense evil in people. I'd never let anyone like that get close enough to hurt me. So you wouldn't have to worry."

Megan sat up very straight. "You mean . . . you mean you would know who hurt Jenny?"

"I think so. I can't promise. But I think so."

If Juliet could identify the cruel, sick person who had sabotaged Jenny's car and created the twisted picture, Lakeside could return to its normal, peaceful way of life.

Megan sat, lost in thought, while Juliet said nothing more. She was Juliet's *only* chance at getting back one short week of the lifetime she'd missed? There was no one else? What had happened to Juliet was horrible, tragic, and so unfair. No one should die so young. It wasn't right, it just wasn't right at all.

"Maybe I'll think about it," she said finally. That scared her so much, she added hastily, "But that's a *maybe*, understand?"

The plume began dancing with excitement. "Oh, of course, Megan. *Maybe* gives me hope. When my father said *maybe*, he almost always meant *yes*. But please," the soft voice begged, "use your open mind and your kind heart, okay? I'll come back when you've had time to think. Good night, Megan. And thank you, thank you for listening."

Megan sat at the window, looking out over the lake, for a long while. But every time she started to think about Juliet's proposal, she had to put it out of her mind. It was too scary to think about at night. Maybe tomorrow . . .

When she finally got up and crawled into bed, she slept poorly. Her grandmother's voice echoed in her dreams. "Anything is possible, Megan, you remember that."

She tossed and turned all night, her nightclothes and hair soaked with sweat.

The next morning, on the way to school, Megan tried talking to Justin about Juliet.

"Justin," she began cautiously, as she climbed into his car, "what do you think happens to a person, well, after they die? Do you think their spirit stays around?"

Justin looked over at Megan. "Those are pretty strange questions. Thinking about Jenny's accident?"

"Well, it's just . . . something weird is going on at my house."

"At *your* house!" he exclaimed as he pulled away from the curb. "Listen, your house is probably the only place in town where weird things *aren't* happening. Someone screwing up Jenny's steering, now *that's* weird!"

"Justin, I — "

"So tell me something," he interrupted, "do you think Donny's behind this stuff? Richardson?"

Maybe it was just as well Justin was distracted today, Megan thought. If she told him about Juliet, he might start to think she was really flaky. He'd told her once that she wasn't like other girls because she listened. *Really* listened, he'd said. That was fine. She'd been flattered. But being "different" because she was a good listener was one thing. Seeing purple plumes in her mirror was something else. Justin might think she was just plain weird. She wouldn't tell him. Not yet. Maybe never.

"I don't know," she answered thoughtfully. "I don't think so. I told him no when he asked me out, and nothing bad has happened to me."

Justin swivelled his head to look at her in surprise. "Donny asked you out? You didn't say anything about that when Hilary was talking about him yesterday."

Megan fidgeted on the seat. "Hil would have made a big deal out of it. And it wasn't a big deal. He asked me out and I said, 'No, thanks.' "

Justin's sandy eyebrows met in a frown. "How did he take it?"

"Okay, I guess."

"Look, just steer clear of him, okay? His alphabet might be missing some of its letters."

"Justin," she said, remembering the strange drawing, "have you ever heard of any famous horse named Jenny? A champion racer, maybe?"

After thinking for a minute, Justin said, "No. Why?"

She told him about the drawing, and when they parked in front of school, she showed it to him. "I figured out Barbie and Cappie," she said, "but why is the horse where Jenny should be?"

"That's not a horse," he said. "Look at the ears.

233

It's a mule. And it's wearing a necklace. Nice touch. Know what a female mule is called?"

"A jenny?"

"Right. Where did you get this, Megan?"

She explained. But before they could discuss it, the first-period warning bell rang.

"Meet me at the *Scribe* office after school," Justin said as they hurried to class. *The Scribe* was Philippa's newspaper. Justin was its editor. "Don't forget. We'll talk about your artist friend then."

The feeling of being watched slipped over her again, as chilling as a wet sweater. She tried ignoring it, in vain. Yet each time she glanced around, no one seemed to be paying the slightest bit of attention to her.

At lunch without Justin, who'd had an errand to run, Hilary said with disgust, "Guess who's back?" She unwrapped a strange-looking sandwich, brown and unidentifiable. Hilary was into health food. "That viper, Vicki Deems! The snake only got one week's suspension for cheating on that Spanish test. I was hoping they'd suspend her for life!"

"Just ignore her. She's not in any of your classes, is she?"

"She's in my *life*, Megan. She makes my skin crawl. I know Ken Waters was going to take me to your party. He hadn't asked me yet, but I could tell. One look at Tricki Vicki in that red halter top she's glued into and Hilary Bench is history."

Megan sipped slowly from her milk container. She didn't want Vicki Deems at her party. Maybe I'm just jealous, she thought as she peeled a banana.

234

Vicki is sexy, sophisticated, everything I'm not. Thank goodness Justin isn't interested in that type.

Or was he? Hadn't he called Karen Tucker "sexy"? Compared to Vicki Deems, Karen was Snow White.

But it wasn't jealousy that made Megan nervous around Vicki. It was the way those cold, dark eyes looked at a boy that made Megan shiver: black spider eyes spotting a nice, juicy fly. No wonder Vicki had no girlfriends. She had only boyfriends, and plenty of them.

After school, Megan went to the art room to check her cubbyhole, just in case.

She found another drawing.

Her stomach lurched. This one was on dark blue paper. The drawing itself was nothing more than a simple curved line, in bright pink crayon, like a giant bump on the paper. It went up and curved back down. That was all. It looked like a mound or . . . a hill.

A hill. Hilary!

Megan raced to the auditorium, where Hilary and two boys from the lighting crew were tying up loose ends after last week's junior class play.

Breathless, her heart pounding furiously in her chest, Megan was running down the wide center aisle in the auditorium when her best friend since sixth grade leaned out over the catwalk high above the stage to retrieve a loose rope.

And fell.

Chapter 7

Megan and Hilary screamed simultaneously as Hilary began to plummet. Arms in a crisp white shirt and legs in blue denim shorts flailed wildly in the air as she plunged toward the hard wooden stage below.

Megan watched in horror as her best friend began to descend toward certain death.

And then, in the blink of an eye, one of Hilary's grasping hands came into contact with a rope dangling on her left.

The hand grabbed.

Clutched.

And held.

There was a moment of breathless silence as the three onlookers stood paralyzed with shock below their dangling friend.

Megan, with a little moan of relief, sank to her knees on the worn red carpeting. Hilary's life had nearly ended.

Like Juliet's had, so long ago.

"Help!" Hilary called weakly, her voice hoarse

with panic. "Get me down! Hurry! I can't hold on!"

The two boys ran for a ladder.

On shaky legs, Megan got up and hurried down the aisle, her gait as disjointed as a toddler's. She kept her eyes on Hilary as she climbed the wooden steps up to the stage. "Hang on, Hilary, don't let go," she urged. "They're bringing a ladder. Hang on!"

When Hilary, her face an unhealthy gray, her body shaking violently, had been rescued and was lying on the stage trying to catch her breath, Megan, kneeling beside her and holding Hilary's hand, asked, "What happened? Did you slip?"

Hilary shook her head. "Didn't. Didn't slip. Pushed."

"Pushed?" Megan sank back on her heels. The drawing. A definite warning.

Hilary couldn't stop shaking. Her arms and legs rapped against the wooden floor like the wings of a frightened bird. But anger quickly began to replace the panic. "Of course I was pushed. I certainly didn't jump. Ken Waters isn't *that* great." She looked up at her fellow crew members. "You guys see who it was?"

One had been busy sweeping up backstage, the other had been returning equipment to the prop room. And Megan had been too far back in the auditorium to see or hear anything.

"I don't like this at all," Megan said slowly, helping Hilary sit up. "If you hadn't grabbed that rope . . ."

"You probably fell, Bench," one of the boys said.

237

Hilary shuddered. Her blue eyes, still glazed with shock, glanced up toward the catwalk. "I did not fall," she said firmly as the boys helped her to her feet. "I am not a *falling* sort of person. Anyway, I know every inch of that catwalk as well as I know my own bedroom. Someone pushed me."

"Well, we didn't see anything," one of the boys repeated. "Boy, were you ever lucky! Talk about quick reflexes. You ever do any gymnastics, Bench?" There was awe and admiration in his voice.

"No. And I don't see how you can joke about this." Hilary bit her lower lip. "It's a long way down from up there." She closed her eyes briefly, another violent shudder shaking her body. "I'm reporting this to Mr. Shattuck."

"He'll just blow it off, Hil," the other boy said. "Nobody saw anything."

"I don't care. I *felt* it." Hilary bent carefully to pick up her books and purse from the floor. "You coming with me, Megan?"

Megan had planned to go home and seek out Juliet. But she couldn't leave a shaky Hilary.

Should she take the drawing to Mr. Shattuck? How could she? It was only a curved line on a piece of paper. It had been meant only for Megan. Whoever drew it knew she would understand. And she had. But Mr. Shattuck wouldn't.

"Of course I'm coming, Hilary. Here, let me carry your stuff." She reached for Hilary's things. "You're not going to pass out, are you?"

"No, I'm not going to pass out," Hilary said in a slightly steadier voice. "If I were a *passing-out* kind

238

of person, I'd have done it when I was hanging from that rope like a piece of meat in a butcher shop. And I can carry my own things."

Megan felt relief wash over her. Hilary not only was not hurt, she was getting back to normal very quickly. She was a very lucky girl.

So was Megan. What would she ever do without Hilary?

As they made their way up the aisle, Hilary managed a weak smile. "I'm sorry I don't have a broken wing so you could feel sorry for me and fix me up, Megan. You're so good at that."

"Hil! I'm *glad* you're not hurt." Impulsively Megan turned to give Hilary a hug.

"Oh, Megan, I know you're glad. I was just teasing." Hilary paused, and then added, "Megan, you believe I was pushed, don't you? I mean, I wouldn't make up something like that."

Megan felt guilty about not sharing the drawing with Hilary. But Hil was already so shaken. Proof positive that she really had been a target would only upset her more.

"Of course I believe you."

"Well, don't you think it's scary? First there's Jenny's accident, which turns out not to be an accident at all, and now someone sends me off into space from the catwalk. Something really nasty is going on here."

Hilary continued to fume about the incident, but Megan wasn't listening. She was lost in her thoughts. Why would someone push Hilary? Push her, knowing that such a fall would kill her? And it had to be the same person who was drawing those pictures.

That meant someone at the school, someone who had access to the art room. Donny, rejected by so many girls? Vicki Deems, Viper Extraordinaire, who always had that cold, hungry look in her eyes? Was she viciously trying to destroy the competition, and keep all the boys for herself?

Megan and Hilary were both still very shaken when they arrived at the principal's office and told their story. But the boys had been right. Because no one had seen Hilary's attacker, Mr. Shattuck, a cautious man, chose to regard the incident as an "unfortunate accident." He then called Hilary's mother to come and take her home, being very careful not to alarm her.

While they waited in the hall for Mrs. Bench, Hilary said angrily, "He didn't believe me. So he won't have it investigated, and whoever pushed me will get away with it, just like he's getting away with the car tampering."

"He won't get away with it. The sheriff is still investigating, according to my mom."

Hilary shrugged.

"Are you sure you're okay?" Megan asked with concern. "Your face is the color of my old gym socks. And your eyes look glazed, like you're not really in there."

"I'm fine. I'm just mad now. Quit worrying. Let my mom do that. It's her job."

When Hilary had been deposited safely in her mother's very competent hands, Megan went to look for Justin. He had said he'd be in the *Scribe* office.

Walking down the hall, the sight of Hilary falling, falling, returned to Megan's mind, and she closed her eyes, feeling like she'd been riding on an out-of-control Ferris wheel. If Hilary hadn't caught that rope . . . Megan leaned against the wall until the nausea passed.

Why was all this happening? In the past two days *four* girls had narrowly escaped death. And every one of them was a good friend of Megan's.

Was she in danger, too? Was that why she felt shadowed? Because someone *was* watching her? Watching . . . and waiting . . .

Shaking her head to erase the image of Hilary's dreadful fall, Megan continued on down the hall.

The door to the *Scribe* office was open when she arrived. As she stepped inside, the tiny hairs on the back of her neck rose. Justin was seated at his desk as usual, a pencil nesting over one ear. But seated on his desk, not at all as usual, was Vicki Deems, a bright red halter top and a black leather miniskirt fitted snugly around her beautiful body. She was leaning forward, a curtain of silky black hair draping one tanned cheek. She seemed to be whispering in Justin's ear.

And what was worse, he seemed to be listening.

Megan froze in the doorway. What if she'd waited too long to ask Justin to be her date for the party? What if he asked Vicki? After all, Justin was a healthy, normal, red-blooded American male. And that was *some* halter top.

241

"Oh, hello, Megan," Vicki said in a husky voice that set Megan's teeth on edge.

Megan allowed herself the satisfaction of seeing Justin glance up guiltily, his gorgeous face flushing scarlet, before she turned and ran. Even when she heard him calling out her name, she kept going.

She ran all the way home in a vain effort to escape two awful images. One was of Hilary plunging toward the stage, a picture that sent Megan's stomach into sickening nausea. The other image was of Justin with his head next to Vicki's. That one filled her with fury.

When she was safe in her own room, in her own house, she grimly put all thoughts of friends in danger, vicious vipers, and treacherous males out of her head. She had more important things to think about.

Because ever since Hilary had grabbed that rope and hung on for dear life, ever since they'd put that ladder up there and a shaky but unharmed Hilary had slowly climbed down to safety, Megan had known that she was going to trade places with Juliet. She just hadn't been ready to admit it to herself. Until now.

The idea no longer seemed so crazy, so impossible. The way she felt now had something to do with four of her closest friends almost losing their lives but being lucky enough to survive. Luckier than Juliet. And all Juliet wanted was one tiny little week. That wasn't very much.

Her gratitude that Hilary's body hadn't crashed into that hard wooden stage made her feel generous.

Scared, *terrified* even, but generous. What was a week, anyway? Practically nothing.

Hadn't Gram said Megan marched to a different drummer? Maybe it was time to prove that. Something deep inside her, something she had never listened to before, was willing to do this incredibly frightening thing. It was time to pay attention to that part of her.

Dropping her books and purse on the bed, Megan took a deep breath and walked over to the mirror. "Juliet, are you there?" she called softly. "I want to talk to you."

The mirror remained clear. There was no plume of purplish haze, no faintly glowing silvery light, no whispering voice. There was nothing but glass and Megan's own reflection.

Chapter 8

When the mirror stared blankly back at her, Megan fought a mixture of relief and disappointment.

Where *was* Juliet?

Every five or ten minutes during the evening, Megan called out Juliet's name. But there was no answer.

After phoning Hilary to make sure she was really okay, Megan crawled into bed, but she wasn't planning on sleeping. She would stay awake and continue trying to summon Juliet.

But the horrors of the day had exhausted her. She fell asleep.

And was awakened during the night by a terrifying nightmare, the worst she'd ever had. A dense forest of cobwebs, soft and furry as caterpillars, imprisoned her. She struggled frantically to break free, but the steel-strong network refused to release her. Off in the distance, a giant spider approached slowly on thick, black, hairy legs.

Megan thrashed and moaned, desperately seeking freedom. But the web held.

Somewhere in the distance, she heard her name called softly. But she was powerless to answer.

Panicking halfway between sleep and wakefulness, she bolted upright in bed, suddenly wide awake. Stunned, she looked around her, but could see nothing in the pitch-black. The dream had been so real. She had felt so absolutely trapped. The feeling of helplessness stayed with her. Her stomach lurched, her head ached with a pain that hurt her eyes, and she was very, very cold.

And then she realized that the cold came from the now-familiar plunge in the room's temperature.

Megan shivered, desperately wanting the darkness to disappear. She could still feel the threat of that enormous hairy spider ambling toward her in the dream web. Shuddering again, she wrapped her arms around her chest and watched numbly as the mirror began to fill with the shimmering lavender image.

"I'm sorry I didn't come earlier," Juliet apologized. "I heard you calling me. But I was scared you'd decided not to trade, and I couldn't stand to hear you say it." Then, "Megan, what's wrong? You look awful!"

"I'm okay." Megan took a deep breath and exhaled. "Juliet, I've thought about it. I want you to explain again about trading."

The plume danced with amazement and joy. "You do?"

"Yes. Exactly how would we do it? Tell me everything."

"Oh, it's so easy!" Juliet's voice rose and fell with

245

excitement. "Once you agree, all you have to do is step into this mirror. And I will step out . . . as you. It takes only a second."

"And I will be invisible, but you will be able to hear me?"

"Yes. And nothing from your world can touch you."

"But . . . it can touch *you*. And you will be *me*. That scares me, Juliet. It means that whoever hurt my friends and pushed Hilary off the catwalk, could go after me . . . you . . . next. Are you *sure* you can protect yourself better than I could?"

"Yes, Megan, I am sure. I'll be careful."

Megan wished she could have talked to someone about all of this. But who would believe her? She hardly believed it herself.

Reading her thoughts, Juliet warned, "You can't tell anyone, Megan. I know it's hard, but that would ruin everything. The only one who can know is the lender, and that's you. No one else."

"You think you know enough about me to act and talk like me?" she asked Juliet.

"It's only for a week, Megan. I can handle that."

"And you will look just like me?"

"I will *be* you, Megan. I will look like you and talk exactly like you. But inside, I'll still be me. And you'll still be you. No one can take your real inner self from you."

Juliet's voice was calm and reassuring, as if they were discussing taking a walk around the lake.

Megan tried to relax. "We would have to practice switching before I agreed."

246

"Of course. There's nothing to it. You step into the mirror and I step out. As you."

She was right. There wasn't anything to it. After each transformation, Megan felt nothing but a peculiar sense of weightlessness, the way she imagined a soap bubble might feel. She disliked the dark emptiness of the mirror, but Juliet reminded her that there was no need for her to remain there.

"You can go anywhere you want, as long as you don't leave the lake area."

They switched back and forth four times without a hitch. The strangest part was looking out from inside the mirror and seeing her physical self, now Juliet, standing there before her. When Megan wanted to be herself again, she simply said, "I am Megan, and I want to be me again." And she was.

Her voice quivering with excitement, Juliet said after the fourth trial, "When can we do this, Megan? It has to be soon. There's hardly any time left before your birthday."

Megan made up her mind. She had thought about her friends, all nearly losing their lives so young, like Juliet. Narrow escapes had saved them. Juliet hadn't been so lucky. Juliet had this one chance to live again, for one tiny little week. It would be wrong not to let her have that. One week wasn't such a big deal.

And there was something else. If there was any chance at all that Juliet could somehow sense who was responsible for the pain and fear in Lakeside, Megan had to take that chance.

"I've already decided," Megan said quietly. "It

has to be tomorrow night. You'll have a full week, and we'll switch back again next Saturday night in time for my party on Sunday. I *have* to be at my party." Setting a definite time for the trade sent butterflies of fear fluttering around Megan's stomach. But she had made up her mind. She wouldn't go back on her word now.

Juliet shrieked with joy. "I can't believe it! At last! Oh, it's going to be so wonderful!" The plume began dancing in excitement. "I'm going to have a whole week!"

The shadows in the room lightened a bit. It was almost dawn. "It's today already," Megan murmured, her heart sounding a drumroll in her chest as she thought about what the evening would bring. "It's Saturday now."

Juliet moved happily in the mirror. "And you promise you won't change your mind, will you, Megan?"

Megan shook her head.

"Then I'll go now. I'm so excited! I hope the day passes quickly. Just call my name tonight when you're ready, and I'll be here. And Megan, thank you, thank you, thank you!"

As the mirror image faded, and the room brightened, Megan fought a wild desire to call Juliet back and tell her she'd changed her mind, that the whole idea was impossible. But she turned away from the mirror decisively. She'd given her promise.

Megan took an early shower and spent the day running errands in preparation for her party.

Hilary called to tell her that Jenny still wasn't

248

allowed visitors, and that there was no news from Sheriff Toomey. "I don't think he's even questioned anyone," she said, adding darkly, "*I* could give him the names of a couple of good suspects!"

Megan hung up, feeling traitorous. Here she was doing this incredibly strange, scary thing and she hadn't shared any of it with her best friend. But Juliet had made it clear that telling anyone would ruin everything.

Justin called twice, calls Megan didn't return. Let Juliet deal with him. Juliet would have to ask him to Megan's party, too, because it was the only thing left undone on the lists. There it was, in black and white: *ASK JUSTIN*.

Walking over to the mirror after dusk, her hands trembling, her knees like pudding, Megan called Juliet's name softly, wishing fiercely that she could have told her parents what she was doing. But of course she couldn't have. They would never understand. Never!

Before she and Juliet actually made the switch, Megan asked tentatively, "There's just one more thing, Juliet. I was wondering — "

Juliet interrupted her. "Yes, I'll ask Justin to your party. And he will say yes, don't worry."

Unable to think of a good reason to stall any longer, Megan nodded, took a deep breath, and stepped into the mirror.

Chapter 9

To Megan's distress, the sensations that came with the final transformation were very different from the practice switches. Instead of the lightness she'd felt before, there was a horrible wrenching sensation, as if steel arms were tugging and tearing at her.

And when those awful sensations passed, leaving her with no feeling at all, the blackness in which she found herself was unrelieved and icy cold. Beyond the darkness, she could see her room. But it seemed very far away, as if she were looking through a telescope.

Wild with fear, she cried out, *"Juliet! Juliet, are you there? I don't see you. Where are you?"*

And a girl who looked exactly like Megan Logan appeared in front of the mirror, a happy smile on her face. "I'm right here, Megan. I hear you. Relax!" Her voice and speech sounded exactly like Megan, too. "Remember, you can talk to me any time you want."

Her words failed to dilute the abject terror Megan felt. *What have I done?* she thought wildly. "*Juliet, I feel terrible. So far away from everything. It's not like it was when we practiced. Why does it feel so different now?*"

"It's because you're not practicing this time, Megan. But it's just a week. Anyway, you'll feel better soon. Don't worry."

Then, touching her cheeks, her hair, her arms with wonderment, Juliet said, "Oh, I can't believe this!" A radiant smile lifted her lips. "I'm going to have such a wonderful time!"

The seven days that had earlier seemed so brief to Megan now stretched ahead of her like a dark, endless tunnel. *This is horrible,* she thought miserably. *I feel like I've been sucked into a bottomless pit. I'll never be able to stand this for seven whole days!*

Only Juliet's obvious joy kept her from reneging on her promise. Megan forced herself to calm down, to tell herself that it would be all right.

She let herself be distracted by Juliet's excitement. "*You'd better chill out,*" she warned gently. "*I'm not a bouncing-off-the-walls person. People will be suspicious.*"

"You're right. I'll try. But I'm so excited. And right now I'm off to the bathroom to take a wonderful bath and put on just a tiny bit more makeup. Then I'm off! This is Saturday night. I've got places to go, people to see."

Juliet paused in front of the mirror and said, "Megan, thank you! You won't be sorry."

But Megan was already sorry. And scared.

Before Megan could utter any one of the thousand new questions spinning around her, Juliet, with a happy wave and an equally happy smile, was out the door.

The thud it made as it closed felt to Megan like the closing of a tomb.

I'm overreacting. Being silly. I'll just get out of this dark, cold place, and everything will be fine, just like Juliet said.

But it wasn't. When she left the mirror, the sensation of darkness, of coldness, of being totally separated from the world she knew was devastating.

No one can see me. No one can hear me. As far as the world is concerned, I'm not here. Is this how Juliet felt all those years? So isolated? How lonely it feels not to be a part of the world!

The only way to ease the feeling was to go where there were people. There was no reason for her to stay in the bedroom, alone. So Megan went downstairs.

Her family was gathered in the kitchen. Megan remembered then that Thomas was in a play that night. He had the lead in a production of *Peter Pan* at Circle-in-the-Square Theater.

Although the loneliness Megan felt was eased somewhat by being around people, watching her family was like looking at one of those What's Wrong With This Picture? drawings.

I'm watching myself eat and laugh and talk . . . but it's not me. It's Juliet. And no one in this room knows that but the two of us. How can my parents not know? Can't they see that Juliet is laughing more and talking more than I do?

And then there was Juliet's makeup.

She looks like someone straight out of a forties movie. I never wear blue eyeshadow, and she must have at least eight coats of mascara on those eyes. I should have gone into the bathroom with her and helped her out.

"You're not wearing all that goop to my play, are you?" Thomas asked Juliet.

She stared at him. "Play? I'm not going to any play. I'm going to the mall."

Megan groaned silently.

"You're not going to the play?" Megan's mother echoed. "But we've planned this all week. I thought you and Justin had agreed to meet there. Isn't he doing a write-up on it for the school paper? And Hilary will be there, too. Betsy's in it, remember?"

Megan told Juliet, *"Betsy is Hilary's little sister, Juliet. We've been planning for weeks to go to this play tonight."* Talking and knowing only Juliet could hear her made her feel even more isolated.

Juliet laughed. "I was just kidding," she told the family quickly. "Of course I'm going to the play. I wouldn't miss it. It'll be fun."

"Well, good," Megan's mother said. "Because we definitely don't want you wandering around town by yourself. Not until Sheriff Toomey can tell us there's no risk involved. You'll be safe with us at the theater, and I won't have to worry."

While they finished eating, Megan wrestled with a strong desire to call off the whole thing. Watching Juliet being her was so much harder than she'd

253

thought it would be. She had expected it to be like watching herself in one of her dad's homemade videos. But this wasn't anything like that. She always knew that was *her* on the television screen. No matter how silly or how stupid she felt, she always knew she was watching *herself* on tape.

But watching Juliet as Megan Logan made her feel the way she'd felt in the nightmare . . . trapped, imprisoned. And knowing that she couldn't reach out and touch her parents, touch Thomas, increased her sense of desolation.

How was she going to make it through a whole week of this?

Miserable, frightened, and more lonely than she had ever been, Megan followed her family to the Circle-in-the-Square Theater.

Chapter 10

The theater was air-conditioned and packed. Megan noticed that hers weren't the only parents accompanied by teenagers. Hilary had told everyone who would listen that she'd been pushed off the catwalk. Most of the parents had believed her. Fear shone from their eyes.

"What's with the war paint?" Hilary asked as she joined the Logan family in front-row seats. "Have you been sampling the goodies at Phar-Mart's cosmetics counter?"

Juliet laughed and shrugged. "I thought it was time for a change. I *am* going to be sixteen, Hilary. Have you seen Justin?"

"He's parking. He'll be here in a minute. So, did you ask His Royal Cuteness to be your birthday date yet?"

"I'm asking him tonight. And he'll say yes," Juliet answered.

Hilary looked impressed. "Wow! I guess it's true what the ads say about makeup. You *are* a new woman!"

Megan warned, *"Careful, Juliet. Don't overdo the 'new woman' bit or Hil will guess that you're not only a new me, you're not even a me at all."*

If Justin was surprised by the enthusiastic reception Juliet gave him when he arrived, he hid it well. At intermission in the lobby, she chattered, laughed at his quips, and held his hand the whole time.

Megan, watching miserably, reminded herself that Justin, after all, thought that it was Megan flirting with him. And he certainly seemed to be enjoying himself. But seeing Juliet having such a good time with him was hard to take. Megan wanted so much to touch Justin, the way Juliet was doing. And she couldn't. For one long, endless week she wouldn't be able to touch him or smile at him or talk to him.

Megan now realized that it was going to be the longest week she'd ever known.

After the play, Constance Logan insisted that everyone come back to the house, squelching Juliet's plans to be alone with Justin. "I know you think I'm a worrywart," Megan's mother said apologetically, "but I'd really feel better if you were at the house. Humor me, okay? Justin and Hilary can come along, too."

"But it's Saturday night!" Juliet protested. "Everyone will be at the mall."

Mrs. Logan shook her head. "I don't think so. I talked to a lot of the other parents tonight, and they're keeping their kids home, too." She patted a disconsolate Juliet on the shoulder. "It's just for a few days, honey, until Sheriff Toomey catches whoever tampered with those cars and pushed poor Hilary off that catwalk. I'm sure everything will be back to normal in time for your birthday party."

Juliet looked stricken. Her eyes widened and her face paled as she drew in a deep breath of dismay.

She's seeing her week of fun going down the tubes. I tried to tell her this was a lousy time in Lakeside. But I guess it was now or never. Poor Juliet.

When they got to the house, Thomas and his father took the boat out. Mrs. Logan went down on the dock to "relax and enjoy the night sky," and Justin talked Hilary and Juliet into watching a science-fiction movie in the den.

Since Justin seemed to be enjoying Juliet's company so much, Megan began to wonder if he would be disappointed when the week was up and the "old" Megan returned.

I could never be like her, all sparkly and giddy and outgoing. No wonder she was popular forty-five years ago. I couldn't be like that . . . could I?

Hilary, Megan noticed, didn't seem to be having very much fun, though. She looked almost as lost and lonely as Megan felt. And she kept looking at Juliet, obviously confused by her friend's un-Meganlike behavior.

Poor Hil can't understand why all of a sudden I'm Miss Personality. I wish I could have told her what was going on.

Megan decided to join her brother and her father

out on the lake. Maybe being out in the open would ease her misery.

The lake was crowded with boaters trying to escape the heat, including many of Megan's friends. She was happy to see Barbie Winn, a bandage across one side of her face, in a canoe with her boyfriend. She'd been luckier than her older sister. Donny Richardson went by in a boat crowded with people Megan guessed were relatives. The two boys who had rescued Hilary with the ladder went by, and so did Vicki Deems, surrounded by boys Megan didn't recognize. From a nearby town, probably. Vicki must have already conquered the entire male population of Lakeside and been forced to seek out fresh new territory.

Unfortunately Megan found that being outside with the trees and the lake around her did nothing to help her mood. Neither did venturing into the depths of the lake, where she discovered the cold and the wet couldn't touch her. Frustrated and unhappy, she surfaced, only to be again surrounded by laughter and chatter from the boats on the lake.

I would rather feel the wet and the cold than this terrible, empty feeling. Nothing could be worse than this. Nothing!

When her father aimed the boat toward home, Megan went, too.

As they neared the dock, something moving in the water caught her attention. Megan moved in closer to get a better look. What was it?

A tree branch? Remnants of someone's lakeside picnic?

Megan saw hair, splayed like seaweed on the water. She saw two arms, two legs. . . .

A voiceless scream soared up through her.

Her mother was floating, facedown and unconscious on the water.

Chapter 11

The sight of her mother's limp form floating like debris on the black water made Megan feel as helpless as she'd felt in the spiderweb dream. *I've got no voice, so I can't scream. I've got no body, so I can't drag her out of the water. And if she dies, it'll be all my fault. If I hadn't traded places with Juliet, I could save Mom now.*

Thomas's frantic shout broke through Megan's frustration. In a second, he was out of the boat and plunging through the shallow water to Constance Logan, crying out to his father. He grabbed at her shirt, ballooning out around her, full of air and water. His frantic shouting, "Mom, Mom!" was high and shrill with fear. His father arrived at his side, and together they lifted the unconscious woman and carried her up the embankment.

Megan wanted, needed, desperately to help her family. There was only one way she could do that. She raced up to the house. *Mom, Mom, please don't be dead!*

Inside the house, she sought out the only person

who could hear her cry for help. She found Juliet in the den with Justin. They were seated, very close together, on the velvet settee. Hilary was nowhere in sight.

"*Juliet! Juliet, quick! Dial nine-one-one! It's Mom! In the lake. Hurt. Hurry! I'll tell you what to say.*"

Juliet flew off the settee and rushed to the telephone on the table beside the bookshelves. At that moment, Thomas ran into the room, crying. He repeated the chilling news. In his panic, he failed to notice that Juliet had already dialed Emergency Services and was beginning to repeat the words Megan fed her.

"Dad's doing CPR on her right now," Thomas told Justin. "But she's . . . she hasn't moved."

As Juliet hung up the phone, Thomas turned to her. "I'm scared. She isn't even *moving*."

"Let's go!" Justin urged.

"Emergency Services will be here right away," Juliet said as they ran out of the house and down the slope. "I told them to come straight down to the dock."

"Do you have a crystal ball you haven't told me about?" Justin asked Juliet as they raced through the darkness.

"What?" Juliet asked.

"You had already gone to the phone *before* Thomas came in. How did you know something was wrong?"

"Oh," Juliet said, startled. "I saw them. Through the den window. I knew something was wrong."

Apparently satisfied with that explanation, Justin nodded and increased his speed.

When they reached the dock, Megan's mother was half sitting, half lying against her husband's chest. Although she was choking and coughing and gasping for breath, they were all relieved to see that she was conscious.

A siren in the distance announced the approaching ambulance.

"You okay, Mom?" Thomas asked, kneeling at his mother's side. "What happened? You're a good swimmer."

"I wasn't swimming," she answered weakly. "I was sitting. On the dock. Just thinking, enjoying all of the lights out on the water. And . . . and something hard hit me from behind. That's all I remember." She tried to smile. "Like they say in the movies, everything went black." She moved one hand to the back of her head, and when she brought it back down, the light from the boat lantern shone on a red, sticky mess.

With a dying shriek, the ambulance arrived. Megan's father rode with it to the Medical Center. He asked Justin to follow with Juliet and Thomas.

Megan, too, went in the ambulance. While the attendants cared for her mother, she fought rising panic. First, her closest friends had been attacked, nearly killed. Now someone had deliberately hit her mother on the head and watched as she fell into the lake, leaving her to drown.

But who? Everyone liked Megan's mother. Like the other victims, she had no enemies. Until now.

We have to switch back. Now! I hate to go back on my promise and disappoint Juliet, but I can't just stand by and watch while some maniac hurts my family. I hope Juliet understands. I never should have agreed to switch in the first place.

When Constance Logan had been comfortably installed in a hospital bed, a thick white bandage on the back of her head, her husband announced that he was staying with her all night.

"No!" she cried, her eyes, clouded with medication, snapping open with alarm. "I want you home with the children. I don't want them in the house alone, not now!"

"Yes, I suppose you're right," Tom Logan agreed, and he took his family home.

When Juliet had told Justin good night and gone upstairs, Megan followed.

"Juliet, I'm scared. Seeing my mother lying there in the water made me realize how helpless I am like this. I mean, I couldn't pull her out, and I couldn't scream. It was really terrible. I don't ever want to feel like that again. We have to switch back. Now!"

Juliet, searching through Megan's denim shoulder bag, scattering papers and old tissues every which way on the bed, had just located the hairbrush she'd been seeking and had begun to brush the dark curls absentmindedly. At Megan's words, she dropped the brush, her eyes filling with tears. "Oh, no, Megan, you can't mean that!" she cried. "You can't! I haven't even had a whole day yet!"

Megan felt like she was yanking the wings off a butterfly. *"I know. And I'm sorry, Juliet, I really am. I know I promised you a whole week. But I didn't expect anything like this to happen. Not being able to help my mother, Juliet, it was . . . it was horrible!"*

To her dismay, Juliet burst into tears. Between sobs, she begged, "Megan, please, please, don't do this! Your mother's going to be fine, the doctor said so. This means so much to me! It's the only chance I'll ever have. I'll help take care of your mother for you, I promise!"

Oh, God, I want this to end now, Megan thought even as Juliet's pleas tore at her resolve. She had never seen anyone so desperate. *"Juliet, it's just such a bad time —"* she began weakly.

Juliet interrupted with fresh tears. "Megan, I told you," she gasped, "there *isn't* any other time for me!" Skinny rivulets of mascara streaked her face. "Any other time will be too late for me." Her voice fell to a heartbroken whisper. "Too late, too late . . ."

The last ounce of Megan's resolve disintegrated in the face of Juliet's anguish. She had never in her life caused anyone so much pain, and she couldn't stand it. *"All right,"* she said with a helpless sigh, *"we won't switch back tonight. Now stop crying, okay?"*

Juliet lifted her head, her face filled with hope. "You mean it?"

"I . . . I guess so. We'll give it a little more time. But if anything else bad happens, Juliet, to my family or my friends, we're trading back."

"Of course, Megan." Wiping her tearstained face

264

with a towel, Juliet smiled and nodded. "But no more bad things are going to happen. I can feel it. Everything's going to be fine." Happy again, she slipped into Megan's white pajamas and climbed into the canopied bed. "If we hadn't switched," she said calmly, "you wouldn't have been down on the dock to find your mother and rush up to the house to call for help. So it's not all bad, is it, Megan? Being me, I mean?"

She had a point. But Megan wasn't consoled. The days and nights loaned to Juliet felt like years, centuries. On this, only the first night, they stretched ahead of her like an endless, dark, deserted highway. How would she ever get through them?

"Oh, by the way, Megan," Juliet said cheerfully as she pulled the sheet over her legs, "when Hilary left, I asked Justin to your party. And he said yes. So now you can quit worrying." She slid down in bed and closed her eyes. "Everything's going to be great. Your mom will be fine, and Justin is coming to your party. So relax, okay?"

"*Juliet, what happened to Hilary tonight? Why did she go home so early?*"

"Oh, I guess she felt like a third wheel. Good night, Megan. See you tomorrow."

A minute later, the sound of her deep, even breathing told Megan that Juliet was sound asleep. Just then, something on the worn blue carpet beside the bed caught Megan's eye. She knew what it was immediately, and the realization sickened her. How could another drawing have found its way into her home?

265

She knew she had to look at it. Otherwise it would lie there all night like some dreadful insect, tormenting her.

The picture was on lime-green paper. There were two crude crayon drawings. One was of a man in a gray-and-black-striped uniform. A convict. The second drawing was of a leg, awkwardly bent to emphasize the knee. CON. KNEE. Connie. Mom.

She remembered Juliet pulling things out of her shoulder bag. The drawing must have been in there. But how had it got there?

The mall. Someone had to have slipped it into her purse while she was there. If she hadn't been so distracted all day by the thought of what was ahead of her that evening, she would have noticed the drawing sooner. Then she could have done something, anything, to protect her mother. She could at least have warned Juliet not to leave her mother alone for a second.

At least her mother was alive. And she was going to be okay. She'd be home tomorrow, safe and sound.

But . . . it might not be over. What if there was another attack, this time on Juliet? Juliet had said she could prevent that. What if she couldn't? Maybe she was wrong.

If she was . . . if something happened to prevent their trade on Saturday night, something that kept Megan from returning to her own body . . . what would become of Megan?

Megan had to know, and she had to know *now.* *"Juliet! Wake up, Juliet! I have to talk to you."*

"What . . ." a sleepy Juliet mumbled from bed. "What is it, Megan?"

"There's one thing you haven't told me, and I must know. What would happen to me . . . if you were . . . if something happens to my body while you're in it? I need to know that, Juliet."

"If something happened to stop you from returning to your own form by midnight Saturday," Juliet said slowly, "you'd . . . you'd be trapped in my world."

Megan gasped. *"And you weren't even going to tell me, were you?"*

"I didn't want to frighten you, Megan. Because nothing bad can happen to me. I can steer clear of evil better than you can. Your body is safer with me than it would be with you."

Megan heard none of what Juliet was saying. All she could think of was being trapped in this horrible, empty world . . . forever. It was too terrifying to comprehend.

Megan went out on the terrace roof to try to fathom what Juliet had just told her. Everything was perfectly still. Not a single leaf on the oak tree stirred. The lake was quiet, lying between the two shores like a giant ink stain. One by one, the lights in the houses bordering the lake went out, until, with no moon visible in the pouting gray sky, the darkness was complete.

Megan had never felt so alone in her life.

Chapter 12

Residents of Lakeside were severely shaken by the attack on Connie Logan. There was talk of hiring a private security patrol for the area. But the proposal was voted down because of the expense.

Megan called Juliet's attention to the drawings. *"Keep your eyes open for more of these,"* she said. *"If someone else is going to get hurt, you might get another one. Check the art cubbyhole every day and the mailbox here at the house. And Juliet,"* she warned, *"I think Mom is right. I don't think it's a good idea to go out alone. It might not be safe."*

Juliet didn't argue. She didn't want to be alone, anyway. She wanted Justin with her, preferably at all times. "I know he's your boyfriend," she told Megan happily, "but it's okay because he thinks I'm *you*. So it's not like I'm doing anything wrong, right, Megan?"

She didn't seem to be taking the drawings seriously. That bothered Megan. How was she going to keep watch over Juliet *and* her family, too?

Megan wished she could feel as confident about

Juliet's safety as Juliet seemed to. If there was a list of potential victims somewhere, Megan's name was surely on it. Everyone who had been hurt was close to her. If *she* could be next, that meant *Juliet* could be next.

She couldn't forget Juliet's answer to her question the night before. *"Juliet,"* she said as Juliet checked out the clothes in Megan's closet, *"I wish you'd pay more attention to what's going on in town. You don't seem to care at all. But if something happens to you . . ."*

Juliet selected several outfits and carried them to the bed. Spreading them out like food on a picnic table, she said nonchalantly, "Goodness, Megan, nothing's going to happen to me! I told you, I'll know if something evil comes near me."

But that wasn't good enough. It was making her crazy. *"But if something* does *happen . . . I'd have to stay . . . like this . . . forever?"*

"The same thing would happen to you that will happen to me, come midnight on Saturday. I'll disappear, poof!" She smiled happily. "But it'll be okay now, because you gave me this week. Stop worrying. Nothing's going to happen to me before Saturday."

Poof? She would go poof? And disappear? Forever? The sharp-toothed edges of Megan's trap closed around her. She could only pray that the hours and the days would fly by quickly.

And that Juliet was right about being able to protect herself.

* * *

Megan's father brought his wife home from the hospital at noon. While she slept, he gave Juliet permission to go to the library with Justin. Reluctant at first to have any family member leave the house, he relented when Juliet pointed out that she had a report due in social studies.

"Nobody is going to attack me in the library, Daddy," Juliet pleaded. "Besides, Justin will be with me."

He gave in then, and Juliet ran happily upstairs to change her clothes.

But Megan wasn't so sure the library was perfectly safe. The auditorium at Philippa should have been perfectly safe, too. But it hadn't been for Hilary, had it? Maybe no place in Lakeside was safe. And if Juliet and Justin got lost in each other the way they had the night before, an army of attackers could surround them and they wouldn't notice until it was too late.

By the time Justin arrived, Juliet, in a full white skirt and a silky red long-sleeved blouse and red sandals, was waiting at the front door. Her makeup was still slightly exaggerated, but she looked very pretty.

The look on Justin's face as Juliet came down the stairs depressed Megan. Would he wear that same expression when she was herself again?

When Justin had learned from Mr. Logan that Megan's mother was okay and sleeping comfortably, he and Juliet left, hand in hand.

Megan left, too. The only advantage to this horrible feeling of separation from the world was her ability to watch and listen without being seen or heard. She might as well use it. But it didn't take her long to realize that she wasn't going to learn anything on a dismal, cool Sunday afternoon in a village whose residents were too scared to venture from their homes.

The town was virtually deserted. A damp gray mist fell steadily on a lake empty of boats, on streets bare of automobiles and bicycles, on lawns free of children and pets, on deserted tennis courts and pools. Curtains and blinds were drawn on every house, gates closed and locked, garage doors firmly latched.

And Megan had no idea what to look for. A stranger with maniacal eyes skulking through backyards seeking out victims? Or someone familiar who *seemed* no different — but on the inside was sick and twisted?

It had to be someone she knew, someone who knew *her*. Someone who knew which art cubbyhole was hers, since there were no names on the boxes, someone who knew that denim shoulder bag belonged to her.

All kinds of people had been in the lake area last night. Which one of them had attacked her mother? And who did they intend to attack next?

Vicki Deems had been out on the lake. But if Vicki wanted Justin Carr for herself, how would hurting Connie Logan help her get him?

Maybe Vicki just hates everyone in Lakeside. That was a scary thought. But, picturing Vicki's cold, dark eyes, Megan found it easy to believe that

271

the girl could hate someone enough to hurt them.

Discouraged because there was nothing to see or hear, Megan explored the lake for a while, then moved through the cool gray mist toward home.

She arrived to find Justin's red car parked in the driveway, facing the lake. That was no surprise. What was a surprise was finding Juliet and Justin still in it, seated so close together they looked like one person.

And they were kissing. Intensely.

Justin had kissed Megan before. But never like that. It had been more of an I-like-you-Megan-and-I'm-glad-we-know-each-other kind of kiss. Not a Wow-are-you-ever-terrific kind of kiss, which was what he was giving Juliet this very minute.

It was so hard to remember that Justin believed he was with *her*, Megan. She wanted so much to tell him the truth, to shout, "Justin, it's me, Megan, over here. That's not me you're kissing, it's a ghost named Juliet!"

But he wouldn't be able to hear her.

Justin pulled Juliet even closer. Mist clouded the windshield and the windows, obliterating the outside world. The pair didn't seem to mind.

Megan fled.

Twenty agonizingly long minutes later, when Juliet entered the bedroom, a dreamy smile on her face, Megan was waiting for her.

"*Juliet,*" Megan said, "*someone could have come up behind that car and pushed it straight into the lake, and you and Justin wouldn't have known it until your shoes started to get soggy. I don't call that being careful!"*

Juliet threw herself across the unmade bed, rolled over on her back, and thrust a lace-edged pillow under her head. "Sounds to me like somebody's jealous," she said with a grin. "Gosh, Megan, I don't see why. Justin thinks that was *you* he was kissing." Another grin. "And kissing and kissing and . . . listen, I was doing you a big favor. Jump starting his motor for you."

"Justin's going to get suspicious. He knows I'm not that . . . that outgoing."

Juliet grinned, catlike. "He doesn't seem to mind."

Just then the phone rang.

"Oh, hello, Hilary." Juliet's voice became ice cream, smooth and cold. "Yes, my mother's fine. She came home this afternoon." She listened for a moment and then said, "Well, I just don't think I have anything to apologize for. You're too sensitive, that's all."

There was an audible click on the other end.

Juliet shrugged and replaced the phone.

Megan had been listening. *"What did you do to Hilary? Why does she want an apology?"*

"Because she's silly, that's why. And because she never learned that three is a crowd. My goodness, Megan, I learned that when I was two years old."

Megan, thinking that the last thing in the world Hilary needed right now was to have her feelings hurt, said, *"She didn't really leave last night be-*

273

cause she was tired, did she? Juliet, what did you do?"

The heat wave had finally broken, and a gust of wind sent a cool mist into the room, stirring the curtains. Juliet jumped up to close the window and then went to the closet and grabbed a white terrycloth robe hanging on the back of the door. "I simply said that it was too bad she didn't have a date on Saturday night and had to hang around with Justin and me. The next thing I knew, she was calling her father to come and pick her up, and five minutes later she was out of here. It's really not my fault, Megan. I didn't mean to hurt her feelings, but I wanted to be alone with Justin."

"You told her she was in the way? Juliet, that's awful!"

"I didn't hear Justin complaining." Her eyes became cloudy with pleasure. "Megan, if I'm going to make the most of this week, I can't do it with Hilary hanging over my shoulder."

And without waiting to hear any more, Juliet left to take a bath.

Megan stared longingly at the telephone. If only I could pick it up and fix things with Hilary. She must be so down right now. How am I ever going to make this up to her?

But there was nothing Megan could do, except wait. Six more days. Six long days.

Chapter 13

It became very clear to Megan the next morning that Juliet wasn't going to be much help to a recuperating mother, in spite of her promise to Megan to "take care of your mother."

"Dishes? Gosh, I don't have *time*! Justin's picking me up in two minutes. Can't Thomas do them?"

Thomas, gulping down the last of his cereal, howled a protest. "I have to put air in my bike tires. I don't have time for dishes."

Megan, watching, disapproved of both Juliet's attitude and her outfit. The perfectly innocent white peasant blouse Megan was so fond of looked very different on Juliet, who had pushed the tiny, puffed sleeves off her shoulders, baring them.

"I don't wear it like that," she had told Juliet upstairs.

"It's more fun like this," had been Juliet's response.

Hearing that her father had decided to take the day off to stay with his wife, Megan followed Juliet to school. Leaving Juliet alone for any length of time would be not only dangerous, but foolish. After Juliet had left, Megan heard her father turn to Thomas and say in a perplexed voice, "Now, what's got into that girl? She didn't even tell your mother goodbye."

Megan hoped that Juliet's behavior at school wouldn't cause the same reaction from her friends and teachers. Would everyone be chorusing, "What's got into Megan?" by the end of this week? Maybe even by the end of this day?

But none of that mattered as much as being sure that Juliet was safe. *Maybe my being around her won't protect her, but if I don't know that she's okay, I'll go crazy worrying.*

Fighting her anxiety, Megan searched the halls and classrooms at Philippa Moore for Juliet. The complete silence in the building seemed to Megan positively freakish. There was no laughter, no chatter, no footsteps clattering down the halls, no slamming of locker doors. The building itself seemed to be holding its breath, waiting to see where disaster would strike next.

Being in the school but separated from it by the hideous invisible wall between her and her familiar world made Megan wish ferociously that she hadn't daydreamed her way through so many classes. *I took it all for granted,* she scolded herself, *and now, if anything happens to Juliet, I might never get it back.*

No. That couldn't happen. It couldn't!

Megan found Juliet in the cafeteria with Hilary.

But her relief was short-lived when she realized they were arguing.

Juliet and Hilary were sitting at a corner table in the sparsely occupied room. Hilary's face was scarlet, her short, squat body rigid with anger. Juliet seemed perfectly relaxed.

Uh-oh. What's going on?

"You could at least say you're sorry!" Hilary said. "You embarrassed me in front of Justin. That stinks, Megan! I could have had a date Saturday night if I'd wanted one, and you know it."

Toying with a plastic fork on her tray, Juliet said, "Then why didn't you? I mean, Hil, you keep telling me to go for it with Justin. How do you expect me to do that with a chaperone around all the time?"

Hilary's mortified flush was painful for Megan to see. "Oh." Hilary's voice sank to a near-whisper. "I guess . . . I guess you're right. I'm sorry. I wasn't thinking. I didn't realize I was in the way."

Why isn't she fighting back? Hilary always fights back. She doesn't sound like herself any more than Juliet sounds like me.

Megan realized then that Hilary's plunge toward death had affected her far more deeply than she'd let anyone know.

Jenny and Cappie and I always knew that as tough as Hil was on the outside, she was a soft, warm marshmallow inside. She would die before she'd hurt anyone on purpose. And the idea that someone would deliberately hurt her, for no reason, has really shaken her.

And Juliet, whether she knew it or not, was making it worse.

Hilary stood up, clutching her books to her chest as if they might somehow protect her. "See you," she whispered, and hurried out of the cafeteria.

As angry as Megan was, she decided it would be foolish to confront Juliet here in the cafeteria. Juliet could hardly sit in a public place and reply to an unseen Megan's questions. She'd look like an idiot, talking to herself. Megan would have to wait until they were both back home.

As Juliet got up and left, Megan noticed that she was not the only person watching. Vicki Deems, seated alone off to Megan's right, had fixed her eyes on Juliet. They smouldered with . . . was that hatred? Why? Because Vicki wanted Justin?

If Vicki was evil enough to have hurt so many people, would Juliet be able to *feel* that when she shared an English classroom with Vicki later that day?

Before she left school, Megan went with trepidation to the art room. Approaching the cubbyhole cautiously, she said a quick prayer that it would be empty.

It wasn't.

The sheet of paper was a bright sunny yellow. It took her a few moments to decipher the message drawn in vivid purple. The crude strokes depicted what looked like a drum. A round, squat drum with a green zigzag trim bordering the top and bottom edges. Two short, skinny drumsticks with padded ends lay crisscross on top of the drum.

278

It's not a drum. It's a tom-tom. Thomas. Tom. There are two of them in my family: Big Tom and little Tom.

Was this drawing a threat to both of them? Her brother *and* her father?

Megan's cold and lonely world began spinning wildly around her. The tomblike silence of the building shouted at her, "Watch out for your family, Megan!"

Why hadn't Juliet told her about the drawing?

"I didn't go to art," was the answer Megan got when, at home, she asked that question. "Justin had to go pick up some stuff for *The Scribe*, so I cut and went with him. I hope you're not mad. I mean, nobody seems to think anything of it. Gosh, if I'd ever cut a class, my father would have killed me!"

"Not your mother?"

"My mother died when I was nine."

"Oh, I'm sorry, Juliet." What terrible things had happened to Juliet. First her mother's death, and then her own. And all she wanted now was this one week.

Still, Megan wished with all her heart that she had never given the week away. She wanted it back. But how could she do that to Juliet? It would be so cruel.

"Juliet, did you cut English, too?" Like art, English was an afternoon class. She shared it with Vicki.

"Yes. But I promise I won't do it again. I wouldn't want your teachers to be mad at you because of me."

Megan was bitterly disappointed. She had counted on Juliet to let her know if she sensed anything evil from Vicki. But she didn't want to say anything that might influence Juliet's reaction to Vicki. It would just have to wait.

As would another evening of fun for Juliet, as she discovered at dinner when Megan's father put his foot down.

"You're staying in tonight," he said emphatically as they finished their meal. Juliet had asked permission to meet Justin at Lickety-Split, the ice-cream store in the mall. "No one in this family is stepping one foot outside this house. Do I make myself clear?"

He looked tired. Worry lines etched a pattern across his forehead, and his thick white hair stuck up all over, a sure sign that he'd been nervously running his fingers through it.

What happened to Mom has really upset him. Poor dad. Then she remembered the new drawing. *If only there was some way I could warn him and Thomas.*

This time, Juliet didn't argue. She seemed to understand that arguing would get her nowhere. Although she pouted over the change in plans, she did the dishes and swept the kitchen floor before going upstairs.

Megan expected her to call Justin immediately to cancel their date, but she didn't. Instead, she took a shower, changed into jeans and a pretty green blouse, blew her hair dry, applied fresh makeup, and then sat down on the bed, a paperback novel in hand.

And stayed there until she heard Thomas go into his room and close the door, and shortly after that, the plodding footsteps of a very weary Tom Logan on the stairs. A minute later, the door to the master bedroom clicked shut.

And Juliet, with a whispered but triumphant, "Yes, yes, yes!" picked up the denim purse, tiptoed down the stairs, and out of the house. Megan knew she was on her way to Lickety-Split to meet Justin as planned.

Her disobeying Megan's father was more than annoying to Megan. It was frightening. Going out at night now was a risky, stupid thing to do. Juliet's need to have fun this week was easy to understand, but Megan couldn't just let her go. Anything could happen to her. And anything that happened to her happened to Megan, too.

The only solution was to go to the mall and make Juliet come back home before anyone knew she was gone.

Thinking again of the new drawing, Megan made sure that both her brother and her father were safe in their own beds.

Then she followed Juliet.

Chapter 14

Megan arrived at the mall to find Hilary arguing vehemently with Vicki Deems in the corridor outside of the ice-cream store. Justin and Juliet were inside, sitting opposite each other in one of the pink-and-white-striped booths. They were the only customers in the store, and they seemed blissfully unaware of the argument going on outside.

"Talk about the pot calling the kettle black!" Hilary shouted. Her voice echoed with a hollow ring amid the potted trees and park benches. Except for her and Vicki, the corridor was deserted. It was late. The only store open was Lickety-Split, which kept longer hours to attract the after-movie crowd. "You've got a lot of nerve calling Megan a flirt. Your own Flirt Alert is on attack status twenty-four hours a day, Deems. A living, breathing male passes within fifty feet of you and you're all over him like jelly on peanut butter!"

Megan felt a warm rush of affection for Hilary. Juliet had hurt her feelings, yet here was Hilary defending her.

"At least I'm not a hypocrite," Vicki fumed, her mouth twisted in contempt. "Little Miss Muffet in there pretended to be so sticky-sweet until she caught me talking to Justin. Then she bared her fangs."

"You never stood a chance with him. He's only interested in Megan. Give it up, Vicki. Get a life!"

Vicki's face went white with rage. "I don't *give* up. Ever. If Megan hadn't come into the *Scribe* office that day, Justin would have asked me to her party. I'm never wrong about things like that."

"In your dreams, Deems."

Enraged, but aware that Hilary wasn't going to back down, Vicki turned on her heels and stalked away. Her long, dark hair swayed on her shoulders like a black silk cape.

Megan wished fiercely that she could hug Hilary to thank her. She wouldn't have blamed her best friend if she'd agreed with Vicki, after the way Juliet had hurt her.

She'd never seen Vicki so angry. Did she really want Justin that much? And how far would she go to get him?

Inside the restaurant, Hilary refused to acknowledge the existence of Justin and Juliet. Head up, shoulders squared, she marched straight to the counter, where she ordered a half gallon of Triple Trouble ice cream. Then she waited, her back resolutely to the couple.

"Hil?" Justin called. "Come on over. You're not still mad, are you?"

Hilary half turned. "I wouldn't dream of intruding," she said stiffly. "I'm just here to pick up dessert. Ignore me. That shouldn't be a problem for you."

Justin got up then and came over to the counter. Draping an arm around Hilary's stiffened shoulders, he said, "Come on, Hil, ease up. We didn't mean to hurt your feelings the other night. We feel bad about it."

Hilary glanced over at Juliet. She was chewing on a straw and smiling at Justin. Her smile excluded Hilary.

"Yeah, I can see she's all broken up about it."

"Look," Justin said, "tell you what. I'll ask Megan's father if we can take his boat out. The weather stinks, but it'll be fun, anyway. Come on, Hil. You can't stay mad forever."

A strangled sound from behind them made them both turn around. Juliet, in the booth, sat up straight and rigid as a pole, her face muscles contracted in fear. "Boat?" she choked. "Justin, you didn't say anything to me about going out in a boat. I won't go!"

Megan was watching. *Poor Juliet. Look at her face. She's terrified of the lake because that's where she died. But they're not going to understand. They think she's me, and I would never react that way to a boat ride. They know I love the lake.*

But Hilary was no longer surprised by anything her best friend did. "Look," she said while an amazed Justin stared at Juliet. "I just came to get dessert, that's all. I had to promise my parents I'd be back in fifteen minutes. If I'm not, they're sending the militia after me. They're totally paranoid right now."

She paid for the ice cream and left without saying a word to Juliet, who didn't seem to notice.

Justin hurried over to the booth. "What was that all about?" he asked Juliet, peering into her face. "Since when aren't you ready and willing to take a boat ride?"

And Juliet, reaching out to grasp Justin's hands in her own, leaned across the table and said sadly, "Since my mother ended up floating in the lake. That really upset me."

That excuse made sense to Justin. Megan could tell that he had accepted it by the understanding look on his face.

"Oh. Yeah, sure. But you'll get over it, right?" Justin wasn't a great swimmer, but he loved boating.

"Sure. Of course. Now, let's talk about something else."

"What did you decide to do about the drawing you showed me?" Justin asked Juliet. "You planning to take it to Toomey?"

It took Juliet a moment to shift gears. "Drawing?"

"Yeah, you know. The one of Jenny's car."

It's a good thing I showed it to her, or she wouldn't have the faintest idea what Justin was talking about.

"Oh, right." Juliet shook her head. "I don't think he'd pay that much attention. It's just a drawing. Someone with a sick sense of humor could have

285

drawn it. It's not proof of anything."

Justin doesn't know about the other two drawings. I never had the chance to tell him. But Juliet does. Why isn't she telling him?

When Justin went to pay the bill, Megan finally had a chance to speak to Juliet. *"Juliet, you have to get back home before Dad notices you're gone."* Juliet jerked upright with surprise when Megan spoke to her. *"If he gets mad enough, he'll cancel the party. And it's not safe out here, anyway."*

As the words registered, Juliet's heavily mascaraed lashes fluttered with alarm. "Cancel? He can't do that."

"Yes he can. You'd better go home, now."

Immediately contrite, Juliet whispered, "I'll go right now Megan. I couldn't stand it if your party was canceled." She sighed heavily. "I guess I've been a real pain. I'm sorry. I'll try to shape up, I promise." She waved a hand in dismissal. "Now go away, quick, before Justin gets back."

Justin arrived, saying with a grin, "Talking to yourself, are you? They say that's the first sign of old age."

Megan stayed just long enough to witness Juliet gifting him with a brilliant smile. Then she went home, where she checked on her sleeping family and waited anxiously for Juliet's return. They had things to talk about.

To Megan's great relief, Juliet managed to get back into the house without waking either parent.

"Whew!" Juliet exclaimed when she entered the

bedroom and realized that Megan was present. "I made it! See, Megan? Nothing terrible happened. Your father doesn't even know I was gone."

Megan wasn't interested in talking about Juliet's little escapade. *"Why didn't you tell Justin about the other drawings? If he knew there were three, I think he'd agree that you should take them to Sheriff Toomey."*

"Oh, Megan, they're just *pictures*. The sheriff would think I was crazy if I came waltzing into his office with a bunch of crayon drawings. Anyway," she added with a shrug, "I don't want to spend my time with Justin talking about creepy stuff like that. It's not very romantic."

"You promised you'd help."

"And I will, Megan. I'll pay strict attention to everyone I meet tomorrow. If I sense anything from anyone, I'll tell you about it, I promise. Okay?"

"Juliet, listen, you have to be more careful," Megan said. *"I'm not talking about upsetting my best friend and cutting classes. I'm talking about taking so many chances with your . . . my . . . safety. You've got to be more careful. Can't you see how important it is?"*

Juliet sighed and nodded. "You're right, Megan. I guess I was just so excited, I . . . I freaked out. It's not a very good way to pay back a favor. I'm sorry. I'll be more careful, I promise."

"Thank you." Megan drifted toward the window, intending to go outside, when she spotted a small white card on the dresser. According to its bright blue printing, Megan Logan had a hair appointment

at Cut It Again, Sam, a hair salon in the mall, on Saturday afternoon at one o'clock.

"*Juliet, what is this? I don't have a hair appointment.*"

Juliet looked up from the bed in dismay. "Oh, Megan, it was supposed to be a surprise! You forgot to put it on your list, so I made the appointment for you."

"*But I don't want to have my hair done.*"

Light laughter. "Of course you do. Megan, you can't go to your Sweet Sixteen party with" — she lifted a hand and gave a black curl a careless toss — "this."

"*Yes, I can. I like my hair the way it is,*" Megan said. "*Just don't make plans without asking me first, okay? And cancel the hair appointment.*"

Visibly disappointed, Juliet agreed to cancel the appointment. "I can't do it tonight. I'll do it tomorrow. But I still think your hair should look special for your Sweet Sixteen party, Megan. I wouldn't have dreamed of not going to the beauty parlor before my party."

"*Well, you're not me, are you?*"

That struck Juliet as being very funny, since, for the moment, she *was* Megan. She was still laughing to herself when she went to brush her teeth.

Megan hadn't found it that funny.

When Juliet had fallen asleep, Megan went outside. The lake and the surrounding area looked deceptively peaceful.

How am I going to keep an eye on Juliet and on Thomas and Dad? Even in this form, I can't be in

288

three different places at the same time. But any one of them could be attacked at any time.

The thought of anything bad happening to her father or brother sickened Megan.

But a threat to Juliet was even more terrifying.

What do I do if something happens to my body and I can't return to it? Oh, God, I can't think about that. I won't!

But the question wouldn't go away. It pounded at her relentlessly, slapping at her, demanding to be answered. What would she do if something interfered with the exchange Saturday night?

She found no answer in the thick gray mist. Or in the night sky, black as coal. No answer in the smooth, glassy surface of the lake.

There was no answer anywhere.

Chapter 15

For the next two days, Megan stayed close to Juliet.
She had decided, after a lot of agonizing, that since
two of the drawings had been placed in her art box
at Philippa, Juliet was in more danger at school than
her father in his office or Thomas in his elementary
school.

Each day seemed to pass more slowly than the
one before it. Every minute became an hour, each
hour an eternity. How could this week ever have
seemed short to her? "Such a little thing" she had
called it. How wrong she'd been!

And each day, anxiety clung to her like the furry
cobwebs in her spider nightmare until her brother
and her father arrived home safely.

Juliet did shape up as promised. She attended all
of Megan's classes, helped around the house, visited
Jenny in the hospital, and seemed content to stay
home in the evening as long as Justin joined her
there, and sometimes Barb and Cappie and Hilary,
with whom Juliet had spent twenty minutes on the

phone Tuesday morning in apology. Hilary had forgiven her.

There were no more notes.

But Megan reminded herself that the warning in the last drawing, the tom-tom, hadn't been fulfilled yet.

Maybe it wouldn't be. Maybe whoever had been doing such cruel things had repented and given up. That was possible, wasn't it?

Anything was possible.

Wednesday afternoon, Donny Richardson joined them at lunch. Although he said little, nervously tugging on his skinny little mustache the whole time, Megan noticed Juliet watching him carefully. His bright pink shirt gave his skin a yellowish cast, and he chewed on his lower lip while he listened to the conversation.

Why was Juliet watching him like that?

"There's something about him," she told Megan later, at home. "I'm not sure what. Maybe he's just a creep. But I definitely felt something. I'm going to keep my eye on him."

"You think it's him? Hurting people, I mean?"

Juliet shrugged. "I'm not sure. But I'll keep my eye on him, Megan, you can be sure of that."

She would have to, because Megan couldn't add one more person to her list of people to watch. It was hard enough keeping track of three.

When Megan's feeling of isolation became especially overpowering, she tried to focus on the fact that, in spite of everything, Juliet seemed happy with her week. The thought wasn't enough to lift Megan's spirits, but it kept her from drowning in despair. She was glad she was making someone happy, especially someone who had once known her grandmother.

Juliet talked a lot about the changes in the world in forty-six years. Although she was careful not to express amazement around other people, with Megan she was more open.

"You have so many fun things now. Stereos and videos and MTV, and your supermarkets are unreal! When I lived here, the lake was our only entertainment." Juliet shuddered. "I never liked it here, but my father did. He wouldn't move back to the city, even though we were much happier there."

"The accident must have been horrible for him."

"Yes, it was. He was devastated. He loved me very much. And I him." Juliet was silent for a moment. Then she added softly, "I warned him about this place. Martha told me there had been deaths here. But he wouldn't listen." With a regretful sigh, she changed the subject to more pleasant things like compact discs and hot rollers.

Megan's mother continued to improve and was up and around, relieving Juliet of the heavy housework burden. Although that allowed her more free time, Megan's father stuck to his rule about no one leaving the house in the evening.

"Sheriff Toomey hasn't learned anything new," he said when Juliet begged for permission to go out for pizza. "You can order pizza in and eat it here."

"It's so frustrating!" Juliet complained later, sitting on the bed with a pizza box at her side. "I think your father's being silly. Nothing's happened since Saturday night. And I don't think anything is going to. Whoever did all that stuff must have decided it was too risky."

"You don't know that, Juliet. Dad isn't taking any chances, that's all."

Megan felt sorry for Juliet. This week couldn't be what she had hoped it would be. No one was giving any parties, the mall was deserted, and nothing fun was going on in town. Not that Juliet was complaining. She had Justin.

"I told you, Juliet, that this wasn't a good time."

Wiping a blob of tomato sauce off the blue print comforter, Juliet sighed heavily. "I know you did, Megan. But I didn't have any choice. It was either before your birthday or never. Anything is better than never."

"I guess." Megan wished she could believe that Juliet was right about no more harm coming their way. The tom-tom note had been placed in her cubbyhole on Monday. This was Wednesday. If something were going to happen, wouldn't it have happened by now? None of the other drawings had appeared so far in advance.

But she didn't believe for a second that it was over. The sheriff hadn't arrested anyone. Jenny's accident and her mother's attack and Hilary's fall off the catwalk couldn't be dismissed just because there were no clues. There had been someone out

there when those things happened, and that someone was still out there.

But what was he waiting for?

And who would be his next victim?

Megan got her answer the very next day.

Chapter 16

The Logan house, like other homes facing the lake, backed up to the boulevard. An enclosed back porch with a row of windows across its width looked out over the wide street, Thomas's route home from school. It was there that Megan went Thursday afternoon when she realized that her brother was fifteen minutes late.

The tom-tom drawing danced across her mind, taunting her.

I should have gone to school to follow him home. Justin is bringing Juliet, so I was free to leave her, and Dad is still at the office. I could have gone to Thomas's school to make sure he was all right.

Peering out into the drizzle through the faded yellow curtains, she hoped that her mother, peeling potatoes in the kitchen, wasn't watching the clock. If she noticed that her son hadn't arrived yet even after repeated warnings to come straight home from school, she'd become frantic.

Megan saw the truck before she saw Thomas. It was an eighteen-wheeler. They didn't ordinarily come through the village, preferring instead the open highway circling Lakeside. This one must have had a delivery at the mall. It was huge, its cab bright yellow and shiny black. It wasn't going very fast, probably only thirty-five miles an hour. But its size alone made it no match for a skinny little boy on a bicycle.

Afterward, Megan told herself over and over that even if she'd had a voice, even if she'd been able to run, she couldn't have stopped any of it. It happened too fast.

The truck heaved its lumbering bulk around a corner just as Thomas came whizzing down the street. Megan thought he was whistling as he turned the handlebars. It seemed to her that his mouth was pursed when he looked up and saw the truck bearing down on him.

He can stop, Megan told herself. *He has plenty of time. All he has to do is use his brakes.*

He tried. She saw him try. She watched as his hands clenched the brake levers again and again, saw the muscles in his thin arms strain as he squeezed with all his might.

Nothing happened. The new red-and-silver bicycle, Thomas's tenth-birthday present from his parents, never even slowed down. It aimed straight for the mammoth metal truck as if it were magnetized.

Thomas, still pumping the brakes frantically, closed his eyes as the truck loomed menacingly over him.

Sound and time stopped as the truck and the bicycle collided.

And as Megan silently screamed, *No, no, not Thomas!* her brother's skinny little body flew up into the air as if shot from a cannon. It somersaulted twice before slamming back down to the ground, landing on a thin strip of green dividing the boulevard.

People began running out of their houses to gather in horrified silence at the scene. A woman in a blue bathrobe took one look and ran back inside to call for help. The few cars on the boulevard came to a standstill. A man in a gray suit, a woman in a yellow raincoat, and two teenaged boys in sweatsuits left their cars to run to Thomas's aid.

In the kitchen, Megan's mother heard the truck's brakes screaming and instinctively sensed that they had screamed too late. Her eyes flew to the clock. When she saw the time and realized that she hadn't heard Thomas's familiar back-door slam, her jaw went slack, and her hands went to her mouth. She ran to the back porch windows.

Megan, watching in agony, knew the exact moment when her mother recognized the red-and-silver bike lying on the ground. With a half scream, half moan, Connie Logan raced for the back door and out of the house.

There was time for him to stop, to get out of the way. And he used his brakes, I saw him. Why didn't he stop?

Thomas couldn't give her any answers. He was

unconscious, bleeding from the nose. Although the ambulance attendants said nothing as they gently lifted him onto a stretcher and took him away, accompanied by his weeping mother, their faces were grim.

As the ambulance pulled away, Megan felt the same horrible wrenching sensation that had torn at her when she'd entered the mirror for the final switch. What was happening to her family? First her mother, now Thomas.

The sounds of the street, the birds singing as if something terrible hadn't just taken place, the boat motors out on the lake, the small crowd whispering about the accident, it all seemed vague and distant, as if it were taking place at the far end of some long, dark tunnel.

Megan cried soundlessly, seeing Thomas's limp, broken body being lifted onto the stretcher. *You have to be okay, Thomas, you have to.*

Although she needed desperately to get to the Medical Center, she stayed behind to wait for Juliet and tell her what had happened. She was about to go into the house to wait when she saw Juliet standing on the corner, watching the ambulance shriek down Lakeside Boulevard.

"Thomas has been hurt," Megan said quickly, anxious to get going. *"Did you see it happen? Where's Justin?"*

Juliet nodded. "I saw it. Justin had to drop me off at the library. He had some stuff to do there. I walked the rest of the way. How bad is Thomas hurt?"

298

"Bad. I'm going to the hospital. You'd better come, too."

"I will. I'll call Justin at the library. He won't mind coming to get me when he finds out why."

He didn't. While they were waiting for him, Juliet asked Megan, "Your party won't be canceled now, will it?"

Megan was stunned. *"The party? Cancel the party? Juliet, Thomas could die! You don't think I care about that stupid party now, do you? I don't care if it's cancelled."*

"You don't mean that," Juliet protested. "I mean, maybe you think you do now, because you're upset. But believe me, you'll be sorry later, when Thomas is okay and you didn't get to celebrate your sixteenth birthday. I know how that feels, Megan."

What was taking Justin so long? *"Juliet, I know you were really disappointed about your party, and I'm sorry about that, but I just don't feel the same way you do. Did. Do. I can have a party any time, but I only have one brother."*

When she arrived at the hospital, Megan hovered near her distraught parents, awaiting news of Thomas's condition. Slowly, she went over the accident in her mind. The red-and-silver bike was new. Those brakes should have worked. Why hadn't they? Had someone deliberately destroyed Thomas's brakes the way Jenny's steering mechanism had been destroyed? Or was it really just, a simple, tragic accident?

No. It wasn't. Or there would have been no tom-tom drawing.

Who would hurt a little kid?

Not Vicki. Even she wouldn't do something that nasty.

Unless . . . unless she was totally crazy. Out of her mind.

Because that's what it would take for someone to target an entire family. And wasn't that just what someone was doing?

Megan watched Juliet take a seat beside Megan's mother. *She doesn't belong there. I belong there.*

It seemed years before the doctor arrived to tell them that Thomas would be a patient at Lakeside Medical Center for some time. He had a fractured pelvis, a broken leg, and a concussion. He was out of surgery now and would sleep all night. They might as well go home and get some rest.

Connie stayed, but she sent her husband and Juliet home, telling them they would have to take her place at Thomas's bedside the next day, so they needed a good night's rest.

When they got home, Megan's father went straight to bed, while Juliet checked the answering machine in the kitchen to see if Justin had called.

There were messages from Hilary, from Cappie, and from Mrs. Tweed at Cut It Again, Sam, informing Miss Logan that the operator scheduled to do Miss Logan's hair on Saturday afternoon had taken ill, but another operator could take care of her beauty needs at two o'clock if that would be all right. If not, could Miss Logan please give them a call?

"I told you to cancel that appointment," Megan said.

Juliet shrugged and concentrated on additional messages. "Oh, golly, Megan, I forgot," she said as Justin's deep voice began speaking. "I'll do it tomorrow, first thing, I promise."

Megan didn't feel like listening to Justin tell Juliet he missed her or he loved her or whatever he was telling her these days. All those things he'd never told Megan. She went upstairs, mentally preparing the speech that would put an end to this nightmare. Surely Juliet would understand that with a second member of her family injured, it was now time for Megan to become herself again.

But when Juliet came upstairs a few minutes later, she surprised Megan with, "Wait till you see what I've got!" Swinging the denim shoulder bag over the bed, she turned it upside down and dumped out its contents. Out came six or seven sheets of folded construction paper and a handful of brightly colored crayons.

It took a minute or so for the booty to register. Then Megan said, *"What is this? Where did you get all this stuff?"*

Juliet grinned. "In Donny Richardson's locker. This is the first chance I've had to show it to you."

"Donny? You broke into his locker? Juliet, what if someone had seen you? Someone like Donny, for instance? If he's the one behind all this terrible stuff and he saw you —"

"Megan, I didn't do it as *you*," Juliet said. "I did

301

it as *me*. So no one could have seen me."

"*As you?*" Megan asked. "*What do you mean, as you?*"

"Megan, I'm still me. I told you that before. I can leave your body if I need to. And I needed to. It was the only way I could check out Donny's locker."

"*You can leave? Where was my body while you were going through Donny's locker?*"

Juliet laughed. "Asleep in the school library with your head down on the desk."

She can leave? Just like that? Whenever she wants?

"Listen, never mind that now," Juliet said. She gathered up the paper and crayons. "I'm going to take this stuff and the drawings you found to the sheriff tomorrow. I figure, if he arrests Donny, things will calm down. And then," she added brightly, "your parents will let you have your party. Especially now that we know Thomas is going to be okay."

"*Juliet, I —* "

"Don't thank me, Megan. My goodness, I owe you so much! This is just my tiny little way of thanking you." Stuffing the colored paper and crayons back into the shoulder bag, she added, "I told you everything would be okay. And it will be. Now I've got to go eat something. I'm starved. Night, Megan."

Her step as she left the room was light and happy.

I should feel like that, too. What Juliet did today,

what she found, doesn't that mean an end to all of this? If the sheriff arrests Donny tomorrow, and why wouldn't he, I won't have to worry about something happening to Juliet before Saturday at midnight. I'll still be here, in this awful place, but it'll only be for two more days and then it will all be over.

So why didn't she feel better? Because she didn't. Not at all.

Chapter 17

When Megan came inside the next morning after a long, lonely night out on the lake, Juliet had already gone.

She must have left early to talk to Sheriff Toomey. Will what she has to show him stop this awful nightmare? It has to!

The room was a mess. There were clothes everywhere, and the closet door stood open. Inside something black and very pink caught Megan's attention.

Megan moved to the closet. Hanging between her new party dress and a pink robe was a short, black, strapless dress with a hot-pink cummerbund and a full skirt. Not the kind of dress anyone wore to a pizza place or the mall or a movie. This was very definitely a party dress.

Where had it come from?

I would never wear a dress like this. It's too sophisticated. More Juliet's speed than mine.

But Juliet wasn't going to the party. If there *was* a party, Juliet wouldn't be going. So why did she need this dress?

Does she have a big date with Justin tonight? Is he taking her some place so special that she had to go shopping?

The date must have been made earlier in the week, because Justin wouldn't suggest a big date with Thomas hurt and in the hospital. In fact, if they'd planned a date, Justin had probably canceled it when he heard about Thomas. Juliet would have to take the dress back.

Megan spent the day at the Medical Center, encouraged by Thomas's condition. He wasn't talking much, lying pale and listless in the bed, but he was conscious. And by late afternoon, he was more concerned about the damage to his bike than his own injuries.

But Megan felt drained and weak. If Sheriff Toomey didn't put Donny away, her father could be hurt next. Tom-tom. Only one Tom was in the hospital so far. Or Juliet could be the next victim. It was lucky that she hadn't been hurt so far, probably because she was always with Justin or Hilary or Barb and Cappie. There really must be safety in numbers.

Hoping for good news, Megan went to school at the end of the day to ask Juliet about her visit to the sheriff's office.

And the first person she saw leaving Philippa was Donny Richardson, unaccompanied by Sheriff Toomey or a deputy, no handcuffs on his wrists. Strangely enough, he looked like an ordinary, lonely boy walking home from high school alone. There was nothing sinister about him.

305

Bitter disappointment drowned Megan. Why hadn't he been arrested? And with the disappointment, feelings of doubt surfaced. Donny Richardson certainly didn't look like a killer.

But wasn't that how killers got away with their terrible deeds . . . by looking ordinary?

Juliet had found the evidence in Donny's locker. He might look ordinary on the outside, but on the inside he had to be evil.

Still worried, Megan continued to look for Juliet. Unsuccessful at school, she decided to try the house.

No one was there. Each room was silent, still, as if waiting patiently to see what would happen next.

Where is Juliet? Megan's cold, empty world suddenly began to spin around her. Something terrible had happened to Juliet. Something that had stopped her from going to the sheriff. That's why she wasn't at the hospital, wasn't at home. With only one more day left in Juliet's week, Megan's worst nightmare was upon her.

If Juliet is hurt or . . . dead . . . what will happen to me? Oh, God, please don't let me stay like this forever! Please! Let me have my life back again!

Juliet could have gone straight to the hospital from school. Racing over there, Megan prayed, *Be there, Juliet, be there!*

She wasn't.

But Sheriff Toomey was.

When Megan saw him, she was terrified. Had he come to tell her parents that the body of their daughter had been discovered, lying in a field somewhere? *I will never be me again. This horrid, empty world is all I'm ever going to know, because Juliet is gone, and I can't switch back now.*

"So," the sheriff said to Thomas, "you're saying you couldn't stop? That you tried and failed?"

He was there to talk about Thomas's accident.

The darkness lifted around Megan. The sheriff was there about Thomas, not Juliet. All hope wasn't lost.

A pale, bruised Thomas nodded. "Is my bike okay?" he asked anxiously. "It's practically brand-new, you know. Mom says you guys took it to check it out. Is it okay?"

The sheriff smiled. "Sure, son. Your bike'll be fine. One of my deputies took it over to Mickey Ryan's bike place. He can fix anything. It'll be good as new in a couple of days."

"Yeah," Thomas grumbled, "but it'll never be the same. Darned truck."

When the sheriff asked Megan's parents to come outside and speak to him, Megan followed.

In the corridor, Sheriff Toomey shook his graying head. "Go figure," he said. "The guy in the truck says he tried to stop and couldn't, just like your son. We're looking into it, but I don't expect we'll find anything more than we found in the Winn girl's accident. Or your accident, Connie. No leads, no clues." Another grim shake of the head. "I remember, thirty, forty years ago, when your mom was young and theirs was the only house out there on the lake. Owned twenty acres. Everyone else lived in town. Martha told me they never locked their

doors or windows, not even at night. No reason to."
He let out a weary sigh as he turned to leave.
"Times sure have changed."

He never said a word about crayons or drawings
or warnings of any kind.

Why had Juliet changed her mind about telling
him? And where *was* she?

She was home, Megan discovered when, desperate, she returned to the house again. A wave of
relief washed over her when she moved into the
bedroom and found Juliet rummaging around in the
closet.

"*Juliet, where have you been?*" Megan demanded. The terrible things she'd imagined happening to Juliet during the past few hours had
nearly driven her crazy. "*I've been looking all over
for you.*"

"Justin and I went for a ride."

"*A ride? You knew I was waiting to hear what
Sheriff Toomey said, and you went for a stupid
ride? I thought something terrible had happened to
you.*"

Juliet laughed. "Well, I'd scold you about your
overactive imagination, but if you didn't have an
imagination, you probably never would have heard
my voice in the first place."

Megan had been too terrified to be so easily pla-
cated now. "*You should have gone to the hospital
after school. Mom and Dad could use some
support.*"

"I was there first thing this morning. Thomas
seemed so much better, I decided to come home and

308

rest up for my date with Justin tonight. We were going out to dinner downtown."

The black dress.

"But Justin decided that wouldn't be such a hot idea, with Thomas in the hospital. So we're going over to the Medical Center for a while and we'll check in on Thomas and Jenny. Then we're going to Justin's house. Cappie and Barb and Hilary are coming, too, I think. It'll be fun."

"Juliet, did you talk to Sheriff Toomey? What did he say?"

"Oh, Megan, he wasn't even there. I rushed right over there when I got up this morning. Didn't even eat breakfast. But he wasn't there, and his deputy was talking on the phone for hours. If I'd waited, I'd have been late to school, and you told me not to cut any more classes. I went back again after classes, but he wasn't there then, either."

He'd been at the hospital.

"Juliet! This is not a simple shoplifting crime we're talking about! My friends and my family have almost been killed! It can't wait! The only reason I didn't tell you last night that we had to switch back right away was you let me think Donny would be arrested today. Now you tell me you haven't even seen the sheriff yet. So nothing has changed, Juliet, nothing at all. You're . . . I'm . . . we're still in as much danger as we always were. Something could happen to you at any minute, and that would be the end of me. You said so yourself."

Hearing the intensity in her voice brought fear to Juliet's eyes. She still had one more night and day. "Megan, think a minute. Thomas is in the hospital, and your parents are safe there, too. They're staying the night, they told me so. And I'll be safe at Justin's house. Nothing more is going to happen tonight. I'll see the sheriff first thing tomorrow, I promise. And by the way, Megan, this should cheer you up. The party is still on."

"*It is?*" Megan asked, surprised.

"Yes. Isn't that wonderful? Your mom said she wanted to show the whole village that the Logans weren't going to be intimidated. She said it would do everyone a world of good to have a party. And Thomas would still be in the hospital, asleep, by the time the party started, anyway."

"*I still can't believe it,*" Megan said.

"Well, it was your mother's decision to 'carry on' as she said."

Megan was silent for a minute as Juliet looked into the closet for an outfit for that night.

"*Juliet, where did that dress come from? The one right there in the closet? Black, with pink trim?*"

"Oh, Megan!" Juliet cried, "you are such a snoop! I bought that dress for you as a surprise, and now you've spoiled it."

"*I have a dress.*" Juliet had said the same thing about the hair appointment, that it was for Megan. But Megan hadn't wanted her hair done any more than she wanted the black dress. Juliet knew the dress wasn't her type. "*I don't need another dress.*"

"Megan," Juliet said firmly, "after all the work I've done with Justin this week, you're not going to blow it by showing up at your party in a dress as juvenile as that green one, are you?"

"You said it was pretty. Before, in the mirror, you said it was a great dress."

Juliet shrugged and began digging through the pile of shoes on the closet floor for a suitable pair. "It's okay, Megan, but it's not very . . . interesting."

Interesting? She meant sexy. *"Juliet, I'm not wearing that black dress to my party. I'm wearing the one I picked out. So you can take that one back tomorrow."*

"Oh, all right. But I think it's gorgeous, and I think you're crazy." Her words drifted off as she unearthed the shoes she wanted and slipped them on.

It's hard to believe she and my grandmother were friends, Megan thought. *They aren't anything alike.*

While Juliet was dressing in the white skirt and a royal-blue short-sleeved sweater, Megan remembered Sheriff Toomey's remark about her grandmother's house being the only one on the lake forty years ago. Then where had Juliet lived?

"Juliet, where did you live? When you lived here, I mean? Was it on this street?"

Before Juliet could answer, the telephone shrilled.

"Oh, hi, Cappie," Juliet said when she'd picked up the receiver. "You're going to be at Justin's tonight, aren't you? The only reason my folks are letting me out of the house at night is I'll be where there are lots of people and two of them, Justin's parents, are grown-ups." She wrinkled her nose in distaste. "I guess it's better than nothing."

Megan was swept up in a wave of overpowering envy. Maybe a night at Justin's surrounded by friends was only "better than nothing" to Juliet, but it sounded wonderful to her. She couldn't wait to be back in that world again, *her* world. Only one more night and one more day . . .

Megan didn't remind Juliet that this was her final outing. Why ruin it for her?

Hearing the arrival of her parents downstairs, Megan went to see how her brother was. Juliet could be on the phone for hours.

According to her parents' conversation, Thomas was doing much better, but Connie still intended to return to the hospital as soon as she'd showered and changed.

The idea of her father being alone in the house until Juliet came home later only made Megan more anxious. Anything could happen. *I can't keep an eye on both Dad and Juliet when they're in two different places. Why didn't Juliet invite everyone over here? She knows how worried I am about the tom-tom drawing.*

Megan hurried upstairs, intent on asking Juliet to call everyone and switch the gathering to the lake. That way, her father wouldn't be in the house alone.

But she was too late. When she entered the room, it was empty. Juliet was gone.

Chapter 18

Megan spent a long, lonely night, not leaving the house until her father went to bed. Even then, she stayed in the den for a while, waiting for Juliet and thinking.

Only one more day . . . and then she'd be herself again. Thank goodness nothing had happened to Juliet so far. It was a miracle, really, that she was still okay. And by this time tomorrow night, the whole awful week would be over — nothing more than a horrible memory. If only Sheriff Toomey would arrest Donny — then the horror really would be over.

Tiring of waiting for Juliet, Megan left the house, assured that her father was safe in his bed, and went out to roam the lake.

This is the last time I'll ever be able to do this, but I won't miss it at all. I'm not a bird or a bat, and I shouldn't be flitting around out here with them — especially when so much is wrong in my own world.

It was very late when she returned to the house.

Juliet was in bed, sound asleep, her clothes in a pile on the floor beside the bed.

Megan was disappointed. And surprised. She hadn't expected Juliet to be able to sleep at all, knowing that she had only one more day. *If it were me, I'd spend the time until morning walking along the lakefront, maybe with Justin, waiting for the sunrise, squeezing the juice out of every last minute.*

Thinking that surprised Megan. It didn't sound like her. It sounded like . . . someone who wanted to fill up every minute of life with interesting things, instead of withdrawing from it by living in a dream world.

Maybe that's because I'm so terrified that I won't get to do those things ever again. That something will happen to keep me from doing them. Maybe that's why I feel different.

When morning finally arrived, Megan was torn between a ferocious anxiety on this last day and a tentative sense of relief. It was almost over. Almost.

Juliet went to see the sheriff as promised, and Megan went with her. He wasn't there. The deputy in charge said he would be back around dinnertime, which seemed to Megan eons away. But there was no choice other than to wait.

I should be getting good at that. But I'm not.

When they returned from running errands, they found Megan's father up on a ladder on the stone terrace, stringing brightly colored lights above the lakefront lawn.

Since Juliet was safely home, Megan concentrated on keeping an eye on her father. When he climbed down from the ladder to get a glass of iced tea in the house, she followed. Juliet wasn't in the kitchen or the living room. Megan searched the first floor thoroughly. No Juliet. She hadn't gone out again, had she?

Anxiously Megan went upstairs and into the bedroom.

Juliet was lying on the bed, her eyes closed, legs straight, arms at her sides. She was wrapped in the white terrycloth robe. The shades were drawn, the room dark, lighted only by a cluster of short, squat candles on a blue metal tray on the nightstand.

Dumbfounded, Megan thought, *What is she doing? What are all these candles for? It looks like a séance. Is she taking a nap on her last day? That doesn't make any sense.*

Candle shadows flickered across Juliet's face, giving it an eerie yellow-gray glow. She was lying so perfectly still. Not a finger curled, not a muscle twitched, not a lash blinked. Her skin looked smooth and waxen, like the face of a department store mannequin.

Suddenly there was a startled shout from the terrace. It was immediately followed by the sound of shattering glass, a slam that shook the house, and then silence.

Juliet sat bolt upright, wide awake, and jumped from the bed. "What was that?"

Megan flew to the terrace, with Juliet right behind her.

315

The ladder had fallen. The upper half of it had thrust itself through the big picture window Megan's father had installed less than a month ago. He was lying on his back in the midst of shards and slivers and chunks of glass. A gash on his cheek bled profusely, and his hands and sandaled feet were measled with red. But he was conscious and seemed more abashed than pained.

"Dad," Juliet scolded, rushing over to help him up, "you shouldn't be up on the ladder in sandals. It's dangerous."

"No kidding." He got up very carefully. "But . . . it wasn't my fault. The ladder just . . . tipped right over."

A pensive Megan watched from a distance as Juliet helped Tom Logan douse his wounds with antiseptic and bandage those that needed it. Megan couldn't help feeling that something very weird was going on. Had Juliet really been asleep when that ladder fell? She hadn't looked asleep. People didn't look like that when they were sleeping. They looked relaxed. Sometimes their mouths hung open and their bodies got all loose, as if their bones had been removed.

But Juliet had been as stiff and rigid as a piece of wood. Like . . . a statue or a slab of cardboard. Like . . . there was no one in there.

She said she could leave my body any time. When she left before, it was to look through Donny's locker. What was she doing this time when she left? When the ladder fell? Where did she go? Someplace far away? Or . . . only as far as the terrace?

Worry and suspicion began to gnaw at Megan. Wasn't it just a bit too coincidental that the ladder had fallen at the exact moment when Juliet didn't seem to be in Megan's body?

But that was crazy. Juliet had no reason to harm Megan's father. Why would she?

She wouldn't.

I'm being ridiculous. It's all this tension, trying to get through this last day.

But the worries wouldn't go away. Megan watched Juliet wash her father's wounds with a soft rag. *Juliet was never worried about something happening to her,* Megan thought. *I worried about that all by myself. And I thought that was because she couldn't be hurt physically. Because she had already lost her life and had nothing to lose.*

Then Megan thought of something else. *She can leave my body so easily. She can go anywhere, do anything, without leaving a trace. No fingerprints. No one can see or hear her. There would never be any witnesses because Juliet would be invisible.*

Megan thought about the night of her mother's accident. Juliet had been with Justin in the den, watching a movie. Megan had watched movies with Justin more than once. He became completely lost in them. Several times, Megan had left to get popcorn and drinks, and he'd never even noticed her absence. It would only have taken Juliet a second to leave Megan's body and dart out to the dock to attack her mother. Justin wouldn't even have noticed that the girl beside him was as quiet and motionless as a doll.

Maybe Juliet knew all along that no disaster would befall her because . . . because she *is* the disaster. *Think about it,* Megan told herself. *Makes sense, right?*

No. No! Juliet couldn't have done those things. It's not possible.

Juliet helping Megan's father made a nice picture: the loving daughter taking care of an injured parent with tenderness.

Was it fake? Had Juliet herself *caused* those wounds?

No, she couldn't have, Megan realized. *She couldn't have done any of it, for one very good reason. She had waited too long for this one short week of life. She would never have deliberately set out to wreak havoc on her precious seven days.*

But look at her! Think, Megan, think! Does she look like someone whose time is almost up? Is she nervous? Depressed? Is there a look of dread in those eyes?

No. Not at all. Juliet is as calm and peaceful as the lake at night.

Juliet finished her nursing duties and, warning Tom Logan to "stay away from ladders," ran lightly up the stairs.

The dark, devilish thought, once born, became relentless. It crept up on Megan steadily, like the big, black, hairy spider of her dream. It circled around her, teasing, taunting, wrapping her in its web.

318

The dress. The black dress with the pink cummerbund. The hair appointment.

They hadn't been intended for Megan. They had been intended for Juliet.

Because Juliet had never meant to have only one short week. She had never planned to give back Megan's life.

She was going to keep it for herself.

Juliet was going to have her birthday party after all.

Juliet had tricked her! Right from the beginning . . .

Megan raced up the stairs and into the bedroom.

Why? Why would Juliet do this? She had sounded so sad and sweet in the mirror, so full of yearning.

But she had done terrible, vicious things.

Why?

Juliet looked up when she felt Megan enter the room. The blinds were still closed, the flickering candles providing the only light.

"You know, don't you?" she asked calmly. "You've guessed."

"Yes. But I don't understand any of it."

"You want to know why? Is that why you're here?"

"Yes."

Juliet settled back on the bed, her skin yellow-gray from the candle shadows. Expressionless, she said, "Then I'll tell you. Why not? It's too late now for the truth to do you any good."

Megan waited.

"It's because of Martha."

"Martha? My grandmother?"

Juliet nodded. The candlelight transformed her eyes into glowing, greenish-yellow coals. "Yes, Martha, your grandmother."

Again, Megan waited.

"She was my stepsister."

Chapter 19

There was a long silence before Megan said slowly, *"That's not true. My grandmother only had one stepsister. Her name was Etta. She died three months after my great-grandmother married her father."*

"Etta!" Juliet spit the word out with disgust. "I am *Julietta*. My new stepmother — your great grandmother — said my name was too fanciful and ordered everyone to call me Etta. Horrid name! But my father said I had to respect my stepmother's wishes." Juliet's voice was her own again.

"I don't believe you."

"I was fifteen when my father married Lily Lewis." Juliet's upper lip curled in a sneer. "I hated her on sight. I hated Martha even more, her and her stupid brothers!"

Megan's mind was reeling. *"Why did you hate them?"* she whispered.

"Because we didn't need them. We didn't need anyone. I told my father when my mother died that I'd take care of him." Juliet's voice lifted, became

321

happier. "It was wonderful for a long time. I was my father's hostess when he entertained. I had beautiful dresses to wear, and everyone treated me as if I were grown-up. Then," her voice hardened, "we came here on a vacation and he met that horrible Lily. We moved here, to this awful place, and everything changed."

In shock, Megan spoke slowly. *"That's why you never told me where you lived. You lived here, in this house! I wondered when Sheriff Toomey said there weren't any other houses out here that long ago."*

"I hated this house. A country house, boring and dull. I was used to living in the city. Nobody here knew anything about museums and art galleries and theater. Instead of dinner parties, they had picnics!" Her voice oozed contempt.

"I've seen pictures of my great-grandmother. She was very beautiful."

Agitation made Juliet's voice erratic. Her sentences came in spurts. "She was shameless . . . chasing him. A widow, with three children to support . . . she knew a good thing when she saw it. I tried to warn my father that she only wanted his money, but he wouldn't listen to me."

"He must have really loved her."

"Love? Love?" Juliet screamed, her features sharpening, her skin draining of healthy color. "We didn't need her or her dull, stupid children. But he married her, and we moved to this awful house and that horrid lake." Her voice lowered, became edged

322

with bitterness. "He never had any time for me after that."

"No one has ever talked about that time very much," Megan, completely stunned, murmured. *"I knew you died, but I never knew how or why. No one ever said."*

"Well, of *course* they didn't! If *you* had killed someone, would your family talk about it?"

Megan gasped. *"Killed? You said it was a boat accident that took your life."*

"It wasn't the accident that killed me!" Juliet shouted. "Our boat hit a rock and we were both thrown overboard. But the crash didn't kill either of us."

"Us?"

"Martha and me."

The candles flickered as the wind, growing stronger every minute, rattled against the closed blinds, as if knocking to get in.

"I was struck unconscious. But Martha wasn't. She wasn't hurt at all. She could have saved me. But she didn't. Your sweet, kind grandmother," Juliet said with hatred, "clung to the side of the boat and watched while I sank like a stone. And then she watched me drown."

"She wouldn't have. Never."

Juliet jumped up from the bed and began a wild pacing, back and forth across the faded blue carpet. There was nothing in her face now that resembled Megan. Her skin was dirty-white, her mouth pinched and twisted, and thin strands of her hair

323

traced a spiderweb across her cheeks.

Megan watched in disbelief. She doesn't even look human anymore, she thought, and wondered how she could ever do battle with such a creature. Because it was clear now that, to save herself, she was going to have to fight Juliet.

But *how?*

"You can't have my life, Juliet. I won't let you."

"She stole *my* life!" Juliet cried. "She hated me as much as I hated her." Her eyes grew colder. "I would never have got into that boat with her, but my father insisted. He said it was my fault she was lonely. He implied that I had stolen all of her friends."

"I think you did," Megan said softly. *"I think you hurt her because you were jealous when your father found a new family."*

Outside, the wind began to pick up speed. It blew across the lake with a low moaning sound that penetrated the walls of the bedroom, bringing with it a chilly dampness.

Juliet's eyes began to glow yellow like the candle flame. "I don't care what *you* think! But I cared what my father thought. I hated Martha for turning him against me. And I told her so. In the boat, when we were out on the lake where my father couldn't hear."

"You fought with her?"

"I told her I hated her. Martha said some terrible things to me. I ordered her to turn the boat around. She refused." The heels of Juliet's sandals dug into the carpet with each angry step. "I tried to take the oars from her. But she fought me. Then we hit the rock."

As she neared the window, the wind-tossed curtains whipped around her, shrouding her in white lace. "And Martha let me drown."

"I don't think so. I think she tried to save you. You couldn't have known, because you were unconscious. I think you hate her so much, you don't want to believe she tried."

Juliet turned away from the window, lace still coiled around her neck and shoulders. She ripped it away from her. "*She* was the one who should have died! I was the pretty one, the popular one. Dull old Martha with her books and her piano and her bird-watching, *she* got to live!"

Then, before Megan could respond, Juliet stopped her pacing and faced the big oval mirror. "But it's all right now. It is. I'm getting even, at last. You've seen for yourself that I, too, can hurt people, just like Martha hurt me." She smiled an evil smile. "Your mother never knew what happened to her. Neither did Hilary."

"You did it all? Everything?"

"The car accident, Thomas's bicycle, your father's ladder. Even the drawings. I did every bit of it. And loved doing it."

"But why us?" Megan asked, bewildered. *"My friends and family never did anything to you. Jenny, Barb, Hilary, they never even knew you existed. Why did you try to kill them?"*

"Because *you* care about them. And Martha cared about *you*. I never had the chance to pay *her*

325

back. Until you moved in. I knew she loved you. And I knew I could take my precious revenge on you and your family and friends. It was even better that way."

"We never did anything to you," Megan cried angrily. *"And I don't think my grandmother did, either."*

Juliet's face contorted in rage. "What I've done is simple justice. Your grandmother loved you. I couldn't punish her, so I punished you. You love your friends and family. Not one of them has remained untouched. Can't you see that's justice?"

"You let me think it was Donny. Or Vicki. You wanted me to think that. And they hadn't done anything. It was all you."

"They didn't matter. They're unimportant. And now you, your grandmother's favorite person, will take my place, in *my* world, and I will take yours. Forever. That, too, is justice." She smiled vaguely, her anger gone. "You know, Megan, it is uncanny how much you look like her." She laughed wildly, a sound that rocketed off the walls and slammed into Megan. "Isn't that funny? I'll spend my whole life looking exactly like the woman I hate most. Are you laughing, Megan? Don't you think that's funny?"

Frozen in shock, Megan heard the back door slam. Her father was returning to the hospital to be with Thomas and her mother.

"Now," Juliet said briskly, "I have to get ready to go out. Justin broke our date because of your silly little brother's accident." She giggled. "I'll have to go find Justin, won't I?" Her face began to rearrange itself into Megan's features. Her voice became Megan's again. "You do get it that the only reason Justin wasn't hurt is that I want him for myself, don't you? I'm going to take very good care of him for you, I promise."

Megan, shaken to the core, watched as Juliet went to the closet to pick out an outfit. Fighting to gather her senses together, Megan said in an unsteady voice, *"I am Megan, and I want to be me again."*

Nothing happened.

She said it louder, *"I am Megan, and I want to be* me *again!"*

Still nothing.

"Forget it," Juliet said calmly. "I left out one very important detail when you agreed to switch. Remember when I said your consent was necessary for the trade? Well, so is mine. That's fair, isn't it? I guess I forgot to mention that part. It's supposed to be an honor kind of thing. You give me your life for a week, and I give it back, willingly." She laughed. "Only I seem to have misplaced my honor. Can't find it anywhere." Her face twisted in anger again. "I guess I lost it when I drowned in that lake, thanks to your grandmother."

Holding up a red leather skirt and examining it carefully, Juliet said, "What do you think your chances are of getting my willing consent to switch back before midnight tonight, which happens to be all the time you have left?" Her laugh this time was almost a cackle. "I'd say that's about as likely as Justin wishing I were you again."

"*Juliet, you can't!*" Megan shrieked. "*You can't do this. You have to give my life back to me. You can't keep it!*"

"Just watch me!"

A dizzied, tormented Megan watched in revulsion as Juliet preened before the dresser mirror. *That's my face, my body . . . and no one will know that the inside of it is evil and decay, like rotten fruit.*

"*Juliet, you had your week. I gave that to you. You can't pay me back for that by stealing what's mine.*"

"Oh, yes I can. And I'm going to."

Satisfied with her appearance, Juliet moved to the door. "See you, Meg," she said cheerfully. Then she stopped and slapped herself lightly on one cheek, laughing. "What am I saying? I won't be seeing you at all, will I? As of midnight, you're history."

"*I'm not leaving, Juliet,*" Megan promised grimly. "*I'm not giving up. I'll get back what's mine before midnight.*"

Juliet's laugh was scornful. "Don't try to scare me, Megan. You're no match for me. At midnight, the clock in the den downstairs will go *bong, bong,* twelve times, and you will disappear like a puff of smoke. Forever." She grinned. "Better you than me."

"*Juliet, stop! Wait! Please, you can't —*"

328

"Kind of like Cinderella." Juliet opened the door. "Except that you won't turn into a pumpkin. You'll turn into . . . nothing. Absolutely nothing!"

"How can you be so evil?" Megan cried. *"I hate you!"*

The smile disappeared. The eyes became cold, green glass. "It isn't me you should hate, Megan. You should curse the day Martha Lewis was born. As I have cursed it for forty-six years."

Alone in his room, Justin had been thinking about Megan. He was probably being loopy minding the change in her. Most guys would have been wild about the new, livelier, more affectionate, girl he was spending so much time with these days.

But the truth was, he missed the "old" Megan. The one he could talk to about anything while she listened, and always understood. The Megan who never flirted with other guys, and was nice to people, and cared about her family.

What had happened to that Megan? Hilary blamed it on raging hormones, due to a sixteenth birthday coming up fast.

Then Justin remembered a comment Megan had made a few days ago. Had that been last week? Or this week? What was it she had said? "Something weird is going on at my house." And she'd said more than that, too. Something about death . . . if only Justin could remember what it was. Maybe then he'd understand why she'd changed. Or why all those horrible things had started happening to her family.

What had Megan said? And why hadn't he listened?

Justin sat up very straight in the hard-backed wooden chair. Megan's best friends, her mother, her brother, all had been hurt. Why hadn't he realized that she could be next?

Justin jumped to his feet and ran out of the room.

Even as Megan reeled in shock and terror, she was conscious of the time passing. There wasn't much left.

The only thing Megan knew for sure was that she wanted her life. Juliet couldn't have it. It didn't belong to her. And Megan was going to get it back.

But how?

Juliet had said she had to give her consent for the reverse switch. How would she ever get it? Megan tried desperately to concentrate, but she was so frightened. And the clock on her dresser ticked away stubbornly.

Juliet would have to give it up. Willingly. What would make her do that?

Think, Megan, think! There has to be a way! Juliet would obviously never give up out of the goodness of her heart, that was for sure. No, Megan would have to do something to make Juliet *want* to let go. She'd have to scare her. But what was Juliet afraid of? Then Megan remembered the scene at Lickety-Split, when Justin had suggested a boat ride.

The lake. Juliet was terrified of the lake.

How terrified? Enough to make her leave Me-

330

gan's body willingly to escape the deep, dark water?

And how would she get Juliet out on that water?

She'll never go near it. Not for me. I can't make her go out there.

But . . . was there a chance she'd go out on the lake with someone she liked and trusted? Someone she liked being alone with? Someone like . . . Justin?

Megan's mind raced. *Was it possible? But how would I communicate with Justin? Juliet didn't say I could. Still . . . we both have open minds and we're such good friends. . . . And he acts like he's in love with Juliet, which means maybe, maybe he's in love with* me. *It's worth a try. If only I can find him before Juliet does.*

Megan went in search of Justin.

Justin made it to the Logan house in ten minutes flat. No one answered his ring. They were probably at the hospital with Thomas.

It was late. They'd be home soon. He'd wait. He really needed to talk to Megan.

Justin went down and sat on the dock. To wait for Megan.

Chapter 20

Megan found Justin sitting on the dock behind her house. The wind had died down, and the lake was empty of boats. Everything was peaceful and quiet, as if nothing were wrong. But it was — terribly wrong. What if Justin wasn't able to hear her?

She'd be lost. At midnight, she would disappear forever.

He has to hear me. He has to! Oh, please, please, Justin hear me!

"Justin, it's Megan. Can you hear me?"

The moon made little silver ripples on the water, a boat's motor died somewhere in the distance, and an owl called out a question, but Justin didn't move. His long legs dangled over the dock, and he trailed a long, thick branch back and forth in the water. He gave no sign that he had heard Megan.

"Justin, please hear me! It's important! I'm right here. Open your mind and listen."

Justin lifted his head, tipped it slightly. But he said nothing.

"*I can't do this without your help. You have to hear me, Justin. It's me, Megan.*"

This time, Justin looked around. Although he saw nothing but water and darkness he *felt* something. Megan was near. He knew it. "Megan?" he said tentatively. "Where are you?"

Sudden warmth enveloped Megan. Justin had felt her presence. There was hope. "*Yes, Justin, it's me. I know you can't see me, but I'm here. All I want you to do is listen. Will you do that, Justin?*"

He continued to peer into the darkness. There were lights all along the shore, some from docks, others from houses close to the water. But as the moon took refuge behind a cloud, the darkness thickened.

"*Even if we had lights,*" Megan explained, "*you wouldn't be able to see me. So just listen!*"

"If you're hiding," he said, "you'd better give it up. I'm not in the mood for games."

"*I'm not hiding, Justin, I promise.*"

Justin climbed to his feet. His mouth looked grim. "I don't get you, Megan. Playing games after everything that's happened. Doesn't seem like you." He uttered a short, harsh laugh. "But then, lately you just don't seem like yourself. I miss the old Megan, the one I knew so well."

"*You still know me well, Justin, or you wouldn't be able to hear me.*"

"It's so strange, Megan. I know you're here — I can feel it." Justin's eyes explored the dock area. "But I can't see you anywhere."

Through an open window, Megan heard the

grandfather clock in the den strike the quarter-hour. Quarter past eleven. She had exactly forty-five minutes to explain this whole thing to Justin and enlist his help in getting rid of Juliet. That couldn't possibly be enough time.

"I'm not hiding, Justin. I promise. I need to tell you something. You're going to find it very hard to believe, but you must. My life depends on it. And you know I'd never lie to you, not ever."

"Megan," Justin said slowly, "does this have something to do with what you were trying to tell me a few days ago — about the strange things going on in your house?"

"Yes, Justin."

"I wish I'd listened to you then," Justin said as he sat down on the dock. "Well, I'm ready to listen to you now. And I hope it's not too late."

"So do I," Megan agreed. *"So do I."*

Telling him the story was harder than Megan had imagined. When she'd traded with Juliet, she had believed she was doing the right thing. How could she have known that Juliet was deceitful, vengeful . . . *evil?*

"The reason you can't see me, Justin," she began, *"is that . . . I've traded places with a . . . with someone who died . . . a long time ago."*

"What?"

"I know, I know how it sounds, Justin, but please, just hear me out. It's really important that you listen and that you believe me."

"You traded places with a . . . ghost? Is that what you're telling me? Megan, come on. Quit kidding around. I'm in no mood for this." The disbelief in his voice chilled Megan.

But she had to keep trying. *"It's true, Justin. She was my grandmother's stepsister. She showed up a week ago, in that old mirror in my bedroom, and she asked me to trade places with her for one week. At first I said no. I was scared. Terrified. But she kept begging me. I started to feel sorry for her."*

"You were talking to a ghost in your mirror? Megan . . ."

"Just listen to me, Justin, please. She said that all she wanted was one week. And after I'd thought about it, one week didn't seem like so much. It seemed like such a little thing. And she was so sad and seemed so sweet."

"A little thing? To give your life to somebody else?" Justin's voice held amazement, but the disbelief was gone. He could hear the urgency in her voice, and he trusted her. "Why didn't you tell me? I guess you tried to — but I was too worried about Jenny's accident to pay any attention."

"I wanted to tell you everything. But I couldn't. She said not to tell anyone. I thought she was sweet and nice, and it wouldn't hurt to give her just one little week out of a whole lifetime. Does that . . . do you think that's crazy?"

Justin sat in stunned silence. "I knew there was something . . . but this . . . I'd never have guessed this." He shook his head, his eyes focused on the water.

"I thought Juliet was gentle and good, and I felt

335

sorry for her. But she isn't. She's evil. She did all those things . . . caused all the accidents — Jenny's, Hilary's, my mom's, Thomas's. She hated my grandmother, and she's getting even. That's why she's here.

"*Anyway . . . we were supposed to trade back tonight at midnight. That's what she told me. But . . . but Juliet never intended to. She was lying the whole time. I just didn't figure that out — until today.*"

"But, Megan . . . what does that mean?"

"*It means . . . that if I can't find a way to force her to switch back before midnight tonight, Juliet will keep my life, and I'll be trapped in this horrible place . . . forever.*"

Megan had told her story. There was nothing more to say. She could feel the seconds ticking away, her time running out. Would Justin believe her?

Justin sat silently for a long moment. Then he said, "So, how are we going to make her switch back?"

He was going to help. He believed her, and he was going to help. "*Oh, thank you, Justin! Thank you!*" But there was still a battle ahead of them, Megan thought. "*The only thing I could think of was this: Juliet is terrified of the lake. It's where she died. Remember that night in Lickety-Split when you talked about a boat ride? Remember how scared she got? I thought, if we could get her out on the lake, maybe she'd be so frightened, she'd leave*

336

my body. *That's what has to happen. She has to leave it willingly."*

Justin stood up, but he didn't know where to look. The sound of Megan's voice came from all around him, not just from one place. "What do you want me to do?"

"You have to find her, Justin. Right away. There isn't much time left. I'll help look for her. And I'll stay with you the whole time, but I'll have to be careful. If she senses that I'm with you, she'll know there's something wrong, and you'll never get her out on the lake."

There were no boats on the lake now. It was quiet, as if it had gone to sleep for the night. Justin looked out over the black water. "If she's that afraid, what makes you think I can get her out on the lake?"

"You can do it, Justin. I know you can. Promise her a special romantic boat ride, just the two of you in the moonlight. She loves being alone with you and she loves romance. It's our only hope."

"You think she'll agree to it?" Justin's voice was doubtful.

"Her fear of the lake is the only thing I know for sure about Juliet. So I don't have any other plan if this one doesn't work. That's why it has to work. I know the two of us together can beat her. I know we can!"

The determination in her voice weakened Justin's doubts.

"Come on, then," he said, and added with a wondering laugh, "wherever you are. Let's go get Juliet and offer her a nice midnight boat ride."

"Before *midnight*," Megan warned as Justin began running up the slope toward the house. *"Midnight would be too late."*

Under the terrace lights, Justin glanced at his watch. It was eleven-thirty. Drawing in a quick breath of alarm, he began running faster.

And ran into Juliet as he rounded a corner of the house. He almost called out her real name in surprise but caught himself just in time.

"Justin!" Juliet cried, obviously happy to see him. "I've been looking all over for you! This town is completely dead tonight." She made a face of disgust. "They're all a bunch of scaredy-cats. There was absolutely no one at the mall, so Cappie and I went to a movie. The theater was practically empty. And no one was eating pizza, either." A note of petulance crept into her voice. "Where have you been, Justin?"

Megan, staying a safe distance away, saw Justin struggle to speak. It was one thing to listen to a story about Megan changing places with Juliet, and something else to be staring at the proof.

Snap out of it, Justin! There's no time for that! And if you're not careful, she'll guess that you know something. Remember the boat ride. Get her down to the dock. Hurry!

"Hey, gorgeous," Justin said then, throwing an arm around Juliet's shoulders, "I was looking for you, too. I've got a great idea. Your folks aren't

338

home. I checked. So how about if you and me take a little boat ride, just the two of us? I know this great little island on the other side of the cove. . . ."

Caught off-guard, Juliet pulled away from him, backing up against the house. Her eyes were wild with fear.

Good. That's a start. I want her *to be afraid.*

"I've . . . I've got a terrible headache, Justin," Juliet stammered. "I came home to get some aspirin and go to bed. I don't want to be all puffy-eyed for my party tomorrow."

Justin pulled her close to his chest. "I thought you said you were looking for me," he said softly.

"Well, I was. The headache just came on, a minute ago. It's a real killer, honest."

"Oh, come on, Meg. Just the two of us. A nice, quiet boat ride out to this little island I know is just what you need."

Juliet shook her head. "No, honestly, Justin, I can't. I told you, I don't like the lake anymore. My mom — "

"Oh, your mom's fine," Justin said impatiently. "You're being silly." He reached down and tipped her chin up toward him. Smiling down at her, he said, "Megan, I thought you were really growing up this week. You seemed so different, like you were ready to stop being Mommy and Daddy's little girl. But if you're afraid to be alone with me . . ."

Juliet hesitated. Megan knew she was thinking that being Megan wouldn't be nearly as much fun

339

if she didn't have Justin. "Why can't we be together inside?" she whispered. "You said no one was home."

Hurry, Justin, hurry! Make her quit stalling!

"Juliet," Justin said firmly, "I am going for a boat ride. If you won't come, I'll find someone else who will." He paused, then added, "Vicki loves the water."

The den window was open. Breaking the stillness, the chime signaled the quarter-hour.

Fifteen minutes! I have only fifteen minutes to get rid of Juliet. That isn't nearly enough time! She's going to win. Oh, no, she can't! She can't win!

Justin softened his voice. "A moonlit boat ride," he said softly, holding Juliet close. "What could be more romantic?"

Without waiting for an answer, he placed a firm grip on Juliet's elbow and began leading her down to the dock. When they reached it, she pulled back. "There's no moon," she complained, her voice shaking. "What fun is a midnight boat ride without a moon?"

"It's just hiding behind a cloud. It'll come out in a minute." Justin grinned. "It's waiting for you to make up your mind. C'mon, let's go!" He jumped into the motorboat and held out his hand to Juliet.

But she hung back. As Justin started the motor and the lantern came on, Megan could see that Juliet's face was pale and strained. She was chewing on her lower lip.

"Megan, what's with you?" he said, deliberately layering each word with suspicion. "You're looking at this boat like it's a two-headed monster. You're acting really weird."

Then there was one long, scary moment as Juliet debated with herself. Megan could see her wavering between her horror of the lake and her determination to hold onto Justin. She didn't want to lose him now, now that she thought she *owned* Megan's life.

Megan waited. *She's thinking the boat ride will be a short one. She's thinking that it's not as if she actually has to go into the water. And she's wondering just how much fun my life would be without Justin in it.*

"Nothing's more romantic," Justin said softly, "than two people alone on an island at night."

Juliet stepped into the boat.

341

Chapter 21

Juliet took a seat, her hands clenched into tight little fists, as Justin started the motor.

"You'll love this place, Megan," Justin said soothingly. "It's very private."

"I can't stay long." Her voice was nervous. Her eyes swept the lake as the boat picked up speed. Megan knew she was searching the water for rocks, although there were none in this open part of the lake. "It's late, and I've got to get some sleep so I'll look really good tomorrow." She was sitting stiffly on the seat, her hands gripping the sides of the boat. "You haven't forgotten my party, have you?"

My *party*, *you mean*, Megan thought angrily. She remained a cautious distance behind the boat, fearful that Juliet would sense her presence.

The boat began to veer toward the cove.

Juliet's body shot up straight in her seat, propelled by alarm. "Justin, what are you doing?" Anxiety made her voice shrill. "There's no island over there. Just the cove."

"Have to go through the cove to reach the island," he said cheerfully. "There's a little opening off to one side. Relax, Megan, we'll be there in no time."

"No! I don't *want* to go to the cove! I hate that place!"

Justin half turned his head to look at Juliet. "Since when?" he said, a hint of mockery in his voice. "I thought you loved the cove."

"I don't. It's too dangerous. People die there."

"Tell you what," he told Juliet calmly, "I'll just scoot around the edge, okay? We'll be there in no time. Relax."

Megan could see Juliet fighting with herself. Megan was worried. Her plan wasn't working. They'd been on the lake for a while, but Juliet hadn't given up.

And there were only ten minutes left.

Would being in the cove — the rocky, treacherous spot where Juliet had lost her life so long ago — be enough? Would that scare Juliet away forever?

What if it didn't?

Hurry, Justin, hurry! Megan cried.

Justin sped up the boat, aiming straight for the cove.

Juliet jumped to her feet. "Justin, you lied! You're not going around it! You're going in there!" Her voice, filled with alarm, rang out above the noise of the motor. "Slow down! What are you doing?"

343

Leave, leave now, Juliet! Megan screamed silently. *You know you want to. Do it! Give my body back to me! It's mine!*

"Justin, turn this boat around, right now! I want to go home!"

It's not your home, Juliet, it's mine. And I want it back. Leave!

"Sit down," Justin ordered Juliet. "Sit down before you fall down."

"Justin Carr, I demand that you turn this boat around right this minute! It's cold out here, and it's getting windy. Take me home!"

She was right about the wind. In just minutes, the trees lining the shores of the cove were bending low against powerful wind gusts, and the surface of the water was churning and boiling. Gray clouds flew past the moon, and the boat began to pitch and toss. Juliet moaned and sat down, clutching the sides of the boat, her face distorted with a terrible fear. The choppy water slopped up into the boat, drenching both of them.

"Justin!" Juliet screamed against the wind. "Please!"

Megan felt new hope. There was desperation in that voice. That was what Megan had been waiting for.

Megan decided it was time to let Juliet know that she was there. Learning that Megan and Justin had planned this together, that Justin knew the truth, might be exactly what was needed to send Juliet over the edge.

There were only five minutes left. She had to try.

344

"Juliet, I'm here. It's me, Megan."

Juliet's head snapped up, her hair sodden now. She jumped to her feet, awkwardly straddling the bottom of the boat. "No! You can't be here! Go away!"

Justin continued to steer the boat, at high speed, straight toward the cove.

"I can be and I am. This little excursion was my idea."

Juliet, battered by wind and spray, peered into the darkness. "That's impossible. You can't communicate with Justin. I'm the only one you can talk to."

"That's not true. Justin and I think alike. We both have open minds, and Justin has a kind heart. You said that was all it took, remember?"

The boat sped the last few yards into the cove.

"Stop him!" Juliet screamed, teetering dangerously. "I can't go in there! I can't!"

"Then don't. Leave. Leave now. Leave willingly, Juliet."

And for one small, agonizing second, Megan thought it had worked. She could feel Juliet's frantic need to flee, to escape the place she hated and feared so passionately.

But in the next second, a violent, ugly rage replaced the fear. "It's not that easy, Megan!" Juliet screamed. "I'll turn this boat around myself!" And in one sudden, fierce movement she leaped at Justin and began clawing at him, struggling to gain control of the boat.

"Turn it around!" she screamed, pounding at his

hands. "I'm going back! And you can't stop me!"

Justin, fighting against the sudden attack, lost control of the boat. Megan watched in helpless horror as the small craft rushed straight ahead through the churning waters. . . .

. . . And slammed into a rock looming like a glacier above the surface of the lake.

Upon impact, Justin was knocked backward to the floor of the boat.

But Juliet, with a blood-curdling scream, was catapulted up into the air and then down, down, down, into the boiling black water waiting below.

Chapter 22

Justin pulled himself to his feet. The sound of Juliet hitting the water paralyzed him for one shocked second. He stood in the motionless boat, frozen, as she disappeared from sight.

The boat's lantern had been dislodged during the collision with the rock and now floated aimlessly an inch or two beneath the surface of the water. Battery-powered and waterproof, it cast an eerie glow over Juliet as she resurfaced, thrashing about violently.

Justin saw her trying to scream as water flooded her mouth and nose.

Megan's mouth. Megan's nose. He drew in a sharp breath. That was *Megan's* body drowning.

Justin poised himself on the edge of the boat, preparing to dive into the lake. The violent wind raked at his long hair, tore at his body.

"*No, you can't!*" Megan cried. "*Justin, you can't save her. Not yet. She has to leave my body willingly. She'll do it, any second now. I can see it in her eyes. She can't bear to be in the water. We have to wait."*

Hearing Megan, Justin paused. But, watching Juliet thrashing about in the wind-blown water closing around her, he thought, What good will it do if Juliet leaves, but Megan's body is lost forever?

And, although Megan cried out, *"Stop, Justin, no!"* he could see no other choice. He dove into the wild, dark water.

Desperation seized Megan. She had gambled on Juliet's absolute terror of the water to make her abandon Megan's body. But being in the boat hadn't done it. And now being in the water wasn't doing it. Juliet was still in there, and only three minutes remained.

Why was Juliet still struggling? Why hadn't she given up?

Then the answer came: She was fighting, still, because she believed that Justin would save her. *She doesn't know he's not a good swimmer — that he'll never be able to get to her. She thinks she'll be free of the water in a minute or two, so she's hanging on.*

Megan felt time racing by. It was too late. She had gambled and lost. There was no more time.

I am drowning now, she thought in despair. *My life is ending, there in the water. And so is Justin's, because there will be no one to save him.*

No. That is not going to happen! We're going to live our lives, Justin and me. Juliet isn't going to rob us of the time that's ours. I want it! I want my life! And I'm going to get it back from her!

348

And so Megan went to Juliet, who was going under for the second time. Justin was trying to reach her, but the wind had whipped the water into a fury, and although he struggled valiantly, he was losing the battle.

Submerged, the light from the lantern surrounding her with a sickly yellow-green glow, Juliet's features became misshapen, grotesque. Her eyes were wild with panic.

"*Give me back what's mine,*" Megan demanded. "*Justin can't save you, Juliet. The wind is too wild. The current is too strong. You're going to die here. Again.*"

Juliet answered her mentally. *You're lying. It's not true.*

"*Listen to me! HE CAN'T SAVE YOU! No one can. And my body is dying and will do you no good now. Give it up. Give it back to me.*"

Justin came up for air, gasping, his eyes wild. He began fighting again to reach Juliet. Foundering, he grasped her collar. With a massive, supreme effort, he heaved her up out of the water, straining desperately to grasp the side of the boat. He failed, and they both sank.

In her mind, Megan heard the grandfather clock beginning to strike midnight. *Bong, bong, bong, bong . . .*

"*Juliet, you've lost.*" Then she began repeating, "*I am Megan, and I want my body back. I am Megan, and I want my body back. I am Megan, and I want my body back. . . .*"

Juliet's eyes had become deep sockets of glowing

yellow. "No-oo," she wailed, "no-oo. My party, my party . . ."

"No, Juliet. It's my party. And there won't be a party, if you drown. I am Megan, and I want my body back. I am Megan, and I want . . ."

The glowing eyes closed in despair. *No party? No party? Justin will not save me?*

"No, Juliet, he can't. You are drowning. Again. Just like before."

Bong, bong, bong, bong . . .

Juliet's mouth made a round O of agony. *Me-gan! Here it is! Here is your body. I give it back to you willingly. I have no choice. I cannot stay here in this terrible place. Take it, and know that you will never see me or hear me again.*

Then her lips twisted and from them came a bellow of rage so despairing, so filled with anguish and torment, every creature within hearing distance shivered with fear. Animals hid in burrows and tree branches and bramble bushes, and people in their houses on the lake slid deeper beneath their bed coverings, taking refuge from the obscene sound.

Bong . . . bong . . . bong . . .

With a joyful relief so overwhelming it made her weak, Megan reclaimed her body as the wailing Juliet left it.

Bong.

As the blood-chilling cry echoed out across the lake then slowly, slowly, trailed off into silence, the feeling of weightlessness left Megan and she found herself in the water, supporting an exhausted Jus-

350

tin. The wind softened to a whisper, the lake became as still and subdued as a pond.

"It's me, Justin," Megan gasped. "It's really me. Juliet is gone. Forever."

Justin was too drained to do anything but nod weakly.

Helping each other, they struggled into the boat, and lay in the bottom, breathing hard and shivering with cold, but relieved.

After a while, Justin reached out for Megan's hand. They linked fingers. Although their flesh was clammy and cold, each took warmth and reassurance from the other's grasp.

When she felt her strength returning, Megan got up and found two blankets in a metal chest under one of the seats. Then, wrapped in gray wool, she tried the motor. It coughed, choked, and started.

Justin stood close beside her as she backed up the damaged boat and turned it away from the cove. Then he put an arm around her.

"Someday," he said quietly, "you can tell me the gruesome details. I want to know all of it. But right now, let's go home. We're going to a very important party tomorrow, remember?"

Megan smiled and nodded.

She aimed the boat toward home, exhausted but happy, as the moon slid out from behind a bank of gray clouds and began shining down on the dark, peaceful water.

And only the wildest of the forest creatures continued to hear the echo of a despairing, tortured wail in the soft whisper of the wind.

FUNHOUSE

FUNHOUSE

Chapter 1

Tess Landers would always remember exactly where she was and what she was doing when The Devil's Elbow roller coaster went flying off its track, shooting straight out into the air and hanging there for a few seconds, before giving in to gravity and plummeting straight to the ground. The crash killed Dade Lewis, destroyed Sheree Buchanan's face, and separated Joey Furman forever from his left leg. And it sent a dozen other roller-coaster riders and ten passersby on the ground to the Santa Luisa Medical Center in screaming ambulances.

Before the crash, Tess was buying a hot dog. With everything. And fries and a large Coke, at a stand not far from where the multicolored cars were making their labored, rattle-clackety climb up the last and most treacherous leg of their journey. The rattle-clatter didn't bother Tess. She had lived in Santa Luisa all of her life and she was used to the sounds of The Boardwalk, the amusement park lining the oceanfront of the Southern California community. Thanks to a mild climate, The Boardwalk was open year-round. Good thing, too, Tess often thought, since without The Boardwalk half the population of their little town would be unemployed. And closing the park, even briefly, would drive most of Santa Luisa's teenagers stark, raving mad. Some worked there, in the shops and arcades and restaurants and booths. Most just played there. What else was there to do in town?

She would always remember what she'd been wearing that night, too. Jeans, boots, and a heavy, white hooded sweater. She'd been waiting patiently for Gina Giambone, her best friend. Gina was always late. Their history teacher, Mr. Dart, teased her nearly every morning. "Hey, Jam-boney, heavy date last night? Looks like you overslept!"

Usually, he was right. Gina dated a lot. Because everyone, girls *and* guys, liked to be around her. She was fun and cute. As short and round as Tess was tall and skinny, with short, dark, curly hair framing her olive-skinned face. Her dark brown eyes were her most outstanding feature. Gina was part of a large Italian family of six kids. Her parents had been married practically forever and seemed very happy, unlike Tess's parents who had recently separated.

Of course Shelley wasn't her real mother. The first Mrs. Landers had died when Tess was nine years old. When she was thirteen, Guy Joe Landers, Sr., had married Shelley, fifteen years his junior. Their marriage had lasted until six weeks earlier, when Shelley had packed her things and left, taking

356

Tess with her. Now Shelley was about to go gallivanting off to Europe for two weeks with her best friend, Madolyn.

"You can go stay with your father and brother," Shelley had said blithely as she packed. "Or you can hang out here by yourself. Whatever. Lord knows you're old enough at seventeen to take care of yourself."

Well, maybe the Lord knew it and maybe Shelley knew it, but Tess wasn't so sure. The exclusive condominium complex called The Shadows was set deep in the woods, on a hill above town. It was beautiful during the day, but it could be cold and lonely when darkness fell.

But Tess didn't want to go stay with her father and her brother, Guy Joe, Jr. No friend of Shelley's was a friend of her father's now. And Tess couldn't forgive Guy Joe for choosing to live with their father.

"But why?" she had asked him tearfully. "You don't even *like* him!" The two of them, father and son, had never been close. The father had been too busy for the son.

"At least he's my *real* parent," Guy Joe had answered.

Okay, so Shelley was their stepmother, and not such a hot one at that. But at least she could be fun. She talked to Tess as if Tess were actually a real human being, something Tess's father hardly ever did. So when Shelley had offered Tess a bedroom in her new home, and Tess's father hadn't said,

"Please don't go," she'd gone. Thank goodness the condo was large enough that she and Shelley weren't tripping over each other.

"Hi!"

Lost in thought, Tess jumped at Gina's sudden greeting. A blob of yellow mustard squirted from her hot dog, landing smack in the middle of Gina's navy blue wool blazer.

"Oh, darn, I'm sorry!" Tess grabbed a paper napkin and dabbed frantically at the greasy mess. Straight, fair hair flew around her thin face. "You shouldn't sneak up on people like that! You scared me half to death. My hair probably turned white!"

Gina laughed and brushed away the napkin. "Your hair is still the same mousy shade it always was. Anyway, forget about the jacket, okay? It needed a trip to the cleaners before you did your dirty work."

"Well, you're in a pretty good mood tonight," Tess said crankily, because she herself was not. She straightened up, tossing the crumpled napkin into a nearby trash can. "How come?"

Gina grinned. "Because I see Doss Beecham over there, working in the ring toss booth. I think I'm making some progress with him. He's stopped calling me Jam-boney. He actually said, 'Hey, you!' yesterday. Don't you think that's a good sign?"

Tess frowned. "What do you see in that guy, anyway? He looks totally Neanderthal to me. You could have any guy in Santa Luisa and you set your big brown eyes on a bruiser in a white T-shirt who

358

spends more time combing that mess of black hair than he does anything else. I just don't get it!"

Gina shrugged. "I think he's cute. Besides, I feel sorry for him. In case you've forgotten, he used to be one of us. Just because his father lost all their money, everyone looks down on Doss now. Well, I don't. He's the same person he always was." She grinned impishly. "And I intend to make my presence known to him."

"People look down on him," Tess pointed out irritably, "because he's a grouch who walks around looking like the world owes him a living and isn't providing it." Maybe Gina just felt sorry for Doss. Although it wasn't as if the Beecham family were starving to death. They'd managed to hang onto that big brick house of theirs up on the hill. Someone had told her that the Beechams had paid cash for the house, years ago, and all they had to do now was pay the taxes on it. Doss probably paid those. Which meant, Tess guessed, that Doss was no bum. He hadn't let his family get tossed out on the street. That was something in his favor.

"Where's Beak tonight?" Tess asked pointedly.

Another shrug. "Oh, he's around somewhere. Probably playing Skee-Ball." She glared at Tess. "And you're about as subtle as a jackhammer. I like Beak, you know that. But Doss is . . . well, he's different. I'm ready for different. Besides," she added, grinning, "how would *you* like to date a guy named Beak?"

The nickname no longer suited Robert Rapp. At

eighteen, his features were perfectly proportioned, which hadn't been the case when he was younger and his nose had been the most prominent feature on his thin, bony face. But the nickname stuck. Tess liked Beak. Except for a penchant for pulling practical jokes, he was nice. She'd always thought he was good for Gina. Apparently, Gina didn't share the thought.

"Maybe Doss will buy me a hot dog," Gina said. "*Without* mustard. So, where's Sam?"

Sam. Pain sliced through Tess's chest. Where was he tonight? And who was he with? "How should I know?" she snapped, turning back to the counter to discard her Coke cup. "I don't own Sam Oliver!"

"Wow!" Doss Beecham commented as he joined them, "who rattled your cage? What'd you do, overdose on sourballs?"

"Never mind," Tess said, embarrassed. She didn't know Doss well enough to behave like a shrew in front of him. "The smell of hot dogs brings out the beast in me."

Doss nodded. "I saw Sam back there. He was alone. You two split?"

She didn't know him well enough to confide in him, either. "Forget it," she said airily. "You guys order your food while I check out the girls' room, okay? Be right back." She didn't feel like hanging around while Gina "got to know" someone who was probably all wrong for her.

But then, who was right for anybody? And how did you know? Her father hadn't been right for Shel-

360

ley. Just when Tess had thought they were going to have a nice, normal family at last, the marriage had fallen apart. And not too long ago, she had thought Sam Oliver was perfect for her. Wrong, wrong, wrong! The support system her school counselor had said she needed to help her cope with her anxieties was rapidly dwindling. Maybe even disappearing forever.

She pushed open the creaky old metal door to the rest room opposite The Devil's Elbow. Rattle-clatter, clackety-clack. It screeched and groaned its way up the rails over her head. She had ridden it once, when she was nine years old. Never again. She didn't mind some of the other scary rides of The Boardwalk, but the roller coaster had taken her breath away, left her knees feeling like pudding, and kept her heart thudding for hours after the wicked ride was over and she was safely on firm ground.

She washed her hands with cold water and ran a comb through her straight, shoulder-length hair. The face in the mirror was a sober one. Maybe *unhappy* was a better word. Well, why not? Feeling almost totally alone didn't exactly bring a smile to a person's face, did it?

She came out of the girls' room just as The Devil's Elbow reached the pinnacle of its last and highest climb. Reluctant to rejoin Gina and Doss, she leaned against the wall and, tilting her head upward, watched as the roller coaster began its last thundering descent.

She could feel the ride as if she were actually

sitting in one of the cars: The wind slapping her face with such brutal force it stole her breath away, the air heavy with screams and shouts, the sheer terror of the rush downward. The last plunge would seem to take forever, although actually it took only a second, so fast was the speed of the roller coaster. There would be just time enough to appreciate the gentleness of that last curve before coasting into the departure gate.

That was the way it was supposed to happen. That was the way it always happened.

But not this time. This time was horribly, shockingly different.

Because as Tess stood against the wall, the lead car, a brilliant orange trimmed in bright yellow, reached the bottom. But instead of following the track and taking that last gentle curve toward home, it sailed out into the air. The car hung there for a second or two, then plunged downward to The Boardwalk below. It took the remaining eleven cars, some occupied, some empty, with it. The cars hit the ground in rapid sequence. The crash of each one seemed, to Tess's disbelieving ears, louder than the one before it. The screaming that accompanied the fall wasn't the playful kind from moments earlier. These were the screams of terror, and Tess didn't even realize that her own voice was among them.

There was screaming on The Boardwalk, as well. People passing by were struck with large and small chunks of falling metal. Some were hit so hard they were tossed like dolls into nearby booths. A mother ran to snatch her small child from the path of a falling car and both were buried beneath the bright blue metal.

Tess, not breathing, huddled against the wall outside the girls' room, unable to believe what she was seeing and hearing. When the last car had fallen and crashed into bits, a brief, shocked silence filled The Boardwalk.

Some distance away, under the last, gentle curve in The Devil's Elbow, a figure slipped out from underneath the tracks. In black slacks, black turtleneck sweater, and black ski mask, the figure blended into the darkness. But even without darkness, total chaos on The Boardwalk would have made it difficult for anyone to notice the figure, or the long, thick, steel pipe in its hands.

Beneath the ski mask a satisfied smile edged its way around the lips. Then the figure in black turned and loped away.

Tess, shaking her head to clear her mind, looked up just then and the moving shadow caught her eye. It wasn't much more than a blur in the darkness, but something about it struck her as strange. Then she realized what it was. Instead of rushing to The Boardwalk to help, the figure was moving *away* from the scene.

Maybe it was rushing off to call for help?

Then why wasn't it rushing *toward* The Boardwalk, where the nearest phones were located?

363

And what had it been doing under The Devil's Elbow in the first place?

Before Tess could think of any reasonable answers to those questions, someone called her name, jerking her back to the chaotic reality in front of her.

Chapter 2

They asked for it. They did. They had it coming, all of them. They get no sympathy.

No one suspects. They think it was an accident. Wrong!

It was *so* easy. Climbing up the inside of the roller coaster's white wooden support system, climbing like a monkey in a palm tree. Then jamming the lead pipe up through the rails at exactly the right moment. That old Devil's Elbow took off into space like it was propelled by jet fuel. Easy, it was so easy.

Dade, Sheree, Joey . . . three out of eight, all at the same time. Not bad. Three out of eight's not bad.

Not bad.

Five more to go.

And no one suspects. Because they don't know what I know. And I'm not about to tell. Not until the job is done. Then I'll share my little discovery with all of them.

But right now, it's time to plan the next step.

Chapter 3

As Tess returned abruptly to reality at the sound of her name, the wooden boardwalk vibrated with feet pounding toward the scene of the crash. The air was filled with screams and moans and shouts for help. Tess's ears rang. Her eyes worked at focusing on the scene before her. Booths had been toppled, their wooden sides collapsing like accordions. There was brightly colored metal everywhere, bits and pieces and chunks of it. Some larger chunks partially hid their victims, revealing a skirt and legs or an arm clutching a purse or someone's very curly red hair. A little boy cried out in pain, wanting his mommy.

Tess shuddered. A siren wailing in the distance told her someone had called for help. The person she'd seen beneath The Devil's Elbow? Maybe.

The smells of popcorn and cotton candy and hot dogs were sickening.

Gina and Doss were running toward Tess. "Tess, are you okay?" Gina cried, her face bone-white. "You're not hurt?"

366

Tess shook her head. But she continued to lean against the wall. She didn't trust her legs to support her all by themselves.

"Were you standing right here when it happened?" Gina's dark eyes, wide with horror, surveyed the disaster scene. "You could have been killed! You sure you're all right?"

"I'm okay. But," she added, pointing shakily to the injured, "they're not. Shouldn't we see if we can help?"

An ambulance shrieked to a halt just beyond the steps to The Boardwalk. Several paramedics in white jumped to the ground and began running, medical equipment in hand.

"They're going to need more than one of those," a deep voice commented in Tess's ear.

It was Sam, in jogging shorts and a red sweatshirt, earphones draped around his neck. His dark hair curled damply across his forehead. "Looks like someone dropped a bomb. What happened?"

"I don't know," Tess answered honestly. A second ambulance arrived, then a third, followed by a black-and-white police car. "The roller coaster just sailed off into the air."

The policemen immediately began trying to disperse the crowd. But no one wanted to leave. People seemed frozen in morbid fascination, their eyes wide, mouths open in disbelief.

"Come on," Tess urged, tugging at Sam's hand. "Let's see if there's anything we can do to help."

The scene that greeted her eyes when she and her friends had pushed through the crowd, made her stomach curl up in fright. Scattered among the bright chunks of broken metal were many of her friends, their bodies crumpled like used paper napkins. Some were unconscious. Some were not as lucky, and cried out in pain.

"There's Sheree Buchanan," Gina whispered, pointing. "There, lying beside the hot-dog stand. I ran into her earlier. She was wearing a purple shirt just like one I bought last week."

Tess moaned low in her throat. Poor Sheree. She would never be the same.

"Dade Lewis is dead!" a girl standing behind Sam cried out. "He's dead!"

A collective gasp of dismay rose up from the crowd.

Dade Lewis? Tess couldn't believe that. Dade was obnoxious, but he was so healthy, so full of life. The girl must be mistaken.

A boy in jeans and a T-shirt ran past Tess, his hand over his mouth, his face sweatshirt-gray. Doss followed him, returning a moment later to say without emotion, "He just came across Joey Furman's leg. Minus Joey. Shook the kid up real bad."

Gina gasped as her hand flew up to cover her mouth. Tess leaned against Sam, all breath completely stolen from her. Joey Furman? He was on the track team, with Guy Joe, Sam, and Beak. Every time she'd seen Joey lately — on The Boardwalk, in town, or at school, he'd been running. And now he'd lost a leg to The Devil's Elbow?

Doss Beecham was an insensitive clod, she thought, as Doss left to help on The Boardwalk.

Talking so matter-of-factly about what had happened to Joey, as if the loss of his leg were no more important than a pimple on his chin! Didn't Doss have any feelings?

She spotted Beak among the volunteers, bending and stooping, his lanky form lifting metal and tossing it aside, as he tried to stay out of the way of the paramedics. His thin face was flushed with exertion and distress.

"There's Beak," she told Gina, nodding toward their friend. She was relieved that he hadn't been a passenger on The Devil's Elbow when it crashed. It was his favorite ride.

Gina simply nodded when Tess mentioned Beak. She was still trying to take in the nightmare around her.

"I'm going with Beecham," Sam told Tess, handing her his earphones. "You stay here with Giambone. And stay *out* of the way."

Ordinarily, Tess's temper would have flared at the command. But nothing tonight was ordinary. Besides, she figured, in this case Sam was probably right. She and Gina could be the most useful by helping to move the crowd back. The policemen weren't having much luck getting onlookers out of the way.

Tess and Gina spent most of the next hour cajoling bystanders, gradually talking them into moving back from the accident scene, leaving the site open for emergency personnel and the cleanup crew.

When the last of the ambulances had departed,

369

sirens wailing mournfully, and the crowd had wandered off, Tess and Gina collapsed to sitting positions, their backs against a cotton-candy booth left untouched by the disaster. Tess's thin face and Gina's round one were totally devoid of color, their eyes full of pain and shock. Doss and Sam joined them, their own faces and clothes dirty. Sam had a small cut on one hand. They sank down beside the girls and rested their heads against the booth.

Tess's brother, Guy Joe, a tall, broad-shouldered boy with a square, handsome face and deep gray eyes, arrived, his denim cutoffs smeared with grease from his cleanup efforts. Trailing along behind him was Sam's sister Candace, a pale, thin, blonde girl. Candace never wore jeans, and the pink dress she was wearing now was much too large for her, billowing around her like a tent. A heavy hand with an eyebrow pencil made her look far more ferocious than she really was. Tess couldn't understand why Mrs. Oliver, who was tall, beautiful, and very elegant, never took the time to teach her own daughter about clothes and makeup. But tonight, that didn't seem very important.

"Well, at least you weren't on that thing when it went," Guy Joe said to Tess, patting her shoulder awkwardly as he slid to a sitting position beside her. "When I saw the bulletin on television, I thought of you. I know this place is your favorite hangout."

"Guy Joe," Tess said stiffly, still uncomfortable around the brother who had "deserted" her by staying with their father after the separation, "you

370

know I never go near the roller coaster. Haven't since the first time I ever rode it."

"According to the bulletin," her brother argued, running his fingers through his unruly hair, "you didn't have to be on the thing to get clobbered. For all I knew, you could have been creamed by one of the falling cars."

Tess knew he was right. One elderly woman had been tossed into a food booth. Two little boys had been slashed by flying metal chunks, and at least half a dozen other people walking along The Boardwalk at the time of the accident had been sent to the Santa Luisa Medical Center.

"Thanks for worrying about me," she said politely, "but I'm fine."

A tall, big-boned, very pretty girl with thick, blonde shoulder-length hair ran up to them. Dressed in beige silk slacks over a red leotard, she carried her large frame gracefully, moving with quick, light steps across The Boardwalk. When she reached the group, she sank into a crouch beside Gina. Tess noticed that she was careful not to let her silk pants touch the wood, gently bunching them slightly at the knees.

"Isn't this just awful?" the girl breathed, her blue eyes wide. "I can't believe it! My daddy's going to have a stroke! Something like this happening on his beloved boardwalk, it's just terrible! Has anybody seen my little brother?"

The girl was Trudy Slaughter, a classmate of Tess and Gina's, and the "daddy" she spoke of was chairman of the board of directors that ran The

Boardwalk. Trudy was a popular, powerful force at Santa Luisa High, having held at least once, every available office. Tess hadn't voted for her since the day she saw Trudy lose her temper in the school parking lot over an English grade lower than the one she'd been expecting. Seeing Trudy violently ripping at sheets of paper and slamming her books against the windshield of a car had not been a pretty sight. It had given Tess chills, and she knew she'd seen a side of Trudy that not many other people had witnessed.

"I saw Tommy," Gina said, referring to the brother Trudy had asked about. "He's fine. He's with one of Beak's kid sisters. They weren't hurt, either."

"I was at ballet class," Trudy breathed, "when we all heard this horrible sound. Debbie Wooster thought it was an earthquake and ran screaming into the bathroom. But Madame Souska said it wasn't, because the chandelier wasn't shaking. She let us turn on the radio and that's how we heard. We were excused from practice, can you believe that? She never excuses us for anything!" Trudy's chest heaved in a heavy sigh. "I suppose that means we'll have to make it up another time."

"Poor thing," Tess said sarcastically, too tired to ignore Trudy's callousness. "And yes, we're all fine, thanks for asking."

Trudy blushed. "Well, I can *see* that! I heard about Dade, though. I can't believe it. How did it happen, anyway?"

"No one knows," Guy Joe said wearily. "Maybe a loose rail."

"I saw someone," Tess said quietly.

Everyone's eyes focused on her. But she could tell that her words hadn't registered. "Under The Devil's Elbow," she added, flushing because she hated being the center of attention, and already wishing she hadn't said anything. "Right after the accident. Running away."

"Well, don't keep us in suspense," Trudy said anxiously. "Who *was* it?"

"You saw someone?" Sam asked quietly, leaning forward to peer into Tess's face. "Running away?"

Tess nodded. "I think so. It was awfully dark and I couldn't see very well. But there was something . . ." A lack of conviction forced her words to trail off weakly.

No one said anything for a moment. They think I imagined it, she thought resentfully. I never should have said anything.

Then Doss surprised her by asking calmly, "Who did it look like, Tess? Was it someone we know?" He seemed to be assuming that she hadn't imagined the shadow.

Sending him a grateful glance, she admitted reluctantly, "No, not really. But I thought . . . well, I thought there was something familiar about the way it moved."

"The way what moved?" Beak asked as he joined them. Sweat from his work with the cleanup crew streaked his thin, intense face. Swiping at it with the sleeve of his navy blue sweatshirt, he sank down beside Gina.

"Tess thinks she saw someone running away from The Devil's Elbow," Gina told him. Although she said *thinks*, Tess felt that Gina, too, believed her, and she sent her best friend a warm smile.

"Running *away*?" Beak asked, leaning back against the booth. "Why would someone be running *away*? Are you hinting that you think someone *did* something to The Devil's Elbow? Deliberately caused the accident?"

That thought hadn't even crossed Tess's mind. Wide-eyed she stared at Beak. "No, I . . ."

Sam interrupted her. "Maybe you should talk to the police. Tell them what you saw."

Tess looked doubtful. What could she possibly tell them? That she'd seen a shadow? Wouldn't they laugh at her?

"Relax," Doss said lazily. "Chalmers will look into it. That's his job. If he finds even a hint of tampering, then Tess can go to him with what she saw."

Sam laughed. "Chalmers? Our distinguished police chief? He couldn't find his own nose without a mirror. Besides, the board got him elected in the first place, to make sure their precious Boardwalk was protected. If he does find anything, whether it was faulty equipment or actual tampering, he's not going to announce it publicly. Either way, it'd be bad for business."

"Oh, Sam," Gina scolded, "you're so cynical! The

board wouldn't hide something like that. And the police would never cover it up."

Sam shrugged. "We'll see."

An uncomfortable silence followed. Then Tess asked, "Anyone know who called the paramedics?" Maybe it had been the shadow she'd seen. That would explain why it had been there and she could forget about it.

Doss nodded. "Martha did," he said, referring to an elderly woman who ran the shooting gallery. "I never knew she could move so fast. The minute that thing took off, Martha raced for the nearest phone."

Of course, Tess told herself. Because that was what you *did* in an emergency. You ran *toward* the phone, not away from it.

Unless you weren't interested in getting help.

Unless you were only interested in running away. Because you had good reason to run away.

Telling herself she was letting her imagination do some pretty fancy running, Tess pushed all thought of the shadow out of her tired, aching mind. All she wanted to do now was go home and crawl under the covers and sleep, and forget about this dreadful, horrible night.

As if it could ever be forgotten!

Chapter 4

I found it in the attic. I was looking for ski clothes. Found no ski clothes. Found the book, instead. A journal. A little red book, hidden in the bottom of an old trunk. The name on the front, in cheap gold letters, was LILA O'HARE.

O'Hare? No O'Hares in this family. None in Santa Luisa, for that matter.

I read that journal. Took me all day, but I read it. Every page. Hot day, stuffy attic with its tiny windows and sloping walls and smells of cedar and mothballs. Sat there all day, sweating and reading.

Glad I read it. Even though it changed everything. When I finished reading it, I knew that nothing would ever be the same again.

But I'm not sorry I read it.

The journal was written by this woman named Lila, who was married to a guy named Tully O'Hare who owned The Boardwalk. Reading that seemed weird, because I'd never thought about who owned The Boardwalk before my father and his friends bought it. Now I knew. Someone named Tully O'Hare.

Lila and Tully ran The Boardwalk together. Very happy, the O'Hares were. Pretty boring stuff, but I read it anyway. Nothing better to do.

Then suddenly the entries changed.

I wish someone could help us. We can't pay the back taxes on The Boardwalk. Tully's worried sick. He's afraid we're going to lose everything.

What would we do without The Boardwalk? It's our whole life. Tully's granddaddy built it and it's all we've got. I don't know what Tully will do if it's taken away from us.

We were both so excited about the baby coming. We've waited and hoped for so long. Now Tully is afraid we won't be able to take care of our child.

He's going to the bank to see Buddy about a loan. Maybe that will save us.

Who was Buddy? Was there a banker in town named Buddy? Not that I knew of.

Turns out, there were a *lot* of things I didn't know.

Chapter 5

When Tess announced that she was going home, Sam insisted on walking her to the parking lot. Almost empty now, it seemed strangely eerie and quiet. As uncomfortable as she felt around Sam after their fight earlier in the week, she was glad she wasn't alone.

Lights began flickering off at The Boardwalk. Someone had made the decision to close early. Good idea. Tess shuddered. Who could have a good time there tonight?

Sam moved forward to stand beside her. A breeze off the ocean picked up stray strands of his dark, wavy hair and lifted them gently. "So, Shelley take off yet?" he asked brusquely.

Oh, no. Were they going to have *that* discussion again? Their argument had been about Shelley. When Sam found out that Shelley was leaving for Europe, he'd made some snide remarks about her abilities as a parent. Because Shelley had wanted Tess when no one else seemed to, Tess had defended her stepmother. The argument had escalated, and

Sam had left her house in a fury. She didn't want to get into that again, especially not when she was feeling so shocked and shaken.

"Yes," she mumbled, turning toward her little blue car, "she's gone. Left around five o'clock." Would Shelley have gone if she'd known about The Devil's Elbow? Probably.

"Then I'll drive you home," Sam said in that commanding voice she hated. "You can come back and pick up your car tomorrow."

It would be nice, when she was feeling so sick inside, to let Sam take over. But that would just reinforce his notion that she needed looking after. Even though sometimes — like that night — she wouldn't have minded letting him decide things for her, she certainly wouldn't admit that to *him*. If he wanted someone to take care of, let him buy a puppy!

"I can drive myself home, thank you very much," she said, her voice as cool as the night air.

"You are so stubborn!" he said heatedly, throwing his hands up in the air in disgust. "You never give an inch!"

That seemed funny to Tess and she almost laughed. She'd been giving inches all of her life. People told her what to do and she did it, because it was easier than arguing. If she was arguing now, with Sam, maybe it was because doing what people told her hadn't worked out so well. Just when she'd thought she was finally going to have a happy family, like other people, her father had said, "We're divorcing," and that was that.

So if she'd been giving Sam a hard time lately, maybe it was because she was getting just a little tired of having other people make her decisions for her.

"I'm going home," she said flatly, opening the door of her car.

"Fine! Great! You do that!" And he stalked away, broad shoulders jerking in anger with each stride.

Watching him go, she was unpleasantly surprised to discover that she was analyzing his walk, comparing it to the movements of the figure she'd seen running away from The Boardwalk. Afraid that he would turn suddenly and see her watching him, she ducked into her car and settled behind the wheel. If Sam *had* been running under The Devil's Elbow, he would have said so when she'd mentioned what she'd seen. He would have said casually, "Oh, that was me. That's the route I take when I jog." And that would have been the end of it. She would have put the figure out of her mind completely.

But Sam hadn't said that. So it hadn't been him.

Then who *was* it? And why had they run away, instead of rushing to The Boardwalk to help?

Maybe the person *had* helped out. It suddenly occurred to Tess, as she headed up the hill toward home, that the figure she'd seen could easily have joined the crowd of volunteers without her knowing it. After all, she hadn't recognized the person, so how could she say whether or not they had returned to the accident and pitched in?

She'd been jumping to conclusions, as usual. She

had no real reason to believe sinister things about that figure. Might as well put it out of her mind right now.

She had always loved the drive home, up the hill. Random house lights scattered throughout the woods on both sides of the road eased the darkness, like candlelight in a dark room. It had always seemed peaceful, even romantic.

But not tonight. Not with those terrible screams echoing in her ears.

At the top of the hill, she took a sharp right turn into the long, tree-lined driveway leading to The Shadows, the exclusive condominium complex she and Shelley called home now. Their unit was all the way at the back, overlooking a lush green valley. Tess loved the daytime view, but at night it seemed isolated and lonely. This would be her first night alone in the house and she wasn't looking forward to it. Shelley's timing was the worst! Why did she have to leave for Europe on the very night that the worst disaster in Santa Luisa's history had taken place?

The patio beside their carport was surrounded on three sides by tall, thick oleander bushes, their narrow green leaves swaying in the night breeze. A small, black, metal gate separated the carport from the patio, which sat directly outside the condo's kitchen. Tess hurried from the car to the back door, unlocked it and went inside, quickly flipping on the kitchen light switch as she entered the house.

It seemed so empty. No Shelley fixing a drink in

the kitchen, no loud jazz music blasting through the rooms, no coat, purse, car keys, scarf, magazines, and newspaper left in a trail behind Shelley as she advanced from one room to another.

Tess swallowed hard. Even when Shelley was in town, she wasn't home that many evenings. What was so different about tonight?

What was different was that something atrocious had happened and Tess wanted someone there to share her pain.

While flooding the kitchen with light made the room feel a bit more friendly, it also seemed to magnify the wide, gaping blackness of the big picture windows over the double sink and the French doors opposite the breakfast nook. Shelley didn't believe in curtains or drapes. She said she liked to "bring the outdoors in," and usually added, "where it belongs," which Tess found funny.

It didn't seem the least bit funny tonight. Tess couldn't have said why, but the bare, black windows left her feeling raw and exposed.

When the phone shrilled, she jumped, banging her elbow on the kitchen counter and dropping her purse. Her lipstick fell out and rolled under the oval wooden table in the breakfast nook.

It was Gina calling. "Just wanted to make sure you got home in one piece. You seemed pretty rattled."

Tess laughed nervously. "I guess I still am, a little. Aren't you?"

"I feel just horrible. All those people hurt. Poor

Joey! And Sheree! And then there's Dade . . ."

They both fell silent. Then Gina said, "Are you all alone or is Sam playing bodyguard? I saw him leave with you."

Tess switched on the breakfast nook chandelier, a hanging fixture with lights shaped like candles ensconced in copper holders. Shelley had left the sink full of dishes, as always. Tess hooked the black rubber phone grip over her shoulder and began loading the dishwasher as she talked. "I'm alone. Shelley's off to sunny Italy. And I didn't feel like dealing with Sam tonight." She paused, before adding seriously, "Gina, hasn't The Boardwalk been in business for about a hundred years?"

"Give or take a year or two. Why?"

"And there's never been an accident there before tonight, right? Not a really bad one, I mean." Gina's father, like most of the parents Tess knew, including her own father, was on the amusement park's board of directors. And since Mr. Giambone, unlike Tess's father, actually *talked* to his daughter, Gina might know something about The Boardwalk's history.

Gina thought for a minute. "Not on The Devil's Elbow," she answered. "But something might have happened in the Funhouse. Don't know what, exactly, but I remember my dad saying something about it once. Whatever it was, it happened before our dads and their friends bought The Boardwalk and remodeled it. I can ask him about it if you want me to. Why? What's up?"

She's already forgotten that I told her I saw something, Tess thought, annoyed. Maybe I'm just jealous of her ability to shut out bad things. No wonder she's never nervous! "Well, don't you think it's kind of weird?" She tipped a glass half full of milk into the sink and rinsed it under the faucet. "I mean, after all these years, all of a sudden there's this terrible accident? Whatever happened in the Funhouse couldn't have been as bad as this, or we'd all have heard about it. So why did something so awful suddenly happen?"

"Tess. If you were almost a hundred years old, don't you think you might break down a little, too?"

"Maybe. But I hope things wouldn't be falling *off* me! Tell the truth, Gina. Do you really think it was an accident?"

She could almost see the frown on Gina's face as her thick, dark eyebrows drew together the way they did when Gina concentrated. "It's that shadow you saw under The Devil's Elbow, isn't it, Tess? That's what's spooking you. So, what are you thinking? That someone put a bomb on the rails? Santa Luisa isn't exactly terrorist territory!

"Tess, you got this idea from Sam, didn't you? Did he say something to you after you left here? You know how cynical he is! Why do you listen to him when he's saying gloomy things?"

"Gina, I didn't *get* this idea from Sam. *I'm* the one who saw something, remember? With my own eyes."

Gina wasn't giving in. "Why don't you just wait and see what the police come up with? I'll bet my

384

new purple blouse that it was just a worn-out rail in the tracks. You'll see."

Her new purple blouse, Tess remembered, was exactly like the one Sheree Buchanan had been wearing earlier. Tess didn't want it. "No, thanks. No bet. I'm not in a gambling mood."

They might have continued arguing, but Tess's eyes, scanning the white brick floor for her lipstick, spotted something else. A piece of crisp white paper was sticking out from underneath the French doors. Had Shelley dropped something on her way out? It would be just like her.

Telling Gina she'd see her tomorrow, Tess hung up. Then she bent to pick up the piece of paper.

It was folded once, into a small white square. She turned it over. Scrawled across the front, in bright purple Magic Marker, was her name.

She didn't recognize the writing. It wasn't Shelley's, she was sure of that. Besides, she told herself, Shelley wasn't the type to leave notes for people when she went somewhere. She just went.

Her breathing slightly uneven, Tess leaned against the counter as she unfolded the note.

The words, like her name, were written in that same vivid purple. Her eyes wide, her hands beginning to shake, Tess read:

> *Dade and Sheree went up the hill,*
> *With Joey right behind them,*
> *Now Dade is dead and Sheree's ill,*
> *And Joey's leg can't find him.*

385

If Dade was one, and Sheree two,
And Joey number three,
Who will be next? Could it be you?
Why don't we wait and see?

Chapter 6

I delivered my little note to Tess. I hope it shakes her up. A lot. Serve her right.

She doesn't even know why. No one does. No one knows what I found in the attic. I'll tell them when I'm good and ready.

The little red book held secrets. I kept reading, that hot, sticky day a few weeks ago, before the air had turned cool and crisp.

After Tully O'Hare went to the bank to get a loan from his friend Buddy, Lila O'Hare wrote:

I can't believe it! Buddy turned us down. He and Tully have been friends since grade school. Now Tully is drowning and Buddy won't throw him a rope.

Why not?

And what are we going to do now?

Bad Buddy the banker. Who *was* he? If there was a banker in town named Buddy, I'd never heard of him. Maybe he'd dumped the nickname. Maybe he'd dumped the bank. The journal was dated a long time ago. Years ago. Lots of things could have changed in that time.

The next entry explained the one before it.

We found out why Buddy turned us down at the bank. He and a bunch of his friends want The Boardwalk! As an investment. They say they have the funds to turn it into a huge money-making proposition. And we don't.

But it's ours! It's all we have. They can't take it from us, can they?

Why was I so sure the answer to that question was yes, they can. Maybe from watching my father make so many deals over the years. He had the money and the power, and he always won.

I was right. Because the next entry read:

It's gone. The Boardwalk. Buddy and his friends now own it. Tully is devastated. So am I.

What will happen to us now? How will we take care of our baby when it gets here?

The next few pages were blank.

Chapter 7

The blood in Tess's veins turned to sleet as she read, and then reread, the note's purple words.

Who will be next? What did that mean? Next, as in, next after Dade and Sheree and Joey? As in, look what happened to *them?*

Sheree's ruined face swam before Tess's eyes. Then Dade's lifeless body did the same, and Joey's leg . . .

Her knees, which had been threatening all evening to buckle, did so now. Her body slid down the cabinet until it collided gently with the floor. She still held the note in her hands, clenched so tightly her knuckles were blue-white. Unable to stop herself, she glanced down at the little square of paper again.

The purple letters hadn't rearranged themselves into a friendlier message. The words still conveyed the same ugly, threatening meaning.

Her mind, fogged by shock and exhaustion, fought to make sense of it. Was it a joke? Who did she know with such a bizarre sense of humor? And if it wasn't a joke, then what was it?

She read it one more time. How could the meaning be mistaken? Wasn't it proof that what had happened tonight at The Boardwalk was no accident? Or could someone with a twisted sense of humor simply be using the crash to scare her? Hinting that something else equally horrible might be in the works, just to tease her?

No. That would be too cruel. No one she knew had such a sick sense of humor.

Okay, then. How about someone she *didn't* know? Was that possible? There *were* people like that, weren't there? People who thrived on tragedy and horror and used it for their own benefit? Like people who read about kidnappings and then send a fake ransom note to the parents? Couldn't the person who had written this purple poem be someone like that?

Tess stood up. She kept her eyes away from the blackness of the windows and the French doors. The person who had written the poem could be watching. Watching her. His or her sick, horrid eyes could, at this very instant, be fixed on her building.

I shouldn't stay here tonight, Tess thought nervously. Her father's big, very solid, well-protected house beckoned. She'd be safe there. Miserable, especially if her father was home. He'd start right in on her about Shelley, for sure. But at least, she'd be safe.

Or she could call Sam. He'd come and stay with her. But she was so rattled by the accident and now the note that she'd probably throw herself into his arms. And that would be a major mistake!

With shaking fingers, she dialed her father's telephone number. She let it ring eight or nine times. No answer.

Why wasn't Guy Joe home? He couldn't still be at The Boardwalk. Maybe Trudy had talked him into giving her a ride home. If she had, who knew what time Guy Joe would finally call it a night? Trudy didn't have a curfew. Her parents were very busy socially and seldom home. So Trudy saw no need to be, either.

If I have to spend the night alone, Tess decided, I'd rather spend it here, in my own house, surrounded by my own things. Besides, she told the grandfather clock as she passed it, that stupid note was probably a joke. A bad one, but still a joke.

Locking all the doors and windows was the first step. Then, feeling just a tiny bit silly but willing to take no chances, she pushed the heavy oval table in front of the French doors. That done, she thought about calling Gina to read her the note, but decided against it. It was too late. Why wake up the whole Giambone family? Especially since Gina would probably just confirm what Tess had already decided: that the note was a rotten joke.

But when Tess left the kitchen, she didn't turn off the light. The note still in her hand, she made her way through the spacious condo, flipping on light switches as she went. All of the rooms were large and airy, decorated by Shelley in French country style, the walls painted a soft gray-blue or wallpapered in tiny floral prints. The furniture was comfortably cushioned in blue-and-rose plaid. Shelley had added wicker baskets, hanging plants at the windows, and an abundance of white floor-to-ceiling bookcases. This home was prettier, warmer, and cozier than the Landers' mansion.

But as Tess passed from kitchen to dining room to wide, open, French-doored living room, she suddenly found herself wondering how she would defend herself if someone broke into the house. She'd never had such thoughts before. They made her skin feel as if something ugly were crawling on it.

Picking out a heavy brass poker from the set beside the white brick fireplace, she settled, still fully dressed, on the roomy couch. Covering her legs with a quilted throw, she turned on the television set for company and positioned the poker at her side. She wouldn't sleep. She couldn't. She'd stay alert tonight and sleep during the day. People didn't break into houses in broad daylight, did they?

But the horror of the night had exhausted her and the need for sleep won out over her resolve.

When she finally gave in and closed her eyes, every light in the house was still blazing brightly.

Chapter 8

Tess awoke, stiff and headachey, to sunlight streaming in through the French doors and a cartoon blaring at her from the television set. When the memory of the previous night's events flooded back into her mind, she made a decision.

Fifteen minutes later, after pulling on a full, flowered skirt and a white short-sleeved blouse, and clipping her hair on top of her head with a wide gold barrette, she grabbed her purse and the note and drove straight to the police station.

Chief Chalmers wasn't there.

"Doesn't come in on Sundays," the desk sergeant informed her. A heavyset balding man with a mustache and round eyeglasses, he sat with his feet up on the desk, which was littered with papers. No one else was in the small, wood-paneled front office. Dying plants lined the windowsills behind the policeman and half filled coffee cups seemed to be everywhere.

"Sunday's his day of rest," the desk sergeant continued. He shook his head. "Not today, though.

Today's he's seeing to that mess over there at The Boardwalk." Another shake of his balding head. "Terrible thing, terrible thing."

"I need some help," Tess said, extending the note toward him.

"You got a problem, little lady?" he asked, swinging his feet to the floor and sitting up straight. His light blue uniform was clean except for a tiny coffee stain on his navy blue tie. "What's the matter, you missing a boyfriend? Nah, that can't be it. Fellow'd have to be crazy to walk out on a pretty little thing like you." He smiled at her, obviously expecting her to return the smile.

She didn't. Standing up very straight, grateful that she'd worn her black heels, she said crisply, "I'm not little. And my problem isn't a boy. It's this note." She tossed the white piece of paper onto his desk. "Someone slid it under my door last night. I need to know what I should do about it."

He picked it up. "What's this? A love note?"

"Not exactly. Could you look at it, please?" The emptiness of the station wasn't very reassuring. Didn't Santa Luisa have more law enforcement than this? Where was everyone? Did they think criminals took Sundays off, like Chief Chalmers?

She watched as he read the note. Now, maybe he would take her seriously. The note should worry him, shouldn't it? It had certainly worried *her*.

But it didn't seem to worry him. "This thing doesn't make any sense at all. And it looks like a kid's handwriting to me. Written in crayon, right?"

"Magic Marker." Did he think crazy people who

394

wrote threatening notes used only the finest writing tools? "It wasn't written by a kid," she insisted. "Don't you recognize those names?"

"Sure. They're the kids hurt last night. Devil's Elbow. Bad business, over there. Terrible accident."

Tess leaned forward, placing the palms of her hands on his desk. "But doesn't that note sound like the crash wasn't an accident? And doesn't it sound like the person writing it was warning that there might be other accidents?"

The man reread the note, pursing his lips in concentration. When he'd finished, he looked up and said, "I don't see that here. Where does it say that?"

Impatiently, Tess pointed to the words *Who will be next?* "There! Isn't that a warning?"

"Could be, I guess. Hard to say. Could be a joke. Someone trying to scare you. You have a fight with your boyfriend lately?"

Stunned by the question, Tess fought the telltale flush that crept up her cheeks.

"I thought so." The policeman nodded with satisfaction.

As if, she thought bitterly, he'd just solved the crime of the century.

"Look, miss, I'm not trying to give you a hard time. It's just that we get stuff like this in here all the time. Young fella gets mad, says things he doesn't mean, the girl comes in all worried and upset and we have to calm her down. Lots of times, the guy writes notes. Never amounts to a hill of beans."

"My boyfriend," Tess said coldly, "would never

scare me like this! He would never write a crazy note like this."

The frown on his face then told her she'd worn out her welcome. "It's like this, miss. Chief Chalmers has his hands full right now with this Boardwalk business. But soon as he comes in, I'll give him your note and see what he thinks. You can rest assured that if there's anything connecting this note with that crash last night, the chief will take care of it. He'll probably call you. Okay?" And with that, he turned away from her, picking up a sheet of paper and studying it.

Tess knew she'd been dismissed. And she hadn't accomplished anything.

"Could I have my note back, please?" It suddenly seemed important to have it. That was probably the only way to keep it from sailing straight into the wastebasket the minute she turned her back.

A dubious shake of the man's head. "I'd better keep it, miss. We intend to follow up on this, I promise you that." Opening his desk drawer, he dropped the note into a jumble of papers.

She'd have to leave. *Without* her note.

"It's not that I don't believe there was a note, Tess," Gina said half an hour later, as they shared a booth at Kim's, an ice-cream shop not far from Gina's house. "I do. You wouldn't make up something like that." Wearing the red silk dress she'd worn earlier to church, she sat opposite Tess, who was toying with the straw sticking up out of her vanilla milkshake. "It's just that it *has* to be a joke.

A really mean one, but a joke. I hate to see you get all upset over it."

Tess began tapping her long-handled spoon on the Formica table. "I told you exactly what it said. Doesn't it sound to you like it means the crash was no accident?"

But she knew it was hopeless. Gina's cheerful, uncomplicated way of looking at things didn't include deliberate acts of terror or threatening notes. That was just the way she was. Which, Tess decided in all fairness, was probably why she smiled more than most people. There weren't any scary demons or ghosts running around in her head.

"Let's wait and see what the police say, okay?" Gina urged. "And by the way, I did ask my dad about any other accidents at The Boardwalk," she added in an obvious effort to make peace. "He hates talking about stuff like that, so it didn't make him very happy."

Like father, like daughter, Tess thought drily.

"But he did say some guy committed suicide in the Funhouse a long time ago. Hung himself."

"Yuck! No kidding? No wonder I was never crazy about that place. Who was it?"

Gina stirred her Coke with her straw. "Daddy wouldn't say. And Mom made us change the subject."

"I wonder why we never heard about it before?"

Gina shrugged. "It happened a long time ago. Before we were born. I guess it's not the kind of thing people like to talk about."

As they left the restaurant, Gina tried one more

time to cheer up Tess. "Let's just wait and see what Chief Chalmers comes up with before you start running around town like Henny-Penny, shouting that the sky is falling. Okay?"

"Just don't be surprised," Tess said darkly, "if it turns out that I'm right. And I *am* going to say I told you so."

Gina laughed. "Of course you are. Anyway, we probably won't hear anything about it until tomorrow. So, since you're so jittery, why not stay at my house tonight? No school tomorrow, did you know that?"

Tess hadn't known. She was relieved to hear it. The atmosphere in school would have been grim.

"The school board gave everyone the day off out of respect for Dade," Gina continued. "We could see a movie this afternoon. Something really funny, to take your mind off all this stuff."

More relief. Tess had been reluctant to invite herself to stay at Gina's, even for just one night. The Giambone house was already packed to the rafters with kids and toys and bicycles and pets. She usually stayed overnight only when at least one Giambone was doing the same at someone else's house. "Thanks," she said gratefully, "that'd be fun."

It almost was. The movie was funny, and she felt perfectly safe in a theater full of people.

And what could hurt her at the Giambones'? The house, messy and cluttered, noisy and busy, shouldn't have been relaxing, but it always was. Gina's parents welcomed her warmly, the smaller children gave her hugs and begged her to read to them, which she did. And The Devil's Elbow crash wasn't mentioned once.

So Tess should have felt blissfully safe. She should have slept like a baby all night in the big, crowded house.

But she didn't. Because vivid purple words kept dancing in front of her eyes. *Who will be next? It could be you . . . it could be you . . . it could be you . . .*

Chapter 9

She went to the police with my poem. I was watching. I watched her house all night. Silly girl. The police probably think she's loony-tunes. Laughed at her, I'll bet!

Have to hand it to her, though. I thought she'd split when she got my note. She didn't. Stayed right there. Had every light in the condo on, though. The place looked like one giant light bulb!

She stayed at Giambones' last night. Okay by me. Plenty of time. After all, a few weeks ago I didn't even know what I know now.

Until I read Lila O'Hare's journal.

After that bunch of blank pages following the entry about losing The Boardwalk, she began writing again.

My Tully is gone. I know people are saying that what he did was cowardly, but Tully was no coward. He did it for me and the baby. He didn't know, that poor, sweet man, that the insurance company wouldn't pay off in a suicide case.

How am I going to take care of our baby when it comes?

The man was *dead*? That was pretty gruesome. I wondered if those guys who took The Boardwalk from him felt guilty. Maybe not. I knew what my own father would say. He'd say, "Look, the guy couldn't hack it. Is that *my* fault?"

Well, yes, actually, I guess it could have been. *If* my father had been in on the deal. I hoped he hadn't, but after all, the journal was in this trunk in this attic in this house and I had a sneaking suspicion that meant something. Lila went on:

Buddy came to see me. He said I shouldn't worry, that he'd take care of everything, that they all felt guilty about buying The Boardwalk, that they never thought it would drive Tully to suicide.

They didn't buy The Boardwalk. They stole it!

But I have to let Buddy help me. I have no choice.

She was going to let this creep help her out, after what he'd done. She must really be desperate.

Tiny little hammers tattooing the inside of my skull made me put the journal down.

Chapter 10

When Tess went home the next day, Gina insisted she take one of the Giambone cats with her. "For company," she said. "Take Trilby. She's the most affectionate. She has a thing for laps and she loves to be petted. You can keep her until Shelley gets back."

"Is Trilby trained as an attack cat?" Tess joked, in an effort to calm the nerves that were stretched taut from uncertainty and lack of sleep. What had that purple note meant? And who had written it? And *why*? Had it really been just a sick joke?

The cat was beautiful, a sleek Siamese with clear blue eyes. She purred with gratitude when she was allowed to lounge in Tess's lap all the way home.

Tess had barely had time to change into jeans and a yellow sweatshirt when the phone rang. It was Gina. "Listen, I know you're not going to be crazy about this idea," she warned, "but just hear me out, okay? My dad asked me this morning if I could get a bunch of kids together to go to The

Boardwalk sometime this week. Just to show people that it's safe, you know?"

But *is* it? Tess wondered.

"I thought," Gina continued, "since we have the day off, this afternoon would be a good time. I've already talked to Beak and Sam and they think it's a good idea. Sam said he'd call Guy Joe. And I think Trudy and Candace might come, too. Trudy told me she was planning to sleep all day, but when I told her Guy Joe was coming, she changed her mind. And Sam said he'd bring Candace."

"I don't want to go down there," Tess protested. The oval table was still firmly pressed up against the French doors, a reminder that Saturday night's note hadn't been imagined. If the author had had something to do with the roller coaster crash, he might be hanging around The Boardwalk. Returning to the scene of the crime. Didn't criminals do that sort of thing? "Why can't we do something else?"

"C'mon, Tess, please? First of all, there *isn't* anything else to do. Secondly, my dad's worried about what the accident will do to business on The Boardwalk, and I don't blame him. Look, he hardly ever asks me for anything. I don't want to turn him down." Gina's voice took on a stubborn note. "I'm going over there this afternoon. You coming?"

Tess hesitated. Gina's father had always been kind to Tess. If he was really worried, she should help out.

"Okay, I'll come. What time?"

"Oh, great! Listen, we'll just hang out in the

Funhouse, okay? No rides, not when you're so up-tight. I wouldn't torture you by forcing you on The Dragon's Breath or Helicopter Hell. But the Funhouse is perfectly safe. We're meeting at the entrance at two, but I thought maybe you could pick me up?"

"Sure." The Funhouse wasn't *always* safe, Tess thought grimly. Someone had committed suicide in there, a long time ago. But then, it wasn't as if someone had attacked him in there. He'd taken his own life.

"The Funhouse isn't my favorite place to be," Tess said before she hung up, "but at least it doesn't have any windows so it won't have a view of The Devil's Elbow. That's about the only place on The Boardwalk that doesn't. So maybe it won't be so grim."

Gina laughed. "If it was grim," she teased, "they'd have to call it the Grimhouse. And nobody would visit it and the whole boardwalk would go out of business and we'd all be poor."

Tess hung up.

And realized immediately that she'd forgotten to ask Gina if her father had heard anything about the investigation. The police should know something by now, shouldn't they?

She'd ask this afternoon. Beak might have heard something if Gina hadn't. His parents were on the board of directors, too, as were Sam's and Trudy's. And Chalmers would probably go to the board with whatever he found before he shared it with the general public.

Too bad she couldn't call her own father. Well, it wasn't that she *couldn't*. She just didn't *want* to. If she told him how nervous the note had made her, he'd tell her she was being illogical and unreasonable and overreacting.

She'd rather find out what she needed to know from Gina or Guy Joe or any one of her friends. They wouldn't lecture her. Before she left, she gave Trilby a small bowl of water and a dish of the cat food Gina had sent with her.

Gina hadn't heard a thing about the investigation and neither had anyone else. When Tess complained, Sam lifted one dark eyebrow as if to say, "See? What did I tell you?"

The roller coaster frame had been roped off and tagged with large cardboard signs commanding NO ENTRY and STAY OUT! and CLOSED FOR REPAIRS. Everything else on The Boardwalk remained open. And just as Mr. Giambone had feared, few people were taking advantage of the fact. After all, something terrible had happened there. Something terrible could easily happen again. Why take a chance?

Tess understood that feeling. It was slinking around in her own head, tugging at her and making it impossible for her to relax. The purple note had mentioned a *next*. But it hadn't said when to expect it. Which meant that today couldn't be ruled out, could it?

Gina, trying to keep everyone's mind off the crash, chattered cheerfully as the group headed for the Funhouse. A bright red scarf tied around her dark curls, she trotted purposefully ahead of them in knee-length red shorts and a red-and-white flowered shirt. The sight of her, looking as if she hadn't a care in the world, should have perked up Tess's spirits, but it didn't. She had already begun gnawing on the fingernails it had taken her months to grow. She shouldn't have come. Keeping her eyes averted from the silent Devil's Elbow frame didn't keep the screams and moans and cries for help from echoing in her head. And she found herself continually looking over her shoulder, consumed by a creepy feeling that someone was watching her.

The Funhouse was a long, narrow tunnel built in an L shape, the foot of the L built out over the beach and supported by wooden stilts. The dark wooden structure contained several small areas of open railings dividing one passageway from another, where people could momentarily relax and enjoy the scenery and salt air before going on to the next challenge. Tess, her stomach rebelling after conquering the challenges of the rolling wooden walkway and then the tossing and tilting of a moving padded tunnel, took advantage of the second of these open balconies to catch her breath and settle her insides. Gina, Trudy, and Candace went on ahead to the third event, a nylon-padded tunnel whose footing consisted solely of heavy metal chain links.

Tess breathed in the cool air and tried to relax. But it was impossible. She was uncomfortable being anywhere near The Boardwalk, and she couldn't stop thinking about the man who had committed suicide in the Funhouse.

"You sick?" Guy Joe asked suddenly, coming up beside her. His yellow sweatshirt matched hers. But his complexion wasn't green, as she was sure hers must be. He looked tanned and healthy, as always. His stomach was stronger than hers.

"Uh-uh. Just catching my breath. You go ahead with the others." She should tell him about the note. But if he believed it was really a threat, he'd just tell her to move back in with him and their father, and she didn't want to do that.

"Beak's still back there," he said, inclining his head backward. "He got hung up on the rolling tunnel. He was on the floor as much as he was on his feet. Clowning around, as usual. Sam went back to give him a hand."

"Guy Joe," she said because she was sick of *not* talking about it, "do *you* think the crash was an accident? Tell the truth."

He shrugged. "Who knows? Anything is possible, right? The question is, why would someone do something so awful?"

"Yeah," she agreed solemnly, "that *is* the question." And although her imagination was pretty vivid, she couldn't come up with any reason why someone would commit such a horrible act.

Sam and Beak caught up with them a few minutes later. They took a break, relaxing on the balcony briefly while Beak told a few stupid jokes, and then they all went on together.

The hardest part of the Funhouse for Tess was always the chamber where there was no solid floor, only a cluster of constantly whirling metal saucers. They were slippery, always moving, and there was nothing to grasp for balance except the softly draped black nylon folds on the walls, almost impossible to hold onto, no matter how desperately you clutched. She had discovered long ago that the only way she could make it across was by lowering herself to a sitting position and scooting from saucer to saucer. It took longer, and seriously dented her dignity, but it worked.

She was in the process of doing just that when she realized that she wanted, very much, to go home. She wanted out of this crazy place with its skeletons rattling and its fake bats flying overhead and its dragons breathing foul-smelling smoke in her face. She was tired of feeling like a fool, arms and legs flailing helplessly as she tried to keep her balance on moving boards, linked chains, whirling circles, and rubber tires.

She'd had enough.

Although there were wooden steps exiting the Funhouse in several different places, Tess and her friends always chose the steep metal chute that slid directly to the beach. The walkways were for more timid souls. It was fun to sail down to the beach and land on the sand, legs sprawled every which way.

With a strong sense of relief, Tess did exactly that.

408

Trudy, Candace, and Gina were already comfortably seated on the beach, watching the waves pounding the shore. Beak, Sam, and Guy Joe followed Tess down the chute.

"Listen, guys," Tess said as she dusted sand from her jeans, "I'm going to split. My head is cracking right down the middle. I need to sleep." Ignoring Gina's protests, she reached into the back pocket of her jeans. And groaned.

"My keys are gone!" she cried in dismay. "I put my key case in my back pocket so I wouldn't have to lug my purse around with me in there," she said, waving toward the Funhouse. "They must have fallen out." She groaned again. "My stomach can't handle that place again, not this soon! It hasn't recovered from that stupid rolling tunnel!"

Gina stood up. "I'll go. I know your key case. The red leather one with your initials on it, right?"

"You'll never find that key case in there," Beak argued. "Get maintenance to look for it."

"Why doesn't Tess go herself?" Trudy asked. "They're *her* keys."

"Why don't we all go?" Sam said as Gina turned to leave. "Tess can show us exactly where she did most of her usual acrobatics so we'll know where the keys would most likely have fallen out of her pocket."

"No, that's silly," Gina said, waving a hand in dismissal. "I'll go, and I'll be right back. I know the Funhouse like the back of my hand and," she added with a grin, "my stomach's cast-iron, everyone knows that." And she turned and ran up the beach.

"Where's she going?" asked Doss, as he joined them.

"To find Tess's car keys," Trudy answered. "She lost them in the Funhouse."

"Then why is *Gina* looking for them?" Doss asked.

"Oh, for heaven's sake!" Tess cried, "I'll go, I'll go!"

The thought of entering the Funhouse again made her sick. But it was true — the keys were hers, she was the one who had lost them, and Gina shouldn't have to look for them alone. She turned to follow her up the beach.

Entering the Funhouse, Tess wondered how they would ever find the key case. The place had so many little nooks and crannies, so many cracks in the wooden floors, and then there were all those open spaces between the whirling circles. The keys might even have fallen through to the beach. If they didn't find the case in here, they'd have to sift through the sand next.

"Gina!" she called as she entered the rolling wooden walkway and clutched at the padded walls. "Gina, wait up!"

She had hurried through the tilting tunnel and was headed for the first of the open balconies, when a sound stopped her in her tracks.

It was a piercing scream that sent slivers of ice sliding down her back.

That scream wasn't a normal part of the Funhouse. It hadn't come from a witch's cackling mouth or a dangling skeleton or a bloody corpse. That scream had been real.

And the voice had been familiar. Very familiar.

Although she didn't want to believe it, the voice had belonged to Gina Giambone.

And it hadn't been an Oh-gosh-I'm-scared Funhouse kind of scream. Tess could recognize a scream of genuine fear when she heard it.

Calling Gina's name, Tess tried desperately to run. But it was impossible, given the footing underneath her as she entered the puffed-pillow passageway. She stumbled and fell several times before reaching solid footing again. Her breath came in ragged gasps, threatening to stick in her throat. Calls to Gina brought only silence in return.

Safer, more solid wooden walkways around each challenge brought her quickly to the chamber of metal saucers. They were separated by small spaces through which glimpses of the beach below could be seen. The spaces were so tiny they provided no danger, as only a toothpick-sized person could slip through and fall to the hard-packed sand below.

Unless . . . unless one of the large round circles was missing.

And one *was*.

Tess stared at the gap in the flooring, her mouth open, eyes wide as she realized that she could see, quite clearly, to the beach below. She could see the tan sand, flat in some spots, mounded into little hillocks by the wind in other places. She could see a small green plastic pail left by a careless child. And she could see . . . Gina.

She was lying on the sand, her left leg sticking out at a sickening angle, her face, in profile, twisted in agony.

And she was lying very, very still.

412

Chapter 11

Stupid Gina! Getting in the way like that. If it hadn't been for her goody-two-shoes helpfulness, it would have been Tess who fell through the hole, just as I'd planned. Slipping the key case out of her back pocket was a cinch, and the plan would have worked perfectly, if it hadn't been for Tess's weak stomach and Gina's Girl Scout instincts.

It was Tess's fault more than Gina's. The keys belonged to Tess. And that hole was designed for her. She really screwed up my schedule. She'll have to pay for that. I can't let people get away with fouling things up for me. I'll have to think of something special for her. To punish her.

Like I wish I could punish that Buddy in Lila's journal.

Buddy came to see me today. He says he knows a wonderful family who will give my baby a good home when it's born. I couldn't believe it! Does he think that just because Tully is gone, I would give away our child? I threw him out.

The next entry was several days later.

*Buddy keeps pressuring me to give up my baby.
He comes back every day, saying I'll never get a
job on The Boardwalk because the new owners don't
want me there. They think I'll make the customers
uncomfortable after what Tully did right there in
the Funhouse. He says I'll never be able to earn a
living and support my baby. And then he said his
friends, who want a child more than anything,
could give my baby everything.*

*He keeps saying that if I really cared about my
baby I'd give it up. What am I going to do?*

A few days later:

*Buddy was back again today. He told me this
family that wants my baby has offered to pay my
rent and my expenses until the baby's born. The
only strings attached, he says, are that they get the
baby when it's born, and I don't let anyone know
that I'm pregnant. When I asked him why, he said,
"My friends wouldn't want anyone to know the baby
isn't theirs. The woman has gone to Europe and
expects to be given the child when she returns, and
she'll tell everyone she had the baby in England."*

*I have to let him help me now. I have no choice.
I have so little money left, and no one will give me
a job. So I'll have to accept their money for now,
for my baby. But I'll think of something before the
baby's born. I'm not going to give up my baby.*

Chapter 12

Tess's only thought as she struggled through the remaining passageways toward an exit was, No, not Gina. Not Gina! Fake bats swung down from the ceiling, diving for her head. Dragons on the walls breathed hot smoke in her face. Skeletons rattled their bones in a crazy dance. She brushed them all aside and kept going. Don't be dead, Gina, she prayed. Don't be dead like Dade Lewis!

What would she ever do without Gina?

Gina wasn't dead. But she was unconscious. Tess's companions had already gathered around her limp body. Beak was kneeling by her side, holding one of her hands, with Doss on the other side. Beachgoers gathered around the small group as the sun sank beneath the sea.

"Someone call an ambulance," Beak cried as Tess, gasping for breath, her face tear-streaked, arrived and knelt at Gina's side. Someone called, "I'll go," and Beak turned back to Gina, calling her name repeatedly.

She didn't answer.

415

There didn't seem to be any blood. But Tess hated the fact that the big dark eyes refused to open. The smoothly packed sand was almost as hard as wood, and Gina had fallen a long way.

Jim Mancini, The Boardwalk's manager, pushed through the growing crowd. A short, squat man wearing tan pants and a white shirt with the sleeves rolled up to the elbow, he made a soft sound when he saw Gina lying on the sand. "What happened?" he asked as he knelt beside her and lifted her wrist to check her pulse. "She's alive," he said. A murmur of relief rose from the crowd. Turning toward Tess, he asked, "Did she hit her head? How long has she been unconscious? What's wrong with her leg?"

There was definitely something wrong with Gina's leg. No normal bone could make such a crazy angle.

"It's broken," volunteered Sam, whose father was a doctor. "Fractured, probably. Doesn't look like a clean break."

"I don't understand how this happened," Tess said in a bewildered voice over the sound of an approaching siren. "Why was that circle missing?"

Mancini's eyes narrowed. "Missing? What was missing?"

With tears in her eyes, Tess answered, "One of the spinning circles in the Funhouse. It was . . . gone. It had been there when we went through earlier. But this time, when I followed Gina into that passageway to see why she had screamed, one of the circles was gone. There was just this great big hole. Gina probably didn't see it in time and fell right through."

Mancini would have questioned her further, but the ambulance arrived just then. Tess wanted to ride in it with Gina, but the paramedics discouraged her.

"Call her parents," one of them said, "and have them meet us at the Medical Center." As he turned away to help carry the stretcher, he told his colleague, "I was on duty the other night when that roller coaster went. Some mess! And now this! I'm keeping my kids away from here from now on."

Tess turned away, intent on going straight to her car and then to the Medical Center. She wanted to be with Gina.

But Mancini stopped her. "Look," he said, "your friend's in good hands. You can see her later. Right now, I need you to show me where this happened. So it won't happen to somebody else."

Tess realized he had a point. That missing circle was dangerous. And she probably wouldn't be allowed to see Gina for a while, anyway.

She nodded. "Okay, come on. But I need to call Gina's parents first." She bit her lip anxiously. "They're going to be so upset."

"Someone already called," Candace said softly, putting a sympathetic arm around Tess's shoulders. "I heard someone say so."

"Good!" Mancini said. "Then we can get right to it. Come on, miss, show me what you were talking about."

417

Which Tess would have been happy to do, except for one thing. When she led Mancini and her friends into the chamber, there was absolutely nothing to see.

Because not a single circle was missing.

Tess stared at the spot where the gaping hole had been. It was now filled by a whirling, innocent-looking saucer, just as it was supposed to be. The disk stared right back at her as if to say, "But I've been here all along. You were imagining things!"

She could feel everyone's eyes on her after they'd searched in vain for anything out of the ordinary. "I don't believe this," she said slowly, feeling a flush rise up out of her neck and spread to her face.

"Well, *I* don't get it!" Mancini said, eyeing Tess suspiciously. "There's nothing wrong here. What were you talking about down on the beach?"

"It was gone!" she cried. "It was!" She knew, even as she said it, how crazy that sounded. After all, the circles were huge. Someone couldn't just lift one out and walk away with it without being seen. "The one in the middle was missing. There was a hole there! That's how I could see Gina, lying on the beach."

No one said a word. And that silence told her, very clearly, that no one believed her.

"Honestly, Tess," Trudy said lazily, "first you see some dark spirit under The Devil's Elbow and now you're seeing missing saucers. I thought people like you always saw *flying* saucers."

And even though Candace said, "Trudy, don't be so mean!" and Sam moved closer to Tess and said,

418

"Take it easy, Tess. You're upset about Gina," Tess began to shake violently. Her arms and legs trembled and Sam had to take hold of her with both hands to keep her upright.

"I know what I saw," Tess managed to say. "And if I didn't see it, then exactly how *did* Gina end up on the beach?"

Mancini shrugged toward the passageway up ahead. "Tumbled over the railing, maybe."

The railing was high, to protect small children from accidental falls. And Gina wasn't clumsy. "She couldn't have fallen over that railing," Tess argued. "It's too high."

"I think you'd better talk to the police, miss," he said coolly. "Something fishy here. I had my assistant give them a call. They should be here by now. You were the only person in here when your friend fell. They'll want to talk to you."

The police? A chilly fog descended upon Tess. "But I want to go to the Medical Center," she argued as they all left the Funhouse, taking the wooden stairs.

"That will have to wait," the manager said sternly, taking her elbow as they reached the foot of the stairs. Dusk had fallen and the air had turned chilly. Tess shivered. But she wasn't really cold. She was frightened. "We need to clear this up right now. I don't want any questions," Mancini went on, "about The Boardwalk's safety."

"Too late," Sam said drily. "Two accidents in one week makes for a lot of questions."

Ignoring his remark, Mancini gripped the sleeve

of Tess's yellow sweatshirt and led her to his office. Her friends followed, grumbling their support for her to themselves. Candace looked even more pale and frightened than usual, and Guy Joe's lips were drawn together tightly in anger. Tess could feel people along The Boardwalk staring at them, and knew that by nightfall the story of Tess Landers being dragged into Mancini's office would be all over town. Her face felt feverish, and she kept her eyes on the ground.

The police questioning wasn't as bad as she'd feared. There were only two uniformed men and they were more polite than Mancini had been. They asked her to take them back to the Funhouse and point out the spot where Gina had fallen. When they could find no evidence of any circle having been tampered with, they walked away from her, talking in low voices. But Tess heard every word.

"Isn't this the girl who brought that note in?" the taller one asked his partner. "You know, the one in purple crayon that Boz showed us?"

Boz. The desk sergeant, Tess guessed, and her cheeks burned with humiliation as the second policeman answered, "Yeah. One of those rich kids, lives up on the hill. Broken home and all that. Probably gets everything at home except attention, know what I mean?" He shook his head sadly.

She couldn't just let them dismiss her as some kind of attention-getting kook. "Excuse me," she said politely.

They turned around.

"If the saucer really wasn't missing," she asked

420

them, "how could Gina have fallen? There isn't any place here for her to fall through to the beach. Not with all the saucers in place."

"Good question," the tall policeman said heartily. "And you have our word, miss, that the matter will be investigated thoroughly. We may have to call on you again."

They wouldn't call on her again, and she knew it. But she also knew there wasn't any way to convince them that she was telling the truth. She had no proof.

"Look, kid," the taller policeman said, "you can go collect your friends now. We'll look into this, I promise. You're probably anxious to find out how your friend is."

He was being nice. Trying to smile, she admitted that she was anxious to get to the Medical Center. Now if only Gina was fine.

Gina wasn't fine. And they weren't allowed to see her, Tess was informed by the emergency room nurse. "You can wait in there," she said crisply, pointing toward a room at the end of the hall. Tess, seeing Mr. Giambone pacing the hall outside of the waiting room, ran to see if Gina's parents knew anything about her condition.

They didn't. No one had told them anything.

The sight of Gina's normally cheerful mother weeping, her hands over her face, shocked Tess. She wanted to say something to comfort the woman who had always been so good to her, but nothing seemed right. Quietly, Tess took a seat beside her.

"The doctor said she'd be in there a while," Doss

said, his usual swaggering air gone as he gestured toward the emergency room. He seemed as worried as everyone else in the room.

But suspicion had taken a firm hold on Tess and was growing with every passing minute. Two accidents in less than a week! In a town where things like this never happened. She didn't care *what* explanation for Gina's fall the police came up with, they'd never convince her that the saucer hadn't been missing. It *had*. Someone had taken it. She didn't have the slightest idea *how* someone would do such a thing. She only knew that someone had.

But who?

The person who had written the purple note, of course. The intention was clear from that awful poem. The police, and then Gina, hadn't taken it seriously. Maybe they should have. If there'd been no more accidents, Tess would have agreed with them that it was just a sick joke. But now Gina had fallen, and it was clear, at least to *Tess*, that the note had been for real.

What frightened Tess most was the fact that every single person who had been *seriously* hurt so far, with the exception of some innocent bystanders injured in The Devil's Elbow crash, had been her age, in her group of friends: Dade, Sheree, Joey, and now Gina. Why would someone target them?

And then Tess thought of something else, even more frightening.

Whoever had slipped that purple note under her door had known where she lived — that she lived with Shelley in the condominium, not with her father anymore. Only a few people knew that. Only her closest friends.

But that was impossible! None of her friends could ever do anything this horrible. Never! Could they?

Tess glanced around the room nervously. Could shy, quiet Candace be harboring feelings of hatred and anger toward her fellow students? Why? Because she felt left out? If people didn't pay that much attention to Candace, it was because she was so quiet. Maybe underneath that quiet, she was full of rage. Maybe she wasn't who they all thought she was.

Beak? Lover of practical jokes? Even he couldn't possibly find The Devil's Elbow crash funny — could he?

Trudy? Remembering the temper tantrum that Trudy had thrown in the school parking lot, Tess watched Trudy for a long moment. Wearing an expensive pink jumpsuit belted in rich leather, Trudy was filing her nails with an emery board, glancing up every now and then to smile at Guy Joe, who lounged against the wall. Could Trudy have some reason for wanting the people she knew well to suffer?

I can't believe, Tess thought unhappily, that I am even considering the possibility that one of my friends could have done such horrid things! It's just not possible, that's all!

Then who had? And why?

Doss, she thought, as she looked across the room at him, slumped in one of the hard plastic chairs.

Doss would know the Funhouse inside and out. And he'd know how to remove those metal saucers and replace them, wouldn't he?

The trouble with that theory, she realized instantly, was that Gina would be the last person Doss would want to hurt. Anyone who had seen the expression on his square, dark face when he looked at Gina would understand that Doss would rather break his *own* leg than Gina's.

That was when she remembered something, and sat up straight. Of course! The missing saucer hadn't been intended for Gina. The missing keys belonged to *Tess*. The hole in the saucers had been created for *her*. And those keys hadn't slid from her pocket at all. They'd been deliberately removed. That's why she hadn't been able to find them anywhere, and had to get a lift back home to pick up her extra set.

But who would have had the opportunity to take her keys? Doss would have. She now remembered he had been standing close to her on The Boardwalk before they'd first entered the Funhouse. He could easily have filched her keys. And then he could have removed the saucer, knowing Tess would return to the Funhouse to search for them.

But how on earth would someone time a stunt like that? And where would they put the missing saucer? There wasn't any place in the passageway to hide something so large.

Never mind. She'd figure all of that out later. Right now, it was enough to realize that Gina's fall hadn't been an accident, that it hadn't been intended for Gina, and that the note had been perfectly serious when it said *Who will be next?*

Tess shivered in her seat.

"Cold?" Sam asked, coming up to stand in front of her. "Want my jacket?" He slipped out of his brown suede jacket and handed it to her, but she shook her head no.

"Not cold," she said quietly. "Just thinking ugly thoughts."

He sat down beside her. "Like?"

She wasn't ready to share what she'd been thinking. Saying it aloud would make it so much more real. She had to do some more heavy thinking before she told anyone.

"Never mind."

He accepted that, and sat quietly beside her, asking no more questions.

"This is such a bad thing," Mrs. Giambone said suddenly. "My Gina, she was in such pain when they brought her in."

"She was conscious? That's a good sign, isn't it?"

The woman nodded, her round face, so like Gina's, creased with worry. "She was awake. But she was crying. And I cried, too." She shook her head, her curly graying hair moving with the motion. "That's not good, for a mother to cry in front of her child. It scared my Gina. But I couldn't help it."

Tess put an arm around Mrs. Giambone's ample shoulders. "She'll be okay. Honest, she will." Because anything else was unthinkable. "And I don't blame you for crying. I cried, too, when I saw her on the beach."

Until she saw Mrs. Giambone weeping, Tess hadn't given a thought to what all of this must be like for the parents. Sheree Buchanan's mother had spent most of Sheree's life bragging about how pretty her daughter was. Joey's parents came to every single track meet, even the out-of-town events. And the Giambones were understandably scared to death.

It's worse for them, Tess thought with conviction. It's worse for the parents.

Her head began to pound furiously. The words *Who will be next?* danced across the white walls, taunting her. *Who will be next, who will be —*

Dr. Oliver, Sam's father, stethoscope around his neck, appeared in the doorway. Mr. Giambone was right behind him.

"Your daughter," the doctor told the parents, "has a fractured leg and a mild concussion. We're going to keep her here for a while. No visitors for a day or two. Except, of course, for you two. You can go in and see her now, before we take her upstairs. She's worried about you."

"We can't see her?" Tess asked, her voice quivering slightly. She wouldn't be certain Gina was okay until she saw that for herself.

Dr. Oliver shook his head. "Sorry. Not yet. Give her some time to get over the shock to her system. A good night's sleep is what she needs right now.

Maybe tomorrow, although the next day would be even better, okay?"

It wasn't okay. But she had to do what was best for Gina. Because in a way, this was all *her* fault. It had been her key case. The hole had been meant for her. So the fall, the concussion, and the fractured leg should have been hers, too.

Perhaps because of her guilt, Tess stayed for a while after everyone else went home, hoping Sam's father would change his mind and let her see Gina.

He didn't, and when she was so tired she felt like she was about to collapse, she left, too.

She hurried to her car, hating the darkness and wishing she had asked someone to wait with her. But who? Right now, she was so unsure about everyone she knew that she couldn't think of a single person she absolutely trusted.

She cried quietly all the way home. Last night she had been safe in the Giambone house, drinking hot coffee and eating homemade doughnuts with a sugar glaze, fresh from Mrs. Giambone's deep fryer. She'd been sitting at the big wooden table in the warm, friendly kitchen, surrounded by large and small Giambones and laughing at the antics of the littlest ones.

Laughing. She'd been laughing! Had that been last night? It seemed like a million years ago.

At The Shadows, she parked the car, jumped out, locked the car doors, and was about to race for the kitchen door when something caught her eye.

There was an object hanging from the black

wrought-iron top of the light fixture on the wall beside the kitchen door. She'd forgotten to turn on the light before she left, so she couldn't see very clearly.

Peering into the shadows, she moved a step closer. The object was white. Not white-white, but grayish-white. A bundle of something? Paper? Rags? What would a bundle of paper or rags be doing on her light fixture?

She took another step closer. It looked soft and furry, like her angora sweater. White and soft and furry? What was white and soft and furry?

Scarcely breathing, Tess moved one more step closer to the light fixture. A sudden breeze sent the object swaying back and forth. Glassy blue eyes turned in the breeze, staring at her coldly.

Trilby.

Tess screamed.

Chapter 13

Poor Tess. What a fright that pretty kitty gave her.

I was in the attic so long that day, that it grew dark. I didn't even realize it until I could no longer read Lila O'Hare's faint scrawl. I pulled the chain on the bulb hanging from the ceiling. I wasn't about to leave until I'd finished the journal. It just got more and more interesting.

Buddy was taking care of her financial needs. He certainly owed her that much, after taking everything she owned. And still that wasn't enough for him. He wanted more. He wanted her child.

Buddy won't tell me who the people are who want my baby. But I think I know. And if it's who I think it is, they certainly could give my baby everything money can buy. And I do worry about that. Maybe I'm being selfish, not considering an adoption that could give my child the best life possible. I know I can't give it to him or her. Buddy says a good mother would care more for her child's happiness than she does her own. Maybe he's right.

Chapter 14

As Tess continued screaming, lights began glowing in first one unit, then another. Doors opened and heads peeked out, turning toward her screams. But no one ventured forth.

A car door slammed behind her. Footsteps hurried across the cement patio toward her. Hands grabbed her shoulders, shook her, repeatedly saying her name.

"Tess! Tess, it's Guy Joe! What on earth is wrong?"

Her brother was standing in front of her, blocking her view of the light fixture and the grisly thing hanging from it. He was flanked on one side by Sam and Trudy, on the other by a white-faced Candace. They were all wearing matching blue Santa Luisa High windbreakers, except Candace, shrouded in a faded tan raincoat and matching hat.

With the swaying animal blocked from her vision, Tess was able to catch her breath. But she couldn't speak. Instead, she pointed a shaking finger past Guy Joe.

Sam moved forward in the direction of the pointed finger. Tess watched in dread as he moved closer to the door. Tilting his head, he examined the object of Tess's terror.

After a moment, he called over his shoulder, "It's not real."

"What?" Tess whispered, sagging against Guy Joe.

"It's not real," Sam repeated. "It's stuffed. It's a stuffed animal, like the kind Candace has overpopulating her bedroom." He reached up and yanked the pile of fluff loose from the cord holding it suspended in the air. Then he returned to Tess, the freed object in his hands. "It's not real, Tess. See for yourself."

"Stuffed?" Tess said softly. "It's stuffed?"

Sam held it in his outstretched hands. "Does look real, though, doesn't it?"

Tess took the soft, fluffy creature in her own hands and turned it over repeatedly, murmuring, "It's not Trilby, it's not Trilby." When she was finally satisfied that it really was not Gina's cat, she let it slip to the patio and began crying quietly.

"Trilby?" Trudy said, taking a seat in a white patio chair. "What's a Trilby?"

"Gina's cat," Tess said quietly, sinking into a chair opposite Trudy because it suddenly occurred to her that if she didn't sit down, she would fall down. "You know, the big Siamese. She looks exactly like . . . that," pointing toward the object lying on the patio stone.

Trudy frowned. "Why would Gina's cat be hang-

431

ing from your lamppost? Honestly, Tess, you just get weirder and weirder!"

Candace came up behind Tess and put both hands on Tess's shoulders. "Shut up, Trudy," she said firmly, surprising all of them. "How could Tess know why it was there? The point is, it was, and it must have been a horrible thing for her. Leave her alone."

And Guy Joe, taking a seat beside Trudy, said, "I don't know about you, Trudy. Sometimes you scare me. You must have ice water in your veins. Ever hear of the word *compassion*?"

Trudy pouted.

Sam sat down in the chair next to Tess's, and took one of her hands in his. "It wasn't real, Tess." "I know it must have looked it, but it wasn't," he said softly. "It's a good thing we decided to drop by tonight."

Guy Joe took a book of matches lying on the round white table and lit a short, stubby citronella candle sitting in a glass dish in the table's center. Tess watched as the resulting light cast an eerie glow over the faces looking at her. Or was she imagining the eeriness? Was she so spooked now that everything and everyone seemed sinister to her?

Well, why shouldn't she be? Wouldn't anyone be, if the same cruel joke had been played on them?

"So Gina loaned you her cat," Trudy said, scooting her chair closer to Guy Joe's. "That still doesn't explain why you thought it would be hanging from your light fixture."

"I didn't *think* it was, Trudy!" Tess said hotly.

"It was! Or, at least, something that looked exactly like Trilby. And I have no idea why someone would pull such a rotten stunt. I also don't know why someone would deliberately sabotage The Devil's Elbow, or remove one of the saucers from the Funhouse or write me a threatening note."

"You got a threatening note?" Guy Joe and Sam said in one voice. And Sam added, "Why didn't you tell me?"

She didn't mention that they'd hardly been on speaking terms. This was not the time. "I didn't tell anyone," she said bitterly, "because so far no one has believed anything I've said about any of this stuff. Everyone says the crash was an accident, and that the saucer wasn't missing even though I saw it with my own eyes, and the police practically laughed me out of the station when I took my note in for them to see. So why would I tell anyone else about it?"

"What did it say?" Guy Joe wanted to know.

She told them. She knew the words by heart and would never forget them.

"Oh, Tess," Candace breathed when Tess had finished reciting the purple words, "that's awful! You must have been so scared! I would have been."

"Of course you would have," Trudy said cruelly, "you're afraid of your own shadow. And you wouldn't have the sense to realize that it was just a big, fat joke. But I'm sure Tess does, don't you, Tess?"

"It doesn't sound like a joke to me," Guy Joe said grimly. "Tess, I think you should move back to the house with Dad and me. At least until good old Shelley comes back. Not that she'd be much protection," he added coldly, "but at least you wouldn't be alone. How about it? Come home with me tonight?"

"That's the best idea I've heard," Sam agreed. "Even if it is a joke, you shouldn't be alone after the shock you just had."

The idea was tempting. Her father's house was solid brick, with an iron gate around the huge property. How could she not be safe there? It would be so easy to just leave the condo and go stay where people could take care of her.

No. She'd always done that. And her father wouldn't "take care" of her. He'd take charge of her. The two things weren't the same at all. She didn't want to take any stupid, foolish chances, but she didn't want to go running home to daddy, either, especially since "daddy" hadn't once called or come to see her since Shelley and Tess had left the house.

"No," she said as firmly as she could manage. "I don't think so. Not tonight. I need to think, and I can do that better here, in my own house."

"I'll stay with you, Tess," Candace said quietly, "if you want me to."

Tess was deeply touched. Trudy had been right earlier: Candace *was* a little like a scared rabbit. To offer her company in a house that might not be one hundred percent safe was a sweet thing to do. It must have taken great effort on Candace's part. Refusing her offer might hurt her feelings. Besides, she would hardly get in the way. Most of the time, people weren't even aware that Candace was around. And while Tess may have been confused about other things, she was sure that there was no way Candace could have had any part in the awful things that had happened. No question there. And it *would* be nice to have some company.

"Thank you, Candace," Tess said, "that would be nice."

"Oh, great!" Sam complained, "now I not only have to worry about you, I have to worry about my sister, too. That's just perfect!"

He was going to worry about her? What about their heated argument when he had said he was washing his hands of her for good? Washing your hands of someone for good didn't include worrying about them, did it?

"We'll be fine," she reassured him. "I'll lock all the doors and windows and put my attack cat in the window. Quit worrying."

She stood up, ignoring the annoyed look on Sam's face. "Now you guys, go home. I've never been so tired in my life! I'm going to bed." She managed a slight grin. "Sam, if you're so worried, you can sleep in a chair out here. I'll even bring you a blanket."

For just a minute or so, she thought he might actually accept. And she wouldn't have minded. It might have been nice, falling asleep knowing he was out there.

"No way," he said angrily. "I'm not freezing my buns off just because you're too stubborn to go back

435

to your dad's. Find some other knight in shining armor. This one's going home to his own nice, warm bed."

"Chivalry is dead," Trudy said gaily, standing up and taking Guy Joe's hand. "Well, Tess, you had your chance to return to the castle where you'd be protected by the moat. If anything terrible happens to you, it's your own fault."

Is that a threat? Tess wondered, and was amazed by the thought. Trudy? Well, why not? She could have tied the cat on the light fixture earlier. Could have written the poem, too. As for the missing saucer, well, Trudy the athlete and ballet dancer was certainly strong and agile enough to handle that.

But the question of motive remained. unanswered.

When they had gone, Tess and Candace went inside. The first thing Tess did was flip on every available light switch. The second thing she did was scoop Trilby up out of her wicker basket and sit stroking the soft, very much alive body until her own nerves settled down. Then she showed Candace where everything was, lent her a pair of pajamas, and gave Candace her own bed, explaining that she wouldn't be using it. She intended to take up her vigilant position on the couch, poker at her side, after making sure that every door and window in the place was locked and the oval table was still firmly pressed against the French doors.

When she finally settled down under the afghan, Trilby was already fast asleep on the couch.

Tess wasn't so lucky. In spite of her emotional

and physical exhaustion, she had a hard time turning off the turmoil in her mind so that she could sleep. Her best friend was in the hospital, the result of tampering aimed at Tess, someone had played a terribly cruel joke on *her* tonight, and what was worst of all, she knew this wasn't the end of it. There was more to come; she could feel it.

What next? she wondered fearfully just before she fell asleep.

She was awakened some time in the middle of the night, by the shrilling of the telephone on the lamp table behind her head. Struggling to wake up, she thought: Shelley. She'd forgotten or ignored the time difference. Typical Shelley.

Swivelling awkwardly, she reached to pick up the phone. It wasn't Shelley.

"It's your fault Gina's in the hospital," a voice she didn't recognize whispered in her ear. "You messed everything up. You'll have to be punished for that. Soon. Very soon."

Tess struggled upward on the couch, trying to comprehend the whispered words.

"Did you like my present tonight?" the horrid voice continued.

"Who is this?" she cried, knowing she wouldn't get an answer.

"Meow!" the voice said, and hung up.

Chapter 15

All I have to do is wait. That's what Lila O'Hare
did. She waited, all those months, for her baby, and
for Buddy to stop pressuring her to sign the adoption papers. She waited for someone to come to her
rescue.

No one did.

And being alone took its toll on her; I could tell
from the way her writing changed. As the journal
went on she seemed more and more tired and hopeless. Buddy's badgering was really getting to her.

The question that had been nagging at me ever
since I'd started reading the journal was still unanswered: Who was this Buddy? Was he still alive
and living in Santa Luisa?

And even more important: What was this journal
doing in my house?

Chapter 16

Tess awoke the next day, bleary-eyed from lack of sleep, to find that the rainy season had begun. Slate-gray skies overhead promised a steady downpour throughout the day.

And like the weather, the atmosphere inside Santa Luisa High School was grim. A sudden, painful acquaintance with multiple tragedies had affected every student and teacher. Even the usually raucous students walked the halls with heads down, talking in hushed voices.

"Doesn't anyone," Tess asked at lunch, "think two accidents in less than a week is a little suspicious? Has anyone heard anything from Chalmers? He should know something about The Devil's Elbow crash by now." She didn't mention her phone call of the night before. While it had terrified her, in broad daylight, it seemed a little fuzzy, and she wasn't sure that it hadn't been a dream. She had a feeling her friends wouldn't be convinced, either. She would keep the phone call to herself, for now.

"I heard it was a loose rail," Beak said casually

as he sectioned an orange, looping the peel around the wrist of Trudy, who sat beside him.

Trudy chose to ignore him, focusing all of her attention on Guy Joe, sitting opposite her, beside Tess. "My dad said at breakfast this morning that Chalmers told him the rail would be fixed, and an accident like that wouldn't happen again for at least another hundred years. A freak thing, he said."

"A loose rail? That's it? A loose rail?" Tess shook her head and sank back in her chair. "Are we supposed to buy that?"

"Tess," Beak warned, "you'd better lighten up or you'll lose it totally. Don't let this stuff get to you, okay? It's probably all coincidence, anyway. No dire plot, no sinister doings, just coincidence. Stuff happens, you know?"

"Leave Tess alone," Sam said lazily, dousing his hard-boiled egg with salt. "She had a rough day yesterday."

"We all did, Sam," Trudy reminded him sharply. "And I don't want to talk about this gloomy stuff anymore. I'm sick of it. And I am *having* my birthday party Saturday night, on the beach, the way I planned. You'd all better be there, or I'll never speak to a single one of you ever again!" A coquettish smile accompanied that threat.

"Promises, promises," Tess murmured. Aloud, she said, "Party? You're having a party? Now?"

Trudy tossed her thick, blonde hair. A fat pink velvet bow sat atop it, matching her short-sleeved sweater. "Yes, Tess, I'm funny that way. I like to celebrate my birthday on the day I was born."

440

"On the day you were born," Beak said with a grin, "your parents wouldn't give you permission for a party."

"Very funny, Beak. I mean, on the anniversary of the day I was born. Quit trying so hard to be cute."

"Oh, it's no effort. Comes naturally. You really having a party this Saturday?"

"What is the *matter* with you people? Don't you understand plain English? I just said I was, didn't I?"

"Holding a party at The Boardwalk," Tess said, toying with her sandwich, which remained untouched in its wrapper, "is like holding a party on a runway at a busy airport! You're just asking for trouble, Trudy. Haven't you been paying attention? People have been getting hurt over there."

Trudy's blue eyes narrowed. "Is that a threat, Tess? You were around both times something awful happened at The Boardwalk. That's a pretty major coincidence, don't you think?"

Tess gasped. "That isn't funny, Trudy! How could you even think such a thing?"

"Cut it out, Trudy," Sam warned. "Tess didn't have anything to do with that stuff, and you know it."

"Shame on you, Trudy," Candace scolded, her ponytail bouncing with the unusual vigor of her words, "Tess would never, ever hurt anyone!"

Unperturbed, Trudy shrugged. "All I know," she said stubbornly, "is that Tess was the only other person in the Funhouse when Gina fell."

That was too much for Tess. For all she knew, Trudy wasn't the only person in school who felt that way. People had been staring at her all day. She'd thought it was because she looked like such a wreck, but now she wasn't so sure.

"Ignore her," Candace said softly. "She's just being mean."

But as comforting as the words were, they weren't enough. Tess, biting her lip fiercely to keep herself from bursting into tears, stood up and hurried away from the table and out of the cafeteria. She was conscious of stares and whispers following her every step of the way.

Fury fueled her steps. Wasn't it enough that someone was torturing her with menacing notes and phone calls? Wasn't it enough that she was alone out there in the condo, without anyone around who cared about her? Wasn't it enough that her best friend was lying flat on her back in a hospital bed? People like Trudy had no right suspecting her. No right at all!

Quit feeling sorry for yourself, she scolded herself. At least you're walking on your own two feet, which is more than you can say for Gina.

After school, Tess went straight to the Medical Center, the heavy rain forcing her to drive slowly. On the way there, she passed The Boardwalk. It was almost deserted, with only a handful of cars in the huge parking lot. That couldn't be because of the weather, she told herself, since most of the amusement park was covered. If anything, The

442

Boardwalk was usually busier in bad weather, since it was one of the few places in town where kids could have fun without braving the elements.

Maybe the thing Mr. Giambone had feared was actually happening. Were people afraid to go near The Boardwalk now, after two serious accidents?

It was at that moment, as she turned a corner toward the Medical Center, that a new thought occurred to her. Maybe . . . maybe people being hurt wasn't the point at all. Maybe the actual target was The Boardwalk itself! The amusement park was hurting for business. Could that have been the goal all along? To cripple The Boardwalk? Or . . . could the target be the board of directors? Dade, Joey, Sheree, and Gina all had something else in common besides being students at Santa Luisa High School. Their parents were all on the board of directors that ran The Boardwalk. And so was her father.

There were eight people on the board. Well, actually only seven since Doss Beecham's father had been forced to resign. So far, four of them had received chilling phone calls summoning them to the Medical Center. Were the others soon to follow?

Pulling into a parking place on the street, she turned off the car's engine and sat quietly behind the wheel, watching the rain slide down her windshield. Should she go to the police with these new theories? On what basis? She had no proof, no new evidence to show them. They were just guesses. They made sense, but she was still missing the one ingredient necessary to clinch her argument: a motive. She had absolutely no idea why someone would want to sabotage The Boardwalk. A disgruntled employee, maybe, seeking revenge? Someone who felt he'd been unfairly fired? How could she find out if there was someone like that?

The best place to seek out that kind of information would be, of course, from one of the members of the board. Like . . . like her father.

She would have to think about that.

Something else occurred to her. Gina! When Gina awakened, she would tell Chief Chalmers and everyone else that the saucer had indeed been missing. Then Chalmers would believe Tess, not only about the saucer, but about the note and the telephone call as well. He'd be convinced, then, that nothing had been accidental. He would know, as she did, that someone in Santa Luisa was deliberately doing these terrible things, and he'd finally do something to stop it.

Gina was the key right now. Because she could also tell Tess who else knew that Tess had taken Trilby home. Only one of *those* people would have hung the stuffed animal from the light fixture. And they had probably done the other horrible things, too. Excited by the possibility of Gina providing answers, Tess hurried into the Medical Center, not even noticing the pelting rain. Now if she could just talk Dr. Oliver into letting her see his patient.

And she did. Gina's head was swathed in white gauze, tiny ringlets of dark hair escaping around the edges. Her cheeks were pale and gray, and her leg was held captive in the air by a torturous-looking pulley arrangement.

444

Relieved just to see her friend, Tess took a seat on a hard wooden chair beside Gina's bed and took off her jacket. When she had made sure Gina was feeling better, Tess leaned forward slightly, anxious for some answers. "Gina, have you thought at all about how someone might have removed that saucer?"

Gina looked blank. "Saucer? What saucer?"

Tess's heart sank. *Oh, no.* But she persisted. "You know. The one that was missing in the Funhouse. Someone took it out and left a hole. That's what you fell through."

Gina shifted uncomfortably in the bed. "Oh, gee, Tess, didn't the doctor tell you? I don't remember a single thing about yesterday. Not a minute of it! I don't even remember going to the Funhouse. My mom says that's where I got hurt, but it's all a big blank to me. Does it matter? You look awfully worried. What's going on?"

Tess sank back in her chair, crushed with disappointment. Gina had been her only hope. Everything would have been so simple if only Gina had remembered seeing the missing saucer.

"I guess," she said slowly, "that means you don't remember if you told anyone I was taking Trilby home with me, right?"

Gina nodded gingerly. "I didn't even remember that you had," she admitted. "How is she?"

Well, she's not hanging from the light fixture, Tess almost said. But didn't. Because she realized she couldn't tell Gina any of the frightening things that had happened. Not now. Not until she was out of that bed and back in her own home again. Gina had enough to worry about. "She's fine. She's good company. Can I keep her until you get back home?"

"Sure. She probably loves all the attention. She doesn't get much at our house. Too much competition."

In spite of her depression and disappointment, Tess laughed, and changed the subject to a safer topic. They were discussing their teacher Mr. Dart's habit of teasing Gina, when Guy Joe arrived with Beak and Sam. Trudy and Candace walked in a few minutes later. All were soaked, their hair and clothes dripping.

"You all look like drowned rats," Gina said with a smile. "And how did you get in here? The rule is no more than two visitors at a time." Her dark eyes registered disappointment, Tess noticed, when she realized Doss wasn't with them. "If Nurse Nasty finds you in here, you'll be sorry. I swear that woman chuckles with glee every time she gives me a shot. She must have majored in torture tactics instead of nursing."

While they all joked about the nurse, Tess watched them. Not one of them looked like the sort of cruel person who could even *pretend* to hang a cat.

But what about the absent Doss? He would have had more opportunity than anyone else to cause trouble at The Boardwalk. And he had a motive: he might be bitter that his family had lost all of their money while the others still had theirs. The board

446

of directors had fired Mr. Beecham because of his drinking, and the man had really fallen apart after that. Doss might be angry about that.

Angry enough to take Dade Lewis's life?

Maybe.

Her eyes shifted to Beak. Charming, funny Beak, who had once replaced a kettle of soup in the cafeteria with a pot of glue. Had poured a thick layer of honey into every pair of track shoes worn by his teammates, had tied two dozen aluminum cans to the back of a school bus, and had once come to American history class on stilts.

But the things that had happened on The Boardwalk weren't funny, and not even Beak could possibly think so. If he'd done those things, then he wasn't who she thought he was.

But right now, she wasn't sure who *anybody* was.

A moment later Doss arrived, standing awkwardly in the doorway until Gina called to him. A very tall nurse was standing right behind him, her mouth pursed in disapproval as her eyes surveyed the crowd.

"Oh-oh," Gina whispered loudly, "that's her! Florence Frightingale!"

In less than two seconds, the nurse had cleared the room of all but Doss and Tess, the two people Gina had asked to remain as her "legal" visitors.

"The rest of you am-scray now," the nurse said in a no-nonsense voice. "This is no recreation room. Run along."

They did. But as Beak straightened up after kissing Gina on the cheek, his eyes landed on Doss, standing beside Gina's bed. Tess saw the resentment in that look and wondered if she'd made a mistake dismissing Beak as nothing more than a practical joker. That was clearly anger in his eyes. It was gone almost immediately, but she didn't think she'd forget it quickly.

There was a moment of awkward silence after they'd all left. Then Gina, holding one of Doss's hands in her own, smiled at Tess and said, "You are going to Trudy's party, aren't you?"

"No, I *aren't*," Tess answered. "I'm not going near The Boardwalk. I think the place is cursed."

"Oh, come on, Tess!" Gina tried to sit up in bed but was defeated by the cumbersome pulley. "I want Doss to go and have a good time, and he says he won't unless you're there." Another smile. "He feels more comfortable with you than he does with the other guys."

Well, that was a surprise! Or did Doss really want her there, on The Boardwalk Saturday night, for nasty little reasons of his own?

His olive skin flushed with embarrassment. "Hey," he told Gina lightly, "don't talk about me as if I'm not here, okay? I don't want to go to that party without you, anyway."

"Neither do I," Tess agreed.

"Yeah, I know." Gina smiled up at Doss. "But the thing is, I have this problem." She pointed to her airborne leg. "The doctor says the only way I can leave here by Saturday is if I go without my leg. And I hate to do that. I like this leg." She grinned. "You might even say I'm attached to it."

Her visitors groaned.

"Okay, okay, so I'm no Robin Williams. Listen, I really want you guys to go to that party. Please? I know Trudy's a royal pain sometimes, but it's her birthday. Her parents are busy that night and without us, Trudy won't have any celebration at all. I can't go, but you two can. C'mon. For me?"

"That's not fair!" Tess protested. "You're in the hospital. You're hurt. People have to do what you ask or they'll feel like slime. Can't you ask me something easier, like taking a chem test for you or giving every pet in your house a bath?"

"Sam's going," Gina said slyly.

Tess knew her face was as red as Doss's had been a moment earlier. "Like I said, ask me to do something easier."

But Gina looked so disappointed. Tess reminded herself that Gina wouldn't be in a hospital bed if Tess had gone looking for her own key case. And Tess couldn't very well explain that her reluctance to attend the party was based on fear, without telling Gina about the hanging cat and the phone call. She knew she couldn't do that.

"Okay, okay, I'll go." She glared at Gina with mock anger. "Now I suppose you'll demand that I have a good time. Well, sorry, but that's too much to ask."

"Promise me you'll *try* to have a good time."

"Absolutely not." Tess stood up. She was beginning to feel like a third wheel. "I won't promise that. I'll go, but that's all you're getting from me. See you tomorrow."

Gina and Doss were smiling at each other when Tess left the room.

Maybe they were smiling because they didn't realize that something awful could happen at that party. Well, Gina didn't, anyway. Tess wasn't that sure about Doss. He might very well know that something awful was going to happen. She hoped not. Because Gina was falling for him, that was clear as crystal, and she didn't want to see Gina hurt any more than she already had been.

It was still raining hard, and her car was a block away. With only her blue windbreaker for protection, she was soaked through when she reached the car. She was still using her extra set of car keys on a small gold ring. They were harder to find in her shoulder bag than the larger key case, and she was concentrating on locating them when she stepped in a puddle of chilly water that soaked her feet to the ankles. Looking down in dismay, her eyes were distracted by something far more disturbing.

The left front tire directly opposite her feet was no longer doughnut-shaped. It was as flat as a deflated balloon.

Groaning, Tess's eyes went immediately to the rear tire. It, too, was completely flat.

A feeling of dread rising within her, she sloshed around the rear of the car to the other side. And sagged against the door as her eyes focused on two more thoroughly deflated tires.

450

One flat tire would have annoyed her, especially in such lousy weather. Two would have surprised her, although she supposed that sort of thing happened sometimes.

But four flat tires was an unmistakable message.

Her breathing was shallow as she bent in the rain to examine first one tire, then the others, more carefully. She found exactly what she had feared she would find.

All four tires had been deliberately slashed.

Chapter 17

Ha, ha, ha. Shredded tires. Now her car won't go!

I think she knows I've been following her. Keeps looking over her shoulder. Reminds me of a deer I saw once when my dad made me go hunting with him. It knew we were after it. I felt sorry for it. But I don't feel sorry for Tess. Why should I?

Lila decided to give up her baby for adoption. I knew it was coming, but it still made me angry when I got to that entry.

I don't know what else to do. I'm so tired. And Buddy's right. I can't provide what a baby needs. I've tried and tried to think of a way, but there is none.

He keeps telling me how much these people want a baby of their own. Doesn't that mean they'll love it and care for it? I hope so.

But anyway, it's too late now. I've signed the adoption papers. I pray I did the right thing . . .

I knew, somehow, that she didn't.

452

Chapter 18

Staring at the shredded tires on her car didn't make them suddenly inflate, so Tess straightened up and looked around her, her heart thudding in her chest. Someone had done this deliberately.

Sagging against the useless car, her wet hair and clothes clinging to her she thought, Gina had a lot of visitors tonight. Every single one of them knows this is my car. Someone I know — one of my friends — is after me and I have no idea why. The thought made Tess feel sick. She heard the whisper again. *"You'll have to be punished . . . soon."*

What should she do now? Call the police? She'd have to tell them who she suspected, the whole long list of names. She couldn't do that. She had no proof. They'd never believe that any child of one of The Boardwalk's directors, the most powerful people in town, was responsible for all the turmoil.

Which child *was* it?

And why were they hurting people in Santa Luisa?

She was stranded. How was she going to get

home? Any minute now, Doss Beecham would leave the hospital and find Tess stranded out here. Although she wasn't *sure* he was the one, that thought made her more nervous than the slashed tires. All she knew was that she wanted to get home, out of the rain, where she could think straight.

Turning, she hurried away from the car and out into the road leading up the hill toward The Shadows.

Halfway up the hill, misery overtook her with full force. She was alone in the dark and the wind and the rain and she was frightened. Where was the tire-slasher now?

Was he watching her? Tess glanced around nervously. The hill and the woods on either side seemed deserted. But were they? Wouldn't the sound of footsteps be muffled by the wind and the rain?

Realizing just how vulnerable she was, walking out in the open up the main road, she decided it would be safer to take a shortcut through the woods. It would be muddier, and therefore slower, than the paved road, but the thick woods might provide some shelter from the weather, and at least she wouldn't feel like a walking target. Out in plain sight on the road, she might as well have a bull's-eye painted on the back of her blue windbreaker.

The thick, tall trees did provide some protection from the torrents of rain spilling out of the sky, but she had no flashlight with her and couldn't see very well. Fortunately, there was a path, and although the mud and deepening puddles prevented her from hurrying, she did feel a little safer in the woods.

The heavy rain had softened the earth beneath her feet into a soggy goo. Walking was difficult. She slid as often as she stepped safely. Low-hanging branches she couldn't see in the darkness jumped out at her, snagging her hair, scratching her face. Several times she hit low spots in the path and sank up to her ankles in cold water and mud. The mud clung to her feet like glue, making her sodden shoes feel as if they were encased in cement. But she struggled on, because she had no choice.

The first couple of times she heard a noise behind her she told herself it was her imagination. The next time she heard it — a soft, padding sound — she told herself it was probably a small animal, a raccoon or a possum. But when the sound came again an uncomfortable feeling began to rise in her throat.

She was not alone in the woods. Someone was following her. The tire-slasher?

She stopped to listen intently. A fluttering sound in the trees overhead reminded her that bats had recently been reported in the area. The reports had frightened her, but Sam had dismissed her fears by saying, "It's not like you make a habit of wandering around outside after dark."

Well, no, not usually. Only when all four tires on her car had been slashed.

There! The sound came again, close enough to be heard distinctly. And it *was* footsteps, she was sure of it. It was an exact echo of the plodding, slogging, dragging-through-the-mud sound she herself was making.

Panicking, she tried to hurry. Her heart was

pounding so thunderously in her chest she was sure her pursuer could hear it. But she couldn't quiet her terror.

The sound behind her drew closer. Soft, soft . . .

Frantic, and sobbing quietly, she tried desperately to run. But her skirt, sweater, and jacket, completely saturated with water, weighed on her like a suit of solid lead. And her feet were imprisoned in a thick coat of gooey mud. Every step she took was a struggle, requiring enormous effort. Running was impossible.

"Te-ess! Oh, Te-ess!"

The voice, so close behind her, shocked her to a standstill. Distorted by the wind and the rain, the voice was unrecognizable. And evil. It was hard to believe that someone she knew well, a friend, could sound like that.

"Te-ess! Wait for me-ee!"

The sing-song was cruel, that of a predator who knows his prey is close at hand — and defenseless. *You'll have to be punished . . .*

Tess almost gave up. Soaked to the skin, with water dripping from her hair into her eyes, and mud up to her ankles, surrounded by dark, silent woods and sheets of rain, she thought about simply sinking to the soft ground and waiting for her tormentor to pounce on her. At least then she'd find out who it was.

No! Maybe he would catch up with her, maybe she didn't have a chance, maybe he was too cunning to be outsmarted. But she wasn't giving up without a fight!

Instead of continuing along the path, she veered abruptly, into the deeper, thicker woods sheltering a housing development. She would soon be trespassing on private property, but even a vicious guard dog would be better than what was behind her and closing in rapidly.

She emerged from the woods to see clumps of pale light ahead of her. A surge of hope overtook her. If she could just get to one of those houses . . .

Renewed hope quickened her steps. The lights grew larger, brighter. She heard a dog barking close by, and turned in that direction. A dog meant a dog owner and a dog owner meant a house and a house meant safety.

Safety. What a beautiful, wonderful word!

She was going to make it.

As she took a step forward, there was a sudden rustling sound behind her and something hit her between the shoulder blades. Already unsure of her footing, the blow threw her off balance, and she fell.

Expecting to hit the ground at any second, she braced herself for the sudden, unpleasant contact with a cold and muddy earth.

Instead, she felt a rush of air and the sensation of space all around her as the earth disappeared beneath her.

She had tumbled into open space. And she was falling, falling. . . .

Chapter 19

I could have finished her off tonight. Easily. But it's too soon. I have other plans to carry out before I take care of Tess.

No guilt. This is simple justice. What those men did was atrocious, and they can't be forgiven. They would never have been punished at all if I hadn't found the journal.

I read for so many hours that day in the lousy light of the attic, that my head felt like it was ready to split open. But I had to finish. By that time, it was as if she were writing only to me. And I had this feeling that she knew I was reading it.

The baby was born yesterday, right here in the trailer, with the help of Buddy's doctor. But I never even saw my baby! The doctor snatched the baby away the minute it was born, and gave me a shot. I was asleep in a minute or two and when I woke up, hours later, they were gone. All of them. Buddy, the doctor, and my baby. Gone!

458

Buddy showed up at the door later that night. When I asked him where my baby was, he said, "In its new home." Then he laid something on the dresser, saying it was a "gift" from the grateful parents, and left, warning me that if I made any attempt to see my baby or reveal who I was, I'd go to prison for a long, long time.

I just sat there in the dark after he left. Then I got up and walked to the dresser. I picked up the gift from the new parents.

It was a check. For a great deal of money. I had sold my baby. I hadn't meant to, but that was what I'd done.

I tore the check into a million pieces. They're here, those pieces, taped into the back of this book. They're the only proof I have of what happened. And I've taped in a list of the names of the others, besides Buddy, who were involved.

I can't fight them. The people who stole The Boardwalk and took my baby are too powerful. Going up against them would be a losing battle. I'm too tired for such a fight. My strength left me for good when they took my baby.

So I'm going to follow Tully. My child will be cared for, and I can only pray that the cruelty its new father showed me will not be exercised on my baby. Can such a man ever love? I can only pray that he can, he and his wife.

Perhaps, some day, someone will find these writings and understand my story. In that hope, I'm hiding this journal in my secret place.

And now, I go to Tully, with a prayer that he, and God, will forgive me.

That was the last entry.

I flipped the pages to the back cover. There, in a small plastic bag fastened with yellowed cellophane tape, were the pieces of paper Lila had talked about, shreds of the check Buddy had left on the dresser after he had taken her baby. And underneath the plastic bag was the list of names she'd mentioned. Every single one of them was familiar. Including my *own* last name. No surprise there. This was just the kind of thing I'd expect my father to be involved in.

Carefully setting the journal aside, I went downstairs to get my own roll of cellophane tape. I was very good at puzzles. I would put the pieces of the baby's "purchase price" together. And I would have the answer I needed.

Chapter 20

Tess's landing, when it came, was softened by a cushion of muddy water. But still it shocked her, knocking her breathless as she landed on her stomach, face down. Upon impact Tess was completely covered in thick, brown sludge. Pulling herself to a sitting position, she scrubbed her face frantically with her sleeve, and realized she was sitting in several inches of rainwater and mud.

Stunned and shaken, Tess slowly became aware of two other things. One, she was at the bottom of a huge, rectangular mudhole and two, there was a dog somewhere above her, barking furiously. The sound comforted her. With an angry dog close by, would the person who had pushed her dare return?

The first thing she needed to do, she decided, shaking her head to clear it, was escape from this watery prison. Dog or no dog, she couldn't stay down here.

But the walls of sodden earth were as slippery

as glass. Clawing at them desperately provided her with nothing but two thick mittens of mud and deep frustration. Getting a foothold on the walls was equally impossible.

Still, she kept trying, slipping and sliding from spot to spot, searching with her hands and feet for something solid to grasp.

It was hopeless. Giving up, she moved away from the wall and shouted in fury through the sheets of rain to the barking dog, "Quit that stupid barking and go get some help! Didn't you ever hear of Lassie?" Then, her anger spent, she sank to her knees, tears of frustration and fear mixing with the rain on her face.

The barking stopped.

A fluttering in the air overhead stopped her heart. Bats! She screamed and covered her head with her hands, trying to shrink her body into as small and invisible a target as possible.

Suddenly, a beam of light shone down upon her and a deep voice called from above, "Hey, down there! Couldn't you wait until the pool was finished?"

Tess shrank back in fear. Who was that? Could it be the person who had been chasing her, who had sent her sailing into this watery hole?

"You okay? I'll get you out of there, hang on!"

No, this voice belonged to an older person. She didn't think it was anyone she knew. Maybe she could trust him. She almost laughed aloud hysterically. Wasn't that backwards? Weren't you supposed to be able to trust the people you knew, but

462

not talk to strangers? How had everything gotten so screwed up?

"Please!" she called, "please get me out of here! Hurry!"

Something dangled in front of her. She reached out for it. It was a thick rope, waving like a flag of freedom before her.

"Can you climb that?" the voice called.

"No." She couldn't. Her strength was gone.

"You weigh much?" The voice belonged to a man. A big, strong one, she hoped.

"No. I'm skinny."

"Okay then. Just grab on, tight as you can, and I'll haul you up."

Tess obeyed. But her normally light weight had been increased by sodden clothing and several layers of mud. The haul upward went slowly. She tried to keep her body away from the wall, but there was nothing solid for her feet to push against, and her face slammed into the oozing wall more than once. Sputtering and spitting, she held onto the rope with every ounce of energy she had left. And finally, finally, she was on firm ground, her weary, shaken body supported by strong arms.

"How on earth did you land down there?" her rescuer asked, removing his tan raincoat and wrapping it around her. He was a big man, and he smiled at her as his flashlight revealed the mud monster she had become.

"I'm sorry," she said, her teeth chattering, "that I used your pool without your permission. I promise it will never happen again."

He laughed, and she recognized him. Trudy Slaughter's father. She had fallen into Trudy's pool?

"You're Mr. Slaughter, aren't you?" she asked as he half led, half carried her toward the house.

"Right. Do I know you? Not that anyone would recognize you right now."

"I'm Tess Landers."

"Guy Joe's girl? You go to school with Trudy, right? Well, Guy Joe's girl, how did you get into my pool?"

She couldn't say she'd been pushed. An answer like that would lead to too many questions, maybe even a visit from the police. She had no answers for them. Besides, she couldn't be that sure that someone had actually pushed her. It could have been a tree branch, blown by the wind, that hit her.

Sure. And The Boardwalk was the safest place in the world.

She couldn't help wondering, now that she knew how close Trudy lived to these woods, had *she* been the one stalking Tess?

Mr. Slaughter was waiting for an answer to his question.

"My car broke down," she said. "I was taking a shortcut home, but I didn't have a flashlight and I guess I got lost."

He nodded. "Hard to see on a night like this. Good thing Beau here doesn't like intruders."

The dog, a sleek Doberman pinscher, trotted along beside them, apparently satisfied that he'd performed his duty well.

When they reached the house, Mr. Slaughter wanted Tess to come inside. "Trudy isn't home, but I'm sure she'd want you to borrow some dry clothes."

Well, of course she wasn't home, Tess thought. She couldn't go running home so soon after pushing Tess into the pool. She'd have to wait a while, so that no one would know she'd ever been nearby. And Tess had no intention of setting one foot inside Trudy Slaughter's house.

"I'd really rather go home, Mr. Slaughter. If you could find an old blanket or something to cover the seat, maybe you could drive me home? I wouldn't want to ruin your upholstery, abominable mudman that I am right now."

He didn't argue with her. Tess suspected that he might have if he'd known that Shelley was out of town and Tess was going home to an empty house. So she didn't volunteer that piece of information.

When they pulled up in front of the condo, Sam's car was parked beside the stone patio wall. And Sam was in it.

He got out when the Slaughter car arrived. Tess was grateful that he didn't laugh as she got out of the car. He didn't look much better, though. He was almost as wet and mud-covered as she was. Her heart sank. Could he have been running around in the woods? After *her*, maybe?

All of this suspicion was making her crazy.

"That your brother?" Mr. Slaughter asked as she got out of the car.

"No. That's Sam Oliver."

"Oh. Trent's boy. Friend of yours, I guess. You'll be okay, then?"

Friend? Who could be sure? "It's okay, Mr. Slaughter," she said, reaching into the car to hand him his raincoat. "I'll be fine now. Thanks for everything. And thank Beau for me. Maybe I'll buy him a nice big bone."

Apparently convinced that Tess was in good hands with "Trent's boy," Mr. Slaughter drove away.

"What happened to you?" Sam asked, removing his windbreaker and draping it across her shoulders. "You look like you just had a mud bath."

"Close," she said cryptically. Then she moved to sweep past him with as much dignity as she could muster, but he stepped directly in front of her, blocking her path.

The words *Who will be next?* swam in front of her eyes again, and she felt dizzy. Not Sam, she prayed, don't let it be Sam.

"I'll take you to your father's," he said. "You can get cleaned up there and get a good night's sleep."

No. Maybe she would go to her father's. Soon. She did want to ask him if any employees had been fired recently from The Boardwalk. But she wasn't getting in a car with anyone. Not until she knew who was sending her purple poetry and making nasty phone calls and following her.

Because it might not have been Trudy. It could have been Sam.

"I can get cleaned up right here in my own

466

house," she said defiantly. "We have plenty of soap and water."

"You're going to stay here alone tonight? I went to the hospital to see if you'd left yet, and I saw what someone did to your car, Tess. That was deliberate. Did you call the police?"

"No. Not yet." And she wasn't going to, either. But she didn't have to tell him that.

"Tess, how did you get so muddy? Something happened, didn't it? I knew it! Beak said you'd be okay, but Candace was pretty worried when I told her about your tires."

"Was Trudy with them?" If Trudy had been with Candace and Beak, she couldn't have been running around in the woods pushing people into unfinished swimming pools.

"Uh-uh. Beak and Candace were at Amy's, scarfing down ice cream." He frowned. "Weren't you just with Trudy? That *was* Kevin Slaughter who brought you home, wasn't it? Trudy's old man?"

They were getting even wetter, with only the driveway lampposts for protection from the weather. "I'm going inside," she said, moving around him toward the patio gate. "Go home." So Trudy hadn't been at Amy's with Beak and Candace. Maybe she'd been too busy for ice cream. *Busy hunting.*

"Tess . . ."

She stopped and turned around.

"I talked to my dad tonight. He said Chalmers will be releasing a statement tomorrow that The Devil's Elbow crash was an 'unavoidable accident.' "

Tess snorted rudely.

"Maybe it was, Tess."

"Since when do you take your father's or Chalmers's word for anything?" she asked rudely. "You never listen to your father, and you were the one who said Chalmers couldn't find his own nose without a mirror. You're also the one who said they'd cover up whatever they found and now when they're doing just that, you're taking their side."

"There isn't any side, Tess. This isn't a war."

She looked straight at him, her chin thrust forward defiantly, tears sliding from the corners of her eyes. "Oh, isn't it?" Then she turned and hurried into the house, slamming the door after her.

She didn't watch to see if he left. Instead, she went through her door-and-window-locking ritual, called a garage to have her car picked up, and headed for the bathroom for a long, hot, comforting shower.

The shower renewed her spirits slightly, and she was about to make a cup of hot tea, when the telephone rang. Setting the blue-and-white teakettle on the kitchen counter, she picked up the phone. If it was Shelley, maybe she'd just give her a piece of her mind, tell her exactly what she thought of parents who left their children to traipse halfway around the world when there were crazy people running loose!

"Happy birthday to Trudy," sang that voice that sent shivers down Tess's spine. "Happy birthday to Trudy, happy birthday to Trudy, may she live till you die!" Then the voice added in a low sing-song,

468

"Which may be soo-on!" Then the line went dead.

Tess held the silent telephone in her hand a moment or two longer. Then she slowly replaced it in its berth on the wall. Turning, she picked up the teakettle, placed it on a stove burner and switched on the heat. Staring at the gas flames as if hypnotized, she repeated in her head the words she'd just heard on the phone.

Something terrible was going to happen at Trudy's party.

Chapter 21

Liars! They're going to announce that The Devil's Elbow crash was accidental. They know it wasn't. There was no loose rail. It was my lead pipe that sent that roller coaster into space.

What good does it do me to punish them if they let the whole town think nothing is going on?

Well, not the whole town. Tess knows. She doesn't know why, but she knows nothing was accidental. She just doesn't know what to do about it.

It's time to do something that can't be interpreted, even by Chalmers and the board, as accidental. Shake them up a little.

They're worried, I know they are. They had a meeting here last night. The driveway looked like a luxury-car dealership. I thought about eavesdropping and decided against it. What could I overhear that I didn't already know? And after the meeting, I ran into my father in the upstairs hall and saw his eyes go to the attic door. Is he beginning to remember about the journal? Why didn't he get rid of it a long time ago? Ego, maybe. Didn't want to let go of the only real proof of his greatest accomplishment.

If he does remember, and looks for the journal, he won't find it. I've hidden it. When my plan is finished, I'll send it to someone I trust, so that none of the men involved can find it and destroy it. The people of Santa Luisa have a right to the truth. Just as I had a right to it. But it was kept from me.

Until Lila told me. Through her written words.

It didn't take me very long to Scotch tape that shredded check together. When the puzzle was completed, there was the signature, big as life.

I'd seen that signature many times before. It had signed my report cards and permission slips for school outings and a number of checks exactly like the one I held Scotch taped in front of me, given to me in place of birthday presents. It was a name I knew well. *Very* well.

It was my father's name.

The attic began to spin around me. My father had "bought" a baby. Considering Lila O'Hare's account, *stolen* was a better word. He'd stolen a baby.

And then I looked at the date on the check. It was my birthday.

Suddenly everything was clear. I wasn't who I thought I was.

My last name wasn't the same as the signature on the check, after all. Not really. My last name was O'Hare.

I was the O'Hare baby.

471

Chapter 22

On Friday, Tess's car was delivered, complete with four brand-new tires. And a brief announcement on the radio and in the newspaper that the crash of The Devil's Elbow had been due to a "loose rail," which would be quickly repaired, ended speculation in Santa Luisa about recent events at The Boardwalk.

When Tess questioned Gina at the hospital about how her own accident was being explained, Gina shrugged and said, "I guess I fell over the railing." And when Tess looked plainly disgusted by that answer, Gina continued, "Tess, I wish you'd quit worrying about it. It's over and done with, and I'm going home soon. You'll drive yourself nuts if you don't forget about it. Daddy said The Devil's Elbow will be good as new and we won't even remember the crash happened after a while. I'll be good as new, too. Can't you relax?"

Tess couldn't. Completely convinced that both accidents had been anything but accidental, but not having a shred of proof, she felt helpless and frightened. This wasn't the end of it, she was sure of that. There was more to come.

She went to Trudy's birthday party on Saturday, hoping to learn something. The people attending all had parents on the board. If she kept her eyes and ears open, maybe she'd come up with some answers. But she went with a sense of dread that something bad was going to happen. She was convinced the phone call hadn't been a joke.

The party was held at night, on the beach below The Boardwalk. Darkness had fallen before Trudy's guests arrived, but the area was bathed in the amusement park's neon glow, with additional lighting provided by tall pole lamps scattered along the beach. The rain had temporarily ceased, and only a few innocent-looking clouds floated now and again across the half moon. A Saturday night with nothing to do in Santa Luisa, combined with the results of Chalmers's investigation, had brought increased business to The Boardwalk. Laughter and music, along with the usual smells of hot dogs, popcorn, and cotton candy, gave the party site the proper atmosphere.

When Tess arrived, Sam and Guy Joe, in cutoffs and short-sleeved sweatshirts, had already built a small, cozy fire. Trudy, unsuitably dressed for a picnic in an elegant yellow jumpsuit, her hair piled on top of her head, sat in a lawn chair like, Tess thought to herself, a queen waiting to greet her subjects. And Candace, cocooned in a dull blue muu-muu, busied herself removing food items from a wicker hamper. Several blankets were spread close

473

together to provide seating and some slight protection against the rain-dampened sand.

Doss arrived shortly after Tess. Beak came next, a huge bouquet of multicolored balloons in hand. Presenting them to Trudy with a dramatic flourish, he asked where the food was.

"Here, Beak," Trudy said, offering him a red box crammed full of chocolate-frosted brownies. "Take this temptation out of my path. We're not having hot dogs until I open my presents, but you can start with these. If I eat even one, the chocolate will go straight to my hips."

Beak selected two very large brownies. Then he donned a party hat of pink crepe paper trimmed with silver and began dancing on the sand, his mouth full of brownie, arms and legs flailing to music from the cassette player Trudy had brought. Grabbing another tiny hat, this one bright yellow, he slid its thin elastic band over his head and clamped the pointed little hat over his nose.

Laughing at his antics, Tess found it hard to imagine that this silly, crazy boy could have had anything to do with sabotaging The Boardwalk.

Then Trudy cried, "Beak, you look like a psychotic chicken!" which wiped the smile from Tess's face. *Psychotic* wasn't a word to be thrown around too lightly these days. And Beak hadn't laughed when Trudy said it. Hadn't he heard her? Or had he decided to ignore it because it hit too close to home?

A sudden hand on her shoulder startled her and she jumped and whirled around.

"For Pete's sake!" Sam said. "Relax! You're as nervous as my old man when the stock market takes a dive. What's the matter with you?"

"Nothing." She twisted a strand of hair around her finger nervously. "But you shouldn't sneak up on people like that."

"Sneak up? You looked lonesome standing over here all by yourself. How come you haven't joined the party?"

Because I don't trust anyone, she wanted to answer, but didn't. Because I'm waiting for doom to strike, her mouth got ready to say, but didn't. Because . . .

"I thought you'd be more relaxed now," Sam said, watching her face carefully, "now that we know The Devil's Elbow crash was accidental."

She laughed harshly. "Yeah, that's a big relief, isn't it?"

"You still don't believe it?"

Beak ran over to Candace and tugged at her hand, insisting that she join him in his crazy dance. To Tess's surprise, Candace did.

"Sure, I believe it," Tess lied, because she couldn't tolerate one more person telling her to forget about it. "Any reason why I shouldn't?"

He knew she was lying, and looked hurt. "No, I guess not. Take a walk down to the water with me."

"No." She wasn't going near the water. A drowning would make a great "accident," wouldn't it? Besides, she should stay here. Since she was the only one who expected something bad to happen, she needed to keep her eyes open. Maybe if she really paid attention, she could somehow prevent another disaster.

"Well, then walk up the beach a little way with me. C'mon."

She hesitated, watching Doss. He seemed uncomfortable, sitting off to one side of the blankets by himself. She knew he had come only to please Gina. Just as Trudy had probably invited him only to please Gina. Although, who knew about Trudy? Maybe she had a reason for wanting all of them there. Doss's father was no longer on the board of directors, but he *had* been. Maybe that was why Doss had been included at Trudy's party.

On the other hand, if it was Doss who had caused the crash and taken the saucer and made the telephone calls and sent the ugly note, this would be the perfect opportunity for him to do more damage. With Gina safely in the hospital, he wouldn't have to worry about accidentally hurting her while he was targeting any of the others.

She wished with all her heart that this evening was already over, and they were all safely back in their own homes.

"Trudy hasn't opened her presents yet," she told Sam.

"Yeah, I noticed. She's too wrapped up in your brother to unwrap presents. Hey, a little play on words there? Wrapped up, unwrap, get it?"

"I got it. I just didn't think it was very funny."

"It wasn't supposed to be funny. It was an accident."

That word again. *Accident*. She had learned to hate it.

Laughter from The Boardwalk echoed out over the beach. People were having fun up there. She wished she could join them. "I wish Trudy would open her presents and feed us. I'm starved!" She was stalling. The thought of food sickened her.

"Have a brownie."

"Too sweet. I want real food." Something as sweet and gooey as a brownie would be worse than trying to swallow ordinary food. "She promised us hot dogs."

"Well, while we're waiting, take a walk with me."

Beak and Candace were still cavorting on the sand, Guy Joe was being held captive by Trudy, and Doss was delving into the brownie box. He seemed to have relaxed a little and he didn't look the least bit dangerous.

Maybe she could leave them alone for a few minutes. It would give her a chance to explain her theory about the board of directors to Sam. If he laughed at her, she'd simply never speak to him again. But if he didn't, maybe together they could figure out what to do. They wouldn't walk very far.

"Okay. But just for a few minutes." Casting one last quick glance across the party group to make sure everything was okay, Tess turned and joined Sam. "And we can't go far."

They plodded silently across the damp sand. The night wind tugged gently at her hair, sent her short, full red skirt billowing around her legs. Because she had her head down, Tess didn't notice until too late that they had been walking toward the disabled Devil's Elbow. The lights trimming its lengthy frame were still on, but the tracks were bare, the cardboard signs still waving on the thick rope fence.

"I don't want to be here," Tess said clearly, stopping in her tracks. "Let's go back."

"Don't be silly, Tess." Sam looked down at her, annoyance bringing his brows together. "The thing isn't even working now. The new cars haven't been delivered yet. What's there to be scared of?"

"It gives me the creeps, that's all. Makes me jittery just looking at it." And it did. She kept hearing the screams . . .

"You're turning into a nervous wreck," he accused gently. "Everybody says so. If you don't relax — "

"Of course I'm a nervous wreck!" she shouted, losing control. "And you would be, too, if you had half a brain! Haven't you even noticed that the kids hurt the worst so far all have parents on The Boardwalk's board of directors?"

He hadn't. She could tell by the startled look on his face. "What?"

"And that's something they all have in common with *you*," she continued. "Your father is a director, too. So is mine." Her voice rose again, "So why *aren't* you a nervous wreck?"

Sam began walking in a small circle around her, his head down. "Never even crossed my mind," he said. "What made you come up with such a crazy theory?"

478

"Facts, Sam, facts," she said crossly. "Can't you *see* it? Can't you even admit that it's a possibility? That someone is out to ruin The Boardwalk and hurt a lot of people at the same time? It's the only answer that makes sense."

He stopped pacing to look at her. "Got any idea who it might be? This crazy phantom of yours? And why he's freaked out?"

She shook her head. "I have a couple of possibilities, but no proof. And it's no phantom, Sam. Phantoms don't send threatening notes and make nasty phone calls." She should have kept the note. It was more convincing than anything she could say. Too late now.

"Look," he said, "I'm not saying you're right or you're wrong. But if you're even close to the truth, why haven't you moved back to your father's house? You'd be safe there. I don't see how you can think what you think and still stay alone in that condo out there in the woods. Makes no sense."

She had been thinking about doing exactly that, moving back with her father and Guy Joe, just until this nightmare was over. But if Sam wasn't convinced that her theory was a valid one, what business did he have accusing her of being foolish? Either there was a reason to be afraid or there wasn't. Sam couldn't have it both ways.

"Then you agree that my theory makes sense?"

"I didn't say that. But if *you* think it does, why are you still in the condo? If Chalmers and the board are covering up something, this is no time for someone like you to be all alone out there in the woods."

479

"Someone like me? What's that supposed to mean?" Occasionally biting her nails and twisting her hair didn't mean she needed a keeper! He was being so patronizing, she thought angrily.

"Someone," he said firmly, "who gets spooked just looking at a roller coaster that isn't even working. Why are you being so stubborn about this?"

"And why can't you take me seriously?" she shouted. "Why can't you admit that everything I've said makes sense?"

In exasperation, he reached out and took hold of her shoulders, as if he was about to shake her. Instead, he pulled her close to him, bent his head, and kissed her. "There," he said as she pushed him away, "is that taking you seriously enough?"

The kiss had unsettled her. Flustered, she said angrily, "What is that, some kind of therapy for people you consider nervous wrecks? Well, it didn't work. I still think I'm right, and until you do, too, I don't want to talk to you. Go away!"

"Oh, I give up!" he shouted in disgust, and turned in the sand to stride away from her, throwing his hands up in the air as he walked.

She watched until he became a blurred shadow in the darkness. She was sorry she'd ever agreed to take a walk with him.

Why hadn't he been willing to discuss her question about the victims being kids of the board of directors? It was worth discussing. It could be the key to this whole, ugly business.

She was *not* going to follow him. Not yet. No trailing after him like a lost puppy. She wasn't wild

480

about staying out here under The Devil's Elbow by herself, but it was better than following Sam as if he were her keeper. She'd sit on the sand for a while to cool off, and then rejoin the party. Laughter and music rang out from the place where Trudy was celebrating her birthday. It sounded like fun. She'd go back in a few minutes.

The sand was damp, and soothed her fingers as she dug into it, molding little hills on either side of her as she watched the surf teasing the shore.

Her left hand touched something hard and sharp, buried in the sand. She pulled out the object and turned toward The Boardwalk to give herself more light. The object appeared to be a small stone — some type of gem. Holding it up to the light, Tess saw that it was blue. And she'd seen stones like this before. It wasn't particularly valuable, she was sure of that. It was something very common.

Of course! It was the kind of stone worn in Santa Luisa High School class rings. She'd bought hers early in September. But it had proved to be so bulky that she seldom wore it, keeping it instead in her jewelry box.

Someone in town wasn't wearing theirs at all. A class ring would look pretty stupid with the stone missing.

She stood up, stone in hand. She looked around, frowning. And looked down at the spot where she'd been sitting. It was directly beneath that last gentle curve in The Devil's Elbow's tracks.

That probably meant nothing, Tess tried to assure herself. Everyone in town wore Santa Luisa

High class rings. And stones probably fell out of them all the time.

Or did it mean the stone belonged to the person who had tampered with the roller coaster?

Anyway, the stone couldn't be identified. Only the rings were identifiable. And she didn't have the ring belonging to this stone.

But she slipped the stone into the pocket of her red long-sleeved shirt. She couldn't have said why. It seemed the right thing to do.

Then she hurried back to the party.

She was halfway there when the quiet hit her. There was supposed to be a party going on ahead of her, but there was no noise. Quiet as a tomb. That didn't make sense. Where had the laughter, the music gone?

Her steps quickened. They hadn't left without her, had they? Left her alone out here? No, they wouldn't do that. Guy Joe wouldn't.

Then, half running across the hard-packed sand, she heard sounds coming from the direction of the blankets.

But they weren't party sounds.

The sounds she heard were moans and groans, sounds of pain. Almost like a muted version of the sounds she'd heard on the boardwalk the night The Devil's Elbow had crashed.

Heart pounding, she ran the last few steps.

And arrived on the scene to find everyone but Sam and Trudy writhing in agony on the sand, clutching their stomachs and moaning in pain.

Chapter 23

Tess ran to Sam and clutched at his elbow. "What? What's happening? What's wrong with them?" she cried, her eyes on her agonized friends.

"Don't know. They just doubled over all of a sudden, a second ago. Trudy," he barked, "get an ambulance! Hurry!"

Trudy ran. When she had gone, Tess turned to Sam in tears. "I didn't want to be right about something bad happening. I *didn't*!"

"I know that," he said, putting an arm around her shoulders. "Let's see if we can do something for them."

But the only thing they could do was cover everyone with a jacket or sweater, and wait.

When Trudy returned, breathless, she began wringing her hands as she saw that nothing had changed. "I can't believe this is happening!" she shrieked. "What is the *matter* with them?" Then her eyes narrowed in suspicion, focusing on Beak, who was rolling from side to side on the sand, moaning. "Beak, if this is one of your practical jokes, I swear I'll strangle you! You're ruining my party."

"Get real, Trudy!" Sam snapped as sirens began, once again, to approach The Boardwalk. "Look at their faces. Does it look like anyone's joking?"

Tess, thinking wearily that she would be hearing sirens in her sleep for the rest of her life, knelt by Guy Joe's side. His pain was so great he had bitten through his bottom lip. A thin stream of blood pooled on his chin. She took one of his hands in hers, but he gripped it so hard, she cried out in pain and he let go. Tess hadn't felt so helpless since the night she'd been trapped in the muddy, unfinished swimming pool.

Sam bent over her. "Did you eat any brownies?" he asked, his voice low.

"What?" What was taking that ambulance so long?

"I said, did you eat any of those brownies Trudy passed around?"

"No. I wanted real food, remember? Why?"

Sam crouched beside her. A distraught Trudy was tossing party things into bags and baskets, muttering in distress to herself, and the injured were too preoccupied with their pain to listen to Sam. Still, he kept his voice low. "Because I didn't eat any, either. And I'm fine. And Trudy's on a diet. But Beak and Guy Joe each polished off a couple of pieces, and Doss had at least one. So did Candace. Get the picture?"

Before she could concentrate on the meaning of Sam's words, the ambulance arrived.

When the attendants had asked about booze and drugs and been assured that none of either were used at the party, Sam handed one of the paramedics the red box, now empty of all but a small chunk of chocolatey cookie. "Brownies," he said brusquely. "They ate them. We didn't."

Asking no further questions, the attendants took the red box with them when they drove away with the patients.

Sam, Trudy, and Tess followed the ambulance in Sam's car. They were sitting in the now familiar waiting room when the parents of the victims began rushing in.

"Tess," her father demanded when he arrived, "what is going on? What's happened to your brother? And where were you when it happened?" He was, as always, impeccably dressed in tan slacks and a pale blue sweater. His thick white hair was perfectly in place. And his blue eyes were as cold as ice.

"I was there," she answered defensively. "And to answer your next question, it wasn't drugs or booze. It was probably brownies."

Thick, white eyebrows aimed for the sky. "Brownies?"

"Trudy had a box of them at the party. Everyone who ate them got sick," Tess elaborated, sinking back into her orange plastic chair.

"Are you talking about ptomaine poisoning?" he demanded. "Who made these brownies?"

"I guess they were a gift," she said vaguely.

"Only we don't know who from. From whom. There wasn't any card on the box. Trudy said she found it sitting on the picnic hamper."

The other parents had joined Tess and her father and were listening intently to every word. Mrs. Beecham, wearing a very expensive-looking but outdated black dress and black shoes with worn heels, hovered on the edge of the group as if unsure of her welcome. Beak's parents, whose formal clothing told Tess they'd probably been enjoying a Saturday night at the Country Club, looked concerned, and Sam's father, in golf clothes, stood beside his son, looking annoyed.

"Are you *sure* you weren't fooling around with drugs?" Mrs. Rapp asked Trudy. "We have, of course, always considered the possibility that Robert might experiment with controlled substances. And he hasn't been himself lately. He seems angry about something, and has been remarkably rude lately. His younger sisters have just about had it with him."

"No drugs!" a teary-eyed Trudy shouted. "We said it wasn't drugs or booze and it wasn't."

"No, it wasn't," a strange voice agreed. The voice came from the doorway.

All heads turned. A tall, thin man in a white jacket came toward them. He wore glasses and carried a clipboard.

"Doctor Joe Tanner," he said. "I've been pumping the kids' stomachs. They'll be okay. Miserable, but okay. We'll keep them here overnight to make sure there's no permanent damage." Then looking

486

at Mrs. Rapp, he added, "These kids are telling you the truth. It wasn't drugs or booze. Their friends were poisoned."

There was a stunned silence. Sam looked over at Tess, the expression on his face grim.

"Poisoned?" Trudy asked in a small voice. "You mean it wasn't just someone making a mistake when they baked the brownies? Like putting in too much of something or not enough of something else?"

The doctor shook his head. "This was no accident, if that's what you mean. Looks like rat poison, although we can't be sure until the lab has analyzed the remaining brownie. But it's definitely poison. Fast-acting." He looked down at the chart in his hands. "Is there a Beecham here?"

Mrs. Beecham moved forward hesitantly.

"Your son can go home tonight. Donald, that's his name?"

She nodded. "Doss. Everyone calls him Doss."

"He must not have consumed as much of the tainted food as the others. Very minor damage to his gastrointestinal system. I'm releasing him."

Maybe the reason Doss wasn't very hungry, Tess thought angrily, was that he *knew* the brownies weren't exactly a health food. And if someone had poisoned food at a party and wanted to avoid suspicion, wouldn't that someone eat just a little bit of that food? Enough to make that someone look like one of the victims?

Was that what Doss had done?

"Are you telling us," Tess's father asked, "that someone tried to *kill* my son?"

Tess shot him a look of disgust. Wasn't it just like him to see the problem only in terms of himself? There were two other boys and a girl in that emergency room.

"No." Dr. Tanner shook his head. "I'm not telling you that. There wasn't enough poison in any of the kids to kill them. Either the guilty party didn't know his toxicology, or he never intended to take anyone's life. Just make them suffer. A lot."

Tess tried to take it all in. Poison! No way could this be called an accident. It had been deliberate. The doctor had said so.

"I've got to get back," the doctor said. "But the police are here and I think they want to talk to all of you, so don't leave, okay?"

Sam and Trudy and Tess nodded silently.

When he had gone, taking the parents with him, a depressed silence fell over the group. Trudy was crying quietly in a corner. But Tess wasn't impressed. Trudy Slaughter had acted the lead in several plays at school. And she'd been very good. Very convincing.

Those brownies had shown up at *her* party. She'd told Tess tearfully that they'd been a gift. But there hadn't been a card.

Trudy could very well have brought them herself.

"Poison," Tess said, in almost a whisper. "I can't believe it." She stared at the white tiled floor and twisted her hair around a finger.

"*Now* will you move back with your dad?" Sam

asked. "This waiting room has been a second home to us lately. I've been thinking of installing my toothbrush in the bathroom down the hall. But if I have to come here again, I don't want it to be because of you."

She lifted her head. "I'll think about it, I promise. But I'm not going back tonight, because Guy Joe won't be there. I don't want to be alone in that house with my father. Maybe I'll go up and see Gina. She should be told about this before she hears gossip around the hospital. And maybe I'll spend the night in a chair in her room. That way, I'd be close to Guy Joe, too." She didn't add, *And I'd be safe there*, although the thought certainly crossed her mind.

Just then Chief Chalmers, a heavyset, red-faced man who walked with a slight rolling motion, entered the room, followed by two other policemen.

Tess was glad to see them. The uniforms were reassuring, in spite of the fact that so far they hadn't been of much help to her. But they couldn't dismiss a deliberate poisoning the way they had the other incidents.

"You still got that cookie box?" the Chief asked when they'd filled him in on the evening's events.

Trudy shook her head. "We gave it to the ambulance attendants. You can get it from the doctor, I think."

Chief Chalmers, looking grim, told them he would want to talk to them again, after the toxicology report was in. Then he left, taking his companions with him.

489

"Well," Sam said when they'd gone, "at least he's not blowing off this one as a prank. That's something."

"I'm going up to see Gina, tell her what happened," Tess said. "You'd better take Trudy back to the beach to get her stuff." She wasn't worried about Sam being alone with Trudy, even if Trudy *had* poisoned the brownies. Sam could take care of himself.

Making her promise to call him before she left for her father's house with Guy Joe the next day, Sam left. Watching a thoroughly shaken Trudy follow him out of the waiting room, Tess found it hard to believe the girl was guilty. She seemed so upset by the disastrous end to her birthday party.

But then, she *was* an actress.

Tess had to sneak into Gina's room. She hadn't realized how late it was. Visiting hours were long over, the halls dim. Gina was sound asleep, with only a tiny nightlight on over her bed. Exhausted, but feeling perfectly safe for the first time in a long while, Tess curled up in a chair and fell asleep.

Chapter 24

The truth of who I was had danced around the attic that afternoon. I could feel it laughing at me. And as it came closer and closer, stealing my breath and wrapping itself around me, I felt every shred of the old me sliding out of my body and slipping along the attic's wooden floor until it disappeared through the cracks.

I was gone. There wasn't any *me* anymore. My whole life had been a lie and when the truth erased that lie, it erased me as well. I didn't exist.

How could I argue with the words of the woman who had lived this story, whose words spoke of truth and pain? How could I argue with the signed check with my father's signature on it? How could I protest a date that said, quite clearly, that although I had indeed been born when I thought I'd been, I hadn't been born *who* I thought I'd been?

I was the O'Hare baby. I was the baby snatched out of its mother's arms on the day it was born. I was the child lied to, never told the truth, never told who its real parents were. I was the kid who had every material possession possible but never an ounce of real love.

Lila O'Hare would have given me that love. I could tell that from her writing. And Tully would have, too, if my father and his friends hadn't driven the man to suicide.

I *wanted* that life, with Lila and Tully. I knew, I *knew* it would have been a good life.

But I couldn't have it now, not ever. It had been stolen from me, just as everything had been stolen from my real parents. They'd even stolen Lila's journal after she killed herself, and my "father" had hidden it here, his incredible ego unwilling or unable to part with it. I shivered, thinking of the horror of it.

The man I'd thought was my father, and his friends, had lied and lied. Because of that, my whole life was a lie. So what did it matter what I did with that lie of a life? No wonder I had never felt that I belonged with this man, belonged with this family. I *didn't*.

They had to be punished. All of them. But what could I do to them that would equal what they'd done to Lila, to Tully, and to me? What would be awful enough?

Suddenly, I knew the answer. It was almost as if a voice were whispering in my ear. "Don't punish the men," the voice said. "Punish their children. The men will suffer the most if you do this." I knew the voice was right.

And the children would be easy to get to. They were, without exception, my friends. I saw them all the time. They trusted me. Why shouldn't they? They didn't know what I knew.

That was how it all started. It's worked out pretty well, so far. And now, I've finally done something that can't be passed off as an accident. It'll be great fun watching Chalmers flounder around trying to explain it. No one will believe that what I did this time was an accident. No way.

It's kind of weird, knowing you're not real. Makes everything easy, in a way. Feels like I'm walking around without a body, as if I'm already in spirit form.

I will be, soon. I've decided that when I've finished with my list of targets, I'll join my real parents. Why not? I have no life here. Those people stole it from me. My life isn't my life anymore. So what's there to hold on to?

But before I go, Tess has to suffer. I've been keeping her scared so she'd seem crazy and no one would take her seriously. And it's worked. But she's not getting off that easily. I have to teach her a lesson.

Because Tess messed things up for me. Now I have to skip one of the names on my list. Chalmers will have to investigate this time and he could trace the poison to my house. The hardware store keeps a record of all poison sales. Chalmers could come knocking on my door any minute now.

What really makes me angry is that I never found out who Buddy was. That was so important. I'd ask around, but I can't afford to make people suspicious. And I certainly can't ask the one person who would definitely know. The man who used to be my father. No, I can't ask him.

But I got most of them. Sometimes I even got to see the pain in the parents' faces. That made it all worthwhile. I was happy to see them suffer! Serves them right. They can't suffer enough pain to satisfy me, after what they did. I wish I could have done more.

The only thing left to do is to punish Tess.

I'm going to take her with me when I go.

Chapter 25

Tess was gently shaken awake the following morning by Mrs. Giambone. "What on earth are you doing here?" she asked with concern, as Tess tried to remember the answer to that question. Before she succeeded, Gina awoke, and when she realized who was in the room, repeated her mother's question to Tess.

Struggling awake, rubbing her eyes fiercely and realizing that every muscle in her body ached, Tess explained.

Gina was horrified. "You'd better go and stay at my house until Chalmers comes up with some answers. Right, Mom?" she said, looking at her parent for confirmation.

But Tess said quickly, "No, it's okay. I'm going home with Guy Joe. I'll stay there until Shelley comes back." She reached up to smooth her hair into some sort of order. "You know that place. It's a fortress!" She was hoping Gina wouldn't ask who Tess thought was behind the poisoning, because she would have had to say Doss and/or Trudy, and she couldn't deal with Gina's reaction to her suspicions of Doss.

Telling Gina and her mother she'd be right back, Tess left the room to find out when Guy Joe was being discharged and how he intended to get home.

Guy Joe was in the shower, but his father was picking him up at nine-thirty, the nurse at the desk told her. Tess left him a note saying she'd be leaving with them and would come to his room before nine-thirty, and then she returned to Gina's room. She stayed long enough to fill Gina in on Trudy's party. There was no point in keeping the details from her, because the hospital would be buzzing with that information. Tess preferred that her best friend hear the gory details from her.

"I thought you were imagining things before," Gina said when Tess had finished. "But I guess you weren't. Something terrible is going on. And you suspect someone, don't you? I can tell. Who is it? *Tell* me!"

But Tess couldn't. What was the point in upsetting Gina? Tess had no proof. And Gina had enough problems right now. Pointing at the clock, she told Gina she had to get downstairs to meet her father and, promising to return later, left the room.

The ride home was a solemn one. The rain had eased, although the sky was gray enough to promise more later. Tess sat uncomfortably on the front seat between Guy Joe and her father. She was anxious to shower and change into clean, fresh clothes. After Guy Joe told her he was glad she hadn't eaten any brownies and that he was feeling weak but fine, and she said she was sorry she couldn't have helped him more, the conversation died. The remainder of the ride was silent.

The only comment from their father was, "Chalmers had better do his job right this time, or I'll know the reason why."

Tess and Guy Joe simply nodded.

The big, red brick house looked gloomy and forbidding, but she told herself that was probably because of the weather. Still, it was hard to regard her father's home as a safe haven. Was any place safe right now?

At least she wouldn't be alone. And neither Doss nor Trudy could get at her here. They would never make it past the front gate.

When their father had deposited them at the front door, he went off to work. She and Guy Joe went straight to their rooms. Tess showered and crawled into bed, and was asleep in minutes. When the housekeeper, Maria, knocked on the door to awaken her for dinner, Tess was shocked to discover that the clock on her bedside table read six-thirty! She'd slept all day! Well, why not? The thought of leaving her fortress to go see Gina made her hands sweat and her heart pound. But she had promised.

Maybe she could talk Guy Joe into going to the hospital with her. If he felt up to it. If not, she'd call . . . who? Who did she trust enough to call? Candace, maybe. Although Candace probably

497

wasn't feeling very well, either. I just can't go out alone, she thought, close to tears. I can't! It's too risky.

Dressing quickly in an old pair of jeans and the red top from the night before, she hurried downstairs.

Dinner was as quiet and unpleasant as the ride home had been. Telling herself it was worth it just to feel safe, Tess ate quickly and asked to be excused.

"I have a meeting tonight," her father said, not looking up from his chocolate mousse. "Robert Rapp is picking me up. You may use my car if you have somewhere to go."

That was a surprise. If Guy Joe wouldn't go with her, she could drive her father's Mercedes and someone watching for her little blue car would be disappointed. "I promised Gina I'd take her something to read. But I'll be back early." Then she remembered what she had wanted to ask him. "Father, I was wondering . . . have you or anyone else on the board fired someone recently?"

His white head lifted, blue eyes met hers. "No. No one besides Beecham. Why would you ask that?"

Tess felt her cheeks reddening. "Well, all of the kids hurt have parents on the board. Doesn't that seem awfully coincidental to you?"

"Exactly right," he said firmly, returning to his mousse. "Coincidence, nothing more. Chalmers will handle things. You go on and have a good time, now."

And that was that. He might as well have said,

"Run along and play now," she thought angrily. End of discussion.

Her father turned to Guy Joe. "Any plans tonight?"

"Nope. Not me," Guy Joe said, standing up. "I'm wiped out. I'm just going to sack out, take life easy."

Tess's heart sank. But she wouldn't push. She didn't blame him. He'd been through an awful experience last night.

Maybe she'd be safe in her father's car. Whoever was watching for her would think that Guy Joe, Sr., was in the Mercedes.

"Very well," her father said. "I'll see you both later." They'd been excused.

"He hasn't changed, has he?" Tess said quietly as she followed her brother up the stairs.

"Did you think he might have?" Guy Joe asked with a grin.

Tess shrugged. "Isn't hope supposed to spring eternal?"

"Not in this house."

Sighing heavily, she went on to her bedroom, planning to look for her old yearbooks. Gina would get a kick out of them.

They weren't there. Maria must have moved them. Put them somewhere out of the way, thinking Tess wasn't coming back.

Well, if she was going to have to search the house, she'd take her Walkman with her. That way, George Michael could keep her company and she wouldn't be disturbing Guy Joe's much-needed sleep. Clamping the headphones over her ears and snapping the cassette player on the metal chain belt circling the waist of her jeans, she began her search.

It took a while. The last room she entered was large and dark. New raindrops slid down the small windows. She switched on the overhead light, a bare bulb with a chain pull. But she had no idea where to begin looking. The yearbooks could be in any one of a dozen boxes and trunks. There, that trunk in the corner, maybe?

Before she could open it, she'd have to unload all that junk on the lid. What were all those things, anyway? Humming to the beat pounding in her ears, she bent over the trunk and picked up the first object: a Santa Luisa High School class ring. Without the usual blue stone. And . . . her red leather key case! What was that doing here? Beside it lay a paper napkin, pale blue, exactly like the ones Trudy had brought to her birthday party. Her initials swirled across one corner: T.S. The tiniest traces of chocolate cookie crumbs clung to one edge.

A pulse in Tess's throat began to beat double-time, out of synchronization with the drums pounding through her headphones.

Then she saw one more object: a large, fat, purple Magic Marker.

She stood stock-still in the corner of the room, holding the key case in her hands.

After a minute, she remembered that she was wearing the same red top she'd worn to the party. Reaching into one pocket, she pulled out the blue gem she'd found in the sand. She placed it carefully into the hollow of the ring on the trunk.

500

It fit perfectly. As she had known it would.

What did all this stuff mean? What was it doing lying there so neatly, so well-ordered, like . . . like . . .

"It's like a shrine," she said aloud, lifting the earphones from her head as she picked up the ring to look for initials inside it.

"Well, good for *you*," a voice said from directly behind her. The headphones had prevented her from hearing footsteps on the attic stairs.

"Because that's exactly what it is," the voice, hoarse from stomach-pump tubes, said. "A shrine. To my mother, actually."

Tess whirled to meet the voice.

It belonged to her brother, Guy Joe Landers, Jr.

Chapter 26

A thoroughly bewildered Tess looked up at Guy Joe. "A shrine? To our mother?"

It was amazing then, the way his face changed, twisted into something strange and terrifying, his gray eyes cold with contempt, his upper lip raised in an ugly sneer. "Not *our* mother, stupid! *My* mother!" Then, more calmly, he added, "We didn't have the same one, you know."

"Guy Joe, what are you talking about? Of course we did!"

He shook his head. "That's what *you* think. I know better." He leaned forward, grabbing one of her wrists and clutching it tightly. "They *stole* me," he hissed in her face, "stole me right out of my mother's arms. And now they're paying for it! And you're going to pay, too. Because it was *your* father who kept the truth from me. He was the one who adopted me and never told me."

Tess felt dizzy. What was he *talking* about? Guy Joe was adopted? He wasn't her real brother? That was crazy. She would have known. Wouldn't she?

Wouldn't *he*? People told adopted children the truth now, didn't they?

But there was something in Guy Joe's eyes that told her he believed every word he was telling her. And it was making him crazy.

Her eyes went to the top of the trunk. The ring, the key case, the napkin with brownie crumbs . . . Guy Joe had put them there. Each of them had something to do with one of the accidents. *Which meant . . . which meant . . .*

"Yes, I did it," he said triumphantly, reading her mind. "I did all of it, and it was easy. So easy! This town is full of fools! Greedy fools. They wouldn't close The Boardwalk because they were afraid of losing a few dollars, so they made it easy for me."

"No, Guy Joe," Tess said softly, "you wouldn't . . ."

"Wouldn't what? Wouldn't kill Dade Lewis and send the others to the hospital? Oh, wouldn't I? It was justice, Tess, pure and simple. They had it coming, all of them. They asked for it. They were all in on it. Your father and his friends. They stole me and then they kept that truth from me. All of them."

"I don't understand." She tried to back away from him, really frightened now. Because she believed him. It hadn't been Doss or Trudy, after all. It had been Guy Joe all along. And now, suddenly, it wasn't safe to be around her own brother. Only . . . only he was telling her now that he *wasn't* her brother. How could that be?

"You don't *have* to understand," he sneered. "All

you have to do is come with me. I have plans for you."

She pulled against his grip on her wrist. "Guy Joe, tell me what this is all about. What's going on? I'm your sister. You can tell me. I won't hate you, I promise."

He laughed, a harsh sound that echoed throughout the attic. "*Sister?* Don't you get it? Weren't you listening? You're not my sister. You're not anybody's sister! Because I'm not your brother. I'm not even a Landers. My real parents were named Lila and Tully O'Hare." He paused and took a deep breath. "And that's all I'm telling you. You don't need to know the whole story. All you have to do is come with me."

"No!" she cried, every instinct telling her he meant her real harm. "I'm not going anywhere with you!"

His hand lashed out and slapped her across the face.

"You will do," he said coldly, "exactly what I tell you to do. You've made enough trouble for me already. Fouling things up in the Funhouse that day! You almost ruined everything."

Tess shifted nervously, eyeing the attic stairs. Could she get to them before he could stop her? Probably not. "What are you going to do?" she asked.

"We're going to have some fun," he said with an evil grin. Then he pushed her ahead of him, toward the stairs. "And if you're thinking of screaming, go right ahead. Maria went home, and your father, in

504

case you've forgotten, is at one of his precious board meetings. So yell your lungs out if you want to."

When they reached the top of the narrow attic stairs, he gave her another push, shoving her down the stairs. He retained his tight grip on her wrist and said casually as he hurried her along, "When we've finished having our fun, we're going to meet my real parents. You'll like them, Tess. They'll be mad at you, at first, because of who your father is, but they'll get over it."

Deciding that the best approach might be to humor Guy Joe until she could think of something else, she said innocently, "Where do your real parents live?"

"Live?" At the top of the wide, curving staircase, he stopped and forced her to face him. "They don't *live*, Tess! Your father and his wicked friends drove both of my real parents to suicide! They're dead!"

Then, as she stared at him in stunned dismay, he added emphatically, "And what was good enough for them is good enough for me. And you, too."

He was talking about two people who had committed suicide. Two people who were dead. He was talking about joining those dead people, and taking her with him.

Tess's knees gave and she slumped against Guy Joe.

He yanked her upright. "Cut it out, Tess!" he said sharply. "Come on, now. I don't have all night. Let's get this show on the road."

Numb with shock and fear, Tess let Guy Joe pull her down the stairs. When he yanked open the front door, windblown rain attacked them. "Can't I grab a jacket?" Tess pleaded. "I'll get soaked!" If he'd let go of her wrist for just a second, she could make a run for it. Sam's house wasn't that far away. Sam. How could she ever have suspected Sam?

Guy Joe snickered and pushed her out onto the porch. "You're worried about getting wet? You really are stupid!"

When he'd shoved her inside his car and taken the wheel, he used his electronic control to lock her door. Then he yanked her seat belt across her chest, and snapped it into place. "If you try to unhook it," he warned as he started the car, "I'll break your arm."

She knew he meant it. Just as she knew he'd been telling the truth about being adopted. How had he found out? Why hadn't someone told him a long time ago? Wouldn't that be a horrible thing to learn when you were eighteen years old? Like . . . like your whole life wasn't what you thought it was. It would be a terrible shock, wouldn't it? In Guy Joe's case, it must have been enough of a shock to send him over the edge.

Her mind felt fuzzy, as if it were wrapped in cotton. She *had* to think, but she couldn't.

"You pushed me into Trudy's pool?" she asked, shivering in her seat.

He nodded, peering into the rain-slicked windshield.

"And the brownies, you did that, too? And then ate some, so no one would suspect you, right?"

"Clever, huh?" he said. "Miserable experience,"

506

he added, shaking his head. "But necessary."

"The saucer. How did you get the saucer up? And what did you do with it after you took it out?"

He laughed, obviously enjoying himself. "Those things wear out so fast they have to be replaced a lot. So they're easy to lift up and out. A baby could do it. The one I took was right there under your feet the whole time. I just slid it onto the one beside it. Afterward I said I was going to call Gina's parents, and on the way I slipped into the Funhouse and replaced the saucer."

Tess remembered the humiliating walk to Mancini's office, and burned with rage. She made one last, desperate attempt to reason with him. "Guy Joe, I don't know how you found out what you think you found out, but you could be wrong. And even if you're right, it doesn't matter to *me* that you're adopted. I mean, I'll always think of you as my —"

Before she could finish he had slammed on the brakes. "It matters to *me*!" he shouted. "You stupid, selfish little witch, it matters to me! If you don't understand anything else before you die, understand that!"

When they arrived at The Boardwalk and he had pulled her out into the parking lot, she felt a sudden surge of hope. She might see someone she knew, someone who could help her.

But the amusement park was deserted. Attendants in the booths and the arcades, passing the boring hours reading or watching tiny portable televisions, never even looked up as Guy Joe dragged

507

her toward the Funhouse. No one paid the slightest attention to them.

Except Doss Beecham, who looked up from the high stool he was sitting on in one of the shooting galleries. But when he saw who was passing by, he barely nodded. She couldn't blame him, after the way she'd treated him. He looked unusually pale after his ordeal of the night before. If only she could signal him that Guy Joe had been behind all of it. But Doss was no longer looking her way.

"Don't you even *look* at him!" Guy Joe ordered under his breath. "He can't help you."

Maybe if she'd been nicer to Doss, he would know her well enough to sense that something was wrong, and come to her rescue.

Too late now.

Too late, too late, too late . . .

The attendant in the ticket booth for the Funhouse never took his eyes off the baseball game on his portable television as Guy Joe quickly paid for two admissions and pushed Tess ahead of him.

"Go ahead and scream," Guy Joe said cheerfully when they were inside the empty Funhouse. "Screaming in here doesn't mean a thing. No one will even notice."

She knew he was right. And now she was alone in this dark and frightening place with someone who had caused the death of one person and had hurt a lot of others. And there was no one to help her.

"Take your shoes off!" he commanded.

"What? Guy Joe, I can't go through the Funhouse in my bare feet. It's hard enough with sneakers on."

He laughed. "You're so stupid. You're worried about your *feet*?"

She waited, knowing instinctively that she wasn't going to like what was coming.

"Tess," he said softly, his cold eyes on hers, "didn't I make myself clear?" He stooped to untie and slip off first one of her sneakers and a sock, then the other, using only one hand. His free hand imprisoned her ankle as he performed his task.

When she was barefoot, he stood up, recapturing her arm. "Little ex-sister," he said in that same soft voice, "this Funhouse is the last place your feet will ever touch."

He smiled down at her. "Because this is where you're going to die."

Chapter 27

As they came out of the dark entryway into the first lighted chamber, Tess fought desperately against Guy Joe's grip, tears of frustration and fear streaking her face. "No!" she screamed as he dragged her into the nylon-padded tunnel with the rolling wooden floor. "No, Guy Joe, *stop!*"

But he ignored her, pushing and pulling at her until her bare feet slid onto the rolling boards.

She tried to plant herself firmly in one spot, but without shoes it was impossible. Clutching at the billowing black nylon fabric that made up the tunnel's sides was equally useless. The loose, black, silky folds waved this way and that, eluding her grasp.

Feeling like a helpless puppet, she continued to struggle. Guy Joe stood on the wooden walkway, watching her, amusement on his face. "I don't know exactly where my father died," he said in a friendly voice, "so I'll just have to pick my own spot. But first," he added with a wicked grin, "we'll have some fun. Isn't that why they call this place the Fun-

510

house?" He chuckled, a sound that sent shivers of fear down Tess's spine.

"Guy Joe, please . . ."

"Guy-Joe-please, Guy-Joe-please," he mimicked cruelly. "Please what?" He stared at her, his upper lip curled in a menacing sneer. "Is there something you *want*, Tess?"

As Tess tried to cross the chamber, she fell twice, landing first on her back, then on her elbows, smacking them sharply against the wood. Guy Joe laughed each time. When she had finally made her way across, she stepped onto the solid wood floor to find Guy Joe waiting for her. He pushed her onward.

The padded rolling tunnel was next. Her bare feet slid on the nylon fabric underneath them. She was tossed to the floor repeatedly as the tunnel bucked from side to side. She felt dizzy, her head was pounding, and her whole body ached from falling down.

"Guy Joe," she gasped as she fell again, "why are you *doing* this? I never knew you were adopted. I would have told you if I'd known. I wasn't keeping anything secret from you."

"I'm doing it because you're *his* child!" he shouted. "His real child! Can't you see that I'm really punishing him, or are you too dense to make the connection?"

"But he's not even *here*," she argued. "He doesn't know anything about this!"

"Ah, but he will." Guy Joe smiled angelically. "It's all in a journal I left behind. Everything that's happened is in there, including our little adventure in here. In graphic detail. He'll know what fun we had before the end."

The end? She didn't want to die.

"Now get up!" he shouted, angry again. "Quit stalling!"

She stayed where she was. Why should she make it easy for him? She stretched out on her stomach, full-length, on the tunnel's padded floor. Let him come and get her. Maybe in a struggle, she could somehow get the upper hand.

"I've decided to hang both of us from those two skeletons in the middle chamber," he said, friendly again, as if they were planning an outing. "Won't that be a hoot for whoever finds us?"

"*Hang* us?"

"Sure. Like father, like son, right? My father did it. Said so in his obituary. I looked it up at the library. Didn't say where, exactly. The writer was too squeamish, I guess. So I get to pick the place. And I choose the skeletons." Taking a penknife from his back pocket, he ripped a long, narrow strip of nylon from the tunnel's side. Then he tore a second strip and stuffed it into the pocket, along with the knife.

Suddenly, without warning, he jumped onto the padding and grabbed Tess, looping the nylon strip around her neck.

"Now get up!" he commanded, tugging on the strip around her neck. "Or I'll finish you off right here!"

They entered the chain-walk tunnel.

"Guy Joe," she croaked, the nylon pulling too

tightly on her throat, "I can't go across those chains in my bare feet. I can't!"

Still holding the nylon strip in one hand, Guy Joe gave her a shove, sending her onto the links. Balancing properly was impossible and she fell again and again into the meshed circle of metal links.

"See," Guy Joe said happily, "what I'm going to do is tie this end of your rope to that hook the skeleton dangles from. You'll be standing on the railing when I do that."

Tess tried desperately to grip the metal with her toes. It was impossible. Down she went again, slicing one of her toes as she fell. She cried out, but Guy Joe ignored her and went on talking.

"Then you'll jump," he went on matter-of-factly. "Bye-bye, Tess, easy as that. Then it'll be my turn. Isn't it nice that there's one skeleton hook for each of us?"

"I won't jump!" Tess cried. "I won't!"

Guy Joe shrugged. "Okay. You don't have to. I'll just push you."

He meant it. She knew that. Whatever Guy Joe had learned about himself, it had stolen the brother she knew and replaced him with this person who had no conscience, no qualms whatsoever about taking her life and his own. She *had* to do something to stop him.

Tess struggled across the remaining chains. When she was on the wooden platform, she said, "I can't walk, Guy Joe. I've cut my foot."

Guy Joe bent to glance down at her foot, giving Tess just enough time to grasp the chain belt at her waist, unsnapping the clasp. In one smooth motion, she yanked the metal belt free from its loops and swung hard, whipping it down across the back of Guy Joe's head.

Stunned, he fell to his knees, releasing his end of the rope.

Tess ran. She raced into the next chamber, where the metal saucers whirled. She knew she had only a second or two. Bending quickly, she reached down with both hands and, stretching her arms across, grabbed at the middle circle and pulled upward. It came up out of the floor easily, just as Guy Joe had said.

She heard footsteps behind her. Lifting the circle, using what little strength she had left, she tossed it into the next passageway. It landed with a sharp clink and then fell silent.

Tess ran across the wooden walkway to the opposite side of the circles. Then, swinging the chain belt with careful aim, she smashed the overhead light in the ceiling, throwing the tunnel into absolute darkness. She crouched there, trembling violently, waiting.

"I'll get you for this, Tess Landers!" Guy Joe's voice, full of rage, cried as he entered the tunnel. "You'll be very—"

He never finished the threat. Consumed with rage and blinded by the sudden, unexpected darkness, his voice became a scream of terror as the hole Tess had created swallowed him up.

514

Chapter 28

Tess would hear Guy Joe's scream in her sleep for many nights to come.

Crouching in the corner, trembling violently, she covered her face with her hands.

"Tess! Tess, where are you?" Tess heard a voice cry out, frantic with worry. *Sam.*

"Here! I'm here! Be careful — there's a saucer missing!"

In spite of the darkness, Sam made his way across the chamber, and a moment later he was kneeling at her side. "You okay?" Lifting her gently, he put his arms around her.

"How did you know I was here?"

"Gina. She called me. She got this weird package at the hospital today. From Guy Joe. A couple of journals. One was his and the other one was an old one, written by some woman." Sam began leading Tess out of the Funhouse, using one of the wooden walkways. The rain had stopped, and the half moon cast a faint glow over the beach. "I didn't have any idea what she was talking about, but she was

515

scared. For you. She told me to find you, right away. I'd just hung up when Doss called me and said you and Guy Joe were here and that Guy Joe looked funny, sort of freaked out. So here I am."

So Doss *had* noticed something strange, after all. And hadn't ignored it. She would have to remember to thank him.

"Where's Guy Joe?" Sam asked.

"Down there." Tess pointed to a spot on the beach. Guy Joe was unconscious. He looked so helpless, so innocent, lying there on the sand, that Tess found it hard to believe that tonight's horror had actually happened. "We'd better call another ambulance. But," Tess added softly, "this will be the last one."

Epilogue

They think I'm unconscious. But I heard every word they said. Dr. Oliver said to that man who's *supposed* to be my father, "We've had our hands full lately with these kids, haven't we? Buddy Slaughter tells me Trudy is just about hysterical after what happened at her birthday party."

I had finally found out what I'd been afraid I'd never know. Trudy's father was the "Buddy" Lila had written about. The only one who hadn't suffered at my hands.

Okay. No sweat. I'd go wherever they sent me. I'd weave little baskets and play Ping-Pong with the other loonies and I'd talk to the shrinks.

But I'd get out some day. And when I did, the eighth man on the board would be waiting. Buddy Slaughter, the man who had stolen everything from me, would be waiting.

So I could wait, too. . . .

P●INT CRiME

If you like Point Horror, you'll love Point Crime!

A murder has been committed . . . Whodunnit?
Was it the teacher, the schoolgirl, or the best friend? An exciting new series of crime novels, with tortuous plots and lots of suspects, designed to keep the reader guessing till the very last page.

School for Death
Peter Beere
When the French teacher is found, drowned in the pond, Ali and her friends are plunged into a frightening nightmare. Murder has come to Summervale School, and *anyone* could be the next victim . . .

Shoot the Teacher
David Belbin
Adam Lane, new to Beechwood Grange, finds himself thrust into the middle of a murder investigation, when the headteacher is found shot dead. And the shootings have only just begun . . .

The Smoking Gun
Malcolm Rose
When David Rabin is found dead, in the school playing-field, his sister Ros is determined to find the murderer. But who would have killed him? And why?

Look out for:

Baa Baa Dead Sheep
Jill Bennett
Mr Lamb, resident caretaker of the *Tree Theatre*, has been murdered, and more than one person at the theatre had cause to hate him . . .

Avenging Angel
David Belbin
When Angelo Coppola is killed in a hit-and-run accident, his sister, Clare, sets out to find his killer . . .

Point Romance

If you like Point Horror, you'll love Point Romance!

Anyone can hear the language of love.

Are you burning with passion, and aching with desire? Then these are the books for you! Point Romance brings you passion, romance, heartache, and most of all, *love* . . .

Saturday Night
Caroline B. Cooney

Summer Dreams, Winter Love
Mary Francis Shura

The Last Great Summer
Carol Stanley

Last Dance
Caroline B. Cooney

Cradle Snatcher
Alison Creaghan

Look out for:

New Year's Eve
Caroline B. Cooney

Kiss Me Stupid
Alison Creaghan

Summer Nights
Caroline B. Cooney